In the Key of Death

In the Key of Death

Robert S. Levinson

FIVE STAR
A part of Gale, Cengage Learning

Detroit • New York • San Francisco • New Haven, Conn • Waterville, Maine • London

Set in 11 pt. Plantin.
Printed on permanent paper.

LIBRARY OF CONGRESS CATALOGING-IN-PUBLICATION DATA

Levinson, Robert S.
In the key of death / Robert S. Levinson. — 1st ed.
p. cm.
ISBN-13: 978-1-59414-647-3 (alk. paper)
ISBN-10: 1-59414-647-0 (alk. paper)
1. Sound recording industry—Fiction. 2. Private security services—Fiction. 3. Murder—Fiction. I. Title.
PS3562.E921815 2008
813'.54—dc22 2007050870

First Edition. First Printing: March 2008.

Published in 2008 in conjunction with Tekno Books and Ed Gorman.

Printed in the United States of America
1 2 3 4 5 6 7 12 11 10 09 08

FOR SANDRA
LVY
LeOlam VaEd

Prologue

There had been times Josh Wainwright woke to the birds gossiping in the light of early morning, stretched out on the manicured lawn alongside Katie's grave at Westwood Memorial Park, on the plot he had purchased for himself. Uncertain where he was. Exploding into tears when he spied her grave marker.

He had the visits under control now, down to maybe a couple times a month and, of course, the anniversary of her death, or days where he had the need to share news and couldn't wait for one of those nights where Katie came to him in his sleep.

To listen.

Comment.

Caution.

Encourage.

Never one to hold back on an opinion, not his precious Katie.

It had been a while since the last visit—Katie concerned about the kids, how he was coping with Justin's increasing rebelliousness, Julie's unpredictable mood swings—but the nightmare of her murder was ever present, playing out like film noir, a mystery in black and white that ended too soon, before the killer was revealed in the final reel.

Josh's movie always opened outside the palace-like Pantages Theater, steps away from the storied intersection of Hollywood and Vine, of course.

Giant klieg lights rotating in the night sky.

A marquee proclaiming:

TONIGHT! 22ND ANNUAL L'CHAIM

'FUND FOR THE NEEDY' TELETHON

Inside the art-deco masterpiece built in the nineteen thirties, two thousand people applaud Jon Voight and Edward James Olmos as they finish reminding television viewers that all monies raised will support more than nine hundred non-sectarian enterprises throughout the world. Drug and alcohol rehabilitation centers. Day schools and summer camps that provide scholarships for underprivileged children. Special housing for low-income families. Programs for immigrants and seniors.

Rabbi Hesh Adler dances out to join them center stage, sends them off with a hug and a mazel tov and brings on James Caan to introduce the next guest.

"She is everyone's favorite entertainer, but you know that already," Caan tells the world. "She spends most of her time nowadays staying home to raise her two wonderful children, but she jumped at Reb Hesh's invitation to join us tonight with her family and help us to achieve our goal of twenty-five million dollars. Ladies, gentlemen, everybody in-between. . . ." The obligatory drum roll, leading into her Academy Award–winning theme song, "Tell Me What Keeps You Alive"—"Give it up, a hot Hollywood welcome for my dear friend and, need I say, the one and only Miss Katie Sunshine!"

Katie, offstage with Josh, Justin, and Julie, takes a last swipe at her hair, takes his usual Break a Leg kiss, takes a megaton breath, locks hands with the kids, and troops out with them.

Josh brings up the rear and falls in alongside her while Katie is accepting the warmth of the audience and settling on her mark center stage.

Justin and Julie fidget, their memories twirling over lines they've been rehearsing for two weeks. When it's their turn, they're letter-perfect.

Now, it's Josh's turn to recite his lines, only—

Stage fright.

He's drawing a blank.

Panic sets in.

Early in his career with LAPD, being a beat cop walking the dark and dangerous killing streets of South Central was easier than this.

How'd he ever let her talk him into it?

Katie taps his shoulder and points to the TelePrompTer mounted above the TV camera, but his attention has been diverted by a person at the back of the house who's moved from a seat to the aisle and, it appears, into a shooter's stance.

Josh can't be certain.

He's blinded by the stage spots.

He squints and shades his eyes with a hand as Katie leans forward and good-naturedly shouts directions to the TelePrompTer over the laughter of the audience.

Katie hardly has the words out when her body jerks away from Josh and rains blood on him and on Julie.

The laughter has obscured the sound of a gun being fired.

A second shot flies by him and smashes into Katie.

Josh screams at stage hands to get his children out of harm's way and sinks to his knees by Katie, testing her for a pulse, but what he sees is enough to tell him the worst.

The people in the audience panic.

They flee the theater, bodies crashing against bodies in a unanimous rush for the exits, and with them the shooter—

In Josh's nightmarish film noir—

A faithful recreation of what happened two and a half years ago—

When Clyde Davenport murdered his wife.

Someday he would have the evidence to prove it, but—

Not yet.

Not now.

For now, that son of a bitch Davenport was still free.

The final reel of Josh's movie yet to splash onto the silver screen.

The ending unknown.

Even to Josh.

Chapter 1

Billy the Kid Palmer's turn to die.

Finally.

A long time in coming.

Clyde Davenport, lounging in the stretch limo delivering him to Billy's place a half hour outside downtown Nashville, nursing a cognac from the courtesy bar, savoring the thoughts, the smile of anticipation snaking up one side of his face and frozen there, trying to remember—

How many on my wish list already checked off? Ingrates who turned their backs on me, dismissed me after they were superstars rich enough, famous enough, arrogant enough, to forget who had made their stardom possible. Ten so far? Eleven? Dead and buried over the years, and no one ever the wiser it was my doing.

He love-patted the lambskin satchel case beside him, containing the exquisitely crafted, pearl-handled .38-caliber automatic he'd personally chosen to help Billy go out in style, feeling the kind of rush that topped anything he ever got from his drugs or his women.

Thinking—

Forgive-and-forget will never be me. Forgive-and-forget is for others, softies fucked over by their own ingrates, who accept the fucking over philosophically and move on, but not me. Not Clyde Davenport. Not me. Forgive-and-remember, that's me. Sweet revenge. Time only improves its taste. It won't be over for me until they're all gone, all of them, every name on my wish list, whenever and for however long it takes.

Clyde rolled the crystal goblet between his palms and studied the amber-colored liquid while reviewing once last time the plan he'd devised, the conversation he expected to have with Billy the Kid. Satisfied, he gave the goblet a few swirls and a hearty sniff that filled his lungs with sweet anticipation, raised it in a silent victory toast to himself, and finished the cognac in a swallow.

The limo's CD player was dusting the limo's posh leather interior with cuts from *Mr. Magic's Golden Greats,* the first compilation album Clyde distributed on his own label, as an advertisement for himself a year after the industry turned its back on him, as if Mr. Magic had run out of tricks.

Mr. Magic.

The nickname he'd gladly accepted and adopted after it was first used to describe him in *Rolling Stone*'s cover story by Ben Fong-Torres, with its delicious Annie Liebovitz photograph of him as a magician in tails pulling his superstar Katie Sunshine out of a top hat.

He had always been a recluse of sorts, maintaining a discreet distance that added to his mystique, but now he was an outcast; treated with iconic respect, but carrying the baggage of a musical history diminished by the deviant sounds that conflicted with the "Symphony of Sound" he'd introduced to pop, country, and, of course, rock and roll; the music of his generation; music that shaped his career and catapulted him into the Rock and Roll Hall of Fame on a unanimous vote in his first year of eligibility.

Clyde shook his head free of the memory, thinking—

Screw them all. My future is in the present, and fuck anybody who believes otherwise. I'll get back to it in Los Angeles, once I'm through shutting down another piece of my past with Billy the Kid Palmer.

"Baby, Baby, Baby," one of Skye O'Neal's four Gold singles from their Platinum *Skye's the Limit* LP segued into "Don't Ever Go," the moody ballad he wrote and produced for Emma Thorne, turning the sloe-eyed unknown born under the sound of Bow Bells into an international superstar and, ultimately, a fire-breathing diva the devil would leap across the street to avoid.

Dead, the both of them.

Earlier casualties in his private war against ingratitude.

And good riddance.

Their deaths, like the death in progress, followed no timetable.

Now, Billy the Kid's turn—

Inspired and set in motion three months ago by a call from Mitchell Dragon, for years his associate producer on the annual "Concert for Big Buddies of America" fund-raiser.

The concert and the personal check for five mil he handed over to Big Buddies year after year kept him in the public eye, got the memory-impaired twelve-year-olds running the business to take his calls, got them to take the occasional meeting, not that they ever panned out beyond a polite *We'll get back to you,* rotten sons of bitches that they were.

His motivation self-serving?

Guilty as charged.

Isn't that what life has always been about?

Clyde Davenport's life, anyway?

Funny thing, though—

He had come to believe in Big Buddies as deeply as Jerry Lewis believed in the MDA.

Something about helping kids in need.

I once was one myself, his standard answer whenever an interviewer asked the question, always good for a laugh and a sound bite on the eleven o'clock news.

Clyde meant it though.

Not because there'd been people around to help him when he was a kid.

Because they weren't there when he needed them most.

Except, of course, for his beloved father.

His mother, with that *You're dumb as butter* look she was constantly throwing in his face, calling him names even when she wasn't coming after him with her favorite leather belt, the one with the large silver buckle—

Never.

The mention of children, that's what got his attention.

That's why he returned Mitch Dragon's call, instead of ignoring him for the disloyal prick he was. Cutting loose from the Concert for Big Buddies two years ago to top dog a series of BBC specials in London; giving overnight notice by E-mail; not even a thank-you for having gotten his first producing break with Clyde. Not then or ever.

"What's this message you left for me about raising bread for a new kid's wing in some hospital, Mitch? Thirty seconds."

"Bigger and more modern than what they got now at the Waggoner Memorial Ranch and Free Clinic in Nashville, where I'm calling from, Clyde. Got a concert in mind like yours for Big Buddies, only this one along the lines of—" putting a carnie barker's pitch to his fruity tenor—"A Salute to Mr. Magic."

"Pass. Good-bye, Mitch."

"No, wait, hold on, Clyde."

"How'd you get the gig, telling the hospital you had an inside track on my bank account? A hundred-grand donation, and that's it. Tell me where to send the check."

"Listen, please. Okay? The hospital people were talking to me about getting somebody like Geffen to front this fund-raiser, but I insisted it had to be you. What you've already done for kids through Big Buddies and, besides, all the country acts you created and charted

with back in the glory days—"

"Stop talking about me in the past tense, you ungrateful little shit."

"Yeah, right, sorry about that." He rattled off some of the acts Clyde had taken into Gold and Platinum territory, several already resident in the Country Music Hall of Fame. "No one can come close to you, it comes to country, Clyde. What'd Geffen ever do in country over at Asylum Records? The Eagles? Okay, them, and Linda Ronstadt, sure. But Cher? Jackson Browne? Joni Mitchell, for Christ's sake? Give me a fucking break. Besides, he's too busy nowadays putting his name on buildings to pencil in something like this."

"You went to him first, Geffen, didn't you?" Holding the reins on his temper.

"No, no, no, negative. Don't hang up, Clyde, please."

Clyde knew Mitch Dragon was lying. His voice betrayed him. He could almost feel the desperation sweat pouring through the phone line, but he had no intention of hanging up.

He hadn't been this excited since early last year, when he got the phone call he'd been anxiously awaiting, telling him Garry Chaplin was the victim of a hit-and-run while out on his regular morning jog, in a coma on life-support systems, and not expected to survive.

Billy the Kid and Bluto wasn't one of the Davenport acts Mitch had mentioned, but Clyde kept close track on all the ingrates.

He knew Billy was living in Nashville, knew where to find Bluto Parks in L.A.

The hospital fund-raiser was all the reason he needed to make Billy the Kid Palmer the next ingrate to move to the top of his list.

And Bluto, him, too.

Clyde strung Mitch along, let him grovel a while longer, and when his pleading became as threadbare as a beggar's wardrobe, he said, "I'll do it, Mitch, but not for you. I'll do it for the children," like the Pope holding out his ring to be kissed. "To my specifications, of course."

Within weeks of the conversation, Clyde had worked out a

plan he wanted to shout to the world was as inspired and ingenious as any of the crazy-quilt instrumental tracks he had ever laid down in the recording studio and set him off on a weeklong, self-congratulatory feast of sex and drugs, only—

To work, his plan needed Bluto Parks, and—

Bluto disappeared on him.

But Billy the Kid Palmer was still in Nashville.

The "Salute to Mr. Magic" was still in place, and—

No better excuse for Clyde being in Nashville was likely to come along anytime soon.

He promised himself he'd have another plan well before he arrived for the concert, one that was failure-proof, because—unlike any of the other plans—this one wouldn't depend on a miscreant like Bluto Parks.

This one would be handled personally by Clyde Davenport.

Who better than himself?

Clyde leaned forward, slid open the privacy window, and asked the craggy-faced black man behind the wheel: "How much longer till we get there, Lionel?"

"Makin' good time as it is," the limo driver called over his shoulder. "A good time of day for Highway 431, trucks galore, but ahead of business folks rushin' home, Mistuh Davenport." A bluesy cadence to his speech that begged to be set to music.

"It's Clyde, Lionel, remember? Mr. Davenport was my father."

"Got to be mighty proud of you, your pappy, for what you're doing for the hospital and our young ones, Nashville not even being your city."

Clyde warmed to the praise. "Only money, Lionel. Got it to burn. You'd been with me yesterday on my tour of the hospital, you'd understand."

"Don't take no tour for me to know whoever said it can't buy happiness can't get past the worm to the butterfly," Lionel said, studying him from the rearview mirror. "Yes sir, that pappy of yours got to be puffed up with pride."

Clyde's eyes had gone moist at Lionel's mention of his father.

He turned away to hide the grief clouding them, as it had at Waggoner Ranch Hospital and Free Clinic after he was led into a cheerless, cramped children's ward that reeked of soiled linens and disinfectant, with scattered crayon drawings taped to faded cream-colored walls the only decoration.

Then, it wasn't the condition of the ward causing them.

It was Dr. Roy telling him about the boy sobbing his heart out, pounding his fists in the air against invisible demons, howling untranslatable words that Clyde interpreted as desperate calls for mommy and daddy.

"Poor little lamb is deaf," the hospital administrator said, launching into an explanation of the rare disease that had robbed the boy of sound and might soon cost him his vision. "It's not unlike what happened to Helen Keller, who lost her ability to speak as well, and—"

Clyde shoved out a hand to turn her off. "It's nothing I need to hear, Dr. Roy. Nothing I don't already know." He averted his face long enough to brush away the tears washing over his lids and down his cheeks. "Does the boy sign, doctor? Does he know how?"

"Better than y'all would suppose from an eleven-year-old. Teddy Jack hasn't been at it that long, maybe six months, but you can see how he still doesn't accept that his hearing is gone and unlikely to return."

"Because?"

"The usual. The almighty dollar. The surgery and what comes before and after is enough to bankrupt a millionaire and Teddy Jack's kin are poorer than mud. There's a valid reason they call this a charity ward, and why your generosity, the hundred thousand dollars you pledged—"

Clyde had heard enough.

He charged down the aisle dividing two long corridors of beds in the ward, past a dozen or so youngsters, to the deaf boy. He grabbed him by the wrists, wrestled his arms still, ordered the boy under control with a hard stare he'd inherited from his mother that had won him bigger battles than this.

The other children quit their hooting and howling for the boy to stop making a racket and began cheering Clyde. The doctor demanded their silence in a merciless tone that rose above the clamor.

Clyde satisfied himself he had the boy's full obedience and released his hold.

He signed: "I want to help you hear again, Teddy Jack."

Teddy Jack didn't react.

Clyde signed: "Whatever it takes, whatever the cost, however long—you will have your hearing restored, Teddy Jack. It's a promise. You have my word on it."

The boy's pale blue eyes fought free of him and chased around the room, as if a wall or the ceiling could explain what he was being told. Finally, his fingers took up the cause, asking: "Who are you?"

Clyde grew the exaggerated smile that over the years had been called warm and inviting by some, deceitful and dangerous by others. He signed: "Santa Claus."

Dr. Roy had caught up with him and was catching her breath alongside Clyde.

Clyde turned to her and, restraining the emotion clogging his throat, said, "Add a million dollars to my pledge. It goes for Teddy Jack's surgery. If you run through that, you call me at my office and let me know. There'll be more."

The doctor shook her head in disbelief. Her toothsome, snow-white smile was genuine, possibly the sun-bleached blondness of hair she wore piled high like a crown on the kind of pretty face that never gave him a smile or a second look back before he quit high school.

"I'd be remiss if I didn't tell you there's no guarantee—"

He cut her off with a flying gesture.

"Dr. Roy, I've learned over my sixty-four years on this planet that nothing in life is guaranteed but death."

"But such generosity for a child you never laid eyes on before today?"

Clyde let the question hang for a moment, then smiled benignly, shifted his head left and right, tossed over his palms, and shrugged, as if he had no more or better answer for her.

The doctor was more giving. She grabbed him, impulsively, her eyes misting over, her body warm and inviting, her voice choking on sentiment, telling him, "You're not a Santa Claus. You're a saint, Mr. Davenport."

A saint?

Hardly.

A devil in disguise more like it.

He drew her closer, resisting the urge to return the chaste kiss she laid on his cheek with something more insinuating. Besides, he had Ava waiting for him back at his penthouse suite in the Nashville Royal Arms.

He said, "Clyde, Dr. Roy. Mr. Davenport was my father."

His father

A constant presence in his memory and his motives, freshly stirred by Teddy Jack, who reminded him of the puny, pint-sized and put-upon ten-year-old he once was, using a textbook he'd found in the library to begin learning blind-deaf signing, a language he hoped would bind him tighter than ever to his daddy and rescue him further from the tyranny of a vicious drunken ogre of a mother.

"Closing in our destination," Lionel announced like a tour guide, maneuvering the limo into an exit lane over the horn-tooting objection of a Hummer that was defying the speed limit. They passed through a mile or so of undeveloped rural acreage and a modest business district, quaint streets full of Depression-era storefronts, before he slowed down, looking for an address in a neighborhood the Nashville Chamber of Commerce would never dare put on a tourist map.

The modest Colonial-style homes, one more rundown than the next, sat decaying at the rear of large, weed-infested lots lining both sides of weather-brutalized streets, their parkways full of what Clyde supposed were magnolia trees either dead or too dying to blossom.

Lionel eased into a parking space across from the Palmer residence and hurried to open the door for Clyde, who immediately upon stepping out of the limo pulled up the collar of his overcoat against the frigid late-afternoon air.

Clyde weaved cautiously along the barely visible path to the front door, unable to mask his delight at observing first-hand and confirming the dreadful condition of the property that he had initially seen in the surveillance reports and photos he'd commissioned three months ago. It had done his heart glad to learn how low Billy's fortunes had sunk in the years since he and Bluto Parks chose to treat their mentor like filth under their fingernails.

Clyde had plucked them from the gutter obscurity of a second-rate rock club in Detroit and transformed "Billy the Kid and Bluto" through the magic of his "Symphony of Sound" into one of the world's biggest recording and concert acts.

They chose the week they were voted a Grammy for their debut album and another as Best New Artists to leave him. And, like so many others, leaving the dirty job to some finger-popper who had crawled out of nowhere, announcing himself a personal manager and saying, "My act needs more than you can offer, Clyde."

Words like that.

"We have to move on, build a team that takes the boys to heights beyond your reach."

Words like that.

And, always, "Thank you for everything you did. We're eternally grateful."

Eternally grateful.

Words they all used on him, every time, picked up from some book of *Fuck You Very Much.*

Today was a day of reckoning, and Clyde could barely contain his excitement.

The oversized door swung open.

Billy stepped out onto the portico to greet him with a wigwag and wide open smile that revealed a mouthful of missing teeth. Billy, gone to bald and bag-of-bones skinny, a skeleton in search of a body, no longer the rugged, dark-eyed rock idol who had starred in the wet dreams of a million teenage girls twenty-three years ago.

"Hey, man, how's life in the big city?" Billy said, like the past never existed, his voice strained through vocal cords the report said was damaged by too many years of too much coke and meth. His eyes were glazed fireballs of restless uncertainty. He called out, "Sweetheart, Mr. Magic has arrived to honor us with his presence." Got a lock on Clyde's outstretched hand and said, "C'mon, man, let's us get your ass out of the cold and some fresh coffee or better in your belly." His words were rushed and hard to follow, like he'd already done better than the coffee.

Much better.

"Traveling light nowadays, Clyde?" Swishing his head around. "Where's your shadow, your factootim"—mispronouncing the word *factotum*—"Peppi Blue, right? The deaf but not so dumb promotion guy? Your chief cook and bottle washer?"

"Back in Los Angeles cooking and bottle washing," Clyde said, feigning a smile while he freed himself from Billy's sweaty grip. Being touched was a business necessity, but nothing he enjoyed. He wiped off his hand on his overcoat and trailed Billy inside, almost feeling sorry for what had become of the son of a bitch.

Almost.

He wondered if death might come as a reward to Billy and toyed with the idea of leaving him to rot in his own life.

No, no way.

This song had been written and only remained to be produced.

If he chose to look at it that way, he was doing Billy the Kid Palmer the biggest favor of his life.

They settled in a living room that looked furnished out of thrift shops and lawn sales, but kept neat and orderly; a lilac scent coloring the air, but not entirely disguising the tobacco smell sticking to the cottage-cheese ceiling; magazines piled neatly on the coffee table; family photos in cheap plastic frames lined up on the fireplace mantle.

Billy's wife, Kristy, joined them after a moment, carrying a cafeteria tray bearing a metal coffee pot, some chipped cups and saucers, and a plate of chocolate-chip cookies smelling fresh out of the oven. She placed the tray carefully on the coffee table, wiped her hands on her apron, and offered Clyde her hand, an uncertain smile.

She said, "Billy's told me wonderful things about you, Mr. Davenport."

"Clyde, please. Mr. Davenport was my father. And you come as a delightful discovery, Mrs. Palmer—"

"Kristy," she said, moving to Billy's side.

"Too good for that galoot, better than he deserves," Clyde said, like a joke, not for the truth it was.

Billy sailed a thumbs-up at him.

Kristy Palmer looked like so many other aging groupies he'd encountered over the years, one of those attractive chicks ready to fall into bed with any rock star who showed interest, pretty enough or cunning enough to turn a wham-bam one-nighter into a wedding ring.

She was in her early forties now. Her face, full of worry quotes at the mouth and eyes, had rounded into a second chin to go with a body begging for a Weight Watchers membership and breasts losing a battle with gravity inside a rainbow-patterned halter dress faded from one wash too many. Hair cut at the shoulders, neat without being stylish. Enough makeup to suggest she still took pride in her appearance and, unlike those other groupies going gray at the roots—

Kristy seemed to really care about the husband she'd caught.

She'd have to, Clyde decided, to stick it out in a rundown house with a shell of a man run over by life, his downfall expedited by weed, drugs, and booze—the Unholy Trinity of too many in the music business who turned rock and roll into rock and ruin.

It showed in the way she looked at him, how she was pampering him now, adjusting the frayed collar of his sports shirt, pampering strands of his hair back over his head and ears. Her hand massaging his shoulder.

Billy laid a hand over hers. "Clyde, when I was going ten rounds with cancer that cost me a lung, Kristy was always there, every single, solitary step of the way. That's the kind of woman I lucked into and thank the Lord for, every minute of every day. My sweetheart never faltered for one second, where other women would've cut and run."

"Oh, hush," Kristy said, blushing, pulling her hand away and tapping the top of Billy's head. "Clyde's come to talk about you, not me, isn't that so, Clyde?"

"Is it too late to change my mind?" Clyde said, making a joke of it, secretly pleased how these few minutes had confirmed how important Kristy was, outside his own gifts for persuasion, to the success of the plan that had brought him here.

Billy finished cackling at the ceiling like a berserk rooster, anxious to show he got the joke, and wondered about their being served something stronger when Kristy started pouring the coffees.

She shut him up with a sharp-edged stare.

"I'll leave you two to whatever," she said. "Got some errands to run and the kids to pick up at school."

"Children?" Clyde said it like he didn't know. Relieved she was leaving and he'd not have to find a reason or a way to be alone with Billy when he sprang the plan on him.

"Two beautiful and talented boys, like my sweetheart there," she said. "If you're still here I return, in an hour or so, you'll meet them, see for yourself."

"That will be delightful," Clyde said, no intention of prolonging the visit beyond the time it took to sell Billy the Kid Palmer on the idea of giving the greatest performance of his life—

His death.

Produced by Mr. Magic.

Chapter 2

Billy waited, tapping his foot impatiently, until he heard the motor catch and their clunker of a Mercedes wheeze down the driveway. He pushed out a gust of relief from his puckered lips and, with a thumbs-up for Clyde, leaped to his feet and stumbled over to a cabinet, found a bottle of vodka, and savored a gulp on his way back to the fractured ebony leather armchair across the coffee table from Clyde, who was on a sofa spurting chicken feathers every time he adjusted his body on the sagging cushion.

Clyde waved off the offer of a slug for his coffee.

Billy added Clyde's to the one he had poured for himself.

Took a healthy swallow.

Dragged the back of his hand across his lips.

"Don't suppose you're carrying, ol' buddy mine, are you?" Billy said, in that combination of pessimism and hope common to every addict Clyde ever knew. "A little nose candy to help our reunion along?"

Clyde shook his head and gestured apologetically. He wasn't here to feed Billy's habit, only his brain, with a different kind of snow. Any sharing he was doing was strictly with Ava back at the suite and that was for the gift that keeps on giving. An acrobatic wonder that one.

Billy shrugged. He topped off his cup again and took a pull from the vodka bottle before setting it on the coffee table. "Minute I heard about you and the deal you got going for Waggoner Memorial, I called on over and offered to be on the bill, but they said you didn't want me or any of your old acts. That producer, what's his name, Mitch something?"

"Dragon. Mitchell Dragon, damn him. Lied on me every inch of the way, right up until it was too late to do anything about it. I told him you, and named some others to go after, so—what wound up on the bill?"

Billy broke in: "Two hours of washed-up stars of twenty and thirty years ago doing their old, mostly forgotten shit. None you ever had anything to do with. All of them looking like they could use free room and board in some retirement home. Surprised you of all people let them get away with it, Clyde."

Clyde threw a hand in the air. "It was a benefit for a wonderful cause, helping children, so in the end no use raising a stink about it, or so help me I would have," he said, papering the truth. In fact, he had made that a condition to Mitch Dragon.

He was moving in new directions, into the future, so—no performers linked to his past.

Mitch had given him an argument, saying it would ruin the "Salute" concept, only until Clyde told him there'd be no deal, definitely no financial pledge, not one red cent, unless all his conditions were met.

"My way or the highway, Mitch."

"Okay, okay, okay. So what else is new, Mr. Magic?"

"You said you want to do the show in the Waggoner Memorial auditorium."

"Free use. What we don't spend goes into the hospital's building fund."

"Except for what gets siphoned off by you, you mean."

"Learned from a master, Clyde."

"I want the show staged at the old Ryman Auditorium."

"Jesus F. Christ, Clyde. It's a relic, a tear down. You know how

many years it's been since the Grand Old Opry moved out of there to Opryland."

He told him, but it was going to be the Ryman or exit Clyde Davenport.

The Ryman was as meaningful a piece of history to him as any part of his life. It was the Ryman stage where he picked up the first of his seven Country Music Association Bullet awards for writing and producing cuts that snap-crackle-and-popped with his trademark "Symphony of Sound," the first singles and albums to catapult from Billboard*'s country chart to Number One on the Pop Top 100.*

"Whatever the cost, I'll write the check," he said. He let the silence run for a few beats before announcing, "Good-bye, Mitch."

"Okay, okay, okay. The Ryman. What else. You must have a what else, right, Clyde?"

"I always have a what else, Mitch."

Billy the Kid freshened his coffee with another slug of vodka, this time not bothering to offer a shot to Clyde. "I was disappointed, I say that?"

"Me, too, Billy."

"Would have gone anyway, just to honor you, but the price of a ticket was way too steep for me nowadays. You look around this dump, you see what I mean."

"No place for a wife like Kristy," Clyde said, setting up his chess pieces. "She seems like quite a woman."

Thinking—

Like the kind of mother I never had.

Thinking—

The look on her face when she spoke those warm words she had about her two sons, and running off to pick them up at school, sheer joy, total adoration, where all my mother ever picked up was something handy to slug me with or her bottle of the cheap screw-top wine she swallowed like soda pop, more and more after Daddy had the accident that cost him his eyes and he lost his job driving a cab in

Manhattan. Taking it out on him, but on me more, after the savings ran out and we lost the house and had to move from Brooklyn to Rockaway, a half block from the shore in a coldwater railroad car basement apartment.

You think I don't remember, you bitch? How you went to working nights at Irish Black Mahoney's Bar and Grill near Rockaway Playland, a fifteen-minute bus ride away on Beach Ninety-Seventh Street, and how I saw you lots of time being dropped off by different guys in cheap silk suits, gold chains around their necks, diamond pinky rings, and lips slobbering all over you? Slamming me black-and-blue the times you caught me at it, threatening me with worse if I said one word to Daddy?

And when I wanted him to learn sign language, how you laughed me into the ground, saying, "You're father's blind, not deaf, you moron."

"But I got a reason for wanting it for Daddy."

"A reason? How dumb can you ever get anymore? You were the daughter I ever wanted, you would understand he can hear a pin drop, you imbecile."

Billy said, "Clyde, you hearing me?"

"Loud and clear," Clyde said, snapping back into the room.

Realized he was answering Billy with his fingers as well as words.

Locked his hands on his knees.

"I swear, Kristy is the only one I never wanted to kick from bed in the morning after the night before," Billy said. "My Wonder Woman, Clyde. Blessed to have her and she blessed me with two fine sons. Without Kristy I'd be dead and gone a long time ago. She's the gift that keeps on giving."

"Maybe it's time for you to give Kristy a gift, Billy?"

"Say what?"

"And your two sons, a gift for them, also?"

Billy placed his hand over his heart, like he was preparing to pledge allegiance to the flag. "You mean like a new hit record with the maestro and a fresh start on life, Clyde, that it? Definitely will drink to that." He reached for his coffee cup.

"Not exactly what I had in mind when I called from L.A. to set up this meeting, Billy."

Billy's face tightened into a question mark.

He leaned forward in the armchair, clapped his hands in slow, nervous anticipation.

"Uh-huh, uh-huh. I remember almost word for word. Something about us maybe doing a turn in the studio, right? Jesus, man. Got my boner going strong just thinking about it ever since. Mr. Magic and Billy the Kid, together again. Bluto, also, Clyde? You said him, too. I ain't seen him, either, in however long, not since him and me split up soon after the label dumped us and everything else."

"Yes, I talked to Bluto, also," Clyde said, mentally cursing Bluto for the disappearing act that led him to personally undertake the arrangements on a death this time.

Maybe he had been too angry about Bluto, had acted too impulsively?

Or, was it Kristy.

The two sons.

That what was causing this crazy introspection?

Developing a conscience after all these years or simply confusing memories with his mission?

Maybe, fuck it, get the hell out of here. All the shit Billy is still putting into his system. The cancer playing an end game with his body. Just leave him be, and let nature take its course?

Billy caught his ear again, saying, "I still got the chops, man, although you might not think it to hear this minute. You remember the Bourbon Street Blues and Boogie Bar over on Printers Alley?" Rushing his words, a slur setting in.

"Of course."

"I've jammed there a lot, although not lately. Chicago blues. Delta blues. I'm still up for that, especially when some heavyweight or other is in there messing. Not just the country shit you showed me and Bluto the way on. After Kristy and me decided to give Nashville living a shot after the bankruptcy and all cost us the pad in Bel-Air, maybe catch on with some other label, but one's a crowd in Music City, U.S.A., and even demo sessions dried up after a while."

Clyde read into Billy's eyes a plea for rescue from the pain of constant rejection, real or imagined, enough for Clyde to wash his mind free of any further doubting. He could chart his death as a favor to both of them.

Signaling Billy to hold off for a moment, he leaned over and retrieved his satchel case. He pulled out a pair of disposable gloves and worked them onto his hands one slow finger at a time while Billy watched with muddled fascination. Out next came the .38-caliber automatic. "For you," Clyde said, as casually as if he were the postman delivering a letter, and settled the weapon on the table.

Billy's face registered confusion. He said, "I don't get it, buddy."

"For you to commit suicide with," Clyde said. "Clear enough? A gunshot at the temple will do it, if you keep your hand steady enough and don't send the bullet off course. The barrel in the mouth, aimed upward, is as surefire a method as they come. It would be my choice, if I were in your position."

Billy went after the coffee cup. It slipped from his two-fisted grip. Bounced off his knee. Emptied the spiked coffee on his pants before landing on the faded grasshopper-green throw rug. "What kind of sick joke you pulling on me, Clyde?" He grabbed for the vodka bottle and drained a mouthful, then another. "You always were the joker, Clyde. C'mon, let me in on it."

"I was never the joker, Billy. I was Mr. Magic and I made

you a star. You repaid me by tossing me out like garbage and telling the press, *Billboard, Rolling Stone,* anyone who asked, that it was me who should be on his knees thanking Billy the Kid and Bluto for letting him take credit for the act's success."

"I was young, Clyde. A kid. I didn't know what I was saying half the time. Bluto and me, we—I would have been nothing without you, Clyde."

"And now I'm giving you a chance to be nothing with me." He pointed to the .38. "Here's the deal, Billy. You blow your brains out within the next thirty-six hours. The arrangement our secret, nothing you'll share with anyone. No one. In exchange, I will set up a trust fund in your memory that takes Kristy and your sons out of this shitty existence your failures and your habits dropped them into. The fund's annual interest, I promise, I swear on my father's grave, will be enough to guarantee they never again want for anything for as long as they live."

Billy didn't know where to turn. He said, "What are you, Clyde, insane?" Got to his feet and paced the room in a meaningless pattern.

"Rich is what I am, Billy. Rich enough to pay for what I want when I want it, and maybe insane, yes, to come here thinking you were smart enough, grown up enough, realistic enough to do the right thing by your family." He had practiced the words back in L.A. and this morning in the bathroom mirror. He presented them calmly, reassuringly, with total confidence. "You'll die knowing you're making Kristy comfortable the rest of her life, Billy. Die knowing your boys will be able to go to college, pursue their dreams, and achieve more than you ever were able to achieve for yourself. Are you so much a basket case, the druggie, the alcoholic, that the truth is beyond you, that you're incapable of acting in the best interests of your wife and children?"

For several seconds, the only sound in the room was a horsefly circling above, uncertain where to land, briefly testing one spot after another before moving on, then—

Billy howled, the rage so profound and deep that Clyde wouldn't have been surprised if his guts followed the sound out of his twisted mouth.

He charged at him, his fists balled, barely able to keep his balance, cursing Clyde.

He stopped a foot away, his stale breath hot on Clyde's face. Rolled his arm like he was getting ready to unleash a punch. Changed his mind and retreated to the coffee table. Swept up the .38 and tried to take steady aim on Clyde's chest. Screamed, "I can do it, you know, you old, washed-up fart, you know that?" His hands shook so badly, there was a chance he'd accidentally pull the trigger.

Clyde berated himself for not anticipating Billy might react to this extreme, but he kept his composure, working through ways to diffuse the situation, get out of here safely, while Billy ranted on the edge of incomprehension.

"I remember you in the studio, out in public, you and all your fucking guns, Clyde. You always sticking them in people's faces and threatening to blow them away, you didn't get what you wanted. How you like it now, Clyde? The picture reversed. Me doing the producing now, Clyde, you bloodsucker."

Clyde chose holding his ground to trying an end run out of the room. However whacked he might be on the vodka and whatever else was hounding his system, Billy was younger, bigger, stronger than he was, giving him the edge. His own best weapon had always been his gift of gab, anyway. He yanked open his sports jacket, exposing his chest, and told Billy: "Go ahead, shoot."

The offer startled Billy and put a puzzle on his face. "Huh?"

"I said, Shoot me. The chest is your biggest and best target, more certain than anywhere else, provided you can get a grip on yourself and stop shaking at mach speed."

"Showing off, giving orders, like always. My turn to show you," Billy said, struggling to get the words out. He raised the .38, arms outstretched, and squinted after a focus.

"Squeeze the trigger, don't pull it, Billy. Pulling the trigger will throw it off-target and put a nice hole in the ceiling, maybe in the wall behind me, that nice framed portrait photo of Kristy and you. When was that taken, Billy? The bright red carnation in your lapel. Her orchid bouquet. On your wedding day, I bet. Correct?"

"None of your God damn business, Clyde." Still unable to steady the .38, but working at it. "I love that woman. A great wife. A great mother. And you got the nerve to show up with that ugly pockmarked face of yours, not ever knowing her yet, and telling me what I should be doing for her and our boys?"

Excellent.

He had moved Billy back on track.

Nurse it now, Clyde told himself. *Take your time getting to the hook. Lay down the melody first, then the message.*

He said, "So what purpose will be served if you kill me, except that it will put you in prison for life, maybe get you the death penalty? It's on the state books, you know? A chance you'll go to your grave having consigned Kristy to her own pauper's grave, maybe the same for your sons. I'd call that selfish, wouldn't you?"

Billy looked from Clyde to the .38 and back again. His combustible look softened, but didn't entirely go away.

"Why not think of me as your Good Samaritan, Billy? The offer I brought you and put on the table gets Kristy and the boys a bottomless pot of gold. Be a good father to your children. Get what's best for them. What you haven't given them in life, with my help, you can give it to them in death. Nothing you'll ever be able to provide on your own hook. You know that. Accept it for the truth it is."

"Fuck you. I don't need you. I'm their father, not you. I can do it without you. I've still got the chops, and—"

"Nobody wants your chops, Billy. Face it. You're history. Maybe a footnote. No more. I'm in the Rock and Roll Hall of Fame. You can't even afford a ticket to buy your way inside."

Billy fired the .38.

The bullet carved a path inches from Clyde's ear and slammed into the ceiling.

Billy, shaking like a dog in from the rain, stared at the weapon in disbelief. "I didn't mean to—Christ! It was an accident." He looked to Clyde for absolution.

Clyde grappled with his composure, determined not to reveal his momentary panic when the gun went off. He smiled benignly at Billy and restated the terms of his offer, stressing, "You have thirty-six hours and that's it, Billy. Less, if that's your choice, but no more. After thirty-six hours, my offer is off the table, never to return."

Billy turned his back on Clyde and crossed back to the armchair. Sank into it, settled the .38 on his lap, and reached for the vodka bottle. "Just go," he said, breaking into tears. "Get the hell out of here, Clyde."

"Is that a yes or a no, Billy?"

"It's a get the hell out of here."

"Should we talk some more?"

"Fuck off, Clyde." He hefted the gun. "Split before I change my fucking mind and murder you for real."

Clyde rotated his palms to the ceiling, heaved his hands upward. He retrieved his satchel, peeled off his gloves, and dropped them inside; snapped the satchel shut, telling Billy, "I'll leave the gun with you, Billy. Thirty-six hours to put it to good use, meet my conditions, or consider it a souvenir of my visit, a reminder of what might have been." Billy was ignoring him. "Apologize to Kristy for my racing off without thanking her for her hospitality and getting to meet your two fine sons."

He was halfway out of the room when Billy called after him, "You and me, we went back into the studio, we could've had another Gold record, you son of a bitch!"

Clyde smiled at what he was confident he heard, a pleading in Billy's voice overtaken by surrender.

He was about to climb into the limo when he got what sounded like confirmation—

Billy shouting his name from the front porch, hanging onto a rail, shouting his name and firing a thumbs-up at him. Shouting his name and telling the world, "Trusting you at your word, Mr. Magic. Trusting you at your word."

Clyde returned the gesture.

What was the harm?

Lionel waited until he was dissecting traffic on Highway 431, heading back to Nashville, to wonder, "Gentlemans I saw back there, looked a lot like somebody my woman and me once or twice heard playing and singing up a storm down at the Bourbon Street Blues and Boogie Bar in Printers Alley. By chance that him, Mistuh Davenport? Name of Billy the Kid Palmer?"

Clyde said, "It used to be," and poured himself a fresh cognac while reminding the limo driver, "Clyde, Lionel, remember? Mr. Davenport was my father."

Chapter 3

Ava was waiting for him in the suite, looking beautiful in the Versace outfit she had gone crazy over their trip last month to New York, saying Madonna had worn exactly that silk blouse, those jeans on Letterman. On the patio, staring out over a city of commerce and high-rise office buildings that weren't there when he first visited Nashville to strut his success and steal pointers from the likes of George Jones and Chet Atkins; Owen Bradley, Wesley Rose, Hubert Long, and other power-brokers who used their slow drawl to disguise the fast shuffle they often applied to business.

She had lasted longer with him than any of the others, since last year's "National Search for Miss American Showgirl" in Vegas, him a judge and Ava one of four runners-up for the title. She was the kind of woman that had always held a special appeal for him, but not available until his reputation preceded him. He was never taken in by the ones who thought they could play him for a meal ticket or a career by sucking his cock or submitting to the sex games he liked playing.

Ava had a taste for the erotic matching his, buried under an air of girlish innocence and a naïve intelligence to go with her fine looks. Enough of a decent voice—a voice, not necessarily singing skills—to let him Svengali her to stardom on his climb back to the top of the mountain, an attractive idea because it was his, not hers.

Deep down Ava was probably a skank, sometimes he thought

he smelled it on her, but to this day all she'd ever asked him for was to make sure he beat her hard enough to get her coming the same time as him. He'd probably miss her when he lost his appetite for her and moved on to whatever came along next, something funky or, maybe, as upscale as Dr. Roy at the Waggoner Memorial Ranch and Free Clinic. Something more than vibes was definitely happening between them this morning, more than his imagination.

At the sound of the door opening, Ava wheeled around, squealed, and came running over. Hugging him like a favorite Teddy bear, tattooing his cheek with her crimson lip rouge, digging into his ear with her tongue and words drowning in sincerity.

"I missed you a bunch, Clyde, honey. I was worried, it getting later than you said you'd be back."

"Taking care of a little unfinished business. Took longer than I thought."

"All finished now?"

"All finished," he said, working his hand through her hair and down her back, weighing her tiny ass inside his palm.

She got the message and reached down to be sure she was reading it correctly. She gave him a squeeze and a devilish smile. "We don't have to go out for dinner, you know? Can be out of these rags faster than I wiggled into them. Later, room service and maybe a nice lounge in the tub. That what you'd rather, honey?"

He patted her cheek and signaled her with a look that said they wouldn't be getting much sleep tonight.

Clyde outlasted her.

The last begging that passed through Ava's bruised lips was for a few hours' rest.

While she slept, his thoughts wandered back to Dr. Roy and

the idea of paying her a visit once the Billy the Kid business was history, see how far he could take it with her. The possibility excited him, sent voltage charging through his body. He'd use the boy, Teddy Jack, as his excuse. Visit the boy, see how he was faring after his operations. That would suck her in, and—

He felt himself drifting off to sleep, finally, images of the boy and the doctor dissolving into a memory of himself, ten years old, his mother chasing after him with a frying pan, ready to bring it down on his head, the third or fourth time he tried talking to her about sign language—

Rescued by his blind Daddy, using his son's pleas of *Stop it, Mommy, please stop* as a compass. Daddy slamming his mother to the floor, finding her thigh, then her belly with the pointed toe of his scruffy black patent leather shoes, shouting at her:

Leave the boy alone, you damned bitch, you know what's good for you.

She flees to the safety of Irish Black Mahoney's Bar and Grill.

His daddy pours them both a jelly glass of his mother's red, diluting his with a splash of rusty water from the kitchen tap, and says: *"Tell me now, son. What was it all about this time, her carrying on like the crazy woman she's become?"*

"Because I want you to learn this kind of sign language I found out about at the library, Daddy, so we can start going to the movies again, like the olden days before the accident. You loved the movies so much, and—"

Daddy presses his fingers to his son's lips and laughs heartily. "What business does a blind man have learning sign language? It's the radio for your daddy now, Clyde." He tilts his head back and empties the jelly glass, feels for the wine bottle and pours a refill after hanging his thumb over the lip of the glass. It's one of the tricks he's been taught in blind class—how to stop pouring when the liquid reaches the tip of the thumb. He's always returning home with some new blind trick or other, Clyde taken to learning them for himself while helping Daddy practice.

"It doesn't have to be, Daddy. I heard about what's called blind-deaf signing and found a book at the library I've been reading up ever since. Practicing every spare minute in front of the mirror. The one-handed and two-handed methods for hand and body contact. Shorthand signs for emotions. Finger spelling. Like that. I'm catching on as quick as I did when I sat down at our old piano, remember that, how natural it came to me, playing the piano? You learn blind-deaf signing, and we can start going to the movies again. I can sign you about the pictures that go with what you hear the actors are saying. Daddy? What do you say, Daddy?"

Daddy taps his picked and bitten rickety fingernails on the walnut door slab on makeshift legs that serves as their meal table while Clyde waits out his answer by picking up the melody in his head and converting it to instruments led by a jazz drum in the style of Gene Krupa.

Finally, Daddy says, "No."

Clyde's desperately hopeful smile folds into a frown.

He doesn't want to cry, but he can't help himself.

Daddy reaches over for his hand, takes it, and says, "We'll learn the blind-deaf sign language together, son. I'll ask next time at blind class where there's a class and get us both signed up. Don't fret none about what the old lady thinks or says when she hears about this. Steer clear of the wicked witch and—"

Clyde bolted upright in bed shouting, "Mommy, quit hitting!"

Ava, rolling over, had flopped a heavy palm on his face.

He slipped out from under the covers and tracked to the balcony, not entirely free of the dream that often came to him. He studied the stars while shaking loose of the worst memories of those days, especially of the last beating from his mother, the one that almost killed him, before she abandoned him, ran away and left him after screaming the usual obscenities for his always siding with Daddy, wishing how he had never been born.

That was the memory that always brought the most pain.

Again, now.

Clyde fought the urge to cry, drawing on his usual anecdote, visions of leading Daddy to the cheap Sunday matinees at the Rockaway Theater. Talking the double bills to Daddy with his hands, with precision, anxious to let Daddy see everything happening on the screen. Everything.

What skilled me at writing lyrics, he signed for the stars blanketing Nashville. The years of describing the most elaborate of the movie scenes for Daddy with an economy of hand and body contact, finger talk that painted as detailed a picture as any painting by Thomas Eakins.

Why I caught on so quickly, so young, after I left home, moved to Manhattan, and began haunting the Brill Building. What led me to create my Symphony of Sound. Daddy and the blind-deaf sign language. Without that I would not have become so rich and famous. I'd be that dumb wimp my mother was always screaming at, until the night I put an end to it by—

Clyde threw his hands behind his back and laced his fingers.

Enough.

That night was no place he wanted to visit.

He quit the thought and padded back to the bed, eased under the covers, and gave Ava a gentle shake. She had slept enough. He needed her again.

"Wake up, you skank," he said. He shook her harder, kept shaking until she rolled over and into his arms, eyes still full of sleep. "Don't you ever even think about splitting on me," he said. "Not until I say so, understand?"

Two days after returning to Los Angeles, a reporter from the *Nashville Tennessean* called Clyde to advise him of Billy Palmer's death by suicide, sketching a few details in a brisk manner that suggested he had been through the ritual dozens of times, wondering if the musician's former record producer wished to comment for his story.

It was the first of the media calls he knew would be coming his way.

They always did after one of the names on his list of disloyal acts died—looking for an easily digestible sound bite from Mr. Magic—and he always found new ways to sound sincere, juggling the same old platitudes into something it amused him to think of as his "Symphony of Words":

A remarkable artist lost to us under tragic circumstances.

A great talent who could have given us so much more, but tragically cut down in his prime, like the immortal Gershwin.

I cherish the memory of my great and dear friend and, especially, the years when our careers merged.

Shit like that, always dressed in mourner's black.

What he wanted to tell the media, but of course never could, was how he had produced the deaths with the same exacting love and precision care he'd introduced to each and every hit record he produced for them before they turned into ungrateful superstars and coldly abandoned him. How their deaths gave him a bigger, better orgasm than the best sex he'd ever had, knowing their disloyalty had finally been rewarded.

Clyde gasped at the news out of Nashville and choked up loud enough to guarantee the reporter heard him. Adopting his usual funereal tone, he said, "A tragedy of the first magnitude. The music community has lost a great one." He paused for effect. "It was an honor and privilege to be involved with Billy at the onset of his career, when the team of Billy the Kid and Bluto skyrocketed to fame under my direction, with songs I wrote and produced."

The reporter said, "His wife told police you visited with Mr.

Palmer a day or so before he put the .38 to his head."

"Yes, correct. I was in Nashville for a benefit concert at the old Ryman, for Waggoner Memorial Ranch Hospital and Free Clinic. Nothing to indicate what that poor soul had on his mind."

"That was for the benefit concert in your honor, A Salute to Mr. Magic."

"Correct, but please don't make your story about me. Billy and Bluto moved on with their careers, but the three of us stayed friends. I would not have dreamed of leaving Nashville without seeing Billy. It had been far too many years."

"Mrs. Palmer says her husband told her afterward that you proposed going back into the recording studio with him."

"Correct. Billy bringing his incomparable voice and talent to my Symphony of Sound. He was so enthusiastic about the idea, so fantastically upbeat. That's what contributes to my shock at the news you brought me." He barely managed to get the last few words out, playing the role he had played with all the other deaths already logged on his play list. "You'll have to excuse me."

"Take your time. . . . I understand from people at the clubs and honky-tonks around here that Mr. Palmer didn't have much of a voice left?"

"Correct. The end product of some bad habits Billy confessed to me he could not shake, but I'd have surmounted them. Made Billy sound good as new. Better than ever. They don't call me Mr. Magic for nothing."

"Mr. Palmer seemed to have fallen on extremely hard times because of those bad habits."

"I got the same impression, damn it. Now, thinking of Billy's devoted wife, Kristy—the awful impact his suicide will have on her and their two sons. . . ." He filled the phone with silence. Put a crack in his voice. "I'll have to do something about that.

In Billy's memory."

"Like what, sir?"

Clyde made it sound like he was giving the reporter's question thought. "Possibly a trust fund, large enough to help Mrs. Palmer through the hard days ahead and help her raise the boys as Billy would have wanted for them."

"You pledge more than a million dollars to the hospital, and there's something I heard about you and a deaf youngster there. Now this. You're a very generous man, Mr. Davenport."

"No, sir, a friend. It's what true friendship is all about."

The interview trailed off after another question or two.

Clyde disconnected and instantly let out a whoop and broke into a little victory dance.

Tonight would be a night for celebration, and what a celebration it would be.

Chapter 4

Josh Wainwright tossed away the *Times,* his anger stoked by the Associated Press story about the suicide of Billy the Kid Palmer in Nashville. "True friendship, my ass," he said. "The only friend Clyde Davenport has ever been true to in his life is Clyde Davenport." He dug into his breakfast melon like he was digging a grave for Davenport.

Josh's ten-year-old, Julie, looked up from her bowl of Lucky Charms and reproached him with her look. "A dime, Daddy. Pay up."

"What's that, sweetheart?"

"A dime for the Penalty Piggy, for the four-letter word you just said."

Her older brother, Justin, sitting across from her at the kitchen table, said, "There's only three letters in ass. A-s-s."

"That counts anyway. Tell him it counts, Daddy." She seemed on the verge of tears.

Josh served Julie a smile and pulled out a handful of coins from the change pocket of his denims. "Don't be such a wise a-s-s, Justin." He sorted through the coins for a dime and slid it across the table to the girl.

Julie blew her tongue at Justin and pushed up from the table. "Be back," she said, and charged through the swinging door, heading for the Penalty Piggy on the knickknack shelf in the den.

The Wainwright family's housekeeper, Niki Beth Jacob,

finished pouring Josh's oatmeal into his metal bowl, carried it over from the stove, and resumed her seat with a suggestion for Justin. "You should try being nicer to your sister," she said. "Kinder. Not contribute to Julie's problems. You're almost thirteen, the age a boy becomes a man, so practice being one, yes?"

"When did you become my mother? Dad, tell her she's not my mother?"

Josh briefly shut his eyes to the latest flare-up between Justin and Niki. "Nobody will ever replace your mother, Justin, but that doesn't give you leave to behave like an ass with Niki." He found another dime and flipped it to his son, who made a mid-air catch.

Justin looked at the coin like it was contaminated. He leaped to his feet screaming, "You always take sides with that bitch," and tossed the dime back before racing from the room.

Josh said, "I'm sorry about that. I'll speak to the boy later."

Niki smiled and showed him she was all right with it. "Eat your oatmeal before it gets cold," she said—

Sounding too much like Katie when Katie would tell him the same thing, or—

Was his imagination playing another cruel trick on him?

Josh was aware Niki had a crush on him, if that was still the word, Crush.

She struggled to keep it under control, but it always revealed itself to him, through the passion lighting her coal-black eyes whenever he caught Niki studying him, the fire he'd hear burning in her voice whenever the two of them fell into casual conversation.

All he felt for Niki was a fatherly concern.

After all, for Christ's sake, she was young enough to be his daughter.

Niki was twenty-two to his forty-one, a graduate exchange student at UCLA, who was looking to trade family household services for her room and board when his brother Lon found her through a placement agency.

This was right after the severe depression that came in the wake of Katie's murder, when his dependency on booze and pills made him fear he'd not be able to take care of the kids, gave him nightmares that the kids would be taken from him if he failed to rediscover the blue in the sky, and drove him to voluntarily commit himself to a rehab facility.

Knowing Lon, he figured Niki's looks, a combination of innocence and sensuality, got her the job. Her only experience, she'd been quick to confess, was helping her mother care for five younger sisters and brothers back home in Iran, which she always referred to as "Persia," and herself as a "Persian Jew."

In the two-plus years since, especially of late, Justin had turned almost resentful of her presence, frequently inventing excuses to argue with her. Josh had no idea what had caused the change. He'd tried to tease the answer out of Justin and, when that didn't work, decided to leave bad enough alone. Justin was still a child. Either he'd grow out of it or learn to live with it.

Julie, on the other hand, seemed to need Niki more and more. She often screamed out in her sleep for her, the way she once had for Katie.

Niki would be at her bedside in an instant, cradling Julie in her arms, whispering words of comfort and crooning her back to sleep with the lullaby her mother used to sing to her to wash away her fears, the words in Ladino, the medieval language of the Jews of Spain adopted by Persian Jews, the melody in a universal language as warm as summer sunshine.

Crush.

Okay, why not?

So what?

Big deal.

Maybe sometime he'd get around to asking her how it translated into Ladino or the informal Latorayi dialect, which she once described to him as the ancient bazaar language of Iranian Jewish merchants, words taken from Hebrew, but "not of the Torah," Niki said, spoken by her parents whenever they didn't want the children to understand them.

Frankly, he'd be lost without Niki, but—

Never as lost as he'd become without Katie.

Crushed without Katie.

Beyond repair until he finally had the evidence that would put the man responsible for Katie's death on trial for murder—

That bastard Clyde Davenport.

Bastard.

Davenport vowing vengeance on Katie for leaving him after he'd turned her into a star, like it was all his doing, Katie a no-talent without Mr. Magic and his "Symphony of Sound."

Making good on his threat—

A public execution viewed by millions.

Josh not able to prove it was Davenport's doing.

Not yet, but only *not yet.*

Josh had made a vow of his own—

To avenge Katie or die trying.

Making no secret of it with Davenport.

Davenport saying, "The largest wreath at your funeral will be from me."

Bastard.

Josh got another dime from his pocket and lobbed it to Niki.

"For the Penalty Piggy," he said.

After Niki drove off with the kids, to deposit them at Murphy-McCracken Academic Academy before heading to UCLA, Josh snatched a rose from the fresh floral arrangement she had made a habit of placing on a pedestal in the entry hall, phoned Keshawna at their office to say he'd be late, and took off for Westwood Village Memorial Park.

He maneuvered his Lexus into one of the few curbside parking spots available inside the cemetery, already full of early-bird sightseeing buses and the camera-toting graveyard groupies who get some special thrill from ogling and trampling on the final resting place of the famous.

Monroe's crypt at the northeast corner wall was the main tourist attraction, a Mona Lisa for the morbidly inclined, but the film buffs among them were also pointing their digital and cell-phone cameras at markers for director Billy Wilder and his favorite co-stars, Jack Lemmon and Walter Matthau, together again for the last time in the Garden of Serenity.

Josh moved onto the center island lawn, weaving a respectful path around dignified marble markers for Burt Lancaster, Lloyd Nolan, and Donna Reed, past Darryl F. Zanuck's notice-me stone, by Richard Conte, between Cornel Wilde and Natalie Wood, to Katie.

He picked at a few weeds the gardeners had missed, substituted his fresh rose for the one he paid to have placed there every day, and sat down yoga-style on his adjacent space. He patted her marker, strained to keep from choking up while telling Katie, "Looks like he's done it again, Sugar. You remember Billy the Kid Palmer? Billy the Kid and Bluto? His act a long time before Davenport latched onto you? Supposedly killed himself. Blew his brains out yesterday, the poor son of a bitch. The third Davenport act to die that way. The eleventh act to quit Davenport and die a less-than-natural death. The first new leads for me to chase since you were—"

He couldn't bring himself to say it.

"You knew her?"

Josh looked up to find the flighty voice, flighty as a hummingbird, belonged to a straw-haired man in his early thirties, wearing shorts and a T-shirt advertising ABBA, his deep-sea-blue eyes blazing with the possibility of discovery.

"I was asking if you knew her—Sunshine Katie," the man said, traces of an English accent seeping in.

Sunshine Katie.

Josh liked that. "Yeah. Why? So what?"

"Brilliant, absolutely brilliant. Sunshine Katie was my favorite, even more than Streisand. More than Celine Dion. More than—"

Josh stopped him with a gesture. "I get your drift. . . . Mine, too."

The man held up a silver-bodied camera the size of a cigarette pack. "I couldn't return home without being here. Without having a souvenir picture made of us. Do you mind taking it for me?"

Josh didn't have to think about it. His whipped his 9-millimeter Beretta from his shoulder holster and aimed. "I mind," he said. "She is nobody's souvenir. Not now. Not ever."

The man broke out of the trance the sight of the 9 M had put him into. He wheeled around and fled in a half crouch, a zigzag course, as if afraid bullets would be flying at him any second.

Josh replaced the handgun in the holster and stroked Katie's marker. "Not now, not ever," he said. "Not now, not ever. Never. I want people to remember you as you were, as I remember you, Sugar—full of life. Okay, Sugar? What do you say? That okay with you?"

Chapter 5

Keshawna Keyes looked up at the click and creak of her office door opening. A grim-faced Josh was homing in on her unannounced. She'd spent enough years with him, knew him well enough—in many ways better than Josh knew himself—to recognize his anger behind the mask. It had to be because of the news about this Billy the Kid Palmer guy's suicide in Nashville and Palmer's connection to Clyde Davenport.

"Here we go again," she thought, time to indulge him, waste more manpower and money chasing after evidence that linked Davenport to Katie's murder. How many weeks or months this time before Josh hit the same brick wall as every other time, before he would agree to her softly peddled urging to shut down the investigation?

He surprised her.

He slumped into a visitor's chair at her desk, arms locked across his chest, legs crossed at the ankles—a poster boy for bad posture—and shook his head.

"Keesh, I'm thinking I should be ashamed about something stupid I just did," Josh said, describing an encounter at Katie's grave with some English ninny who wanted his picture taken. "You think I overreacted?"

"Sounds like improvement to me," she said. "A year ago, same circumstances, I'd figure you to pop him, plant your backup pea shooter in his palm, and claim self-defense."

"All my years on the force, I never played that number."

She feigned horror. "I heard the rumor there was some Goody Two-Shoes in Blue, but never suspected it was you, partner."

"You knew it was me, partner, every mile on the road leading to your resignation and my retirement. . . . What do you think Katie would say?"

"She'd say you're an Eagle Scout."

"About the creep with the camera."

"The truth?"

"As usual."

"Katie would tell you to take the picture for him. She'd be flattered to be so remembered and loved by somebody besides you, Josh. You should feel flattered, too. Honored to be able to share the love with people everywhere in the world who remember her rich talent and the good vibes Katie Sunshine brought into their lives."

"I asked for an answer, Keesh, not one of your ass-kicking Sunday sermons at Adams First Evangelical." He catapulted from the chair and prowled the office, arms reaching for the ceiling, hands doing a palsied dance. "Hallelujah, hallelujah, hallelujah. Okay?"

Keshawna let him wander. She pulled a stack of reports from the in basket and swiveled around to face the view window, the high back of her executive chair turned to him like a wall against any further outbursts. She'd lost count years ago over how many scenes like this they'd played out between them. She knew it was coming even before she answered Josh. It was Josh's hair-trigger response to anything he interpreted as criticism, an insult, or a rebuke. He would cool off internally, then land back on earth as if nothing had ever happened.

The other detectives came to call it "The Keshawna and Josh Show," giving her top billing because she was the senior member of the team, a Detective One working vice out of Hollywood

Division three years before Josh won his badge and was partnered up with her.

From the beginning they fit together like peanut butter and jelly.

It stayed that way after he joined her as a partner in International Celebrity Services.

International Celebrity Services, an organization providing film, television, and sports celebrities and VIPs among the rich and famous what it advertised as "safety and peace of mind for our clients and their families," occupied an entire floor of the Century City Towers building, high enough up to command views from the San Fernando Valley to Catalina Island, north and south, and downtown Los Angeles to the Pacific Ocean, east and west.

Keshawna started ICS in her bedroom within days of resigning from the Los Angeles Police Department, one step ahead of an internal investigation that, ignoring every sign of her innocence, seemed ready to name her a co-conspirator among dirty cops and the not-so-dirty who continued to plead clean hands even as indictments were drawn against them.

"They got it in for me because I'm a woman, I'm black, I got my detective rank by guts, drive and determination, and there's no one braver than me in the line of fire except, maybe, for my partner, Joshua Wainwright," she told the world at a press conference called by her lawyer. "It's a wonder they're not trying to nail Josh, put him behind bars, as well, but he's a man's man, white as a Ku Klux Klansman's sheet, and too smart to fall for the lying tricks being played by Internal Affairs on me and our brother officers."

Keshawna had always been outspoken, blunt in her choice of words. She made offense her defense from her earliest days growing up in South Central in a fatherless family of eight brothers and sisters reared on food stamps by a Bible-quoting mama with soulful eyes, sagging breasts, and a back permanently bent from cleaning jobs for Beverly Hills wealthies, who paid her a fraction of the state's minimum hourly wage and figured Mama owed them thanks for the opportunity.

The one time she saw the man passing himself off as her daddy, he showed up on a day Mama was scrubbing somebody's brown-stained toilets. Keshawna was eleven, street wise smart enough to recognize his tats were handmade prison variety and his restless red, white, and blue eyes spelled out "junkie" in blazing neon.

The moment she let him in, he was ready to rip up the place searching for something that might turn him enough dollars at Fat J's pawn shop to score a fix.

When she warned him off and ordered him to leave, he put a move on her, quick as a hound in heat.

Mama walked in on him holding her helpless and bare-ass naked over the arm of the couch, his pants ringing his ankles.

Not hesitating a second, she grabbed for the steam iron on the ironing board always set up in the front room, where Mama liked to work while watching *The Young and the Restless.* She gave him a whack on his shoulder that sent him flying across the room and slamming into the wall, knocking off all the pictures Mama had methodically hung gallery-style. He was gone before she got close enough to whack him again and prove her threat that "Lord willing, nigger, this next one gonna put you in touch with the devil hisself."

Once satisfied her baby was safe beyond a few bruises, she told Keshawna, "Child, all men ain't like that one, only most, so you never let your guard down on your way to the kind of better life you can come by you always minds your Bible and do what's right and good. Always put your trust in God and God gonna keep his trust with you, see you through to the Kingdom of Heaven."

Keshawna tried hard to honor Mama's advice, but she fell off the Bible more than a few times, mostly when it came to taking up with men who slicked her with cotton-candy promises and took what they wanted from her before taking off for good.

By the time she was seventeen, she'd survived two rapes and two abortions, but nothing put a dent in her appetite for men. She'd love them more than she'd ever trust them, one after the next, but she became the one to end the affairs.

Also by seventeen, Keshawna's cocoa-colored beauty was visible enough to get her voted "Campus Queen" at Jefferson High. It didn't hurt that she had grown into an athletically built six-footer who led Jeff's girls' basketball team to two consecutive Southern League championships and was named All-League and All-City center, all the while managing a 4.0 grade average.

It earned her an athletic scholarship to the University of Southern California, where she majored in business administration until a drive-by shooting took the life of Mama and two of her siblings, Shawn and baby Amir, who got in the way of bullets flying from an Uzi fired by a gang-banger in a boosted Chevy low rider who never got caught.

Neither of her two older brothers could take on the responsibility of the family—one was a speed freak selling his wasted body on Santa Monica Boulevard in L.A., the other doing two-to-seven at Q for robbery—so it fell to Keshawna.

She dropped out of USC into a job an Alumni Association member scored for her at Tower Records on the Sunset Strip. She was made an assistant manager on the night shift after three months and promoted to night shift manager six months later.

Keshawna stayed at Tower until the twins, Latasha and Latoya, were old enough to take over running the family, freeing her to apply to LAPD. Becoming a cop was a goal that formed in her mind after Mama, Shawn, and baby Amir were gunned down and the detectives on the case treated it like carpet dust.

She breezed through the department's entrance exam and finished first in her class at the Police Academy. That earned her a modicum of respect after she had spent months tolerating the prejudice brought on by either her color or her sex. She was unsure which, settling on both after she kept getting handed junk duty assignments at one undesirable division after the next.

Joshua Wainwright was the last and the best of the plainclothes they partnered her with.

Josh brought his own baggage, as well as his badge, to the relationship, and the kinds of cop skills and general savvy that could have taken him high up the chain of command, except for the three circumstances that turned Josh's life topsy-turvy.

The first was standing tall and righteous for her when Internal Affairs was under intense pressure from Top Cop and City Hall to root out the corrupt Blue Crews who for years had made the department motto, "To Protect and Serve," self-serving.

They were getting runaway rich on robberies, burglaries, protection racketeering, drug trafficking, even an occasional homicide, until undone by a couple of busted cops motivated to trade names for a plea bargain.

Busts begat busts, and somewhere down the line Keshawna was implicated.

There was no evidence against her, only the words of a division captain who'd once put the make on her in an empty locker room and, when that didn't work, tried a strong-arm rape that resulted in a busted nose, a broken ankle, and balls she kicked into blue balloons, the captain having underestimated the power Keshawna was capable of putting behind the words *Fuck off, you miserable slimeball.*

She honored the Blue Wall of Silence, of course, but the prick had held a grudge against her ever since, wheezy breathing and a slight limp his constant reminders of the incident, and, despite the lack of any evidence linking Keshawna to any wrongdoing, made certain the public spotlight stayed on her.

He gouged into her heart with one media sound bite after another, made her suspect among some small-minded parishioners at her church, caused neighbors to look the other way when they saw her puppy-strolling the street, wore her down to the basement of the blues, and finally out of the department.

Josh never wavered in his support, never ducked a news camera shoved in his face along with the kinds of questions meant to provoke some comment that would incriminate Keshawna and, maybe, even himself.

His last words on the subject became "The LAPD is losing a great detective and I'm out one damn fine partner."

Then, Josh put a deed to the words, creating circumstance number two.

He and his beloved Katie Sunshine made it possible for Keshawna to move International Celebrity Services out of her bedroom, Katie writing a check large enough to cover an office in the Larchmont district, a small staff, and enough state-of-the-art equipment to make the security company an instant frontrunner.

Katie became her first client, pushed Keshawna's way the recording and concert stars in her circle of friends. Josh did the same, promoting her among the motion-picture and television stars he knew through his movie-star brother, Lon McCrea, or their movie-star-icon parents, the late Harry Wainwright and the ageless Olivia McCrea.

At no time did they ask for a return on the investment, even refusing her offer of an IOU on paper, another act of kindness Keshawna vowed never to forget, to repay in some way someday.

Ultimately, it became a full ICS partnership for Josh, after Katie was killed and he retired from the force.

The Police Central brass read this support for Keshawna as evidence of Josh's disrespect and disloyalty for official position, effectively ending any chance Josh might have at promotions.

He was shuffled from one division to another, every rung lower on the ladder, and assigned to dump duty meant to embarrass anyone whose jacket was stuffed with letters of commendation and blue ribbon reviews from years past.

He was off duty, in a tux, the night the third circumstance occurred:

Shrine Auditorium.

After the Grammy Awards of the Academy of Recording Arts and Sciences, where Josh had participated in a segment honoring Katie's memory—ten minutes that left him drenched in sweat and tearstains as Katie's career was recalled and remembered in film clips dating back to appearances on *American Bandstand* and progressing to her last regular engagement, her multimillion-dollar one-woman spectacular, "Sunshine Katie," at the Klondike Hotel in Las Vegas.

He was outside on the red carpet, in line waiting for his limo while his date, Katie's best friend and girlhood singing partner Connie Reynolds, shared hugs with Barbra Streisand and Stevie Wonder, when he heard shouts for help from a bosomy singer rigged in full bling-bling regalia, who had thanked God and a phone book of friends for her Grammy victory before stutter-stepping off the musician-cluttered stage.

She was screaming for police, anyone, to stop the thief who'd just snatched her diamond necklace and was disappearing into what was still a crowd of celebrity gawkers and autograph hounds on the other side of the frayed velvet crowd-control ropes.

Josh responded instinctively.

He navigated around the lineup of parking attendants in gold-trimmed red vests and elbowing through a gaggle of fans who were making a game of it, chanting "Stop thief! Stop thief!" like it was some hip-hop anthem.

The thief broke into the clear and jumped into the two traffic lanes, both bumper-to-bumper with limos, Cads, Hummers, and Rolls-Royces inching forward to the Shrine's main entrance. He pumped his short legs between and around the cars and, turning, he saw Josh closing the gap between them.

He picked up enough speed to manage a jump onto the fender, hood, and roof of a forest-green Bentley sedan, from there to the hood of a glitzy Porsche and onto the opposite sidewalk. He was aiming for Jefferson Boulevard, where he stood a chance of losing himself in the thick pedestrian traffic, except—

Josh had no intention of letting him get away.

He was taller than the thief, his legs longer, and that gave him an edge.

Josh cut his own path through the cars, adding to the cacophony of angry horns set in motion by the thief, narrowly escaped getting his knees crushed when a bumper tap sent a BMW lurching forward, and turned two pedestrians into ten pins.

The thief jerked his head over his shoulder and spotted Josh still in pursuit.

He cut back through the traffic and turned east on Jefferson.

Josh rounded the corner in time to see the thief duck into the service alley behind the auditorium. He navigated the turn, adding to the sloshing sound of the thief's sneakers in the badly lit alley full of tricky rain puddles left over from the succession of storms that had tried to drown Los Angeles a week earlier.

About fifty yards down, he stopped to catch his breath, bent over with his hands on his knees, and came up after a few seconds to silence.

The thief also had stopped.

He was waiting for Josh, crouched in a wrestler's stance at the far end of the alley, in front of the tall loading doors of the Exposition Center adjacent to the auditorium.

He had gone past the last turnout and was blocked by walls on three sides, by Josh in front of him.

He jabbed at the night air with a thin-handled six-inch switchblade, urging Josh forward with his free hand while hissing in a heavily accented Latino high soprano that Josh would be smart to turn around and split, unless he was anxious to taste death.

A quarter moon had drifted past a bank of clouds, casting the thief in a shallow, revealing light. Latino. Fifteen or sixteen. Cheap street clothes. Pants two sizes too large that bagged at the cuffs. A sweatshirt under a punk club jacket. Broad fullback shoulders. An expression revealing, for all his mouthy bravado, the thief was fearful of the moment, uncertain about his next move if Josh didn't take his suggestion.

In Josh's experience, these were the most dangerous types, young, inexperienced gang-bangers who were cornered and armed. He wasn't. He had intended to pack a piece, but he was ten or twelve pounds heavier than the last time he wore the tux, and it wouldn't have buttoned if he strapped on the shoulder holster.

He approached the punk cautiously, psyching out the situation while doing a slow-footed shuffle forward.

The punk had nowhere to go, except through him.

Josh said, "Give it up, dude. I'm the Man. I'll see to it that you get treated right, you don't try anything crazy-ass stupid." He whipped out his billfold and flipped it open to his badge.

"You stop right there," the punk said. "You packing?"

"What do you think?" Patting his jacket over the heart. Trying a bluff: "Bullets fly faster than a switchblade any day of the week. You got a mama waiting for you at home? Let's make it happen."

"How so?"

"You hand over the necklace you snatched, I let you walk and forget I ever saw you."

"What makes you so goody-goody?"

"Got my own boy at home."

"I ain't nobody's boy." He took a step toward Josh and made a threatening gesture with the switch.

"Easy, easy. Don't do anything dumb."

"And fuck you, too," he said, and—

Those were the last words Josh heard before something hard caught him at the base of his skull and propelled him forward into the Exposition Center doors like a puppet off his strings. His eyes traded a look at the thief's large-toothed smile before they blitzed out on him and—

He woke up in County General he didn't know how many hours later, his head in a mummy kind of bandage, held rigid by a vise-like contraption; his arms and legs strapped to the frame; Connie Reynolds dozing in a bedside chair, an open book on her lap.

Turned out to be days since the Grammy Awards.

The kid hadn't been working the Grammy crowd alone.

He had some accomplice, who'd come up behind Josh and used a lead pipe or something like that to treat his head like a piñata. They were gone before paramedics arrived on somebody's nine-one-one call.

The doctor said a little harder or higher and Josh would be waking up where the gates were pearly.

Josh was never a hundred percent after that.

Migraines became his constant companion and there were the occasional memory lapses, like people he knew who were ten and twenty years older than him, able to recall the minutiae of their Good Old Days better than what happened to them yesterday.

It was all the excuse the brass needed to lock him to the desk job and his own for taking an early getaway on disability.

Keshawna wheeled her chair back around and said, "What else, Joshua?"

He was fiddling with one of the Buddha ivories on her Netsuke shelf. "Meaning?"

"Something else on your mind besides some goof got your goat wanting his picture taken with Katie to get you charging in here like a pit bull, that insane gleam in your eyes I know from past times."

Josh ran a grin of acknowledgment up one side of his granite-jawed face, replaced the Buddha and, crossing back to the desk, told her, "You think you read me like a book."

"Like a booking sheet."

He gave her a thumbs-up and eased into the visitor's chair. "If you heard the news, you know what."

"I heard. I know what."

"Billy the Kid. Not the first suicide I can connect to Davenport."

"Not that you have, or that you were able to get your payoff with anything else we ever checked out since you decided Davenport was behind Katie's murder on no proof, damn it. No proof at all, Joshua."

"This could be the one, Keesh. Tie him to this one, I get him for Katie's murder."

"No connection and there's always the next time, right, Joshua? And the next time after that?"

Josh's face flushed traffic-signal red and his eyes signaled anger. His neck muscles turned hard and sprang a blue vein thick as the one pushing out from his temple, like Clint Eastwood's whenever "Dirty Harry" got on a tear.

"You don't look, you can't find," he said.

"For how many years? How many years already? How many of our ops running down shit on foot we couldn't track with state-of-the-art bigger and better than anything LAPD'll ever be able to afford? Equal to anything the Feebies have."

"Save the old lecture. Deduct it from my salary, my chunk of the business."

"Don't go stupid on me."

"Is that a yes or a no?"

"Have I ever said no to you?"

He let her question settle, then, "Only once."

"But that didn't stop you."

"Or you."

"You needed it and I had it to give."

Keshawna shook her head in disbelief at the turn the conversation had taken, to a place both had sworn a long time ago was off limits and would stay there. She pushed out of her chair and came around the desk. Josh was already on his feet. They manufactured an embrace that felt as natural as the last time. The open-mouthed kiss, too, after her tongue found his—

Josh, the one man who'd made her feel dirty without ever having done her dirt.

Chapter 6

Connie Reynolds wasn't about to give Niki Beth Jacob the satisfaction of squeezing a reaction from her as they went about preparing tonight's meal.

She let every nasty look and gesture Niki sent her sail by unanswered, except for an occasional off-hand question to remind her she was Josh's housekeeper, not his wife.

And that's all Niki was, the housekeeper, the maid, although it had become increasingly obvious to everybody, but maybe not to Josh, that the young Iranian upstart would like nothing more than to trade the dirt rings in the bathtub for a gold ring around her wedding finger.

What movie did this fluttery-eyed vixen think she was living out? One of those romances of the forties and fifties, where the maid sets her avaricious sights on her widowed employer and, next thing you know, Cary Grant and Irene Dunne, Cary and Deborah Kerr or, in this case, Cary and Audrey Hepburn live happily ever after?

If Josh was going to be living happily ever after with somebody new, it was going to be her, Connie Reynolds.

She was here first, not this nymphet.

It was she who pushed Josh and Katie together, encouraged their romance as it evolved from modest sparks of interest to a mutually stoked intellectual and emotional inferno.

She knew—

If two people were ever meant to be together—

Katie and Josh.

Or she would have tried picking off Josh for herself.

Instead, she wound up crawling into bed and an emotional cesspool with—Connie bit down on her teeth; just dredging up a reference to her ex was enough to make her sick to her stomach—with Russ Tambourine, who reserved his greatest love for—

Russ Tambourine, the self-anointed Prince of the Vegas Strip.

Hey, Mister Tambourine Man, Go Drop Dead for Me.

It was only out of love for their son that she never demeaned him to Rusty Jr. for the shit he was. Rusty Jr. was a handful, but Connie was confident he'd grow out of it the way all teenage boys do and eventually discover without prompting the truth about his deadbeat dad, who never met a woman he didn't feel like beating the holy crap out of.

Connie finished setting the dining-room table, adding a few inches to the serving space for tonight's main course, her gypsy prime rib roast, one of Josh's favorites, which she alternated with other of his favorite dishes when she and Rusty Jr. joined Josh, Justin, and Julie for dinner, lately two or three times a week. If the way to a man's heart was through his stomach, as her late sainted Grandma Mollie always used to remind her, tonight she'd be logging another mile on the route she began traveling shortly after Katie's murder.

She double-checked the table for correctness, breath-polished two of the water glasses and Josh's wine glass, and returned to the kitchen.

Niki probably had her own grandmother whispering into her ear. There she was at the kitchen counter taste-testing one of her stupid native desserts, prepared and served with Josh's blessing, because Julie liked them or had been brainwashed into saying she did.

Tonight it was Niki's Makh-Loot, a combination of Faloudeh Shirazi and Akbar Mashti Ice Cream.

So what if it was delicious?

Connie never allowed herself more than a bite, maybe two.

Competition, after all, was competition.

It was bad enough Niki was allowed a seat at the table, when she should have been doing what she was paid to do: serve the food. More than that. She was always dressing for dinner like she was a fashion queen, in clothing too expensive for the modest stipend Josh insisted on adding to her room and board as part of their arrangement. Tonight, a provocatively tight blue-striped v-neck blouse over a virgin white silk skirt that probably would have got her stoned back home in Iran.

If Josh was impressed, he never showed it.

Not so Rusty Jr., his father's genes and teenage hormones in full rage.

Connie was also dressed for battle, in a slinky top that served up a peek at the lace border of her black half bra and enough cleavage to qualify for a full-page photo in the Victoria's Secret catalog and Gap jeans that, even at her age, made her ass an asset and let Rusty Jr. brag to friends that his mom still qualified as a full-fledged member of "The Bod Squad."

Niki heard her coming and, without turning, finished licking her testing spoon and said, "Want to try it, Mrs. Connie? See if you're able to enjoy the Makh-Loot this time as much as Mr. Josh and Julie always?"

"No, thank you," she said, studying how Niki's rich black hair so perfectly framed and suited her exotic heart-shaped face and scolding herself for going with so casual a top knot. "The starch noodles and all that sugar you use, it's a miracle your people aren't fatter than they are."

"That could be," Niki said, and took another taste. "Food such as your heavenly pot roast is something else they devour greedily, indifferent to warnings about high cholesterol that brings on clogged arteries and an early death." She turned and smiled innocently.

Connie answered with an equally insincere smile and retreated.

Nothing would be gained arguing with the hired help.

More important she do something about her hair before Josh got home.

She stepped into Katie's combination office and rehearsal room, snapped on the light and closed the door behind her.

The room was exactly as Katie had left it the night they headed for the L'Chaim telethon at the Pantages Theater. Everything in the house of hers was as she had left it that night, except for Katie's wardrobe, which Josh, after he'd returned from the dark ages of depression, asked her to donate in Katie's name to some suitable charity.

She is who he asked.

He'd asked *her,* Connie.

No one else, same as Josh would have asked her later, after Lon found Niki through the employment agency and told Josh he needed somebody like her to help mind the kids, especially in the hours Josh couldn't be around and mindful that Connie had her own life to get back to.

Lon was being thoughtful, and bless him for that, even though she'd given no indication she felt put upon.

After the horror of the L'Chaim telethon—

Wasn't it she who took charge of the funeral arrangements, the memorial service?

Because over the years, almost from the day they met, she and Katie were as much family as friends.

Wasn't she the one who helped Lon get Josh to rehab?

Lon might just as easily have asked Keshawna Keyes to help out—Keshawna was good people—but Keshawna was his business partner, not Katie's confidante or anything else.

Connie Reynolds was *family.*

Wasn't it she who Josh turned to whenever an event called for someone on his arm, like the Grammy Awards the night Katie was tearfully remembered by her peers?

Connie Reynolds was *family,* entitled to be at the Grammys that night, almost as much as Josh.

Afterward, not because she was asked to or expected to, wasn't she the one who sat by Josh's hospital bedside for hours, day and night, and saw to it that Justin and Julie were being cared for properly, and—

She was *family,* that's why.

Even Katie said so, back when they were kids and found one another growing up in the same low-rent area of Venice Beach. She was Katie Zun then. She would not be Katie Sunshine for years yet. They shared a passion for music and the thrill that came from sneaking into rock concerts at the Forum and flirting past door gatekeepers at Sunset Strip clubs like the Roxy and the Whisky.

They formed a duo before graduation, calling themselves "Connie and Katie," and performed in clubs, restaurant bars and cheap hotels in the beach area and the outskirts of L.A., Katie on piano, Connie on a Fender bass she bought on the cheap at Guitar City and figured to be paying off for the rest of her life.

The act caught on, mainly because of the songs Katie was writing. She'd started after hearing at one of Allen Rinde's "Discovery" nights at Genghis Cohen on Fairfax that record companies were only interested in artists who wrote and performed their own material.

Billboard magazine, reviewing their act at the Golden Bear in Huntington Beach, gave her stuff a name, "Throwback Music," and raved it was a blend of folk, rock, country, and easy-listening designed for ears not meant to accept anything harder or noisier, like rap and rap's first cousin, hip-hop.

The labels came looking for them.

They signed with Clyde Davenport's independent production company, "Mr. Magic Music," hypnotized by the fact that somebody with his reputation, who had changed music with his "Symphony of Sound" and created hit after hit for the biggest names in the record business, would even give a "Connie and Katie" a second thought.

At the time, they didn't know Davenport's career and reputation were sliding and he was desperate for a hit, anything, that would sustain his distribution deal with Majesty Records.

Something else they didn't know—

Davenport wasn't interested in "Connie and Katie"—

Only Katie.

Katie told her all about it later.

There had never been any secrets between them.

She described in the same exquisite detail she brought to her lyrics how Davenport had phoned to summon her to a meeting, instructing: "Only you, Katie. Connie's not to know about this for the time being. For your own good, Katie, for your own good. Trust me about that."

They met in Davenport's office at Majesty Records, at Sunset and Highland, where he had positioned his desk at an angle that, through the one-way picture window, offered a bird's-eye view of Hollywood High across the boulevard. Mr. Magic dripped sincerity, but most of the time kept focused on the young girls traipsing on and off campus, nodding approval at those who were meeting some unspoken qualifications.

"I want you to hear something," he said, after about fifteen minutes of padding her ego with enthusiastic words about how her work in the recording studio more than justified his belief when he signed her—that she could be his next big recording artist.

"Us you mean, Mr. Davenport. Connie and Katie."

"Hold the thought, my dear," he said, moving from the desk to the bank of sound gear that occupied an entire wall. "From our first sessions. I was up nights working on the mixes." He hit the playback switch on a reel-to-reel unit cranked up and ready to go. It was "In the Key of Love," which Davenport had been talking about as either the A or B side of their first single, the twin vocals reinforced by "Symphony of Sound" musicians who'd laid down their tracks before she and Connie added their vocals.

When the song played out three minutes later, her heart was racing and she had to cross her legs to hold in the excitement. She said, "I love it, Mr. Davenport. I absolutely love it. It totally freaks me out. You are positively the genius everyone says you are."

"A gift impossible to deny," he said, "and one I take deep pleasure in sharing with remarkable talents. But now I want you to hear something else."

He hit the switch.

It was still "In the Key of Love," but this time there was a single vocal—hers. It boomed out like cannon fire, threatening to crash through the walls, her voice dominating the song where, before, its power was undermined by the blended voices.

She was confused. Davenport saw it on her face. He returned to his desk and, after a survey across the boulevard, his attention briefly captured by a well-endowed student in a tight cashmere sweater and khaki cut-offs showing off her cheerleader legs, said, "Modern technology lets me play all sorts of games on the soundboard, Katie. In this case, I put you and Connie on separate tracks."

"In what case? I don't understand?"

He waved off the question and dipped into a desk drawer. The next moment, he was inspecting the pearl-handled revolver he'd pulled out. He hefted it for weight while adjusting his chair for a fuller view across the boulevard. He raised an arm horizontal to the desk and used it to balance the revolver barrel. He took one-eyed aim and mouthed a silent *Bam!* without squeezing the trigger.

"That stud athlete in the letterman's sweater strutting his stuff," he said, educating her while he returned the revolver to the desk drawer. "Whenever I see him, he reminds me of the lousy SOB who was always playing me for a fool in my own high school days." He settled his elbows on the desk surface, rested his stubbly bearded chin in his palm, jabbed the air with his forefinger. "From the time I heard you and decided to sign you, I knew it was because of you. You're the real deal. As half of a team, as half of 'Connie and Katie,' you'll go nowhere. Even with your sensational songs and me, Mr. Magic, at the helm, you'll be a one-hit wonder at best, another Patience and Prudence."

"Patience and Prudence?"

"The answer to a trivia question. . . . By yourself—you heard the difference. A world of difference. A world that's ready and waiting for Katie Sunshine, ready and waiting to be her oyster, where the sky's the limit for her."

"Who?"

"You, my dear. You are Katie Sunshine. From this moment on, Katie Zun exists no longer in our world. She becomes a memory, the same as the team of 'Connie and Katie' is a memory from this moment forward."

"I don't think so, Mr. Davenport."

He looked at her like he hadn't heard right, made a silent show of using a finger to clean out his ears.

"She's my best friend—Connie. We share the same dream.

For years. If the dream can't come true for both of us, I don't need it for myself. I don't want it." She looked at her wristwatch. "I have to go now, so that's that."

"Far from," he said. "Sit back down, young lady."

A meek smile. Trying not to sound belligerent. "There were others wanted to sign us, you know, so it's not the end of the world."

"I said sit back down."

Katie was afraid Davenport would reach for the pistol again, only this time aim it at her. She wondered if it was loaded. She sat down. "If it's about the money, the advance, we got when we came with you—"

"Be quiet and listen," he said, speaking so softly she had to strain to hear him. "It's time for you to grow up, Katie Sunshine, so now you're going to hear why it'll be my way or no way at all. The contract you and Connie could not enter into by yourselves, because you're minors, so your parents signed on your behalf? It's legal. It's binding. It says you belong to me for seven years. I own 'Connie and Katie.' I own you individually, as well as owning the team. I own your publishing on every song you've written or will be writing. What's in the can will go out any way I choose. I choose to have it go out from Katie Sunshine, with or without you. You want to quit me, little girl? You won't be the first to quit me. But you can kiss your career good-bye." He put four fingers to his puckered lips and blew them away.

Katie, shaken by Davenport's declaration, trembling with anger, fighting to hold back her tears and catch her breath, struggled to her feet. She gripped the armrest with a hand, afraid of losing her balance. She duplicated his gesture, fingers to lips and blown away. She looked him square in the eye and said, "Definitely not good-bye to my career, Mr. Davenport. Good-bye to you. Seven years isn't that long from now. Not for me and not for 'Connie and Katie.' "

She turned and headed for the door, her back as straight as her path.

Davenport called after her, "You stupid kid. You'll live to regret this."

When Katie reached that point in the story, crying probably as hard as she had in Clyde Davenport's office, Connie wanted to know: "How did you answer him?"

"Didn't, Con. I said what I had to say and after that all I wanted was to get away and breathe clean air instead of that hateful man."

They were wandering aimlessly along the Venice Canal, Connie also crying, reacting to emotions ranging from anger over how Davenport had so callously dismissed her talent to elation over Katie's loyalty, at the same time wondering if she'd have been as resolute if she had been the one Davenport wanted, not Katie.

"Seven years, really, not that long from now," Katie said, adding a buddy tap on Connie's arm.

Connie wasn't so sure, but kept it to herself. She did some wisecracking that lightened the mood until Katie felt good enough to recite some lyrics she had written during a jolt of hot-water inspiration in the shower, hum a melody not yet fully developed, then work the words and music together too fast for Connie to match her when they tried harmonizing to Katie finger-snapping the rhythm.

Katie saw her discomfort. "Don't sweat the small stuff," she said. "We can work on it some more and maybe in a week or so test it out on Pop Night at Rockland U.S.A. What say, girlfriend? Won't be the first time. Won't be the last."

Connie answered with an overcooked smile and a high five she didn't mean.

By the next morning, after bedtime prayers asking for guidance, after a tormented sleep, Connie woke up to the only decision she believed could let her feel clean about herself.

Seven years was a long time from now.

She was not going to allow Katie to risk sacrificing this immediate chance at stardom Clyde Davenport was offering her alone.

If Mr. Magic was wrong, if "Katie Sunshine" bombed, well, there'd always be "Connie and Katie" waiting for her, but—

How to break the news to Katie?

Convince her.

A simple declaration wasn't going to work on someone as stubborn and determined as Katie.

An unexpected phone call from Davenport gave her the solution.

When Davenport's secretary put him through, Connie wasn't past the "hell" in "hello" before he was telling her that Katie had decided to record without her. "My heart goes out to you," he said. "You are a sweet, wonderfully talented girl. I admire you tremendously. But, if Katie wants to go it alone, given she's the one who also writes the songs, I can't very well deny her, can I?"

He made it sound so real, so true, she would have believed him if it were anybody else but Katie.

She told him so.

"Believe what you will," he said, "but you're not the first one where a partnership hasn't worked out. Simon and Garfunkel, you know who they were? Jan and Dean. Peter and Gordon. Sonny and Cher, for goodness sake. Not always for the same reason, but divorce is divorce. Even one of my own acts, Billy the Kid and Bluto? That was a tragedy. Bluto Parks so distraught when Billy quit him, you know what Bluto did?"

"What?"

"Tried committing suicide, that sad boy. Mixed a pesticide in his Jack Daniels, some rat poison or cleaning detergent, I think it was. Went to bed and waited to dic. Only, he hadn't put in enough pesticide. He survived, but he was left with damaged vocal chords, hoarseness, a loss of vocal range, and no chance of ever singing professionally again. Now, don't you go off and try anything so foolish, young lady. Believe in yourself. You'll catch on with a label if you work at it. Sky's still the limit, you know. You're young. You have years ahead of you to make the world your oyster."

Davenport gave her a few more mouthfuls of encouragement, repeated his cautions, and abruptly ended the call, claiming John Lennon was waiting for him on another line.

It would be a long time before Connie came to realize and could accept the fact he had so skillfully manipulated her, planted the seed and spelled out the directions that took her from the phone to the kitchen.

Mom's dishwasher cleanser was blue and white powder, not liquid.

She wasn't sure how well it would dissolve in the glass of milk she'd poured for herself.

Unable to get the ant poison to squish into the glass, Connie returned the container to the supply cabinet and headed for the bathroom.

She felt like Goldilocks discovering the bowl of porridge that was *just right* when she spotted the large plastic bottle of clear liquid toilet bowl cleaner on the lid, next to the stack of old *People* and *Cosmo*s. She filled the lid with the cleaner and dumped it into her glass of milk. Added another splash, to be certain she was mixing in enough to do the job, and retreated to her bedroom.

She sat on the edge of the bed while composing the suicide note she had already worked out in her head, claiming despondency over grades that hadn't been good enough to get her into UCLA. That was a reason Katie would accept. She'd heard Connie moaning and groaning about that off and on throughout their senior year.

Connie pinched her nostrils, bent back her head and emptied the glass of milk in one dreadfultasting swallow. She settled onto the bed and waited to be discovered by Mom, due home any minute from her latest job, waiting counter at Zucky's Deli on the pier.

After she didn't know how much time later, her head spinning like one of Mom's old LPs, no sight or sound of Mom, Connie struggled off the bed and staggered out of the bedroom calling for her. She bumped into a chair, tripped over she wasn't sure what, her eyesight starting to shut down on her, and fell. Pulled herself to her knees and crawled to the phone. Punched in nine-one-one. Got out the word *Help* and half the address before the world quit on her.

When she regained consciousness, she was at Santa Monica Emergency Hospital, Katie asleep in a chair across the room, a Walkman in her lap, a set of earphones clamped to her head. She tried calling to Katie, but the best she could manage were undecipherable sounds stranded at the back of her throat, like she was gargling, like hands were choking the life out of her.

She'd not learn until later that her vocal chords had been severely inflamed and promised permanent damage. In time, with proper therapy, she would be able to speak, but there'd always be traces of hoarseness. Singing? In the shower, perhaps, but professionally? Her vocal chords would be unable to open and close properly, making it impossible for her to ever again sustain a pitch.

Reduced to writing notes, she urged Katie to move forward with her singing career on Clyde Davenport's terms. No argument that Katie could make would be able to restore the team of "Connie and Katie," she wrote. She wrote: *Be Katie Sunshine and let that also be my sunshine.*

Katie reluctantly agreed, but only on one condition: Connie would become her personal manager and accept half of whatever money she earned as Katie Sunshine. Connie refused. The manager part she'd be proud to accept, she said, but half the money was too generous. Managers got fifteen or twenty percent, and that was the way it should be between them. Katie said, fine, twenty percent. Connie said fifteen would be enough. They traded hugs and kisses after settling midway, at seventeen and a half percent.

Connie went into the bathroom and studied herself in the cabinet mirror.

Yes, definitely, the top knot had to go.

She undid the band holding it in place and her hair splashed down around her face, taking the emphasis off the lines that had made a permanent home on her forehead and the age wrinkles that weren't going anywhere without the cosmetic surgery she'd promised herself never to have.

Since she was a kid, she had worked too hard, sacrificed too much, screwed up too often to give up any proof of her lived-in life. Every wrinkle, every furrow, the razor-thin scar on her chin, sliced by Rusty in one of his drunken rages. Evidence. She had worked through too many problems without losing her pride or self-respect. There it all was, worn like the Medal of Honor. A little touch-up from something on Katie's neatly organized makeup shelf, a little lip gloss, that would take care of her outside. Inside—a little happiness one of these days was the makeup she needed there. It was not in the jars on Katie's shelf, but for years it was in Katie's bed. Someday, maybe, Josh. . . . She left the thought unfinished. Turned to studying the labels on the jars. Found the shades that worked best for her.

The phone rang while she was heading back to the kitchen.

Niki held out the receiver. "It's Mr. Josh," she said. "He says he needs to speak to you."

Connie took it from her and said into the mouthpiece, "Let me guess. You're going to be late again."

"That and more," Josh said, his voice sounding unduly elated. "I think we finally got that crazy son of bitch."

"Which crazy son of a bitch is that, Josh? We know a lot of crazy sons of bitches."

"The biggest one of all—Clyde Davenport. He's just been arrested for murder. On his way downtown to be booked now. I want to be there for the moment."

"They linked him to Billy Palmer's death?"

"Better than that, Con. Better than that and closer to home."

Chapter 7

Earlier that day, Clyde Davenport woke up wondering where he was.

It was Clyde's usual confusion after one of his rare nights on the town, the times he was in the mood to test the reality of the world below, outside the gate of Magic Land, his towering Italian villa-styled mansion on Mulholland Drive, twenty thousand square feet of domain on four acres a half mile east of the adjoining estates of Brando, rest his soul, and quirky Jack Nicholson.

The death of Billy Palmer still had Clyde in the mood for celebrating.

Billy the Kid.

His time had arrived.

One more insult avenged.

The ones that turned their backs on him, used him, then abused him by dismissing him like he had outlived his usefulness—

None of them would ever be safe from him until the day he saw to it they outlived their lives.

How many so far?

Including Billy, a dozen?

And no apparent connection, one death to the next, except for Clyde Davenport as an important chapter in their career histories, the media always calling him for a comment; him always finding new ways to say the same old platitudes.

A great artist lost to us under tragic circumstances.

A great talent who could have given us so much more, but tragically cut down in his prime like the immortal Gershwin.

I cherish the memory of my great friend and especially the years when our careers merged.

For Billy the Kid Palmer, it was your basic *I'm shocked—do you hear?—shocked.* Clyde working to sound more shocked than Claude Rains ever sounded in *Casablanca.* Sheer joy, that movie. Time to screen it again? Tonight, maybe, after performing his usual corrective surgery on the sour notes Ava kept hitting in the studio.

Ava, next to him in bed—

The bed covers pulled over her head and muffling the sound of her snoring.

Clyde snaked his hand under the covers until it touched warm skin, a smooth, taut thigh he slid over on his way to verifying a small island of pussy fur. Accounted for, and so were the scars under the nipple-hardy breasts that so bedazzled the judges at last year's "National Search for Miss American Showgirl."

Ava was one of four runners-up, but his kind of winner.

She radiated a girlish innocence and naïve intelligence beyond real or manufactured beauty and could easily be molded to his specifications and desires, with enough of a decent voice—a voice, not necessarily singing skills—to let him Svengali her to stardom and put Mr. Magic back on top of the mountain.

Yes, Ava sharing his silk sheets, all the signs there.

He was concerned it might be the waitress from last night in the upstairs VIP club room at the House of Blues, where he'd gone to monitor acts at a Dead Dogg Records showcase for the "Clyde's Kids" charity concert he created and produced annually for Big Buddies of America.

Her name badge said she was "Brenda."

She began working a gap-toothed smile, teeth the size of

dominos, and her husky-voiced innuendo on him after she delivered Ava and him a bottle of Cristal, compliments of Dead Dogg, and he dropped a hundred on her tray.

She didn't have a clue who he was, only some music-industry type who was free and easy with his Ben Franklins.

Ava, she no longer existed to Brenda.

On the next bottle of Cristal, delivered by Brenda with the old Playboy Club squat that invited a tourist's-eye survey of the valley between the twin peaks of Boob Mountain, Clyde made it two Ben Franklins.

Brenda eyed the two bills hungrily, then turned her appetite on Clyde. "You're far too generous, sir. I can't begin to thank you enough. Rent's due tomorrow, and—"

Ava cut her off by slamming her palm on the table. "Take your tits and toodle off, sister. The man's taken, by me, or are you blind as well as stupid?" Like she was the boss.

She turned to Clyde, her eyes blazing with a demand for affirmation.

Only nobody told Clyde Davenport what to do.

Ever.

His backhanded slap caught Ava on the lips, hard enough to draw blood that filled the quote marks on the right side of her mouth.

She recoiled and threw her hands up defensively, screaming, "Clyde, not my face again," loud enough to be heard over the rap music pummeling eardrums from the stage; drawing the attention of most of the other invited guests.

Clyde ignored them.

He rattled his fist within inches of Ava's Greek goddess of a nose and said quietly, like he was obeying a library sign, "Get your ass out of here now. Now, Ava. Get outside to the limo. Tell Peppi to drive you back to Magic Land, drop you off, and then come back for me."

Ava looked at him like she saw the end of the world coming.

She grabbed her handbag and fled.

The room became animated again.

Clyde looked up at Brenda. "What time do you get off?"

"What time do you?" she said, giving him the kind of lascivious smile his acts used to get from groupies trying to sell themselves past stage-door security.

Waiting for Brenda, he flew solo on the Cristal, then a couple Jack D shooters.

Did a handful of poppers.

Handed over a fifty to a flat-nosed dude in the men's room, the color of an eight ball in matching Armani threads, who laid on him a plump line of primo, barely stepped-on Colombian.

Two-thirty in the a.m.

She was barely in the limo before she made a dive for his cock, but he was already too far gone and, apart from diddling her a little with the .22 he kept stashed underneath the seat, he had to command a rain check.

Now—

What the hell time was it now?

Except for a corridor of daylight streaking through a break in the window curtains, it was too dark for anything but a guess.

Clyde rolled over and slapped around the nightstand until he found the Tiffany's crystal candy bowl holding his goodies. Popped a few. Tracked to the lamp switch and moved his Patek Philippe—a thank-you gift back when from Tony O, for giving him a fifth consecutive Number One—close enough to take a reading.

Two in the p.m.

Almost twelve fucking hours.

Fucking hours.

Good one that.

Exactly what they were.

The blue pill got him going once he was in bed, splitting his time between Brenda and Ava, watching them go at it when he wasn't taking a breather and wondering if he could make his woody last the four hours they warned about in the TV commercials.

Warned?

In his case, his age, he'd be the first to call it a miracle.

A fucking miracle.

That got him cackling.

Not so funny was his sudden recollection of the crazy shit Ava had started laying on him before he ordered her to get dressed and get the hell out of Magic Land. She told Brenda he was a wrinkled gnome, a washed-up piece of recording history whose greatest hits nowadays were on defenseless women.

Bitch talk.

From a skank too wasted to know she was screwing with her future, now her past.

He slammed Ava good for being the drugged-out skank bitch she was.

He dragged her from the bed by her hair.

He yanked her to her feet and pushed her to the door.

Ava wrestled free of him and ran back to the bed, screaming about how Brenda was the one who should be tossed out on her dick-loving ass.

She tried getting Brenda off the bed, but Brenda fought back, returning every insult with insults of her own.

Clyde charged over to them with the Uzi he had pulled from the upper weapons drawer in the dresser.

Cracked Ava's shoulder with it, then a second time; jammed the Uzi into the small of her back, vowing to squeeze the trigger if she wasn't gone by the count of ten.

He started the count at five.

Whatever Ava thought she heard in his voice scared her

enough to send her on her way. Clyde chased after her, calling to Brenda as he passed through the door, "I'll be back soon as I make sure I'm rid of this pile of *dreck.*"

Hey! Minute!

Clyde crash-landed back into the moment, wondering:

If Ava's gone, dumped like yesterday's trash, what's she doing back in bed, and—

Where's Brenda?

He couldn't remember.

His memory refused to cooperate.

More and more lately, all he was certain of retrieving from the fogbank brought on by advancing age and certain prodigal habits was his music, which stayed imbedded in his mind note-for-note, arrangement-by-arrangement, all the way back to his initial schoolboy efforts.

Clyde found the Uzi under his pillow and poked Ava.

Her body moved under the covers, a spasm of irritation, then turned over, moving from back to side, facing away from him. He jabbed her again. Inched closer and screamed in her ear, "What the hell are you doing back here, you miserable, worthless cow?"

Startled, she rolled over and fell off the bed, landing on the floor with a thud and a yelp.

"Answer me, bitch. Who invited you back in?"

"What's it, King Kong?" she said, dragging herself up and into view. "You ready for more of Mama Brenda's patented action, sire?"

Sweet fucking Jesus!

It was Brenda.

Sounding like she had a mouthful of mush.

He had misinterpreted what he had felt, or was it another example of every cheap trick wannabe in show business doing the same pussy shave and titty lift, like it was the guaranteed ticket to stardom?

"You hearing me, sire? Mama Brenda reporting for duty. A line or two, I'll be good as new." Without makeup, her face looked like a battleground.

"Shut it. Where's Ava?"

"I don't know, baby." She reached over for a touchy-feely. He cracked her knuckles with the Uzi. Brenda stretched her rubber lips to her ear lobes and said, "Your yummy-yummy gun again. Wouldn't mind getting plugged some more by you."

He pressed the Uzi against her temple. "I said, Where's Ava?"

Before Brenda could answer, the bedroom door crashed open and two uniformed police marched in, weapons drawn, followed by two men in shabby suits, badges hanging from their jacket pockets, their weapons also drawn. Clyde's man Peppi behind them, Peppi's ring-weary face a study in dread.

It was while patiently enduring the booking process at County Jail, smiling like he didn't have a care in the world, telling out-of-school stories about his celebrity friends who knew their way around a jail cell all too well, even signing autographs for cops who knew Mr. Magic by reputation, mostly from the *Rolling Stone* cover interview he'd done with Jann Wenner himself, that Clyde spotted a familiar face in the crowd—

Josh Wainwright—

Mr. Katie Sunshine.

Josh Wainwright carrying on in a determined way designed to get his attention—

Backslapping the detectives who had cuffed him, told him he was being charged with a homicide—the murder of Ava Garner—read him his rights, shoved him into the back of a filthy squad car, and now, having done the fingerprint thing, were telling him to look into the camera lens, like he needed posing instructions from them.

Nothing like being charged with a homicide to restore one's equilibrium.

Especially the first time, which this was—

For all his trying, Josh Wainwright never able to prove his engraved-in-stone belief that Clyde Davenport was behind the murder of Katie Sunshine.

And try he did.

Was still trying.

Mr. Katie Sunshine, for all his faults, had one shining virtue:

He wasn't a quitter.

Mr. Katie Sunshine kept pushing until he got what he wanted.

Clyde Davenport knew the type because Clyde Davenport was also the type, only—

Clyde Davenport never lost, but—

Mr. Katie Sunshine was going to lose if he continued wasting his life searching for some needle in the haystack that implicated Clyde Davenport in his wife's death, or in any of the other deaths involving acts Clyde Davenport turned into stars before they turned into shits.

In that moment, on that thought, Clyde recognized that in Josh Wainwright he had the solution to his current predicament.

Clyde signaled over the obnoxiously chubby cop who'd been pestering him about an act he had produced with disastrous results, Little Boy Peep, or as Clyde came to call him, "Little Boy Creep." It was a major stain on the Clyde Davenport legacy through no fault of his own, one he had spent years scrubbing off his biography.

Clyde said, "I'd owe you a big favor if you'd do a little favor for me, Officer."

Putting a wink in his words, the cop said, "Delivering a cake with a file inside is out of the question, Mr. Magic."

Clyde aimed a finger at Wainwright. "I'd like to have a few

words with him. Would you mind telling him that and bringing him over?"

"That big favor you mentioned? Any chance of your coming up with the Little Boy Peep single that somehow disappeared from my collection last year? My favorite? 'Pulling the Wool Over Your Eyes.' "

"Also my favorite, Officer. You have excellent taste in music. Consider it done."

The cop gave him a thumbs-up and headed for Wainwright.

Wainwright listened to the cop and shook his head.

Sent Clyde a look as telling as a hangman's knot.

The cop returned, reporting with a shrug and throwaway hands, "Josh says for you to stow it where the sun don't shine."

Clyde flicked a smile and said with the confidence of someone used to having his way, "Mark my words, Officer. The sun will come up tomorrow."

He turned to send the same message to Wainwright, but—

Wainwright was gone.

No matter.

Tomorrow, the sun would come up, and Mr. Katie Sunshine would soon thereafter start helping to prove Clyde Davenport couldn't possibly have murdered Ava Garner.

CHAPTER 8

"He *what?* He wants to hire us?"

"But not without you. You, Joshua. Specifically you."

"For why?"

"To prove he didn't kill Ava Garner. To lead a private investigation and bodyguard him against the killer he thinks was there at his place to take him out and got her instead."

"And you told that lethal son of a bitch—"

"Nothing," Keshawna said. "Was Davenport's lawyer called—"

"R.J. McKay."

"The 'Miracle Worker' himself. In the limo with Davenport, right after springing his client on a million bucks bail, cash money—"

"Pocket change. And you informed McKay I would sooner drop my Jockeys in a West Hollywood alley than deal with his cocksucker of a client. Tell me, Keesh. Word for word. How you explained there are some things Davenport's bottomless bankroll can't buy."

Keshawna rolled her chair away from the desk, rose, and turned to stare out the picture window, her fingers laced behind her. "I told McKay you'd be happy to meet with his client and hear him out," she said, quietly, more to the horizon line than to Josh.

She didn't have to see his face to know it was contorted in disbelief.

The slamming sound was his palm assaulting the desktop. "You didn't."

"Know my own voice as well as anyone's."

The legs of his chair dug into the parquet flooring. It caused a screeching sound as he pushed backward and tramped around the desk like a boot soldier. He gripped her by the arm, spun her around, jamming his face into hers, close enough for her to feel the rage steaming from his nostrils.

"You're putting me on, right?" He read the correct answer in her eyes and let go. "I hope you have a reason I can buy into," he said, retreating to a far corner of the office, by the door, his fists clenched, looking like he'd just challenged her to an impossible task.

"Two," Keshawna said, settling on an edge of the desk, rubbing out the hurt where he'd grabbed her and thinking about the long-sleeved blouses she'd need to wear for a week or two to hide the purple bruises she'd have by morning. She pointed at his chair. "Sit your bony ass back down, you want chapter and verse."

"I want to hear why I shouldn't walk out of here and never come back."

"Because you're stupid, not crazy, partner. Most of the time. Right now, crazy, you don't recognize the opportunity's come your way to get what you want—Clyde Davenport's head on a platter." Keshawna aimed an index finger at the chair.

He thought about it, reluctantly rejoined her, and gestured for her to continue.

"Until now it's been one dead end after the next, you on the outside looking in, chasing after the missing link that'll tie Davenport to somebody's death. Prove what was made to look accidental was in fact a homicide, Davenport's inspiration."

"Tell me something I don't know."

"Tune out your emotions and tune in your intelligence, fool.

Davenport's inviting you into his life through the front door. It's a gift, your chance to get close to that asshole, get inside his head, sort through his lies until you get to the truth, what you need to finally send the bastard on his way to lethal injection."

"He's no dummy. Why would he want to take this kind of risk?"

"Ask him that."

"I'm asking you."

Keshawna shrugged. "Maybe he doesn't think it's a risk?" Josh snorted. "How many times have you struck out? I've lost count."

"You dancing on my head now?"

"I'm thinking about Katie."

"Dancing on my head now," he said, and burned her with a look. He shifted in the seat, propped an elbow on the armrest, and planted a cheekbone on his knuckles. "What's the current status on Billy Palmer?"

"Same as the last time you asked. Zero. Zilch. Nada. Nothing. There's nothing to connect Davenport with his suicide, except for what we already knew, his being in Nashville and calling on Palmer and his wife to make nice-nice."

"Anything new out of her?"

"A fresh barrel of widow's tears. What do I tell McKay?"

"You said *two* reasons. What's the other one?"

"In depth or in a nutshell?"

"Dealer's choice."

Keshawna noticed another chip in her hundred-fifty-dollar French manicure and worked at making it less obvious, but only made it worse with her picking.

She said, "You know what happens when you staff up from the cream of Special Forces, the best military and law-enforcement personnel you can lure into private practice? When they earn merit raises or tough out a contract renewal? What happens when technology upgrades and you have to spend for the gear and the specialized training that lets you stay Numero Uno, keep one step ahead of the competition in protection, personal security and private investigation?"

Josh was watching her pick.

She moved her hands under the desk and kept at it.

She said, "You deploy our resources on your never-ending quest to bag Davenport and revenge Katie and tell me to deduct it from your share, Josh, and because of Katie I can't bring myself to tell you our cash flow situation has about as much flow as the L.A. River. You add in overhead and the boost we're facing when our lease expires next year and—"

Josh stopped her like a traffic cop.

"I should have asked for the nutshell," he said. "Did McKay say what the job's worth to Davenport?"

"He volunteered the information—a blank check. We fill in the amount."

Josh thought about it.

He dry-washed and wiped his hands and told her, "Okay, damn it. Set up the meeting."

Chapter 9

Josh spent the rest of the day and the next morning riffing through his Davenport files in anticipation of the meeting Keshawna had arranged for one o'clock, the hour R.J. McKay told her his client considered his personal sunrise.

If he was climbing into bed with Davenport, close enough to catch his slime, he wanted to double-check on the minutia he'd so meticulously compiled since Katie's murder and a quick course in the details surrounding Ava Garner's death.

Keshawna had pulled together all the police reports and paperwork, as well as the print and TV coverage, even before he agreed to the deal, that confident he'd buy into one of her two reasons, if not both.

The clincher for him was Katie, of course.

Keshawna knew that going in.

Cash flow?

He'd made like that mattered, but—

Keshawna also knew she could count on him to bail out the business, especially if it was tottering like a stilt house on a hillside being eaten away during one of the relentless rainstorms now as common an occurrence as facelift sightings on Rodeo Drive.

It wouldn't be the first time he had written her a check, drawing on the lofty inheritance and good life Katie's career had made possible for the family.

No questions asked.

If he trusted anyone, he trusted Keesh.

So—

Clyde Davenport's blank check?

Take it, take the deal?

Hell, yes; sure; why not?

And no discount on services rendered, if nothing happened at their meeting to decide him against playing Davenport's game of search and rescue.

Curiously, nothing he'd reviewed about Ava Garner's death fit any of the patterns he had constructed around the earlier deaths he considered Davenport's handiwork. Those deaths were produced with the same precision Mr. Magic always put into his "Symphony of Sound."

Not so Ava's death.

Her death was outright murder, Ava's once-beautiful face borne to oblivion by a Glock G36 from Davenport's personal collection, dropped and waiting to be found alongside her body, a contortionist's nightmare on the cobblestone driveway ten or so feet short of the rusted security gate leading out onto Mulholland Drive.

The gate hung by a hinge, offering no defense against intruders. A security camera was attached near the top of a flagpole rising twenty-five or thirty feet alongside the gate, its rubber-encased wiring hanging limp and useless; definitely nothing that would fake out a pro intent on invading Mr. Magic's domain.

Ava was scantily clad, her outfit thrown together in a way that seemed to confirm what Davenport told the suits, that he'd ordered her out of the mansion at gunpoint—with one of the Uzis from his home arsenal, not one of his Glocks—but details after that turned fuzzy.

Brenda, the aging starlet type wandering half-naked and afraid in Davenport's playground of a bedroom, indifferent to the admiring eyes of the crime-scene crew, sometimes going out of her way to be noticed, remembered Davenport saying something to her about getting rid of Ava and how he'd be right back.

Remembered Davenport calling Ava *dreck,* which she translated for the detective running her statement as *poo-poo.*

Remembered Davenport using an Uzi to wake her hours later, almost scaring the poo-poo out of her.

Remembered nothing about the hours in between.

And, if the detective was finished with her, could she maybe bum a ride home with him or one of the uniforms?

Davenport's ride came without his having to ask, of course.

Downtown to County Jail, to be booked on suspicion of murder.

A reading of his rights thrown in at no extra cost.

"He talks out of both sides of his mouth and his asshole at the same time," Connie said last night, after dinner, once the kids settled in front of the television with a communal bowl of buttered popcorn to watch *The Incredibles* for the millionth time. "Whatever Clyde Davenport says when you meet with him tomorrow, it's what he doesn't say that you have to watch out for, Josh."

They were touring the crooked patio path through the flower garden that had been Katie's pride and joy, the scent of every rose a reminder of how much she'd relished putting on a pair of overalls and crawling around in the dirt, patting here, puttering there, talking to the seedlings, the buds on the bushes, urging them to blossom into a healthy life, in almost the same loving, tender tone she used on the kids.

With the roses especially.

How Katie loved her roses, her Anne Hathaways and Lady Jane Greys, her red and pink tea roses, her orange Heirlooms, her pink Floribundas, and over there, preening in the light of the half moon floating aimlessly in the pale blue sky, the delicate white Nastrananas that were one of her special favorites.

After Katie's death, after Niki was hired, he saw it was the rose Niki usually chose for her entry hall arrangements. He asked why. She lowered her face to avoid his eyes, blushed, and with a smile that begged understanding told him, "I know the Nastranana quite well by its other name, as the Persian musk rose. I especially love it for the way it reminds me of home and my dear family."

Josh recognized in that instant how more than coincidence had brought Niki Beth Jacob here.

She had been guided here by Katie.

Katie would be looking after the kids and him through this young woman.

Metaphysical silliness, maybe, but it was a belief Josh couldn't shake.

It gave him comfort and contentment, and a passport to conversations with Katie on his visits to her gravesite at Westwood Village Memorial Park.

Connie tugged at his shirtsleeve and said, "You hearing me, Josh?" She cleared her throat of the cool night air. "All I'm saying is be careful around him. If it's what Davenport claims, if he didn't murder her, if someone was out to get him, but got the Garner woman instead, please don't let him make that an excuse to pin a bull's-eye on you next."

"He wanted me out of his way, he'd have tried it a long time ago. He knows I won't get off his case as long as I have a breath left. Why now?"

"Because he feels like it? Because he's fed up with you hounding him? Because he's Clyde Davenport and believes he can do anything he wants to do whenever he wants and get away with it? Because he needs to feel the power in life he no longer commands in a music business that passed him by a decade ago, although that's nothing he'd ever admit to anyone, much less himself? Why now? Christ, Josh. You're the detective. You tell me."

Connie was swimming in emotion, close to drowning.

Impulsively, he left her side, returned in a few moments with a golden Grandiflora and handed it over.

"What's this for?"

"For caring," he said, at once wishing he had chosen his words better, concerned Connie would confuse his appreciation for a sign of affection.

If she did, she didn't let on.

She pressed the rose against the gamin haircut Katie had fallen in love with and adopted after seeing it on Leslie Caron in *An American in Paris.* Connie had taken on the style as her own in the last year, in a shade of strawberry blond similar to Katie's.

"What do you think, Josh? Go with the goods?" When he hesitated answering, she said, "Better I find a mirror and check for myself." She turned and set off for the house, but quit after a few steps to spin around and tell him, "Just be careful, okay, Josh? Justin and Julie need their father."

Josh used Coldwater Canyon to get to Mulholland Drive, navigating familiar twists and bends past the estate he'd heard was now occupied by Warren Beatty, Annette Bening, and their brood, past the Brando and Nicholson estates, and pulled up to the irresponsible entrance gate to Magic Land fifteen minutes before his one o'clock meeting with Davenport. The gate was wide open, the bands of yellow investigation tape confetti on the cobblestone driveway. Behind him, buried under a blanket of afternoon cloud banks full of smog, was the sprawling San Fernando Valley.

TV vans and news teams, as well as paparazzi, were lined up along the opposite side of the road, poised to spring into action if Mr. Magic showed himself.

He sensed cameras working while he shifted the Lexus into gear and headed up the steep winding drive to the villa, a towering presence rising three stories, ruling over various types of indigenous trees and wild shrubbery defiantly beyond taming by a landscape gardener's touch.

Josh knew the villa well. For months after Katie's murder, he'd parked a discreet distance away, stalking Davenport, monitoring his comings and goings, logging the license plates of his infrequent visitors, praying to discover someone, something, that linked Davenport to the crime.

That was before rehab, while the whiskey and the pills were still helping him deal with his grief; helping him stay awake through the coldest nights parked on Mulholland, afraid sleep might cost him the answer; helping him stay awake in his own bed on the nights he lacked the strength to endure another nightmarish reenactment of the L'Chaim telethon, the shot that ended Katie's life, the spilled blood staining Julie then and possibly forever, and turning Justin into an incorrigible problem child.

While still in his thirties and at the height of his game, Davenport had purchased the villa, once the home of Alfredo Mantegna, a silent movie idol forgotten by time in the wake of Jolson and *The Jazz Singer* and a later sex scandal exceeding Fatty Arbuckle's tribulations and trials.

Mantegna, nearing eighty, his personal fortune wiped out by a depressed stock market, was barely surviving on Social Security and public welfare. As a concession that helped to close the sale at a million or more below market value, Davenport agreed to let the chronically ill actor live out his remaining years in a caretaker's cottage at the rear of the property. After Mantegna's death, Peppi Blue, the only holdover from the glory days of Davenport's production company, "Mr.

Magic Music," took up residence there.

Davenport called Peppi his vice president in charge of record promotion.

Peppi was that, but also more than that.

Peppi Blue was Clyde Davenport's factotum, his silent, unsmiling shadow, whose ties to organized crime had earned him a rap sheet longer than Sepulveda Boulevard, the longest street in L.A. County, seventy-six miles from the San Fernando Valley south to Long Beach.

The sheet's highlight was the hard time he served for manslaughter. It gave him a patina of menace missing from the grab bag of graft carried by all the independent promotion men. It came in handy whenever radio-station managers or program directors balked at adding to their playlists the new Davenport single Peppi was hyping.

As Josh swept around a final driveway curve, pulled up to the villa and maneuvered into a parking spot next to Davenport's limo, he recognized Peppi on the terrace at the head of the stairway leading up to the arched main entrance, commanding the wall like a sea captain on the bridge. He was checking the Lexus against his wristwatch and nodding approval while a ribbon of white drifted aimlessly from the filter-tipped cigarette parked in the trach hole in his throat.

Peppi was a small man, five-four or five-five the most, constructed like a concrete block eroded by time and the weather inside a dark suit shining from a dozen cleanings too many and a powder-blue dress shirt open at the collar that revealed his tracheal cannula, neck plate, and the modest tattooed blue dot of a radiation patient. In his late fifties, maybe older, but the rosy pink skin of an infant on his lean, angular face. Enormous bug eyes. Drooping lids that lacked lashes beneath black eyebrows that looked to have been painted on with a thick brush. A hairpiece the same color, as obvious as the sag on the right side of his mouth.

Peppi ignored Josh's outstretched hand.

He unplugged the cigarette from the porthole, fieldstripped it, tossed it into the breeze. Directed Josh inside with a swing of the chin. Took the lead like he was answering the bell in a boxing ring; thick legs pumping with cocky deliberation; the ham-sized fists of a heavyweight ready to throw a punch.

The entrance hall was the size of a modest museum gallery, furnished with antique tables and chairs that complemented the villa's historical sensibility.

The walls were an entirely different story, full of Gold and Platinum records; ornately framed photographs of Davenport with recording stars, each one autographed and singing his praises; a glass case for his Grammys, his two Emmys and the Oscar he had taken home for contributing what the celebrity magazines said were five words, *be high on love now,* to the lyrics of a Best Song winner he produced.

The wall along the broad wooden staircase leading upstairs demonstrated another aspect of Davenport's rich ego, oil paintings of various sizes and schools, lit to be adored; Josh certain he recognized a Picasso and a Munch and, no question, a Warhol portrait of a Davenport at a much younger age, rendered in reds and greens, Davenport staring arrogantly down on the world like some Dorian Gray.

Or God.

Maybe both.

Peppi pointed him to the one metal door among wooden doors dotting both sides of the central corridor that led to the rear of the first floor. He pulled it open, revealing a small elevator behind a metal folding gate, large enough for three average-size people who didn't mind defying a basic law of physics.

Got in first.

Pressed the down button.

When the elevator hummed to a stop, Peppi drew back the gate and pushed open the door. Josh was momentarily blinded by blinking neon wattage that belonged on Times Square, letters twenty feet tall spelling out

MR. MAGIC—

A set decoration Josh remembered from coverage of Davenport's induction into the Rock and Roll Hall of Fame, on a night MTV and VH-1 captured his brief but revealing flight from humility, Davenport at the podium, waiting for a standing ovation to conclude before he berated the audience behind a meaningless smile, saying: "Bad enough I was eligible to be voted in the first year, in '86, and it took you this long to get to me. That neon should be three times as big. Four times. Five."

And there was Katie at his elbow, looking embarrassed, joining in the audience's nervous laughter, telling him after the show how she now regretted accepting the invitation to introduce him. She had agreed over Connie's objections, after the producers told her she was Davenport's personal choice from among all the acts he had ever worked with. Katie had taken it as a signal Davenport wanted to put behind them the ugly words and threats of retaliation he'd bombed her with after she honored the last terms of her contract and announced she was leaving him.

Katie, in all her sweetness hoping to save the moment for Davenport, wrapped her arms around him and told the audience, "Mr. Magic's greatness as a songwriter and record producer is, as he has just demonstrated, matched by his wonderfully wry sense of humor."

This time there was relief in the audience's laughter.

A wave of applause rippled through the auditorium, only—

Davenport wasn't buying into it.

He steered Katie away from the podium, and when he had complete attention proceeded to recite the names of those already in the Hall of Fame.

"You know what they all add up to?" he said. He gave the silence a moment to jell before launching a downbeat. "Me," he said. "Without me, what you had here until tonight was only a Hall of Shame."

He pushed a *fuck you* index finger at the TV cameras and stalked off.

Later, in a prepared statement issued by his attorney, Davenport apologized for his remarks. He had neglected to take his medication before the ceremonies and that accounted for what he characterized as his "regrettable behavior, maligning a great institution that I'm grateful thought to vote me into its ranks." He went on to apologize to Katie for putting in an awkward position "an exceptional artist who has brought so much sunshine into so many lives for so many years."

Connie had a conflicting analysis. "The bastard knew what he was doing," she said. "He did it for the attention he knew he would get, hijacking the whole ceremony that way. You wait. They'll be replaying that tape year after year from now on."

Time proved Connie right, but Katie, always looking for a rainbow, said, "It could have been because of the meds, Con."

Connie shook her head and coughed her throat clear. "You see his eyes dancing like he was auditioning for a touring gang of whirling dervishes? It's not what Davenport didn't take, honey. It's what he did take." She blew another cough into her fist. "And what he said about you? He wants something. Wait. He'll come crawling out after it some day."

Connie was also right about that.

The lights went out on MR. MAGIC.

Josh squeezed the neon residue from his eyes and blinked for focus.

He scanned the room, measuring it at around twenty by forty feet.

He was in Davenport's recording studio.

Quilted sound baffles covering the walls and the ceiling. Lots of standing mikes and mike booms. A pile of drum shields and absorbers folded and stacked neatly on a set of cloaked risers. A small baby grand hidden under padded movers' blankets. Several bass traps. An ISO booth for the drums and another ISO for vocals, its plastic window facing the smoked-glass window hiding the production booth.

"Welcome, Josh, thank you for coming." Davenport's voice attacked him from all directions. He was inside the booth. "Welcome to a place superior in every respect to anything you saw or experienced while I was working with Katie, or anywhere since. It gives far greater dimension and definition to the term 'state-of-the-art,' as you'll quickly recognize."

Uninvited, Davenport launched into a professorial discourse.

"As I'm sure you know from past experience, Josh, the acoustic properties of a recording studio are the opposite of those for an auditorium in many ways. Where an auditorium hungers after enhanced reverberation, a recording studio should be acoustically dead, with an extremely short reverb time, so the matter of soundproofing becomes of the utmost importance. Here, as in any fine studio—only here to perfection—I've isolated the room from the rest of the villa with a double wall, creating a room within a room. This eliminates the low-frequency sounds of passing aircraft and autos down on Mulholland Drive, any activity in the household, any sound from the heating and air-conditioning systems, any sound that doesn't belong in one of my recordings."

Josh stuck his thumb and forefinger in between his lips and

blasted out a whistle.

"I'm not here for the lecture, Davenport."

"Of course not. I know that."

The lights popped on in the booth, revealing Davenport at the recording console, waving for Josh to join him. "I recognize your time is valuable, Josh, so, indeed, let's you and me get down to the business at hand," he said, at the same time talking to Peppi Blue with his fingers.

Peppi nodded.

He showed Josh the door to the booth and disappeared into the elevator.

Josh passed into the booth.

The door swung silently shut behind him.

Davenport was settled behind the console in a classic Eames lounge chair, wrists resting on his crotch, a two-handed grip on the Glock he had angled at Josh's chest.

Chapter 10

Josh showed Davenport his palms, arms extended parallel to the floor.

"Let me guess," he said. "Nobody will hear the shot."

"The wonders of modern soundproofing," Davenport said. "Keeps the noises in as well as out. As they say in Vegas, 'What happens here stays here.' " He added a brief barking laugh to the sly grin that had slipped onto his face. "You're armed, of course. Let me see, but carefully."

Josh kept his eyes on Davenport's aim while reaching underneath his sports jacket for the Smith & Wesson .38-caliber revolver holstered on his right hip. He held it by the grip, with his thumb and two fingers, the barrel pointing to the acoustically cushioned floor.

"A popular favorite, cops and killers alike," Davenport said. "Several in my collection, along with lots of classic Smithies any gun museum would kill for." That laugh again. "Set it on the console, please. Excellent. And a backup? You carrying a backup, Josh?"

Josh shook his head, studying Davenport's clouded eyes for a sense of his game.

They told him nothing.

He knew Davenport well enough to know his M.O. called for him to be in control.

How many times had he heard that from Katie or Connie?

But, right now, of what, and for what reason?

What was happening here didn't fit the pattern Josh had constructed around every death he'd linked to Davenport.

Davenport said, "No weapon inside your sock or strapped to your ankle? A .22, perhaps? Like those your former brothers in blue have been known to plant on shooting victims, to make a shooting look righteous?"

"You've been watching too many movies, Davenport."

"Reading too many stories in the newspaper, you mean. You ever do something like that, Josh? Make a shooting look righteous?"

Josh dismissed the question with a wave. It wasn't a subject he intended to discuss with Davenport.

Davenport laughed, like he knew what the answer would be. He said, "I know how to make a shooting look righteous, too, Josh. It's not an art limited to cops with nervous trigger fingers. Like here, for example? Us?"

"I'm listening."

"Let's us suppose I've finally grown weary of your accusing me of deaths I could not possibly be responsible for—"

"Inspired or arranged. Not committed."

"Blamed on me in articles I've read, interviews I've seen you give on television."

"Alleged an involvement, not blamed."

"Whatever words to keep me from suing you for libel and slander and destroying your life the way you seem intent on destroying mine."

"All things good come to him who waits."

"But he who gets tired of waiting, never past out to revenge the death of his wife, which he blames on—" Davenport moved a hand from the Glock long enough to poke his chest several times. "He seizes on unexpected opportunity. A lovely and talented young woman is murdered and the object of his intention is booked for the crime. The object of his intention invites him to his home to make an altogether strange request, to look into the murder and protect him against the parties unknown he believes meant for him to be the victim, not her."

"Plain English, Davenport. Who out there would want you dead?"

"You, for one. . . . You keep the appointment and here, in this room inside a room, you impulsively seize on opportunity to avenge your Katie. You decide to be your own judge, jury, and executioner. You draw your .38, but before you can fire, I manage to get my hands on the weapon I keep close for any such emergency and—" He raised the gun, took squinting aim, and—

Tossed the Glock to Josh.

Josh made a one-handed catch and popped out the single-column magazine.

The Glock was loaded and, Josh was beginning to think, so was Davenport, whose laughter had assumed the antic merriment of a hyena. He replaced the cartridge and stored the gun inside his belt, stepped over to retrieve the .38 and returned it to the hip holster.

"Was there a point to the stunt you just pulled, Davenport?"

"A statement, not a stunt. If I ever meant for you to die, you'd be dead by now, but not here, not this way. Not at my home, with a gun from my collection. It would happen a million miles away from me, while I was covered by an alibi as warm as a baby's blanket."

At once, Josh was mad at himself for not having sensed that immediately. It was nothing he intended for Davenport to recognize. "I knew that," he said, "I wanted to hear it from you."

"You're not a good liar, Josh."

"Compliment coming from a master."

"And there are people who call *me* arrogant." He gestured for Josh to take the other Eames lounge chair. "Sit, and we'll get down to the business that brought us together."

"I think I'll stand, you don't mind."

"I do mind. I prefer not to have people towering over me."

"What if I sit and you stand?"

"I don't have to stand to tower over you, Josh."

"And there are people who call me arrogant."

They let a minute pass in silence, then another.

Davenport swung around to the console and checked some settings before running his fingers over a computer keyboard like a piano virtuoso. The board lit up and the sound boxes exploded with a recording never far from Josh's memory—

His Katie singing "Tell Me What Keeps You Alive," the Number-One Academy Award–winning hit she was about to perform the night of the L'Chaim telethon, when she was—

The fucker was toying with his emotions.

"Davenport, you're one venomous prick," he said, and started after the Glock.

Davenport shook his head and wagged a finger. "Shooting off your mouth is one thing, Josh, but thinking to shoot me? A fool's gambit." He continued adjusting the levels to give Katie's vocal greater prominence over the "Symphony of Sound," taking down the brass and doing something with the string section.

"Now you're a mind reader?"

"Among my many unheralded skills, so to speak." Said without pretension. "How else do you imagine I'm able to turn out songs and records that anticipate public taste year after year?"

"Past tense, Davenport. Mr. Magic stopped pulling his rabbits out of the hat when rap came along and fooled the public into thinking it was music, not social commentary to stolen riffs from someone else's hits. The rap-bangers sampled some of your stuff, on their cuts, but you didn't fit into the music scene past that."

"Not sampling. Stealing. And I took them to court, one by one, and they paid dearly for the privilege . . . as you will in court, if you kill me."

"You are a mind reader."

"And a careful one at that," Davenport said. "Look behind you."

Josh glanced over his shoulder.

Peppi Blue was framed in a doorway at the rear of the booth, cradling an Uzi.

"Even the smartest people have been known to do foolish things," Davenport said. "Sitting down makes so much more sense than shooting me, Josh."

Josh showed empty hands and dropped into the Eames lounger.

"Much better. Far more civilized," Davenport said. He sent Peppi a message with his fingers. Peppi answered him in kind, retreated, and the door slid shut in front of him. "So, back to business," Davenport said, his face full of sanctimonious authority.

Everything Davenport said synchronized with what Josh had heard from Keshawna and siphoned out of the police reports. Everything tying him to the Ava Garner murder was at best circumstantial, explaining why Miracle Worker R.J. McKay could sail through the arraignment and have his client out on a million dollars bail in less than twenty-four hours. The D.A. called Davenport a flight risk and asked the court to take his passport, but McKay had successfully argued that his client was a public figure whose reclusive nature as well as current charitable activities precluded the need.

Josh said, "And the drug charges, illegal possession?"

"McKay says they were based on discovery incidental to the nine-one-one call that brought the police to Magic Land. He expects them to disappear before we get to court, in the event this sorry business ever gets that far."

"Not so incidental. Discovered in the course of investigating a homicide."

Davenport looked at him like he knew better and changed the subject, describing with certainty how he was on the verge of making Ava Garner his next major discovery.

They had finished touring the villa and were outside, heading to where her body was discovered.

"Over there," Davenport said, pointing to a spot on the cobblestone drive near the iron entrance gate. Only scattered yellow tape evidence of a crime. On closer inspection, traces of blood that somebody's scrubbing hadn't entirely removed.

Josh said, "Your memory any better now than it has been?"

"No."

"And no idea who called nine-one-one?"

"No idea."

Josh aimed an index finger at the overhead security camera by the broken entrance gate. "Shame that's not working."

"Not for years."

"And nothing to prevent someone from getting into your place. No security system. No motion detectors. No sound alarms. No video cameras. No armed patrol service. No—"

"Better than any of that." He flipped a thumb over his shoulder. "Peppi is my ounce of prevention. Hearing like a dolphin and not much on sleep. A twig breaks outside, a toilet flushes inside—a fart in a windstorm—he hears it from his cottage."

"The shot that killed Ava Garner, he heard that?"

"Yes, he did. It's all there in the statement he gave the police." Davenport's fingers began working, the way Josh imagined Peppi has told his story to an LAPD pro at sign language. "He was awake when he heard, waiting out the possibility of a call from me to take Ava or that pig Brenda home. He grabbed an Uzi and got here in minutes, hardly any time at all before the cops came screeching up."

"Without first checking on your safety?"

"Peppi knows I can take care of myself." He aimed and fired a finger gun at Josh.

"You have yourself, you have him. Why hand ICS a blank check to cover your ass."

"Not ICS without you. It's your ass I'm after, as I'm confident Keshawna Keyes has already made quite clear to you, Josh."

"Because?"

"I'm sure R.J. McKay told her, so—"

"I want to hear it direct from the horse."

Davenport said, "Given your hatred and contempt for me, you'll be so busy trying to prove me guilty of her murder, you're bound to stumble onto the evidence that proves me innocent."

"I'd agree with half of that."

"I am innocent, Josh."

"That's your half."

The legit news crews and the paparazzi had clustered outside the broken gate and were aiming cameras at them, throwing questions at Davenport, urging him to join them and make a statement.

Davenport ignored them.

Two paparazzi passed through the gate.

Peppi stepped out from behind a tree and charged forward, blocking the path. One read the menace on Peppi's face, skidded to a halt and hurriedly back-stepped through the gate. The other attempted to maneuver around him. Peppi grabbed him by the wrist and shoved him to the ground. Ripped off the three digital cameras around his neck and pitched them one after the next at Mulholland Drive. Raised the paparazzo to his feet one-handed, by his shirtfront, and marched him off the property, deaf to the man's screaming threats of a lawsuit.

"Food for the evening news," Josh said.

"He trespassed," Davenport said. "He's fortunate Peppi let him off with a warning."

Back in the villa, in an office wallpapered with rows of Gold and Platinum records and a variety of tribute photos, trophies, and citations, Josh declined Davenport's offer of a drink and settled onto one of the facing conversation area couches while Davenport poured himself a tall snifter of cognac from one of several choice bottles on the portable bar. He swirled, swallowed, and mouthed exaggerated satisfaction before moving to the opposite couch.

He picked up a remote from the end table and pressed several keys.

Music from recessed Quad speakers bombarded the room, at a sound level meant for the Staples Center, not a space the size of an average neighborhood 7-Eleven.

Davenport brought down the level with a few taps as a symphonic mix of strings, horns, and woodwinds dissolved behind a woman's throaty voice, hitting every note out of the ballpark the way Josh had grown up imagining it was for Babe Ruth, Willie Mays, Mickey Mantle, and Duke Snider. It was a combination of rap and hip-hop gift-wrapped in Stephen Sondheim, like nothing he'd ever heard before.

Davenport settled back like a proud parent whose child had just stolen the show at her school's annual Christmas pageant, mouthing the lyrics in sync with the singer. When the song played out after four minutes, before Josh could say anything, Davenport waved him off and did another thing with the remote. "First, you need to hear it again," he said. "How it would sound playing over the car radio or CD system."

This time the performance was muted, but no less powerful; maybe more powerful.

"Great, I know," Davenport said. "You don't have to tell me, Josh. I'm telling you. I was up all night putting the mix together. It still needs minor tweaking, but it's there. In the grooves. A stone cold smash. Mr. Magic doing his thing like no one else can or ever could. And you know whose voice that is?"

Josh knew.

What other reason could Davenport have for having him listen?

He said, "Ava Garner."

"Of course. I'd be disappointed if you gave me any other answer. And you know why I wanted you to hear her? I wanted you to hear her so you'd have more than my word that the girl was a remarkable talent. Had the chops to become an important artist under my direction." Smug in his self-conceit, he studied Josh's face, daring any expression of doubt. Finished the cognac in a swallow. "Why would I want to kill or have killed my next great discovery? There's no reason on Earth I'd want that."

"You mean like you had a reason for wanting Katie dead? All the others?"

Davenport dismissed the questions with a sweep of the hand. "Hear me out before you add Ava to your foolish and misplaced *j'accuse.*"

He rose and crossed the room to his desk, returning in a moment with a sheet of paper he handed over to Josh. It listed in chronological order all the artists who'd recorded for Davenport, left him after achieving superstardom and were now dead. It showed dates and causes. Locations. Where Davenport was at the time. Katie was on the list and, in last position, so was Billy the Kid Palmer.

"I made this printout for you, Josh."

Josh scanned the paper and offered it back. "I already know

it by heart."

"Black and white. I wanted to show you in black and white how Ava Garner's death differs from all the others in a significant way."

"She wasn't yet famous and she hadn't yet left you."

"Brilliant. I sense we're making excellent progress here."

"So that's supposed to mean you had no reason to want her dead?"

"Add what you just heard. I had every reason to want her alive."

"And who do you think it is wants you dead?"

"Find Ava's killer and we'll both know."

"And if I find it is you?"

"That won't happen," Davenport said.

"What if I tell you I'll set up and supervise your security, but at the same time I'll be using your blank check to find evidence of your complicity in the other deaths?"

"Impossible, Josh, but be my guest."

"A challenge, Davenport?"

Davenport shared the hint of a smirk. "Encouragement."

"Sooner or later, I am going to nail you."

"Good enough for me, what happened to Jesus."

Chapter 11

"How did you leave it?" Keshawna asked, after Josh gave her the meeting in broad strokes, tossing off nervous energy while pacing her office, his adrenaline in overdrive long before he pulled the Lexus into his reserved spot on the second underground parking level of Century City Towers.

"Tomorrow, you send the crew in to hotwire Magic Land, inside and out. Cameras and audio surveillance. Motion detectors. Ants parading, we see them. Hummingbirds, we hear them. Keypad locks and silent alarms. Code Red buttons. A tap on the phones. . . . Install a guardhouse at the Mulholland gate and schedule it twenty-four seven, Earl Pulliam on the day shift, Wambaugh and Sawyer our best bets for the overnighters—"

"Sawyer's down with the flu."

"Then sub Goodman for the duration. Wambaugh and Goodman. Video monitors in the recording studio, in Davenport's office and his bedroom. The caretaker's cottage behind the main house. In addition to the feed here, snake a feed to my computer at the house."

"Aren't you the guy who has this jones about taking the office home with him?"

"Now that I'll have that piece of shit in my sight, I don't want to let him out of my sight."

"A blank check is a wonderful thing. Exceptions?"

"The johns, off-limits, as usual. Davenport also wanted to

ban his bedroom, but he was satisfied when I explained how he'd have controls that shut down all or part of the office system any time of day or night. I didn't mention the monitors at my house. Instruct the crew to firewall it from him. With any luck, what Davenport doesn't know will hurt him."

"Anything else I don't know?"

"Stevie Wonder's real name."

"Steveland Hardaway Judkins, although he sometimes claims it's Stephen Morris."

"You Googled it since our bet."

"Detectives do crazy stuff like that."

"And any late-breaking research worth reporting about Billy the Kid Palmer?"

"He's still dead."

"You know how many refugees from Clyde Davenport could claim suicide if they were still alive?"

"Why do I think I'm about to find out?"

Josh pulled the printout from his jacket pocket and walked it over to Keshawna, who reached for her reading glasses. She was smelling good, sweet, that French perfume she loved and cost him half his paycheck for her birthday, back when they were more than partners. She considered the scent evidence of the good life she didn't have growing up and thanked him for his gift the best way she knew how.

Keesh owned a highly developed fashion sense and catered to it with chic outfits usually worn by Vogue models and the country-club set, not by an LA detective in badge-high hock to MasterCard and American Express. She'd never lost the need or the touch. Today it was some Italian designer's flashy blue v-necked blouse and white leather skirt topped by a matching blue gingham trench coat, an outfit that must have set her back a thousand bucks, but looked like a million bucks on her.

She ran her finger down the list. "Three suicides, including

Billy the Kid Palmer." More finger play. "Two hit-and-runs. One from a home fire blamed on his smoking in bed. Four drug-related deaths that could be suicides, an accidental overdose or sheer stupidity. Katie the only one who—"

She couldn't bring herself to finish the sentence, so Josh did it for her:

"Was shot to death," he said. "Until Ava Garner."

"That clinches it for me, Joshua. Davenport's guilty of First-Degree Coincidence."

Keshawna's status-sized office and its luxurious trappings were as much a part of her psychological wardrobe as her perfume, her clothing, the diamonds and the gold bling-bling that crowded visible parts of her svelte figure, but nothing Josh required.

He'd grown up in comfortable surroundings among the rich and the richer yet, a Beverly Hills address on the right side of Sunset Boulevard, with famous parents who practiced the basic values of their Midwestern, middleclass upbringing and shared a love that exceeded the affection showered on them by their fans.

Josh's office was at the opposite end of the executive corridor, sparsely furnished and rarely used. He preferred a desk he'd set up for himself in a corner of the bullpen, an open area of stylish metal desks abutting one another like he'd grown used to during his years on the force.

He liked the access to instant interaction with the ICS ops, the team spirit, the free and easy byplay that often made him the butt of their jokes, like now, as he worked his way through the bullpen to the desk and performed a custom of years standing, rearranging the family photos whether they needed it or not.

Among the E-mails were messages from his brother, Lon,

two from Justin, and one apiece from Connie and Niki, all about tonight's invitational screening on the Paramount Studios lot of Lon's new movie. Lon reminding him of the time and the reception afterward in the studio dining room. Justin making sure it was still cool to bring Rusty Jr. as his guest. Justin's second message asking the same question in an angrier tone. Connie advising she had a meeting that could make her a few minutes late getting to the house. Niki saying that Julie wanted to bring a friend to the screening if Justin was bringing a friend, hinting that she was the friend Julie had in mind.

He answered them all and some E-mails from field ops or clients who needed a fast reply before feeding the computer a report on the Davenport meeting. Glancing at the list Davenport had given him, he was struck by something odd he hadn't noticed earlier. There was a name on it he was certain was not on the list he had compiled. He called up the file. He was right. The name wasn't there, but it was trapped in his memory for another reason.

He found a number for Billy the Kid Palmer in Nashville and told the mechanical voice on the answering machine who he was and why he was calling.

Josh got home late, everyone ready to leave for Paramount except Connie—

Who wasn't there.

Rusty Jr. said, "She and my dad were having this big argument, so she sent me here in a taxi and to say to go on without her and she'd meet up with us at the studio as soon as she could."

Josh phoned her and got no answer on either the house line or her cell.

He left voice mail, saying he'd have Niki drive the kids to the screening in the van and come pick her up, was explaining this to Niki when his cell phone rang. It was Connie calling back, telling him not to bother, she couldn't make it, and would it be all right if Rusty Jr. slept over.

Her voice was a study in poorly disguised distress.

He gestured Niki and the kids off, catching a kiss Julie blew at him and blowing it back while walking out of earshot, and lowered his voice.

"What's going on, Connie? You okay?"

"Thanks, Josh. I appreciate that. I can't tell you how much."

"Your ex, Rusty Jr. told me he's with you. The lowlife is giving you a rough time again, that it?"

"Enjoy the movie and tell Lon 'hello' for me."

"I don't like what I'm hearing, what I'm thinking, Connie. I'm coming over."

"I'd rather you didn't, Josh. Please. I've inconvenienced you enough. I'll be there in the morning, first thing, to fetch Rusty Jr."

"I'm coming over," Josh said, and clicked off.

Chapter 12

Connie snapped the cell phone shut, dropped it in the waiting hand of Russ Tambourine. He stuffed it in his pants pocket. "Good girl," he said, and backhanded her across the face again. "There's your reward for being a good girl." The roughing up had started after the cab came for Rusty Jr., when Russ dropped any pretense of civility, escalating their latest confrontation from vicious words to violent action. She was huddled up in a corner of the living-room couch, Russ hovering over her like an overzealous waiter at The Ivy or The Grill, his hard smile as menacing as his balled fists, his cobalt-blue eyes reveling in the sight of her pain.

He had shown up unannounced an hour ago, moving quickly from a mechanical hug for her and a handshake for Rusty Jr. into a climb up his latest anger mountain. Their ugly history together told her Russ was barely halfway to the peak. He reeked of booze and the body stink from chasing her around the house.

Connie swiped at the corners of her mouth and checked her fingers to verify the blood through the eye he hadn't claimed yet with one of his punches. She couldn't open the other eye past a slit. Last time, it had turned into a black-and-blue Easter egg by morning and it was two weeks before the swelling went down, the doctor saying she was fortunate it wasn't a detached retina.

Russ said, "You know what I get bitch-slapping you? A hard-on."

"Put it where it doesn't belong anymore and you'll get twenty years."

Russ was intimidated by strong-minded women, who recognized the coward hiding behind the violence he directed at them.

Her tough talk usually slowed him down.

Not this time.

He said, "I should shove it down your mouth to shut you up, only you'd like it too much."

"Try me, Russ, and you'll find out my bite is worse than your bark."

"Not after I bash out those expensive caps," he said. He snatched a handful of her hair and yanked hard enough to draw tears. "Get up. I want a better look at you, whore." When she didn't move, he pulled her to her feet and shoved her to the middle of the room.

She had dressed to be noticed at Lon's screening, a fault of pride that had grown over the years. A sequined camisole cut low enough to show off her braless boobs and, if she was careless with her posture, flash nipple. A ruffled hip-length knit wrap sweater in matching pink. Form-fitting indigo cropped denim pants. Platform boots that added four-inches to her height and gave her thighs a showgirl's curve. Diamond studs in her ears, a thank-you gift from Katie the year her "Good-bye, Sunshine!" farewell concerts finished as the highest-grossing tour by a female artist, ranking her fifth behind the Stones, Elton, Nate Axelrod, and Barry Manilow.

Russ made a big show of studying her, one hand on a hip, two fingers of the other hand framing his mouth. Nodding agreement with whatever conclusions he was reaching.

"I can still see what I saw in you," he said, then, "You still fucking him? You still keep that piece of ass in ready reserve for your dead dear friend and client Katie Sunshine's hubby or just down to copping the cop's joint?"

"It never happened, Russ."

"Neither did Vietnam, although I've got the battle scars to prove it."

"Never. Not like you, Mr. Tambourine Man. No zipper strong enough to prevent my husband, the Prince of the Vegas Strip, from making it with every show babe who ever set foot in a Donn Arden production number."

"Not every," he said. "I drew the line at the transsexuals and transvestites." He gave the ceiling a playful glance. "Now, Katie, she was something else again. All woman. Knew how to spread her legs as good as she ever spread that sunshine of hers."

"Never!"

"Sure she did, sure as yesterday ain't never coming back. Soon after she heard about how you took your manager's percentage of her man. I don't know what got Katie's juices flowing more, her learning she had been betrayed by her best friend or plain, old-fashioned jealousy. Case you're wondering, wasn't only the singing department she was better'n you."

"I could kill you," Connie said, words she'd never said to him before, but a thought that repeated itself hundreds of times after they married and Russ revealed himself for the cunning, conniving, career-obsessed, wife-beating cock hound he was.

He was all boyish charm and good manners when they met in '96, a lounge singer at the Sands Hotel. Katie was taking her turn among main-room headliners doing one last gig before the Vegas Strip war horse was demolished, with it the ghosts of Sinatra, Dino and Sammy, Lena Horne and Louis Armstrong, Johnny Mathis, Patti Page and Peggy Lee, Danny Thomas, who had opened the showroom forty-four years earlier, in 1952.

Connie was in the lounge, schmoozing with George Albert, the publisher of *Cash Box Magazine,* listening to his bad jokes and better stories about the good old days with enough enthusiasm to guarantee he'd give Katie a cover for her upcoming "Greatest Hits" album with or without the payoff of a full-page ad. She was giving more attention to the smoke clouds hanging overhead, drifting in from the casino and lathering nicotine on her throat than the singer on stage belting out standards, his vocals straining to be heard over the jumbled chatter of players taking a break from the tables and the slots and the working girls lining the long oak bar over watered champagne, sitting out tricks in Hawaiian shirts in hopes of a high roller pitching them their next roll in the sack.

The singer finished with "I've Had the Time of My Life," nowhere near as mellow as Bill Medley had done it with Jennifer Warnes for the movie *Dirty Dancing,* and bowed off to polite applause after reminding everyone who he was and that he and the trio would be back for three more sets.

About ten minutes later, after George Albert had gone to find his wife, and she was waiting for the barmaid to bring the tab, the singer settled unannounced at her table. "Was hoping you'd still be here, Ms. Reynolds."

"And you are?"

"Russ Tambourine. That was me you were just paying no attention to up there on the stage."

She could have guessed by the show tux, the white carnation on his satin lapel, and the silk handkerchief overhanging his jacket pocket; the open collar and the bow tie at half mast.

"I apologize, Mr. Tambourine. No offense intended. This was the only time I had to take care of some important business."

"Yeah, George Albert. Damn important man. Like you're a damn important woman in our game. I was hoping we'd meet before Katie Sunshine wrapped her engagement."

"And now we have," she said, looking anxiously for the barmaid, "but I really must split. Run some business with Katie before the dinner show."

"You're all business, that it?"

"What's that supposed to mean?"

"I've caught glimpses of you before now. Even long-distance you always struck me as more all woman than all business."

She knew then he was playing her, but with enough charm to make him interesting. She didn't remember the last time a man had complimented her femininity or even noticed. Truth was, she had become all business. Making a career and a life out of Katie and living vicariously in Katie's shadow. Any longing for a life of her own had crept in only after Katie married Josh Wainwright, and—

Connie wasn't sure.

Was it because Josh had replaced her as Katie's best friend, or—

—because Josh looked, thought and behaved like the kind of take-charge guy she had always wanted for herself?

He wasn't exactly handsome, but he had the kind of rugged rectangular face you couldn't help staring at, drawn in by hot-coffee-brown eyes, topped off by a full head of rich brown hair going prematurely gray; one of those thick brush mustaches that LAPD cops wore like a second badge and took away from his sexy pouting mouth; and, an infectious laugh easily set off by the worst jokes and the most outrageous puns.

She wondered about that once, and Josh didn't have to think about his answer:

"The same reason I love children and animals," he said. "It helps to erase the everyday ugliness of the world I work in."

Wondering now about this Russ Tambourine, who was older than her by a decade or more and had the determined face of an underachiever racing the clock. Wrinkles and crevices disguised by a Vegas tan and a heavy layer of pancake. High cheeks at conflict with a receding chin. Troubled eyes. Painted black hair greased back like Valentino's. Like Josh, a six-footer.

Attractive in a glittery sort of way, but, unlike Josh, not her type.

Impulsively, she asked him, "How do you feel about children and animals?"

"I used to be a child myself. In bed—an animal."

So, maybe he did have a sense of humor.

"I want to tell you a joke," she said. He gave her a curious look, then welcomed it with a gesture. "You know what Cleopatra said to Marc Anthony when he wanted to make love? She said, 'Not tonight, Marc Anthony. I have my pyramid.' "

He looked at her curiously, gave it another beat, then broke into a laugh that sailed above the casino noise, the kind she'd have expected from Josh.

"That was a lousy joke," she said.

"Yes, it was," Russ said. "So, tell me, what's doing with your pyramid?" Crooning the question in his unremarkable baritone.

"What time does your last set wrap?" Connie said, and traded her suite number for the answer.

When she awoke midday, tired, aching, happier, and far more satisfied than she had been in years, she was alone. On the nightstand he'd left a homemade CD, *Mr. Tambourine Man,* and a neatly printed note on Sands stationery:

You are all woman.—Your sixty-minute man

They were married a week later.

Within the year, she had him headlining in Vegas.

"Kill me?" Russ said. "For shame. A horrible way to talk to the father of your son."

He stepped forward and without warning punched her in the stomach.

She screamed as her head flew back and her hands rallied to the spot before sinking to the floor.

He straddled her like a gladiator and unbuckled his belt while crooning, "Seems like old times," Connie unsure if Russ intended using it on her or if it was the prelude to him dropping his pants.

He was wrapping the belt around his hand, working it so the buckle would sit on top of his fist, when the doorbell rang.

He moved off her. Put a vertical finger to his lips.

A few moments passed.

The doorbell rang again, then a third time.

They both recognized the voice calling her name through the door:

Josh.

"Your lover boy just couldn't bring himself to honor your request and not come on over," Russ said. "It doesn't end here between me and you, Connie, you don't finally learn to keep your damn fucking mouth shut anymore, from now on."

Josh calling, "Connie, it's me. You in there?" as Russ fled the room. "Connie?"

She tried answering Josh, but was hurting too much to make word sense.

She heard the back door slam shut.

Seconds later, a car door.

A motor gunned. The screech of brakes. The faint scent of burning rubber creeping through the open windows.

She managed to roll over onto her side. Used both hands to push herself onto her knees, then struggled onto her feet. Stumbled a few times while using furniture and walls to painfully work her way to the front door and get it open.

Josh had his revolver drawn.

Looked like he was about to try kicking in the door.

She fell into his arms.

Josh carried her to the bedroom, propped her up in the bed, got wet towels to clean her off; ice cubes wrapped in a dish towel to press against her lips, where Russ's fist had cut into her skin; a package of frozen corn from the fridge, to help reduce the swelling on her eye, an old folk remedy he insisted would help; at the same time, demanding that she let him call for paramedics or get her to a hospital to check for possible internal damage.

She thanked him for his concern and rejected the idea, insisting she'd suffered far worse at Russ Tambourine's hands and only needed a night's rest.

He growled at her over that, excused himself and returned after about five or six minutes carrying a steaming bowl of chicken soup on a serving tray. She denied an appetite, but he was adamant chicken soup, historically, had mystical curative powers.

"If you don't want to take my word, remember it was the Eleventh Commandment of Katie's Bubbeh Zun: '*Thou shalt slurp thy soup of the chicken,* who lived to be a hundred and one,' " he said. "Katie would want us to show respect to Bubbeh Zun."

Josh was making her laugh, like that was also part of the cure. It brought pain to her stomach, where she'd suffered Russ's hardest blow. She bit down on her back teeth to keep him from seeing how much she was hurting and reached out to give his hand an appreciative squeeze.

He sat down alongside her, feet on the carpet, and spoon-fed her the soup.

"I'm going to get that cowardly son of a bitch busted for violating the restraining order you got the last time this happened," he said, barely able to contain his anger.

"No, Josh, please. You see how much good the other restraining orders did. Let me handle it my way."

"What's that, stay Russ Tambourine's punching bag? What was it put your ex on the warpath this time?"

"The new issue of *Inside Stardom Weekly,* just out. A cover story about the Prince of the Vegas Strip that makes him out to be a royal shit."

"And here I thought those rags only dealt in fiction," he said, causing her stomach to hurt again.

She gave him a playful *Quit it!* poke on the arm. "He blamed me for it, said he was sure I called the magazine and blew the whistle. Over there." She pointed Josh to a rolled magazine that Russ had tossed into a corner of the room.

"The story tells how he's months behind on child-support payments, because of all the money he's lost at the tables, and how he's in debt up to his crown at three or four Strip hotels, gambling interests holding markers that will keep him working in Vegas for free for the next fifty or sixty years. Pictures of Russ with the showgirls. Hookers. Quoting some of them about how he gets when he's had one too many or because of his drug problem. How he loves to smack them around."

"Any lawyer will tell you the truth is an absolute defense," Josh said, letting a grim smile play out. He settled the serving tray on the nightstand and padded over to retrieve the magazine. Found the story and worked through the pages. "I'd have figured he'd covet this kind of publicity. When was the last time Russ got the cover of any magazine? When the *Journal of the American Medical Association* wrote about congenital sickos?"

Back beside her, he wondered, "Did you turn the magazine onto the story?"

"You can't be serious."

"Only curious. Did you? He does owe you a wad of child support, and—"

"It's bad enough Rusty Jr. will see me beat up like this again. To let him learn the whole truth about his dad that way, in a magazine? Expose him to ridicule or something worse from his classmates?"

"Rusty Jr. already has problems that a good swift ass-kicking dose of reality might help correct faster and better than you always covering up or making excuses for his daddy dearest?"

"Like what? Tell me."

"For another time. For now, let's take care of you."

Why, she wondered to herself, did Josh only show this depth of concern when she was suffering? Because misery loved company, that why? Because Josh still wasn't ready to accept the finality of Katie's death, that she was never coming back, and he was overdue to get on with his life? Because he was blind to the happiness she could bring him, given a chance? Because—

"Rusty Jr. is fifteen," she said. "His only problem is puberty."

"Sure," Josh said, and abruptly changed the subject. "Anything else daddy dearest have to say before he tore into you?"

Her mind jumped to Russ's claim about making it with Katie.

"There is something, Con. I see it on your face. Spill it."

Connie shook her head. "For another time," she said. Josh checked his watch. "Go on, get," she said. "Catch up with everyone at Paramount. I'll be fine. Party hearty for both of us."

He was reluctant to leave. "I don't know that you should be alone tonight."

"I really will be fine, really. Go."

He resisted. She insisted.

He said, "Sleep in. I'll deliver Rusty Jr. in the morning."

"Don't tell him—"

"Anything."

"Nothing. Thanks, Josh. Thank you."

After he was gone, the aspirin he'd fed her earlier helpless against her growing pain, she searched out the vial of Vicodin in the nightstand drawer and popped a couple dry. They were what remained of the prescription she got after the last time

Russ had paid her one of his surprise visits.

She couldn't remember why he came that time, or maybe it was that she didn't want to remember.

It was worse that time, that she was sure about.

She swallowed another Vicodin for good measure and settled back to welcome blessed sleep, imagining what might have happened if she'd let Josh spend the night. She smiled at the possibility, heard herself whispering, "For some other time, Josh," before darkness rescued her from her pain.

Chapter 13

Lon's movie was in its final pyrotechnic moments, Lon saving the world, as usual, when Josh got to Paramount. He hung in the back of the theater while the audience politely endured the end credits, an eternity of names, except for some television series faces, who banged into him in their hurry to beat his brother and the other big screen stars to the news crews covering the after-party.

When the house lights came up, he moved out of the way of the anxious mass exodus, and checked for Lon and the kids. They were down front, Lon surrounded by well-wishers and Justin, Julie, and Rusty Jr. hanging close enough to share in his celebrity; Julie, especially, who appeared to be letting people know they were related. Niki nearby, in open-mouthed awe of the stars.

Reunited, finally, hugs all around, they marched to the studio dining room followed by the noise of cameras and cries of *Just one more!* and *Look this way!* Lon in lockstep with his gorgeous co-star, Stephanie Marriner, their arms entangled, the family trailing six steps behind. Julie calling, "He's my Uncle Lonnie!" Justin and Rusty Jr. more interested in the swinging rhythm of Stephanie Marriner's derriere. Niki tight beside Josh.

The lot had changed in the years since he and Lon were kids and the folks sometimes treated them to a visit on the set, when they were shooting one of their mega-hits here. More soundstages and hardly any evidence of the old, historical sets, except maybe for the gigantic outdoor Bonanza backdrop of mountains and sky that rivaled the real thing.

The DeMille Gate existed only in photographs, same for the main gate that Erich von Stroheim had driven Gloria Swanson through in *Sunset Boulevard,* on her way to see DeMille himself. The lagoon was long gone, as were the stars who had once occupied the bungalows in the courtyard behind the administration building, facing a putting green installed for Bob Hope and Bing Crosby.

Josh cruised through the buffet line and settled at an out-of-the-way table with A.C. Lyles, who started as a messenger boy at the studio and became one of its most successful producers. Now in his eighties and still showing up every day in his antique red T-Bird, he was one of the few remaining eyewitnesses to Paramount's glory years in the "Golden Age of Hollywood." The only remaining eyewitness, maybe.

A.C. had finished telling stories about his pals Dick Arlen, Jimmy Cagney, and Ron Reagan and was sharing memories about Josh's folks, when Lon joined them, Julie in tow. Justin and Rusty Jr. were off exploring the lot, Lon said, lifting Julie onto a chair and taking the other empty for himself. He did a double handshake with A.C., filched a meatball from Josh's plate, and said, "I heard about Connie and that jerk Russ Tambourine from Rusty Jr. What was that all about?"

"The usual bickering between exes," Josh said, letting Lon see it was not a question he cared to answer in front of his daughter or A.C.

Lon recognized the clue.

A.C. leaned over to Julie, like he was about to share a secret, and said, "Not every union works out long-term and happily ever after like your parents and your grandparents before them, sweetheart. Harry Wainwright and Olivia McCrea. Up there with Jimmy and his darling Bill, Ron and Nancy, that rascal

Freddie March and his Flo, Alfred and Lynn, my Martha and me."

Julie pulled away from A.C. "My mommy got shot and killed. What's so happily ever after about that?"

In tears, she pushed up from the table and fled, A.C. looking pained, apologizing for the unexpected grief he had caused her, Lon telling A.C. he could not have known, Julie would be fine, while Josh excused himself and raced after her, calling Julie's name.

He caught up with her halfway to the parking lot.

He swept her into his arms, hugging her tightly, gently patting her back, sending her wordless love as he had done so many times before tonight, adding his tears to hers on their merged cheeks.

High heels echoed behind him and came to an abrupt stop alongside him. Niki, out of breath, resting with her hands on her knees. "I saw Julie run outside from the party, then you," she said, her face a portrait of concern.

Julie called out for Niki, pulled away from Josh, and reached out for her.

Josh settled her in Niki's arms, and—

Looking past them to the parking lot, he spotted Justin and Rusty Jr.

They were skulking about in the shadows.

Wobbly on their feet.

The hazy light of a tall lamppost revealed a long-necked bottle in Rusty Jr.'s hand.

What looked like a cigarette was protruding from Justin's puckered twelve-year-old lips.

The boys saw him and ducked out of sight.

It was nothing Josh could deal with now.

He gave Julie a comfort touch and instructed Niki to round up the boys and head home while he went back to the dining room for a few minutes, for some last words with his brother.

Katie came to him during the night, waking him from a sleep that had eluded him for the better part of an hour while he wrestled with ideas about Clyde Davenport and the fragile bargain they'd made, but mostly—mostly—the kids, condemning himself as a lousy father, frustrated and full of confusion over how to deal with them.

She was wearing the summer dress he'd bought for her, a floral pattern in a rainbow of colors, on their first date after that first L'Chaim telethon. The date was a test, she said, testing if their meeting was *bashert*—predestined—or inspired by a temptation of the flesh that, at best, would be temporary.

"I suppose we won't know until we put it to the test," Josh said.

"True or false?"

"I've already failed at multiple choice."

"Then we'll fill in the blanks together," she said, Katie's smile as wicked as it was sincere and overpowering.

Theirs was easy banter, comfortable, coming after they'd hardly known each other for fifteen minutes that already felt like a lifetime.

He was still a cop in uniform, moonlighting at the telethon with a half dozen other off-duty officers. Patrolling an area in front of the stage, between cameras, and mesmerized on first sight by this young singer whom Jon Voight was guaranteeing would "steal your heart with her outrageous beauty, her magnificent voice, her sincerity of purpose, and become the idol of all the world by this time next year."

Barely into her number, "In the Key of Love," singing to a background track produced by Clyde Davenport, the "Mr. Magic" of rock and roll and a major supporter of L'Chaim, her eyes locked onto his and stayed there, as if she were performing only for him.

"Katie told me she thinks you're hot," a raspy voice whispered in Josh's ear.

He had been joined by the nice-looking girl he'd noticed earlier backstage, talking to the telethon's yarmulke-wearing floor manager and crew members about the lighting and the sound levels for "my star."

"It's the uniform," he said, unsure how to respond.

"It's what's inside that counts with Katie. I manage her. Name's Connie Reynolds. I could sort of go for it myself if Katie hadn't seen you first."

"Uh-huh," Josh said, staying focused on Katie and increasingly uncomfortable with the way the conversation was going. He breathed relief when an assistant director stepped over and motioned them to silence.

Connie gave him a wink and hurried off.

She sought him out again a minute or two after Katie finished her number to sustained applause from an audience moved to its feet in the cramped KCOP stage on La Brea Avenue. She had Katie in tow and disappeared after making a quick introduction, saying, "You smitten kittens need your privacy."

Katie's proposed test took them up to Santa Barbara for the weekend, a two-hour trip on the 101 full of amiable chatter that quickly became personal and, soon, deeper than that, both of them divulging secrets they swore they'd never revealed to another living soul.

They checked into an overpriced out-of-the-way beachfront motel that mirrored the city's Spanish heritage and at once were ripping at each other's clothing like two animals in heat.

More than once Katie told him, "Yes, *bashert*," always happy, sometimes the word framed by tears of joy.

"Bashert," he agreed. She had to help him get the pronunciation right.

Later, during an evening stroll on State Street in downtown Santa Barbara, along outdoor paseos and through cobble-stoned arcades with their bubbling fountains, plush palm trees, and cascading bougainvillea, Katie spotted the summer dress in a storefront window.

When Katie admired it—

Impulsively, Josh dashed into the store and bought it over her objections, insisting that he owed her a replacement for the outfit of hers he had destroyed at the motel.

"You don't have to do this," she said.

"I do," Josh said.

"I do," Katie said. "I like the sound of those words, *bashert* boy."

She had the dress on when they eloped to Las Vegas and were married by an obese Elvis in a studded jump suit and, at no extra charge, a studded yarmulke atop his bushel of unnatural brown hair. "*Mazel tov,* y'all," he said, showering them with a handful of rice he assured them was kosher before launching into an off-key rendition of "Love Me Tender."

She wore the dress again at the next L'Chaim telethon, when Jon Voight's prediction had been partially realized, Katie having achieved stellar stardom in America and about to embark on her first world concert tour.

She wore the dress to celebrate their first wedding anniversary.

Afterward, she had the dress framed and hung on the bedroom wall over their bed. The dress was more priceless to her than a Rembrandt or a Picasso, she told him, a trophy she had earned by winning the right to be called Mrs. Joshua Wainwright.

He had Katie buried in the dress, and since her funeral, the frame over their bed had hung empty.

Josh felt her presence before he opened his eyes, sat up, and saw her at the foot of the bed, as always, looking terrific in the dress.

"I heard you calling for me," Katie said. "I felt your pain."

"The kids. I'm at a loss. What do I do about our kids, Katie?"

"What you've always managed to do, my *bashert* boy: The right thing."

"I don't know what the right thing is anymore."

"You do," Katie said, and proceeded to remind him in detail.

He reached over for the pad and pen he kept bedside, scribbling furiously to keep up with her.

"And you know what else is burdening me, what I'm doing for the man who had you killed?"

"Yes."

"Something I never should have agreed to take on in the first place, damn it all to Hell. Say the word and I'll quit Davenport cold."

"It doesn't matter. I'm dead. He can't hurt me anymore. Be careful not to let him hurt you."

"Hurt me how? How do you think he can hurt me?"

He was writing down her every word when they began to fade from the page, and her voice grew dimmer until, finally, she was gone, too, and Josh woke up with a memory of their conversation as empty as the frame above the bed.

He fumbled after the pad and pen and snapped on the bed lamp.

Nothing there.

Blank pages.

He stretched back under the covers and tried for sleep, anxious to reconnect with the dream, with Katie, frustrated by his awareness it wasn't going to happen.

It never did.

Josh let breakfast pass without raising any of the business about last night with Justin and Rusty Jr., who was especially distant, not the least curious about his mother and what might have happened between Connie and Russ Tambourine; not so much as a question from him. Probably, Josh thought, because it wasn't an answer he needed or wanted to hear.

After Niki drove off with the kids, he changed into his sweats and crossed over from the bedroom to the gym. He was halfway through his usual morning ritual, on the stationery bike, throwing off enough sweat to wet the pages of the new Jack Higgins he was reading, when his cell phone sang out.

Keshawna.

"Mickey Gubitosi," she said.

"Robert Blake's real name, when he was in the *Our Gang* comedies, before the MGM movies and playing Little Beaver," he said. "How much do you owe me now and what so early in the a.m. besides this round of 'Keesh Loses Again'?"

"Davenport just called on the hot line. In a panic. Saying he scared off somebody trying to crack the mansion last night and, in the last fifteen minutes, a phone call telling him his life wasn't worth shit anymore."

"As if it ever was. What's Goodman say?"

"All he caught overnight was the sound of his pee helping the shrubbery to grow. Our surveillance guys just got there to make our installations, so no eavesdropping to play with yet. I checked into the call he claimed, with our usual unlisted friends. He got one. From a disposable cell. End of the line."

"So, what's it? Davenport commanding my presence to hold his hand?"

"Yeah, but not there," Keshawna said.

Chapter 14

Big Buddies of America was headquartered on the eighth floor of one of the high-rises sending shadows across the shuttered, decaying Ambassador Hotel on the no-longer fashionable stretch of mid-city Wilshire Boulevard that had turned all business and commerce since the years when wealthy matrons dressed elegantly to shop the expensive counters and take tea at Bullock's or wander the high fashion racks at I. Magnin, when the movie stars mixed martinis and meals at the original Brown Derby and loaned glamour and glitter to opening nights at the Coconut Grove.

Josh rounded a corridor off the elevator bank and saw Peppi Blue hanging against the wall about halfway down, an unlit cigarette plugged into his trach, his nose buried in a copy of *Billboard.*

Peppi looked up when he heard him approaching on the faded, threadbare carpeting that may once have been emerald green. He moved a hand inside his sports coat and kept it hidden shoulder-holster high until he satisfied himself it was Josh. They exchanged nods of recognition. Peppi pushed open the office door and directed Josh inside, but did not join him.

Davenport, pacing nervous circles in the small, austere waiting area, hands locked behind his back, flashed relief. "Can you believe it?" he said, hurrying over and offering his hand, which Josh accepted reluctantly. "All of a sudden, I am living in a nightmare. Somebody out to murder me, God knows why."

Josh wanted to say, *And so do I,* or *It's about time,* or *The devil his due,* something like that. Instead, taking back his hand and rubbing the palm on his thigh, he said, "You see him or, the voice on the phone—recognize it?"

Davenport wagged his head.

Josh said, "Talk to me about what happened at the house."

Davenport ran his eyes to the ceiling, then across a wall full of posters, photographs, and commendations, landing them on a mounted poster bearing the date, time, and location of this year's Annual Concert for Big Buddies above a jumbo likeness of Davenport decked out in an Uncle Sam costume, his finger aiming at a message in block letters:

CLYDE'S KIDS NEED YOU.

He said, "I'd gone out for the evening, needing to hang with a familiar face or two after what I've been put through lately. In the mood for lobster tail at the Palm. Sitting in my usual booth up front, under my caricature. Trading words with Bob Fead about the hits we had together in his RCA days, when he was running the show there. Harold Childs and Stan Layton, who I hired to do national promotion when Peppi was battling back from the throat business that put him out of action for a while. Macey Lipman, the indie marketing guy who's painting landscapes nowadays. Jay Lowy, who I knew from his running Jobete Music and NARAS. It was like I'd stumbled into a reunion of guys who mattered when the record business was still a business for record men, not suits who could not tell a bass line from the bottom line.

"I got home early, maybe midnight. My stomach was knotted up. What can happen if you consume a hundred pounds of lobster tail drowning in butter. I sent Peppi down the hill to buy something that would get rid of the ache. About ten minutes later, I was halfway into my pajamas when I heard a noise coming from outside, like someone trying to crack a lock. Not Peppi. He has keys. I got to my gun cabinet and grabbed a Ruger double-action Super Redhawk that's powerful enough to take down a moose. I hit the front door screaming for the bastard to show himself." He shrugged. "Nobody. Nothing. I wrote it off as my imagination playing tricks until the call this morning on one of my unlisted numbers to tell me I was a scum-sucking rat and get ready to die."

Davenport sank into one of the leather chairs dotting the reception room, began tapping out a nervous melody on the armrest. His nails were dirty and desperately needed a trim. His face contracted, as if grappling with a fresh thought.

He looked up and said, "What is it, you don't believe me or are you taking it in as good news?"

"A little of both. Does that upset you?"

"Not as long as you're earning your keep."

"Can you think of anybody new who'd want you dead?"

The subtlety of his innuendo didn't escape Davenport. He was about to answer when an interior door opened and a man in his early to mid-fifties sailed through it as if he were making a stage entrance, shouting "Mr. Magic!" in triplicate, apologizing for making Davenport wait, hugging him, and launching a slurping kiss on the lips. His yellow and blue-striped polo shirt hung high over a protruding belly that defied his snug jeans, which he wore with the cuffs tucked inside a pair of steel-tipped rattlesnake boots that added two inches to his height and turned him into a six-footer. His eyes sparkled on a face otherwise etched by years of hard living. A puff of hair grew under his lower lip, the same shade of magenta as the hair hanging long and loose over his shoulders.

Davenport introduced them.

Josh recognized Terry Jameson's name at once. "I still have every one of your albums," he said, pumping his hand. "I wore out the grooves on most of them."

"You're a man of taste and discernment," Terry said, winking away any suggestion of ego. "None of it ever would have happened, it weren't for Mr. Magic. His Symphony of Sound turned me into a hit maker and it might have gone on forever, I hadn't turned myself into a stone junkie. I'd be dead now, he hadn't done what it took to straighten me out. God bless you, Clyde."

Davenport backed away from another hug. "Ancient history, Terry."

"Not ever in my lifetime," Terry Jameson said, then turning back to Josh: "What he did for me more years ago than I have fingers, he didn't have to do."

"Loyalty repaid. I don't know how many labels tried to pry you loose from me, but you rejected them all."

"Told them to go fuck themselves is what I said to them. I was trailer trash before you caught me at the Whisky and saw something in me nobody else saw, except for me. Not enough money in the world to change my mind about you, Clyde, then or since." He seemed ready to cry. "You want to hear something else, Mr. Wainwright?"

"Josh."

"Hear me, Josh. . . . He helps me straighten out and I know if I get back into the scene again it'll kill me. I have the willpower of an amoeba. I lay it on Clyde. I announce that my love affair with rock and ruin is over for quits. I tell him I want to do some good before I draw my last. I want to get the message out there to kids before they have a chance to skunk up their lives. More than *Just Say No.* More like *Just Say Never.*

"Clyde tells me, 'Say no more, Terry.' He whips out his checkbook and lays one on me for a cool million. And that, Josh, is how Big Buddies of America came to be. Every year since, we get this concert thing going, a bill of big-name artists who also want to give something back. Every year has been bigger and better than the last one, Clyde helping us pull it together. Why, over his objections, I came up with 'Clyde's Kids' as a way to honor him."

"And I still object," Davenport said.

"Oh, for Christ's sake, Clyde. Humility still doesn't sit well on you." Turning back to Josh: "Wouldn't you agree on that?"

"Humility will never be his middle name."

"Good one," Terry Jameson said, giving Josh's back several appreciative slaps. "I should get back to the staff, Clyde. Anything special got you here, or maybe you and Josh would like to hang out in the meeting, hear how we've been adding chapters at the rate of five a month?"

"We were on our way to another meeting," Clyde said, "so I thought to drop up for a quick hello and to get this year's campaign off to a solid start." He extracted an envelope from a pocket of his white silk canvas blazer and handed it over.

Terry Jameson made a show of holding it up to the fluorescents.

"You can open it now," Davenport said.

His check, made out to Big Buddies of America, was for a million.

Now, Terry Jameson was crying, insisting, "Mr. Magic, you are truly one amazing fuck of a human being."

"Let me guess," Josh said later. "You wanted me there to get a third-party opinion, that you're a kinder, gentler Clyde Davenport than I ever give you credit for being, which is no credit at all."

"It was convenient," Davenport said. "Except for my current situation and the need for your services, your opinion is worthless to me. Always has been and will continue to be until you satisfy yourself that, outside of your imagination, I'm guilty of no murders."

"A million's a big spread to make a point, Mr. Magic."

"Chump change. I make that in my sleep on royalties. More than enough to hand over a blank check to ICS. Worth it if it helps get you off my back once and for all."

"And if it doesn't?"

"Don't flatter yourself."

They were in the Lexus, Josh driving, having been summarily drafted after the Big Buddies of America meeting to play chauffeur, Davenport explaining without apology, "I kept Peppi here for protection only until you arrived. He's off now running some errands for me."

Davenport's directions took them south a couple miles down Vermont Avenue, to Adams Boulevard, where he pulled a right turn and cruised in the direction of Normandie Avenue, past restored Victorian-style mansions built at the turn of the last century, when the wealthy upper middle class began moving south and west of downtown.

The Adams District came to represent the center of fashionable society until displaced around 1917 by Beverly Hills. The homes created by well-known architects of the day fell for the most part into decay and ruin, the glitter and awe gone from rows of elegant homes flush with imported wood paneling, stained glass windows, massive fireplaces, grand staircases, sun and sleeping porches, and other accoutrements of gracious living.

Over the years, the crumbling neighborhood slowly changed coloration from white to black as real estate prices fell within reach of blacks working their way out of the South Central ghetto. Mansions were restored to their former glory, frequently by owners who'd once worked in them as maids and butlers, joined ultimately by Latinos and Asians, who also understood that "Upward Mobility" owed more to the color of their money than the color of their skin.

The address Josh was looking for belonged to the only three-story mansion on the palm-lined block, with a high-rise turret that added a special elegance and distinction to a splendor of gables. He found street parking a couple houses down.

At the head of the brick path to the gabled entrance, a modest sign hung from the kind of wooden posts used by real estate companies:

DEAD DOGG RECORDS

Davenport steered Josh forward, telling him with almost feverish delight, "You're after a killer? You're about to meet one, with my compliments."

Chapter 15

Pressing the doorbell produced a musical blitzkrieg piped onto the porch through invisible stereo speakers. The metal-reinforced door clicked through a succession of locks several moments later, following an inspection by invisible video cameras, whose whirring sound Josh recognized as easily as he felt an eye checking them out through the peephole.

A giant of a man in camouflage fatigues, somebody Josh might have expected to see hoisting a shade umbrella over Michael Jackson, opened the door and invited them inside. His twin guided them from the vestibule along an oak-lined corridor lined with Gold and Platinum records to double-doors that swung open onto an office furnished in money, sort of *Nouveau* Filthy *Riche.* Everything else about the office was like every other record company executive office Josh had ever been in, walls of self-adulation and congratulation and sound gear ramped high enough to beat a missile to the moon.

The noise sweeping down the corridor like fire in a wind tunnel was coming from here, high-octane rap pumping out street crude, talking dirty sex and death to dirty cops, or something like that, to a beat built on a Motown sample he thought he might be able to ID before he went deaf forever.

Davenport muttered something under his breath and marched from the door to the floor-to-ceiling black ivory audio shelves.

He found the switch he wanted.

Click.

Quiet settled over the room.

Davenport wheeled around and announced in a voice meant for an audience in the Radio City Music Hall, although they were the only two people here: "If you want to know what it is wrong with music today, that's what's wrong with music today. They've taken all the music out of today's music."

A section of wall slid open.

A cream-skinned black stepped forward with the grace of a runway model dressed for a *GQ* fashion shoot. Double-breasted powder blue pinstripe suit. Blue-tinted eyeglasses among his perfectly color-coordinated accessories. Handmade leather loafers that must have set him back five hundred bucks. Each one. His luminescent curly chestnut hair cut tight. His left ear sporting a diamond three times the size of Ed Bradley's on *60 Minutes.* A silk shirt worn open at the neck, showing off a museum of Fifth Avenue bling-bling.

Josh didn't need a formal introduction to know this was EZ-XTC, the president of Dead Dogg Records. Real name: Ezra Charleson. His handsome face was a fixture on TV and in the fan magazines, the way years ago, growing up in the South Central ghetto, his profile and side view had been a staple of countless booking sheets.

He was in his mid-to-late forties and looked ten years younger. Work had been done by a lazy plastic surgeon to trimline his nose. A sliver of a mustache gave him a Continental air, but his conversation couldn't make up its mind between practiced elocution and pure ghetto.

"Who you dissing, dawg?" he said. "Problem with all you old-timers, you're so out of tune with the times you can't hear how we're poets of the people, the way Dylan was in his day and that whole lot before him, including you with your sugar-coated Symphony of Sound, so I give you props for that much."

"I'm not here to philosophize with you, Mr. Charleson."

"Of course, not. Why would Mr. Magic ever so much as spend a second thinking of quality conversation with some dumb nigger." He glided to the blue leather executive chair behind the cherry-stained marble pedestal desk that dominated the room and settled into it, carefully adjusting his trousers to keep the crease.

"Now who's dissing who?" Davenport said, suppressing his irritation. He rattled off a list of black artists he'd worked with, capping it with Ray Charles. "My record speaks for itself," he said.

"Mine for the California Youth Authority," EZ-XTC said. He leaned forward with his elbows on the desk, his chin resting on his laced fingers. "Ray Charles. Met him before he got played off, Heaven-bound and Saint Pete happy to welcome him, and he never onc't mentioned your name."

Josh watched Davenport draw deep and noisy breaths in a struggle to hold his temper, relished the sight of his face turning fire-engine red.

"He mentioned yours," Davenport said, finally.

That perked Ezra Charleson's eyebrows. "Say what?"

"We were running down masters at his place—"

"RPM Building. Over to 2107 West Washington. Know the address by heart."

"—at his place," Davenport continued. "He wondered if I knew who you were or had heard the sounds you were putting out there. He spelled it out note for note. Said this cat EZ-XTC had something new and fresh going on with his Dead Dogg shit. He said EZ-XTC was putting cool hep into his hip-hop, and people'd be calling him a genius another ten or fifteen years."

Charleson bolted upright. He pulled his glasses down his nose and gave Davenport a challenging look. "You're shitting me, right? Ray Charles say that?"

Davenport raised his right hand like he was taking an oath. "Got a Bible?"

"Matter of fact. . . ." It was a paperback-sized edition, bound in black leather, the pages rimmed in red. He was using it as a paperweight, holding down an unruly stack of files by his left elbow. He picked it up like an old friend, invited Davenport to one of the visitors' chairs across from him and handed it over. "The Good Book where you find the best lyrics ever."

Davenport patronized him with a smile and settled the Bible in his lap.

Charleson said, "Idolized that man. Here now because of him. Gangs was all I knew in the hood. Doing the dirty before I was old enough to poke or tell a hard-on from a hambone. My peeps had me running all kinds of shit for them, paying me off in shit, teaching me how to do a needle. I janked whatever and whenever, tribute to the habit or to help feed my family.

"Got mainy and did a drive-by, sending away a lowlife homie for reasons I never heard. Got caught, but being underage, they couldn't put me on Death Row for a Murder One. I caught soft time full of hard times, people getting their freak on with me day and night. Music and the Good Book got me through in one piece. I came out full of peace of mind and knowing how I'd be seeing those Pearly Gates soon enough, I didn't do better with my days."

He had pushed onto his feet and was using the desk like a pulpit, his words getting as ghettoized as he'd once been, emphasizing every thought with an inflated expression or gesture:

"Didn't matter no more I was too light for football, not tall enough for basketball. I saw what Mr. Ray Charles did with his life, and I heard what music had come around to, no more June-moon cracker-belly shit songs, but telling it like it was by people living the life. I scored enough—not saying how—to fix up a garage studio and signed up my homies to come in and rap. I sold CDs in front of schools and movies from the back of my trunk, me and my crew. I learned fast how to deal with radio and the trades. Got me my own hit that crossed me into the big time. Big money. Big, big. Big, big, big. You know what rich is? I left rich behind my first year. You think you rich, Mr. Magic? I'll see your rich and double you down. And I do it clean. Never onc't poked one of my acts out of their fair share. Performance royalties. Publishing. Silly shit stuff like concert programs and T-shirts. What say? Never much heard that said about you, Mr. Magic."

It was a challenge.

Davenport shrugged it off.

Charleson looked at Davenport like the truth was flashing in neon on his forehead.

He said, "This place? Because of Mr. Ray Charles. Took my inspiration from him. He built 2107 West Washington the ground up. He put the RPM building where it is, a working-class black neighborhood, to put money back into the community, let homies see what a poor blind boy was able to accomplish. I wanted to add to Ray's vision and fuck them what says it's because I stole the place cheap or to be near to downtown, Hollywood, the valley, and a straight shot to the airport. You dig, Mr. Davenport?"

"All six feet," Davenport said, amused. "He were still with us, Mr. Ray Charles would be proud of you."

EZ-XTC liked hearing that. "Never had the nerve to walk up to the man, fall on my knees, and kiss his shiny shoes, not ever even when we were both hanging backstage at the Grammys, so what you're saying will have to do me."

"With all due respect to Ray, I'm saying you don't make music. Millions of dollars, yes, Mr. Charleson, but not music."

Davenport couldn't let it go.

He pushed the Bible back to EZ-XTC.

"So why you here then?" Charleson said. "You don't even do that anymore. You too washed up to ever get a hit again and only making news because the pigs think they got you for murder. I can relate, dude, and because you could talk Mr. Ray Charles, I'll wait out what you come here to say." He plunked into his chair.

Davenport momentarily closed his eyes. Josh thought he could see his mind turning cartwheels, like a Bobby Fischer psyching out his next three hundred chess moves against an IBM mechanical brain. His face drained of anger. He adopted a benign smile. "First, let me apologize for my rudeness, Mr. Charleson. You touched a raw nerve, and I overreacted."

"Not all your shit was shit," Charleson said, signaling acceptance of the truce.

"And I admire what you turned out this year with Cake Mouth."

"He's the big dog at Dead Dogg right now, and don't think he don't know it, either. Three singles on the charts and the new album, *Cake Mouthing Off,* gone Triple Plat and not over yet."

"You know about the concert I produce every year for Big Buddies of America?"

"I'll say that for you. You here for a donation? Double what I pledged last year. No need to shine the light on me or Dead Dogg. Say it's in honor of Mr. Ray Charles. That do us?" He started to rise, as if calling the meeting to a close.

"Not why I'm here, Mr. Charleson." He let the news sink in. "I'm here to ask you for Cake Mouth for my Big Buddies concert."

Charleson showed no reaction at first, then went flat-faced, and began searching the room after flies. His eyes fell on Josh, as if he were seeing him for the first time. Shot a finger at him, as if he were identifying somebody in a police lineup.

"I seen you before," he said. "I know you?"

"Never."

"You got a name?"

"Joshua Wainwright."

"You stand like a cop. Smell like one. You a cop? Mr. Davenport here under some sort of police arrest he not talking about? Police protection?"

"Ex-cop. Retired."

"Only retired cops I ever saw was dead," Charleson said. He outlined Josh with his eyes. Snapped his fingers. "Was my church I saw you. Not lately. Some old calendar. You ever been to Adams First Evangelical Church? Maybe to land on some brother or other?"

"My business partner preaches there sometimes."

Charleson let that sink in. An ear-to-ear grin put his cheeks in overdrive. He finger-snapped again. "It! Where I seen you. Keshawna Keyes trotting you out. You be my old home girl's partner. She mention you in a hot light back when and anytime after that. How she?"

"How she's always."

Charleson smacked his lips. "Don't know how I ever let that woman get away from me. You be sure and spill my love you next see her. Say Easy Charleson wouldn't never no mind hearing from her now and again."

"Consider it spilled."

Davenport coughed to draw back attention.

Turning to him, losing the smile, Charleson said, "Not Cake Mouth. He busy night of the concert."

"I haven't mentioned the date."

"Cake Mouth busy any date you mention." He let the news sink in. Davenport held his tongue. Charleson leaned back in the chair and locked his hands behind his head. "Tell you what, though. Seeing as how you brought me kindness about Mr. Ray Charles and the cop there is tight peeps with Keshawna, you can have Princess Lulu for your show."

"Who?"

"My new discovery. Nobody you saw when you was at the House of Blues checking out my scene." He nodded knowingly. "A young woman with a voice sweet as molasses and a heart to match."

"We're not doing *American Idol,* Mr. Charleson."

Charleson patted the Bible. "What's the Good Book say about judging lest you be judged? You'll thank me after."

"Not the other way around? You thanking me for giving this kind of exposure to someone no one's ever heard of? The press coverage is always massive. If she's as good as you say she is, the Big Buddies concert will—"

"I heard of her, you heard of her, Mr. Joshua Wainwright heard of her."

"Cake Mouth *and* Princess Lulu."

"I can think on it."

"I have to hear her first. Know what I'm getting."

"You mean beside the chance to associate your washed-up ass with the music that did you in, maybe for keeps, and its next big star?"

"I have to hear Princess Lulu first," Davenport said, leaving no doubt he was determined to have the last word.

"I'll let you know," Charleson said.

"Then I'll let you know," Davenport said.

Whatever he was thinking, Davenport kept to himself throughout most of the drive back to Magic Land, until, finally, as Josh turned off Laurel Canyon onto Mulholland, he said, "It went well back there. Two acts for the price of none, one the reigning gangsta hip-hop hero, who'll guarantee me not an empty seat in the house. It was game, set, and match for me." He was clearly soliciting Josh for confirmation and appreciation.

"A draw, the way I see it," Josh said, "mainly because you got into Charleson with that business about Ray Charles."

Davenport angled into the space between the passenger seat and the door, making sure he noticed his burgeoning smirk of superiority. "Did my homework before calling the meeting. That uppity punk of a producer talked a lot in interviews about Ray Charles being his role model. That became a tool in my armory."

"You're saying Ray Charles never mentioned EZ-XTC?"

"Don't take my word for it," Davenport said. "Ask Ray when you see him."

"I'll add it to the list," Josh said, slowing down and honking demands for the small gang of newsmen and paparazzi to clear out of his way.

A gunshot from somewhere outside the estate grounds exploded.

It splintered the windshield.

Narrowly missed Josh.

Davenport yelped and ducked.

The news guys scrambled for cover.

Josh hit the brakes.

He leaped from the Lexus, pulling his .38 Smithie in the same motion, and hollered for Davenport to stay down.

Chapter 16

Later, his fingers flying angrily, Clyde Davenport asked Peppi Blue, "Do you know how close you came to hitting me with that shot?" He was in the hot tub, savoring a martini while the tension eased from his weary bones.

Peppi, across from him, lounging on the master bathroom's gilded toilet seat that would not have looked out of place in Buckingham Palace, took a deep drag off the filter tip in his trach and dispatched the smoke jets through his nose.

"If I wanted the shot to hit you, you'd have been hit with that shot," he answered with his fingers.

The cops and the news hounds had come and gone—no one wiser to the identity of the shooter and Clyde had dismissed Josh Wainwright after they had toured the security systems installed by the International Celebrity Service teams.

"You're positive you weren't seen by anybody? By the surveillance cameras?"

Peppi swallowed and divested himself of more smoke and buried the butt's remains in the toilet bowl. "Did you want me to be seen?" Clyde gave him a look. "Then why ask? I made sure the cameras were turned off before I slipped out and they were still off when I returned. I almost bumped into an ICS technician coming to check the sequenced electric eyes at the sidewall gate. The Magnum was already hidden."

"Excellent. This should settle any doubts in anyone's mind that I was the intended victim, not Ava Garner."

"What about Wainwright?"

"As easy for me to dupe as the rest of the world," Clyde's fingers said. He proceeded to tell Peppi about the meetings with Terry Jameson and EZ-XTC. "Jameson laid it on a little too thick, but Wainwright came away a believer," he said.

"EZ-XTC, a possible problem?"

"I'll know once I hear this Princess Lulu and decide what to do about her. If she has passable talent—" His fingers dissolved into a pair of palms pointing at the gilded ceiling. "If she's his bed meat—" The gesture repeated.

Peppi nodded. "I will pay him a visit."

Clyde refused the suggestion.

"These people aren't like the station managers and program directors you found so easy to intimidate. These are street thugs who strike it rich but never lose their old ways. They're always protecting their turf or their honor. They settle arguments by killing each other."

"We already know people like that."

"Yes, but we're usually on the same side as them. The rules are different. We know how to successfully deal with them."

The wall phone rang.

Peppi checked the ID screen and reported:

Private Name. Private Number.

He clicked on the speaker halfway into its recorded message that the caller had to identify himself by pressing the pound key and reciting his name at the tone.

EZ-XTC.

No mistaking his voice or his attitude.

"Hey, what you hiding out from?" he said, dripping enough sarcasm to refill the hot tub. "Acting like your number still some guaranteed hot ticket to making the charts or the dumb ass Hall of Fame?" He told Davenport when and where he could hear Princess Lulu. "Only chance, my man, so show your face or get erased, dig?" he said, and disconnected.

Clyde didn't know what infuriated him more, EZ-XTC's latest insult or seeing Peppi so bothered by the words that he turned his head aside.

He grabbed the plastic bottle of body conditioner and hurled it at the wall phone without aiming, almost yanking his arm from its socket. Ignoring the pain, he tried again, this time with a glass bottle of hair restorer. He connected. The receiver sailed from the hook and the glass bottle shattered and rained onto the imported custom-cut marble squares drawn from the stone quarries in Carerra, Italy, where, his decorator swore, Michelangelo ordered the marble for his David and Pieta statues.

"That strutting black peacock is on my list, Peppi," Clyde said, his fingers shouting. "Not now. Not yet. No hurry. After the Big Buddies concert, when it gets to be his turn to answer for his insulting way, his insulting words; the idea that—his daring to speak to me that way—like he was a—his thinking he—" Unable to complete a thought, struggling to regain his composure. Peppi pretending not to hear while he carefully picked up shards of glass and dropped them in the waste basket.

Two days later, promptly at eight o'clock in the evening, Clyde's limo pulled up to the guarded entrance to a recording studio on Wilcox Place in Hollywood, south of Sunset, that he knew well from twenty-something years ago. It had been one of Motown's many studios within walking distance of their offices.

He'd slipped in sometimes, on those rare occasions when he was out prowling—maybe checking out Martoni's for industry types he felt comfortable jawing with—and got wind Stevie or Marvin or Smokey, maybe even the grand diva who'd come to demand that everyone address her as "Miss Ross," had something going on here.

It was state-of-the-art, a world removed from the basement

digs Berry Gordy had started out in, in Detroit, and he'd pulled favors off Phil Jones or Tommy Noonan to use it himself, on occasions where his own board couldn't give him the effect he needed, a sound that Motown was cranking out with ho-hum ease.

Clyde laid the sound down better, of course, but he never made that claim openly.

It was there in the grooves and anybody with half an ear knew that without needing to be told.

Clyde recognized one of the two beef trusts at the gate from EZ-XTC's place on Adams. He was the taller and heavier of the pair, but the other one beat him for a menacing glare, like the difference between malice and murder.

"He okay," Malice said, and waved the limo through after Murder had used his cell phone to snap photos of Peppi behind the wheel and the car's license plate. He ran over as Peppi settled the car in a marked space by the entrance to the nondescript building, whose style fit somewhere between California neo-classic and California non-classic, and got out to open the rear door for Clyde.

"EZ say only you inside, not no one else," Malice said, throwing a thumb at Peppi while gasping for breath like he'd just run the mile in a minute.

"I don't go anywhere without him," Clyde said.

"EZ say, you was to say so, I was to tell you good night and point you back out."

Clyde started to object.

Peppi stopped him with a headshake and signed: "He's playing his power to impress his crew. You go listen to the girl. I'll stay here and listen to the Lakers lose again."

"One more thing," said Murder, who had joined them. "You or you packing heat? EZ don't allow no outside heat inside, why I'm asking."

"No."

Peppi signed a reminder of the shotgun under the driver seat.

"What he hand-jivin'?" Murder said.

"Same answer. No."

"Lot of hand-jivin' for *No,*" he said. "Mind we pats you down for insurance?"

"Yes."

"We do it anyway," Murder said, his rich bass rumbling like thunder. "We don't need to add to problems already flying our way. You hear something sound like gunshots, don't forget to duck." He let the advisory stick for a moment, then burst out laughing. "Only playing with your head, man," he said, and guided Clyde into the studio while Malice hung back with Peppi.

The studio was larger and more elaborate than he remembered, the booth a marvel of technology that one quick glance revealed was superior to his own board back at Magic Land. He'd correct that first thing tomorrow. An engineer was lazily reworking levers and knobs while a co-pilot replaced strips of masking tape that marked the points and ID'd the tracks, the samples and loops in red, everything else in black.

Two skinny black girls were stretched out on the sofa against the rear wall, half-asleep, half-hanging out of their halter tops; neither wasting more than a lopsided look at Clyde through droopy lids illustrating the thick smell of weed, tats, and fresh pops on their dangling arms adding to the story, along with half a brick half-buried on a glass-top coffee table holding a mountain of fast-food bags, cartons of Chinese take-out, and greasy paper plates loaded with chicken bones, unfinished burgers, and cold fries. Crushed beer cans.

"Help yourself to anything you like," the engineer said, finally taking note of him. "It's Cherie, that one there, best if it's a suck-off. Got lips and a tongue on her can finish you before you start, no seconds flat. Hey, Cher, you hear?! Show him what I'm talkin' 'bout!"

Cherie pursed her lips and shot out her tongue across half the booth, then folded it in half and did a sort of loop-the-loop before gliding it back inside her mouth.

The engineer hooted. "Your dick get wrapped inside dat like a samwitch, nothing you'll ever soon forget," he said, and turned back to the board.

Clyde put a horizontal hand to his forehead and peered through the glass window into the dimly lit studio.

Nobody there.

Turning back to the sofa, he addressed the other girl. "You Princess Lulu?"

She struggled into a sitting position and leaned forward for a go at the snow brick. She dug into it with a curved green pinky nail an inch-and-a-half long, and filled her nose like she was packing for a long trip. She exhaled satisfaction and fell back onto the sofa without answering him.

"She Princess Lulu?" Clyde asked the engineer.

"She not even a good fuck," he said.

The audio kicked in, the engineer checking out the loops and samples in stereo and mono, tinkering until he found acceptable levels. The co-pilot scurrying to make fixes with the masking tape. Clyde filling time by calling out the titles of the raided songs, the players and the vocalists, making it a game, still batting a hundred percent when Easy Charleson arrived, his arm around the waist of one of the most beautiful creatures Clyde had ever laid eyes on. His eyes, his mind, struggled for words that would do her justice, this girl-woman flawless of face and figure.

She understood his stare. She lowered her head modestly and looked aside, as if bothered by the attention and the signal he was unintentionally sending out.

Clyde wanted her. He couldn't remember the last time he felt this way, so strong about any woman. Then, he could remember, and pushed aside the memory.

The memory still came packaged in the pain of an outcast boy unable to cope with his abrupt dismissal by the object of his adoration or the ridicule she heaped upon him after that. Ever since, all these years, even when the wall he built to keep out that part of his past failed him, Clyde could not bring himself to think or speak her name.

He forced his stare onto Easy Charleson and said, "You're late."

EZ-XTC snickered. "Like you never hear of CPT? Colored People Time? By my clock, you the early bird, bro."

"Of course," Clyde said, certain EZ-XTC had kept him waiting as another show of his superiority. There was nothing to be gained by making it an issue. Giving fresh meaning to his smile, he turned to the girl-woman and, extending his hand, said, "You must be—"

"Princess Lulu herself," EZ-XTC said. "Take the man's hand and welcome him, my little swan." She did as instructed. "She a swan, ain't she, Mr. Davenport? Furthest cry from the ugly duckling what first come on to me asking for a chance. Ain't that so, Anthony? What say, Gary?" The engineer and his co-pilot grunted confirmations. "A gangly thing, all legs and arms, wanting to be a star, up top the mountain with—" He began rattling off names. Counting on his fingers. "Bahamadia. Da Brat. Lil' Kim. Foxy Brown. Lauryn Hill. Eve. And 'course Queen Latifah," he said. "Why Lulu, she got to be a princess for me, 'cause hip-hop already have its queen, dig?" He made a face. "You know any those names, bro? Suppose not. Names you know they more like—" Going goggle-eyed. "Streisand. Dat so, bro? Dat your speed? Madonna, sure. Maybe Rusty Springfield, how she was called?" He got back to finger-counting, dropping a half dozen names he said he knew from the Rock and Roll Hall of Fame.

"I like Mariah, love her to death, and Alicia Keyes," Princess Lulu said, her voice silk and sultry in the shadow of a whisper.

EZ-XTC shushed her with a soft hand to her fertile lips and drove his hand over and around the mound of curly reddish-brown hair that framed the perfectly oval face resting on an elegant neck dressed in strands of perfectly matched petite pearls and diamonds, her only bling-bling. A satin tank-top dress trimmed in sequins showed off her broad shoulders and legs that owned half her treetop height. Three-inch heels dyed to match; toes painted a similar shade. Her face free of unnecessary makeup, except for a dab of satin lip gloss.

"Child going to be bigger'n Mariah, Alicia, and dem all," EZ-XTC said. "Go ahead and show him, my little princess."

She dutifully obeyed him and a minute or two later was inside the studio at a mike the co-pilot was adjusting to her height while she fiddled with the headphones that would allow her to perform live to the pre-recorded backing tracks.

The tracks kicked in.

At once, Princess Lulu's voice broke loose above them, motor-mouthing a sequence of lyrics he could barely understand, catching a word here or there, but able to translate the drama of the story she was hip-hopping by the way she worked over, walloped, caressed, or massaged the material.

As remarkable as she was, Princess Lulu was too good for what she was doing. With the kind of music that took her out of hip-hop and into something with greater international appeal and impact, she was superstar material; a time bomb close to detonating, an artist with staying power that would last for decades.

Whatever else Clyde despised about Easy Charleson, he couldn't fault him over Princess Lulu.

EZ-XTC and Dead Dogg Records be damned.

Clyde had to have her for himself. His mind was plotting how to make that happen even before she played out the last unintelligible lyrics hop-scotching over notes he hadn't heard since Ella at her peak.

Princess Lulu took off the headphones and stared expectantly at the booth.

EZ-XTC punched air with a high five and clicked into the intercom.

"Girl, you tamed the beast," he said, then turning to Clyde: "Cake Mouth, he doing your concert, correct?"

"Your Princess Lulu, she's—" Clyde wiggle-waggled his hand.

EZ-XTC reared back. "I got me niggers on my payroll jive ass better'n you, so quit your pokin' with me. I seen your look and them wheels spinning, hearing what my girl can do. Yes or no? Going to count to five, starting with four, and I better be hearing the answer I want."

There was something in the way he spoke that made Clyde realize there was more going on here than Charleson getting his way and his new act on the Big Buddies concert bill. Positions reversed, he'd already have booted Charleson out the door.

He turned his face to stone and counted off a few beats before telling him: "No."

EZ-XTC pulled his trimmed eyebrows tight and gave him a side-eyed study. Stuck a finger in one ear, then the other, like he was cleaning them.

Aiming his chin at the two girls flopped out on the sofa, Clyde said, "Not until I satisfy myself she's not like those stoned skags, who'd be prowling backstage probably looking to trade pussy for pot I let them anywhere near the show."

"She clean as my mama's oven," EZ-XTC said, his irritation on the rise.

"And your bros at the board, all they're high on is life."

"We don't do no urine tests, so you'll just have to take my say. She ain't never been a hood rat. Already had enough like dat in my stable."

Definitely something going on.

He glanced through the glass at Princess Lulu, and knew what it was.

What he wanted for himself.

What he planned on taking away from EZ-XTC.

Now, pursuing his gamble, he said, "Let Princess Lulu convince me."

"Say what?"

"You want her on the show badly enough, I want it from her lips. Up close and personal. Just Princess Lulu and me alone. Five minutes. All I need."

"You dancing right on the edge, Mr. Magic, you saying my say ain't enough."

"I'm saying I have it on good authority that during your vacations at the University of San Quentin, you earned your high school diploma, your B.A. in English, with a history minor, and an M.A. in business administration, all of which has me believing you talk like a pale imitation of all those slow-motion darkies that used to populate the movies in order to maintain your street cred. . . . Five minutes."

EZ-XTC narrowed his eyes. He brought up a menacing noise from his belly, maybe his bowels, and shoved Clyde against the wall. He pushed his face into Clyde's, sending bursts of hot garlicky breath into an ear, while dropping his voice to a whisper.

"I suggest you not use that tone on me when there are others within hearing distance," he said. "In fact, never, assuming you value your life as much as your reputation, Mr. Davenport."

"Five minutes," Clyde said.

EZ-XTC released him, stepped back to the board, and called

through the intercom, "Baby, I needs yo' body be back in here wit' us."

"Alone," Clyde said. "Just Princess Lulu and me."

It was a modest, windowless room, a battered wooden desk and kind of chair like the ones used by all the instructors and counselors at the juvenile detention center he hated more than the others—the one they all called "Stalag Censored"—and a broken-down sofa full of sagging, stained cushions, the only furniture. Two deadbolts to secure the door. No phone. The air conditioning playing high, probably to help dissipate the stink of weed and cumulative rolls in the hay. The poster for an early EZ-XTC album, *#$!!%+& Thuggin'*, the only wall decoration.

In the ten minutes before Princess Lulu joined him, Clyde sat at the desk, playing an imaginary keyboard, working out the how and what of what he wanted to say to her, to make her understand her greater future was with him, not Mr. Ezra Charleson. He would keep it basic, talk in terms she'd understand. She admired Mariah and Alicia. Fine.

He would regale her with stories about Tommy Mattola, who made Mariah the greatest-selling female recording artist ever, explaining how he had helped power Tommy's career in the beginning, before Tommy's fourteen-year reign at Sony, when he was maneuvering at RCA as the manager of Hall and Oates. Alicia would let him rag on Clive Davis, possibly the only record man Clyde considered an equal—almost; a genius at discovering and minting superstars, whose bag of tricks included a huge handful he picked up from Mr. Magic during his days at Columbia Records and, later, creating and running Arista Records, where Clive's great discoveries included Whitney Houston. He would drop all the names, tell as many tales as necessary, to convince her of the difference between the gutters of rap and hip-hop and the gold-lined streets she'd discover through the music and lyrics of his Symphony of Sound.

Princess Lulu knocked and stepped inside, leaving the door open about ten inches.

Socked him with an apprehensive smile and held up five splayed fingers.

"I understand," he said, his smile more sincere. "Five minutes."

He gestured her to have a seat.

She briefly studied the sofa, registered disgust, and settled instead on the edge of the desk, near enough for Clyde to smell her skin and the barest hint of a sweet cologne.

His hand moved to touch her.

He pulled it back before temptation defeated good judgment.

There'd be time for that later.

"Princess Lulu, my name is Clyde Davenport," he said. "EZ-XTC has probably explained to you that I'm thinking about putting you on the concert I produce every year for Big Buddies of America."

A smile crossed her face, revealing two dimples he hadn't spotted earlier.

She said, "I know why you're here, Mr. Davenport. It was my idea to begin with, after he told me he had agreed to take a meeting with you. I want you to do for me what EZ-XTC can't." She correctly read the look on his face. "What's it? Y'all expecting me to talk like dis way here, dat what? I ain't not one-a his hood rats, dawg." Then, "Columbia University, Mr. Davenport. Julliard." She tapped the face of his wristwatch. "Not enough time. Wrong place. Your place, better. Tell me what works for you."

Clyde struggled after his tongue. "Any time."

"Works for me, too," she said, tapping his nose.

And then she was gone.

Chapter 17

Earlier that same day, Josh and Keshawna got together in her office to play catch-up over a desk lunch catered by Jack-in-the-Box. She'd been gone a day and a half, in Washington, D.C., playing patty-cake with senior officials at Justice and the FBI, angling to snatch some big-budget freelance assignments she had heard via the grapevine would be up for grabs next month.

When it became Josh's turn, he filled her in on Davenport.

Keshawna broke out a *How about that?* face that ballooned into a toothsome smile at his mention of EZ-XTC, but quickly reined in her emotions, not fast enough for Josh to miss.

He said, "Charleson made it sound like you were more than a homie to him."

"Like a part of my life I'd rather forget?"

"He made it sound closer than that and not that long ago. Hanging with him at church, that recent. He asked me to spill his love on you and for you to keep in touch. Anything you'd like to spill?"

"The blood's blood one of these days."

"That close, were you? Why's it you never mentioned him to me?"

"I've never mentioned a lot of other men I've fucked and forgotten. Easy Charleson heads the list of Lousy Choices I Have Made, going back to before high school."

His look encouraged more history, but he wasn't going to get it.

Instead, Keshawna cleared space on the desk for the modest stack of blue-jacketed manila file folders she pulled from her In box and passed the top file over. "This one came in yesterday. Should have gone straight to you," she said.

The folder contained an updated Internet survey and a field op's report about Bluto Parks, a name on the list Josh had been given by Davenport that was not on the ICS compilation of one-time Davenport acts that had suffered curious deaths.

Except for Davenport's list, there was no evidence of Bluto Parks being dead.

In fact, there was no evidence of Bluto Parks at all.

The op's summary noted: *While the Davenport accounting cites a date, location, and cause of death, we were unable to ascertain and verify the correctness of these data. Parks appears to have fallen off the planet, like the fourth ship in Columbus' fleet.*

Josh flipped through the stapled pages to verify what had caught his eye days ago, the news coverage where Billy the Kid Palmer's widow had talked about Davenport's visit and his vision of producing a comeback album for Billy the Kid and Bluto.

He gaveled the page with his forefinger and pushed the report at Keshawna, asking, "Alive or dead, which is it?"

Keshawna studied the paragraph and settled the report aside. "Maybe Mrs. Palmer misinterpreted what Davenport told her husband or maybe the media got it wrong."

"Transcriptions of the TV and radio coverage in the file. The media got it right."

"Maybe Davenport was thinking to replace Bluto Parks, pass the Bluto Parks name on to somebody else. How many times have we seen that? After somebody quits an act to try it solo or retires or gets fired? Or dies. Almost every group ever on Motown, the Supremes, the Miracles, the Temptations. The Beach Boys. War. Three Dog Night. The Who. The Stones. The Fifth

Dimension. The Village People. Blood, Sweat and—"

"Suppose Davenport was handing Billy the Kid Palmer a bill of goods."

"Why, Josh? For what reason?"

"That's an answer Mrs. Palmer might be able to give me—something else she said to the media that the media didn't bother to report—if she'd ever bother to return my calls?"

"Instead, go to Nashville and knock on her door."

"I'm already thinking it."

"I'm surprised you're not already there. . . . What do you want me to say to Davenport when he calls looking for you?"

"Tell him I'm off whittling away at his blank check."

He retrieved the report, pushed from the desk, stuffed the file folder under his arm, and headed out.

Keshawna called after him, "Josh, one more thing." He turned back to her. "Annie Mae Bullock," she said.

"Best you could conjure up? Ike turned her into 'Tina Turner,' " Josh said, throwing her a sympathy smile. He said, "Your turn—Julia Elizabeth Wells," and continued out the door.

Connie insisted she felt well enough to join the family for dinner. Josh agreed to allow it only if she stopped demanding the right to help prepare the meal. She did, until Rusty Jr. guided her through the front door. She gripped his arm and moved on uncertain legs toward the kitchen over the strenuous objections of Niki, who blocked her way inside.

Josh heard the racket and raced over.

He got Connie settled in her usual place at the dining-room table and threatened to send her home at once if she didn't behave herself. No question in his mind she was still suffering from the beating Russ Tambourine had given her two days ago, but at least he had her doctor's assurance it was nothing of serious or lasting physical consequence.

He had hoped to discuss with her what he'd seen Justin and Rusty Jr. doing on the Paramount lot, share his suspicions, and decide on a mutually satisfactory course of action.

Clearly, this wasn't a good time.

Connie's jaunty manner could not conceal her bad case of nerves.

Her hands had developed a mild palsy that carried over to her vocal croak and she was easily distracted.

Any conversation would have to wait for his return from Nashville.

Later, after Connie and Rusty Jr. left for home, on her insistence she was as fit to drive now as she was on the way over, he spent quality time with Justin and Julie in front of the TV, passing the popcorn bowl through an Adam Sandler movie the kids had TiVo-ed and were now watching for the eighth or ninth time.

Justin yawned and excused himself midway into the movie, promising to finish his new homework assignments before ten o'clock lights out.

"How about a kiss goodnight for your old man?" Josh said.

Justin responded with what had become his overworked twelve-year-old look of disdain.

Julie, once certain Justin was gone, finished a mouthful of popcorn, clicked off the TV, and said she needed to ask Josh a question.

She said, "Daddy, did you ever hit Mommy?"

"Never, sweetheart," he said. "Why would you even think to ask me?"

"Rusty Jr. told Justin his dad always hit his mom all the time, so I only wanted to know for sure about you and Mommy, that's all."

"I loved your mother too much to ever do anything like that."

"Do you love me that much, too?"

"Always," he said, drawing her into his arms.

"Me, too," she said.

She gave him a hug and a kiss and scampered off to bed.

The next morning, before grabbing a non-stop to Nashville out of LAX, Josh headed to Uncensored Productions, a television company that had ties to both Clyde Davenport and Ava Garner. He had wangled an appointment after discovering some nuances in the ICS op's update that were only suggested or entirely overlooked by police investigators.

The production company was located in a low-rent industrial park on West Washington Boulevard, about a mile and a half west of Sepulveda, in an arc-roofed building resembling an aircraft hangar recessed behind a blacktopped parking lot. Cars filled half the marked slots, the newest and most expensive in the reserved spaces closest to the main entrance.

The building's metal-plated façade was decorated with a row of framed movie theater–sized posters spotlighting the programs *Censored/Uncensored* produced for television syndication and the cable channels, along with its one long-running network success, *Outside Looking In.* Fresh and faded graffiti in a mixture of colors, languages, and images was slashed over the windows and most of the siding, giving the place a rundown appearance that was immediately echoed inside. The reception room looked like it had been decorated by the Salvation Army.

A perky young receptionist with showy breasts, shoe-polish-black hair, and a nose ring, tucked her bubble gum inside a cheek and auditioned the kind of smile starlets lavish on casting directors. She passed on his name through her headset, and a few minutes later a dapper figure danced through saloon-type swinging doors like a chorus boy in an old Fred Astaire movie, an outstretched arm already aiming for a handshake.

"Mr. Wainwright, how excellent to make your acquaintance,"

Vic Swank said, pumping away, crooning the words in a mellow voice dripping sincerity. "Our mutual pal, Augie Fowler, speaks highly of you."

"And you," Josh said, improvising. Augie was a retired police beat reporter he got close to in his detective days. Augie, who knew everyone, owed him a few favors, so he'd called in one of them when he couldn't get through on his own to Swank.

"I understand this is something to do about poor Ava," Swank said, leading Josh down the corridor and onto a soundstage, where he settled them on the living-room set Josh recognized from *Censored/Uncensored,* the series that gave the company its name and reputation.

"We've wrapped production for the year on *C/U,* so we'll have our privacy here," he said. "The crews are one and two stages over, doing pick-ups, inserts, and re-shoots on *Peekaboo!* and *The Truth Machine*. You know my series, Mr. Wainwright? Josh, is it?"

"By reputation."

"Top Twenty all three, the re-runs Top Fifty. You know how the old saying goes, success begets more success. Spins on reality programming that leaped to my mind watching some of the horseshit making it on the network and cable schedules. All the energy I once put into my feet I transferred to my mind and—*voila!*—thank you, Jesus, my empire was a-building. You ever catch *West Side Story,* Josh? Inspired me to be a dancer. Making money inspired me to turn producer. But look around—" He gestured dramatically. "No bucks wasted on fancy trappings. It all goes into quality production, giving viewers their money's worth, not that the TV Academy has yet taken notice. Emmy looks good on a shelf, but it's not negotiable at Bank of America, if you get my drift."

He gave Josh a hungry look through deep-set hazel eyes awash in bloodshot ego.

"About Ava Garner," Josh said.

"Yes, of course, Ava," Swank said, fishing a breath spray from neatly pressed white chino cargo shorts that showed off his muscular calves the way his arms and pecks inside a T-shirt advertising *The Truth Machine* promoted a man ten years younger than the forty or forty-five Josh figured him for. A string of Gucci gold around his neck and one of those watches that announce the bank balance as well as the time. Barefoot inside a well-worn pair of brown leather loafers that Gene Kelly might have worn in *Singin' in the Rain.*

He resembled Kelly, about the same five-seven or eight and the five o'clock shadow that took layers of pancake to disguise, but a grin more false than embracing and a studied accent that fell somewhere in the mid-Atlantic, between Brooklyn and Brighton.

Swank said, "A sweet girl, that dear Ava. She perfumed the air with her presence here at Uncensored, until—" He seemed reluctant to continue.

"Something happened to change that? Clyde Davenport?"

Swank stopped running circles around the rim of a lipstick stained water glass on the coffee table. "That crazy gun-toting prick? No, not at first. At first it was Merv Bannister, you know who that is, of course. The host who loves you most on *Censored/ Uncensored.*"

"Of course," Josh said, but not because of the show. He knew Bannister from a rap sheet filled with charges that slick lawyers made sure never got past police files sealed by court order. Contrary to his public persona, Bannister was not an aw-shucks, corn-fed All-American Boy Next Door. Bannister never met a perversion he didn't enjoy. "Where does he fit in?"

"How much do you know about Merv, Josh?"

"Quoting the late Will Rogers, only what I read in the papers." It was an easy lie.

"Then you couldn't begin to know how many hundreds of thousands it has cost me over the years to keep it that way," Swank said. "Ava was fine until she got tangled up with Merv. When we hired her, she seemed typical of the wannabes who'll buy into any gig that gets them inside, closer to people who might help their careers take off. She was bright as well as beautiful, did her nine-to-five and kept her playtime off the lot, but only until she got noticed by Merv.

"The next thing, I heard he'd turned her into a games player with friends who made what was *Behind the Green Door* look like a nursery school. Next thing, after I slot Merv to emcee the last *National Search for Miss American Showgirl,* he gets her onto the bill as a contestant. Not a question about her qualifications, only about how she'd qualified. The network brass let it pass, because Merv was adamant. No Ava. No Merv. They didn't want to risk losing the ratings points that came with Merv front and center."

"I read where she finished fourth."

"Third runner-up, actually, on a clean vote that Merv couldn't manipulate, although he tried, and here's where the story gets more interesting."

"Because Clyde Davenport was one of the judges."

Swank rewarded him with an upright thumb. "Clyde's been dropping around here for years—eyeing the chicks, hitting on this looker or that one—ever since the first year, when I brought him on board as my music consultant. I had always been a fan. I knew he was out of tune with the times, so I might be able to get him for a song, metaphorically speaking. It turns out Ava had been flying under his radar since she hit the American Showgirl runway at the Utopia in Vegas and Clyde's dick lit up like the Fourth of July at Disneyland.

"Next thing, Clyde is checking her out with Merv. Next thing, he's hanging around here and her like a horsefly on honey. Next thing, he's telling me he's taking Ava under his personal wing, management and the usual bells and whistles, because of what he knows he can do with her voice—make her his next big singing sensation. Next thing, Ava's packing to leave here and Merv is screaming at Clyde like he's some claim jumper, but that ends as fast as it begins, when Clyde yanks out a gun and quietly tells Merv he is prepared to blow Merv's brains out, although he doubts Merv has brains, unless Merv apologizes to him and to Ava before he counts ten. Merv pees his pants and apologizes as Clyde starts counting. Everyone around is laughing at him, none harder than Clyde and Ava before they split the scene."

"And afterward?"

"Merv bust a gut over it for a while, shifting into fourth gear anytime their names were mentioned, making wild-ass threats about getting even with Clyde, but not lately, almost like it never happened. I didn't see Clyde again until the news about him killing Ava."

"You sound so positive about Davenport being the murderer. From all you've been telling me, it could as easily been Bannister who killed her. Bannister out for revenge."

"That's who I meant," Swank said. "Merv, not Clyde."

Chapter 18

"Where can I find him?" Josh said. "Bannister here?"

"Merv's gone, but not forgotten," Vic Swank said. "As usual, he disappeared two seconds after we wrapped the last segments of *Censored/Uncensored.*"

"A home address?"

"Sure, but don't know how much good it'll do you. It's his habit to head for an exotic port, someplace where the laws aren't as restrictive as ours. Someplace like Holland, where getting in Dutch doesn't get you in Dutch, if you catch my drift? Or Bangkok, when Merv is in the mood to switch hit and bang a little cock. He always returns with dozens of counterfeit watches as slick as the genuine articles, which he passes out like party favors to new lookers who get his Game Boy going." Swank flashed his wrist. "My Tag Heuer is as legit as they get. Merv's phonies don't miss by much."

"So, if Bannister is out of the country, he couldn't be the one who almost got Davenport with a bullet," Josh said, thinking out loud.

Swank checked out the idea with the studio rafters. "Maybe he held off splitting or maybe Merv farmed out the work. We've had our share of lowlifes on *Censored/Uncensored,* including two or three hiding in witness protection and itching for the kind of action that's hard to come by in Duluth or Keokuk. Merv's resourceful that way and, besides, it doesn't mean he didn't take out poor Ava."

"It also doesn't eliminate Davenport as the prime suspect."

"Clyde's screwy, but I don't think screwy enough to murder someone he's investing in and thinks can be his ticket back to the big leagues. You see him, tell him he's welcome anytime to come on *Outside Looking In* and make his case. Meanwhile, my two dollars are staying glued on Merv." He got up, signaling an end to their meeting.

He and Swank exchanged a few more, mostly repetitive thoughts while the receptionist was scribbling down Bannister's address and an assortment of phone numbers for Josh. Swank surprised him with one of those Hollywood hugs meant to convey friendship and usually shared, as now, by people who barely knew one another and weren't likely to become pals anytime soon, if ever, before he disappeared through the swinging doors.

"This, too," the receptionist said, as Josh turned to leave. He glanced at the paper she was holding out to him, flexing her lush collagened lips nervously, in a way that made her nose ring sway. "My phone number."

He tried handing it back. "I'm not a casting director," he said. "I really can't do you any good."

"I know why you came to see Mr. Swank. I can do you a lot of good." She glanced over to the swinging doors and upgraded her rate of speech. "Things I know and can tell you about Merv Bannister and especially Clyde Davenport."

"What kinds of things?"

"Phone me," she said, then into her headset, a smile back in her voice: "Good morning, Uncensored Productions. How may I direct your call?"

When he got to the Palmer home in Nashville, he discovered a "For Sale" sign on the front lawn, dangling from it scuffed wooden plaques announcing "Sold" and "In Escrow." He knocked on the door, then banged on it. No answer. Grumbling, he turned to go and was heading down the rickety stairs when rusted hinges signaled him to turn around.

The woman half-cast in darkness behind the screen door thick with dust said, "I was down in the cellar and thought I heard something. You from the termite inspection people?"

"Mrs. Palmer?" Josh identified himself.

She seemed puzzled for a moment. "Wait. The investigator for Mr. Davenport who left all those phone messages." She pushed open the screen door. "Come on in." Under a bandana that reminded him of Aunt Jemima on the cereal boxes, her cherubic face was soiled, the dirt lining her forehead glistening from sweat. She wiped her hands up and down her dirty apron, held one out for him to take. "A good time for a break anyway. Call me Kristy. You game for some ice-cold lemonade or maybe an iced tea?"

She led him to the kitchen, cleared two kitchen chairs of cartons and made space on the table by moving some stacks of dishes to the sink counter. "Been settled here so long, I forgot what a bear moving can be. Instead of selling, might've been better to go and blow up the damn house to Kingdom Come."

Kristy Palmer laughed, but her face and the false gaiety he recognized in her voice told a different story. She was endeavoring to mask the acute heartache she was suffering over the loss of her husband.

Josh knew the signs.

Those and more.

All the signs.

It wasn't his place to tell her it would get better with time.

He hadn't yet convinced himself of that.

She settled a pitcher of iced tea and two jelly jar glasses on the table.

"Help yourself," she said, and plopped into the other chair

with a sigh. "Thanks for the rescue. Feels good to take a load off for a few. I been on my feet steady-like ever since getting back here so early this morning I woke the birds up. Heard none of your messages until then. I would've got around to calling you, only so much to first get out of the way. My apology if it's what caused you to come on out here all the way from Los Angeles. Cheers!"

"Cheers." They clinked jelly jars.

"Were you a fan of my husband's, of Billy the Kid and Bluto? You never once said so, is why I'm asking. He had lots of fans in his time, you know, all over the world? I'd put on some of his albums for you to hear, only they were the first things I packed back here from El Paso, safe and sound in the car trunk."

She needed to talk about Billy.

Another sign.

Another way of not letting go.

"A big fan," Josh said.

She needed to hear that.

"Me, too," Kristy Palmer said, "and I could give you lots of reasons that you might not need, seeing how you were also a big fan, like so many. Did you know there's a lot of Web sites on the Internet about him? He's remembered, oh, is he ever. He'll be remembered long after you and I are gone to meet our maker."

Josh nodded, sipped his iced tea and showed interest in everything she was telling him. Friends had done that for him after Katie's murder. Even people he hadn't heard from in years, other people he had never considered friends. There was something about a tragedy that often seemed to reveal unsuspected truths about a person, sometimes the bad, but how nice when it's something good and loving, an unsolicited kindness that calls for no reward.

She said, "You know who told me that, although I didn't

need to hear it to know it about Billy? Clyde Davenport told me that. Mr. Magic said it, and he said it to the newspapers and on television. He tell you that?"

She smiled hopefully.

She needed a response.

Josh said, "Yes, not that I had to be told."

"A saint that man, but I don't suppose he told you that." Josh shook his head. "Of course he didn't. Saints are like that. Don't need to have it broadcasted all around, what he said when he phoned to say a check was coming that'd make it possible for my boys and me to get out from under this house and get us a new one in El Paso, same neighborhood as Billy's blessed parents, who they're staying with now, while I finish up here. Two sons, the spitting image of Billy. You have children?"

"Boy and a girl."

"How old?" He told her. "Close enough to my sons, so you best keep your girl away, because she'll fall mighty quick for them handsome devils of mine, spitting image the both of their father. Billy, minute I laid eyes on him, it was like—"

She lowered her head, hands clasped on top of the bandana, like she could find the words she needed on the tabletop. A few seconds later, she was sobbing uncontrollably. A minute went by, then another. At last, she brought herself under control. Cleared her throat and gulped some iced tea. Shared with Josh a wistful smile. Said, "William Bradford Palmer was never perfect but, good times or bad, he was my whole world."

Josh listened politely to Kristy catalog their years together, hopeful her gush of memories would bring her back to Clyde Davenport. After almost an hour, when he was close to giving up, his patience was rewarded.

". . . and he just showed up like that, knocking on the door, like it was only yesterday and there'd never been any bad blood spilled over Billy and Bluto Parks leaving him," Josh caught her saying. Snapping him back to full attention. "Takes a real man to forgive the ills of the past the way Mr. Magic did that day. You know what he said to Billy?"

She seemed to stall on the question.

He gave her a gentle prod: "What, Kristy?"

"Mr. Magic said he wanted to reunite them, Billy the Kid and Bluto."

"Reunite them?"

"You know. Take them back into the studio and get them a hit, get them back on track and back in the ballgame. He said he had already talked to Bluto about it and Bluto was one hunnert percent up for the idea."

"Mr. Magic said he talked to Bluto?"

"One hunnert percent up for it, yes, so you know how excited Billy got over what it'd mean for the family, for me and for the boys, not only for himself. All of us being back in the chips again. Out from under."

"Anything else he say?"

Kristy was puzzled. "Like what?"

How could he answer that and not distress her about her sainted Clyde Davenport?

He hurriedly played out in his head the contradictions raised by what Kristy had said already. If she had her facts straight, Davenport talked like Bluto was alive on a date long past the date on the list he'd handed over to Josh. If Bluto was, indeed, dead, why would Davenport bother lying to Billy? What purpose did it serve? If Bluto was still alive, why list him at all and with all those details, like where and how? If Davenport found him, why couldn't ICS track him down, catch a single whiff of Bluto Parks?

Kristy's face lit with the spark of a notion.

She said, "If you mean like did Mr. Magic tell Billy or me Bluto was going to call us, he did not. Not one single word.

Bluto's call was a surprise."

"Bluto's—" It was Josh's turn to be surprised.

He jerked back, almost tipping over his chair, and made an aimless hand-gesture for balance that knocked over his jelly jar.

Iced tea splattered on the table and rolled onto his lap.

He collected the stray ice cubes and plopped them back in the jelly jar.

Kristy hurried after a dish towel and mopped up the watery mess; seemed about to use the towel on his crotch, but stopped short, and tried to hide her blush.

Easing back into her chair, she said, "Reminds me of Billy, you know? He was always spilling things, especially times he was afflicted with the shakes and couldn't find a straight line to walk it. He was getting better, though. Would've been fine by the time he and Bluto got in the recording studio."

"I'm sure of it," Josh said. He reached across for her hand. "When was this, when Bluto surprised you with his call, Kristy?"

"Same as you, while I was gone to El Paso, that same old sweet voice, a lot older, maybe not so sweet anymore, Bluto saying how he was heading out our way and for us to batten down the hatches. He was always saying things like that, Bluto was. Batten down the hatches."

"But you haven't seen him?"

"No, or heard from again, but hoping he'll show up for Billy's memorial service. He can sing one of their old songs. It won't be the same without Billy, but I know how happy Billy'll be listening from up above."

"Memorial service?"

"No date yet. Still have to work that out with the funeral people, then get out the word. Hoping Mr. Magic will get up and say a few words. You? You'll come?" Her eyes pleading now, as if she feared Billy might play out his last venue to an empty room.

"Yes. Let me know. I may bring my son and daughter, if you promise that your boys will behave around her."

He winked, and she brightened up.

"Swear," she said, raising her right arm and gifting him with her biggest smile of the day. "Billy had a sense of humor like yours. He knew how to make people laugh, but you know what I miss most about Billy?"

"What's that?"

"Everything," she said, dissolving once more into tears.

Josh called Keshawna from Nashville International to brief her on the conversation with Kristy Palmer and have her make a fresh go at locating Bluto Parks. She let him know she wasn't happy with his request, declaring it a waste of manpower, time, and money.

"Besides," she said, "I just got an earful of nothing that would make Billy Palmer's death more than what it already is, a suicide, or in any way tie Davenport to it as anything but a good Samaritan."

"I won't be satisfied until I get an earful of Bluto Parks, assuming we have someone on staff who can do as good a job finding Bluto as Davenport did. Maybe, better we should give Davenport a blank check to handle the job for us?"

She bristled on the other end of the line. "Maybe if we simply asked Davenport and remembered to say 'please'? You think of that, wise guy?"

"That's Plan B. I'll check back when I get in from Vegas."

"Vegas?"

"Just switched my ticket to a one-stop, off an urge I haven't been able to shake, to see a man about a beating."

Keshawna knew at once what he had in mind. "Going after Russ Tambourine. How smart is that?"

"Look at it this way, Keesh. If Clyde Davenport can be a

good Samaritan, so can I."

She poured a sigh into his ear. "Last time you talked that way, somebody wound up dead, remember?"

"A long, long time ago, before Davenport, and it wasn't me, Keesh, was it?"

"A first time for everything, Joshua. Watch your back."

Chapter 19

Outer Space, the town's newest playground, was a five-thousand room resort hotel that easily surpassed for outrageous design and size every planet-locked gambling Mecca on the gaudy Vegas strip. It loomed on Josh's left, a half-mile ahead, as he inched his rental Porsche along the bumper-to-bumper freeway that was Las Vegas Boulevard.

The Porsche wasn't his idea. He had asked for a modest Toyota or Honda at Airport Autos, but—everything here being above and beyond reality—the fluttery counterman who resembled a transvestite in training, pushed the upgrade on him, insisting with a twinkle in his lousy French accent, "Same bargain price *tres extraordinaire, mon ami*. Our traditional midweek special seven days a week."

The Strip's eye-bending stretches of neon flash and pizzazz were in fierce competition with the blanket of stars crowding a desert sky undefeated by layers of auto exhaust and the smokers' fumes rising from tourists doing sidewalk gridlock on both sides of the boulevard.

Outer Space's monstrous missile-shaped marquee in mid-blast-off towered above it all, boldly flashing in a cavalcade of colors:

Mickey Barnum Presents
Absolutely Live In Person!
Tonight and Every Night in the Mother Ship

Robert S. Levinson

THE PRINCE OF THE VEGAS STRIP

Not the Prince's name.

Unnecessary nowadays, but a monumental, easily recognizable Russ Tambourine in space gear, attached by a mock lifeline and clutching a microphone, floated high above the marquee, like one of those giant balloons in Macy's Thanksgiving Day Parade.

Tonight, I'm bringing you down to earth, Josh thought.

After an eternity of traffic crawling, he geared up, jiggered lanes to an outburst of angry horns, and made a squeaker of a sharp turn onto a side street that ultimately got him to a self-parking area behind "Pluto," one of the nine interconnected pods that comprised Outer Space.

During his concert and Vegas years with Katie, Josh had learned that the quickest and easiest way to move through any hotel anywhere in the world is not by the visible public routes, but via the labyrinthine series of back doors, side doors, corridors, and elevators used by kitchen and cleaning crews and other hotel employees.

It took him only a few minutes of exploration to figure out the best route to the three-thousand-seat Mother Ship showroom, a mile-long stroll from "Pluto" to the central core of the hotel, watched every step by security cameras mounted in the ceilings and elevators.

Josh shuffled along as if he belonged, smiling and waving at the invisible eyes keeping track of his progress.

When he reached the elevator that would take him two levels below the showroom, to the dressing rooms and Russ Tambourine's suite, a voice down the corridor hit him with a "Hey you, hold on up!" Male. Gruff. Sounding anxious to enforce the "Show and Backstage Crew Only. No exceptions" signs taped on either side of the elevator doors.

He pretended not to hear.

Heavy footsteps scraped closer as the doors slid open.

Josh stepped inside and willed the doors to close before the voice now insisting, "You hear me? I said wait," reached him.

The doors did, only—

When they opened, waiting for him was somebody whose Herculean chest was near bursting out of a natty black suit, security ID draped over the jacket pocket, eyes closeted in impenetrable shades that mirrored Josh's uneasy reflection, a tightly drawn mouth that ticked nervously at the edges. The guy had age, height, and muscle on him, but he hoped a bluff might get him through.

Josh didn't get a chance to try. The guy took him in a bear hug that whooshed the breath out of him and lifted him several inches off the ground.

"Damn good seeing you again, Mr. Wainwright," he said, before returning Josh to the tarnished linoleum flooring. "Damn good after all this time."

He saw Josh's confusion and removed the glasses. "Gregg Andrews, remember? I was over at the Klondike Hotel before here in Outer Space, helping look after Katie, I mean, Mrs. Sunshine. I mean, Mrs. Wainwright."

"Now I do," Josh said. "You're the one who escorted her from her dressing room to the Good Morning Sunshine spaceship for her entrance."

"And back after the *Up, Up and Away* number. She was something else again—"

"Yes, she was."

Gregg inclined his chin toward Russ Tambourine's dressing room double-doors and frowned. Lowered his voice. "Talking way out of turn saying I wouldn't want to tell you what that one in there's all about. Don't know how his missus, your wife's manager, Connie, ever put up with it the way she did for as long as she did."

"He in there now, Gregg?"

Gregg nodded. His voice sank lower. "Oiling his dick on one of the girls, as usual, until he has to be hoisted up on the elephant to make his grand entrance. That's in fifteen, unless he feels like making it twenty or twenty-five. Keeps the players out of the casino, but he don't care none, and the bosses put up with it, because he fills that damn showroom every night of the week and two shows on Fridays and weekends."

"I need to see him, Gregg."

Gregg sucked in two full lungs of warm backstage air, exhaled, and gave him a *can't be done* look. "Would cost me my job, permitting that, Mr. Wainwright, as much as I'd like to for you, who were always so up front nice with me back then at the Klondike, and in memory of Katie . . . Mrs. Wainwright."

"If you weren't around?"

Gregg answered with a conspiratorial grin. "I'm overdue for watering the daisies," he said, patting his crotch Michael Jackson–style. He held up ten fingers and headed down the narrow hallway, pausing to kibitz with a bulb-nosed clown and a gent in tails who'd emerged from one of the dressing rooms leading a chimp on a chain.

Russ Tambourine was bouncing on a sofa that faced away from the dressing room door, now-you-see-him-now-you-don't fashion, grunting, groaning, and demanding faster action. He apparently got it, because he quit suddenly with a satisfied grunt, and it wasn't Josh he ordered: "Scram, bitch. I got a show to get ready for."

The bitch must have said something he didn't like, because there was a sound of fist on flesh followed by her howl. She leaped to her feet, sobbing, and had finished wrapping herself in a robe too transparent to hide much of her overly endowed body before she saw Josh.

"Oh, man, Jesus, wow!" she said, sounding like a teenager trapped by a cop while doing the nasty in the backseat of her boyfriend's car on Mulholland Drive. He'd caught a couple like that back in his uniform days. This one didn't look much older. Maybe eighteen or nineteen, a pixie hairdo, and a welt forming under her left eye.

Tambourine materialized, mussed-up hair and fucked-out eyes, a lot of silver in the faded black of his hairy chest. Shoulders sagging on a flab-filled body losing to gravity the way his chin already had.

Josh threw him a weak-wristed wave. "Hi, Russ. Looks like you're up to your old tricks with new tricks."

"Who let you in?" the Prince of the Vegas Strip said. "Heads are fucking gonna roll over this, you better believe." Turning to the girl, who was doing a fright dance, bouncing from one bare foot to the other: "Didn't I say for you to get the fuck out of here?"

She fled the suite, the door gliding shut behind her.

"Told her to lock us in," Tambourine said, moving around the sofa and striking a pose like a naked Superman. "Nice of you to drop by, Josh. Great seeing you again. Now, fuck off before I—"

As far as Tambourine got before Josh brought a fist up from the pile carpeting and caught him on the chin with enough force to send him backward over the sofa. He hurried around while Tambourine struggled to his feet and this time connected with a solid straight shot to the chest. Tambourine teetered back on his heels. Stutter-stepped into the wall. Shook his head clear. With an incendiary howl, he charged at Josh, who stepped aside and tripped him, sending Tambourine speeding head first into the opposite wall.

Tambourine did a stumbling turn, took two steps and

dropped to the floor.

Josh stepped over to him. "I've never believed in kicking a man when he's down," he said. He laid a shoe into Tambourine's rib cage. "There are exceptions to every rule," he said, and kicked again, this time connecting with Tambourine's thigh.

Tambourine screamed blood both times and seemed on the verge of passing out.

Josh hunkered down alongside him, tapping his flaccid face until Tambourine opened his eyes. Quietly, like a doctor conveying bad news, he said, "This is all about Connie, in case you haven't figured that part out, Russ. The first kick was a reminder to obey the court's restraining order and keep your distance from now on. The second kick was to remind you that paying child support isn't an option. Everything else, because it always gladdens my heart when I can let a son of a bitch know he's a son of a bitch and that I'm on his case."

The door burst open.

Someone grabbed Josh from behind.

Yanked him to his feet.

Jerked him around.

Trapped him in a headlock.

It was the guy who'd trooped after him upstairs, looking ugly, smelling like dirty laundry, declaring, "Yeah, he's the one I saw trespassing."

"Don't know how he got by me," Gregg Andrews said, twisting Josh's arms behind his back and cuffing him. "Must've been when I stepped away to take a whiz."

He held onto him, averting his eyes, while Dirty Laundry helped Tambourine off the floor and onto the sofa. He apologized for the lapse in security, telling him, "We'll run him in to the locals, sir. Get him charged with assault and battery."

Tambourine wheezed out an urgent, "No!"

He struggled to his feet and shook his fist at Gregg, telling him, "Next time you so much as think about waltzing off and leaving me unprotected from piss ants like him, don't even bother coming back." Fending off offers of assistance and using the furniture for support, he trailed over to Josh. His face previewed his intention.

Josh said, "Women and defenseless men, the preferred territory of bullies, right, Russ?"

"Right as rain," Tambourine said, and caught Josh's cheeks with slaps that almost sent his head flying off his neck. "You're lucky I need to get ready for my show, you fucking cunt, or I'd have them take the cuffs off you and show you what a fair fight's all about."

"You fighting who, the little girl you were beating up on when I walked in?"

"Cocksucker," Tambourine said, and slapped him again, catching the side of his face, flush on the ear; Big Ben tolling in Josh's head as Tambourine coughed up a huge wad of phlegm and spit it in his face.

Turning to Dirty Laundry, Tambourine ordered: "Now get him out of my sight. Rough him up good and plenty before you give him over to the cops."

"You bet, sir," Dirty Laundry said, executing a smart salute.

"With pleasure, sir," Gregg said, with equal enthusiasm.

They kept the cuffs on Josh until they got him to his Porsche, sent him on his way with handshakes all around.

Chapter 20

At one time, jets landed at LAX and within minutes had rolled to a stop at the terminal gate. Nowadays, they touched down miles away and navigated access alleys and runways for what sometimes seemed as long as the flight itself, like tonight. The bump and grinding brakes snapped Josh awake.

He checked his watch.

It was closing in on midnight.

He waited until he was off the plane before flipping open his cell phone.

He'd missed voice mails from Davenport, Niki, Connie, and Keshawna.

Davenport, his voice smooth as pudding, wanted to hear how his visit with Kristy Palmer in Nashville went, no indication how he knew about the trip.

Niki, apprehensive, saying it could wait until morning, not saying what it was.

Connie, choking on emotion—no explanation; Josh suspecting it had to do with Russ Tambourine—saying she would call back, but no callback.

Keshawna, saying in her usual tight-mouthed way that it was *Urgent,* to call the minute he got the message, no matter what the hour.

Keshawna said, "Julie Andrews."

"What about Julie Andrews?"

"You said 'Julia Elizabeth Wells,' and I'm saying the answer's Julie Andrews."

"This is your 'Urgent, call me no matter what time it is'? Our game?"

"Just getting it off my desk before I forget. What's 'urgent' is Bluto Parks. Found him."

"Dead or alive?"

"And kicking."

"How?"

"Intrepid field work inspired by your insistence."

"Besides that."

"Masterson had laid out some chum last time he went out fishing for Bluto. Caught a callback a couple of hours ago from that skid row junkie shelter between Little Tokyo and Seventh, remember the place?"

"Mission Possible. Pissing distance of the L.A. River. Where you sent Moe Gallico packing."

"Fool that Moe was, but not before you caught one in the arm from him."

"His gun hand any steadier and you'd be talking to yourself right now."

"Never did convince IA of that, did we?"

"By then those turds didn't want to be convinced. Bluto Parks. Tell me."

"He got recognized checking in for a square hot and overnight cot by Masterson's inside guy, who's due a bonus hundred for keeping a bead on him until you show up in the a.m. Go home, get some pillow time, but knew you'd want to know ASAP."

"On my way downtown now, while the adrenaline's still flowing."

"Masterson's guy, Raul, gets his hundred either way."

"Should I remember to get a receipt?"

"One other thing," Keshawna said. "Laszlo Lowenstein."

"Who?"

"Exactly," she said, and clicked off.

The fringes of the wholesale district retailed in wasted humans and human waste through the night. It was a camping ground for hundreds who traveled with their life in a shopping cart and hundreds of others who lacked even that luxury. Pimps, prostitutes, and runaway kids who'd fall into the life if they didn't fall from a needle first were also part of a mix that lined the streets and alleys with cardboard cartoon homes or used doorways as a bedroom. Rape was recreation and murder a way of life.

Mission Possible was a safe harbor for the fortunate several dozen who lined up and signed up on a daily basis, first come, first served, and no single stay longer than two days.

The three-story brick building would never be confused with an architectural masterpiece or considered for Historical Landmark status. In its best times, eighty or ninety years ago, it was a cheap hotel for low-end merchants and travelers needing a place to stay between connections at nearby Union Station. Later, a boarding house. Then, for a decade, boarded up and abandoned, a breeding ground for four-legged creatures until some anonymous do-gooder specified a modest annual contribution in his will and the Mission Possible Society took over. That and occasional government subsidies covered food and lodging, but there was never enough to repair the slanted roof covered by plastic sheeting meant to keep rain out of the rot holes where tiles were broken or missing entirely.

Josh parked the Lexus half a block down, underneath one of the street's few unbroken lamplights, and gave his hip holster a comfort pat before double-timing the fifty yards to the shelter, where the hand-printed sign posted on a front door inspired by a prison cell read:

FULL UP. LINE FORMS AT DAYLIGHT.

He kept his finger on the bell until he sensed someone checking him out through the peephole in the safety window that opened a moment or two later, revealing nervous eyes blinking furiously through Coke-bottle lenses.

"Can't you read what it says? You seeing any daylight?" The accent smacked of Boyle Heights barrio.

"You Raul?"

He had to think about it. "You the man with my c-note?" Making it sound like *Seeing is believing.*

Josh found his wallet and rifled after one of the folded hundreds he kept stashed for these types of situations. He stretched it open and held it up to the window. The dome-shaped porch light flashed on for a second, followed by a murmur of satisfaction.

A hand reached through the window.

Josh pulled back the bill. "Inside first," he said.

"You don't trust me?"

"I'll trust you better inside."

"We got no heat tonight, busted pipe or something," Raul said, leading him up the narrow stairs to the third floor, through a doorway missing its door into a room where the walls had been knocked down to create a barracks. Unorthodox rows of folding cots and bunk beds ran the full length and width, all occupied, as were the sleeping bags taking up much of the remaining floor space. Josh couldn't decide which was worse, the snorts and snores, the nightmarish cries, the feverish, unintelligible mutterings, or the smell of dirty bodies inside filthy clothing.

Raul whispered, like waking someone with their conversation would be a sin: "See the bunk by the wall, where the holy cross is, and the picture of Jesus on black velvet? He's in the upper."

Holding his breath against another outbreak of farts, Josh said, "You're certain it's Bluto Parks?"

"Know him? Wouldn't believe it looking at us today, man, but Bluto and me used to share a needle back before we wound up riding different elevators."

Raul showed himself off in the light of a half dozen naked bulbs scattered around the room. A chicken-skinned forties face that could not disguise his hard living. Forehead furrows deep enough to plant corn in. An enviable mane of white hair and a matching Zapata 'stache. A lopsided mouth. A bulky body covered by a Mission Possible sweatshirt and blue jeans a size too large. A faded gang tat on his neck.

"He was a regular for a while back, then gone, man, like I got to figuring him for a body bag," Raul said. "Nobody more surprised than me when he showed his ass here today, man. He give me some tongue and offered a hand job for the bed. Give him the bed for old time's sake."

"And because you knew we were looking for him."

"What you're paying me, a bargain. No way to recognize him anymore if you didn't already know him good enough when he had that beautiful face and was sitting on top of the world with Billy the Kid."

"Go roust him. Bring him over."

Raul pushed away the request with his hands. "Mister, my work's done. Last thing in the world I need is people here spotting me for a scar mouth." He turned and slipped out of the room.

Josh slowly worked his way to the bunk, stepping over the sleeping bags like they were speed bumps, drawing grunts from inside the one or two he caught with a toe or heel. He had a blast of cop's sixth sense, something disturbing the rhythm of the room his radar had locked onto. Shuffling sounds, and—

Hands grabbed his ankles and yanked him off his feet.

Josh plunged face forward, caught bare floor with an impact that sent thunderbolts of pain up his arms and into his shoulder before he rolled over onto his side, then his back.

Hands arrested his arms and legs, pinned him there.

Somebody quickly squatted on his stomach and put a blade to his throat, showered him with foul-smelling sweat, and said, "One word out of you and it's your last," the threat sounding as sincere as a priest's sermon.

Somebody else jimmied off his shoes and after several seconds complained about the size and tossed them aside.

Somebody else dug into his pockets, muttering after a wallet, and came across the .38 in Josh's hip holster. "Hey, see what I found," he announced, loud enough to earn complaints from all corners of the room. He pressed the barrel to Josh's temple, taunting, "Anybody for Russian roulette?"

A gunshot answered him.

It thudded into the ceiling, causing a downpour of paint flakes.

Bums were bouncing up all over, loud and confused, afraid about something more than their usual downtrodden reality. Banging into each other making a fast exit through a door at the back end of the room.

A high beam exposed the bums who had Josh trapped.

The one with the .38 used an arm to shield his eyes against the blinding light and eased back the hammer. He called over, "Whoever you goddamn pirates are, we got him first," shifting his palsied aim to the source of the light.

Josh angled his head and saw it was coming from the door, but was unable to distinguish what appeared to be two figures made shadow black by the flashlight and the hallway light until the taller of the two called across the room: "Do anything stupid, I'll put a bullet in you faster'n you can blink your goddamn eyes, you fucking hophead."

"Who you calling a fucking hophead?"

"You, you fucking hophead."

The one straddling his stomach decided: "Don't listen, Thomas," and: "I'll slice his throat if you don't retreat from here and do it now, lady. Get on back up to your own floor. Leave men's work to us men." He nicked Josh's neck with the tip of the blade.

"He means as much to me as the top of your head. You like it where it is, you get up and off him and your ass out of here like fucking now, you fuck head, or my next shot visits the fried remains of your fucking brain. Then, you, Thomas. Are you ready to die, you hotwired fuck of a former human being?"

"No lady should use that kind of language," Thomas said.

"This sound any better?" she said, and fired into the ceiling again. "See the bulb on the wall behind you?" Thomas dared a glance. "Pretend it's your skull, Tommy boy." Her third shot shattered the bulb.

Summoning up bravery from somewhere, he said, "Like for me to try one on you and your shitty mouth?" He steadied the .38 on his arm, but couldn't quite steady the arm.

"Thomas, don't," the other doorway shadow said. "Lay down the damn gun like she told you, *amigo.*"

"Raul?"

"Let him go, Thomas. You, too, Chet. Put away the pig-sticker, *por favor.* We don't need that kind of trouble again."

The one who had swiped Josh's shoes said, "He got lousy shoes, Raul," while the other one, silent so far, stayed silent. He released the leg he had been holding down and moved out of gunfire range.

"*Tambien* you let go, José."

"Lousy, lousy shoes," José said, and let go. "Waste of time," he said, moving from his knees to his feet. He dusted off his pants, as if it might make a difference, and stalked toward the rear door, calling, "*Vengas,* Arturo." Arturo chased after him.

Thomas watched them leave.

"Fuck it," he said.

He laid down the gun, got up and moved away, urging Chet to do likewise.

"So, Thomas, now you're giving orders?" Chet said. He looked down at Josh, drenching him in more sweat. His hand was playing the knife like a violin bow, a fraction of an inch above Josh's throat. "People always giving me orders, what got me to here in the first place," he said, his enlarged pupils begging for understanding. "People always giving me orders, what got me to here in the first place. People always giving me orders, what got me to here in the first place."

"I understand," Josh said, hoping Chet wouldn't notice his hand sliding for the .38.

"You also want to give me orders?"

"No," Josh said, drawing the word from the back of his throat, keeping his neck as rigid as a steel girder. Chet was whacked on something, and—

Josh's fingers were an inch shy of catching hold of the trigger guard.

Thomas stopped a few steps short of the back door and appealed once more: "Chet, let him be, Chet."

"See what I mean," Chet told Josh. "Orders, orders, orders. Calls for a lesson." He was on his feet in a second, gripping the blade handle like a tomahawk and taking a bead on Thomas.

He flung his arm back for a hard toss.

By now Josh had a grip on the .38.

He got off a shot.

The shot caught Chet in the arm. He dropped the knife, screaming correctly: "I been shot. I been shot." He moved a hand to the wound and checked for blood. Started tongue-lapping it off his palm. Then again. Another time. By now crying over his plight with words that had lapsed into obscurity.

"In the old days you'd have shot to kill," Keshawna Keyes said. She moved aside the flashlight beam so he could have a clearer look at her standing by the doorway with Raul. "Two seconds slower and I'd've had the freak notched."

"Best I could do left-handed and in a hurry," Josh said.

Raul covered the distance to the blubbering Chet, threw his arms around him lovingly. He was guiding him from the room, assuring him the wound wasn't serious and easily patched, when Chet broke free, pushed Raul aside, and fled, shouting, "None of this would've gone down a-tall, a-tall, it wasn't for you, Raul, damn you."

Raul made sure they saw him shrug off the accusation before he chased after Chet.

Josh and Keshawna shared an *It takes all kinds* look.

He rolled over and pulled himself onto his feet.

"What brought you to this neck of the woods anyway?" he said.

"Somebody had to watch your obstinate back, and I elected me. Next time maybe you'll listen when I say wait until morning to pigeonhole Bluto."

"The bunk over there," Josh said, thumbing over his shoulder.

"Which empty bunk would that be?"

Josh wheeled around.

The bunk by the holy cross and the picture of Jesus on black velvet was empty, upper and lower, and so were all the other bunks. The cots. The sleeping blankets. The melee had emptied the room, except for them.

"Win a few, lose a few," Josh said. "Let's us go find Raul. He owes me a hundred."

"And a pair of shoes?"

"They're here somewhere. Borrow your beam?"

Raul said, "You got a Bible. I'll swear on the Bible. I knew nothing what Chet or Thomas, any of them, was thinking to pull on you," Raul said. "We got lots of crazy nights like this. Only sometimes worse."

"Where are they, Raul?"

"Thomas?" He elevated his shoulders. "Chet? I go after the first-aid kit and when I come back." Another shrug. "Also. You look, you'll see his blood on the way out the door."

"And I don't suppose Bluto Parks is anywhere to be found?"

"Out somewhere on the street again, like the others. Back later, maybe, or maybe not. Times like these happen, you never know, unless it's worse weather than now. Could be back for breakfast, maybe not."

"Maybe up on the third floor?"

"Ladies only ever up there, but you're welcome to look. Careful, though. They got their own problem children up there. Same, but only different, and sometimes a whole lot worse."

Josh was tempted.

Keshawna saw it.

She said, "Go home, barefoot boy. Log in with the family. I'll take the overnight watch."

"You'll call if Bluto—"

"If. . . . Beat it."

Josh was back in five minutes.

His Lexus had been stolen.

Chapter 21

It was closing in on three in the morning when Josh paid off the cabbie and slip-slopped into the house on the ill-fitting pair of cheap leather sandals Raul fished out of the donations box and mended with string substituting for missing straps. He figured everyone to be asleep, but he was wrong. A living-room light snapped on, startling him, as he headed through the hallway past the arch, aiming for the kitchen and something to pad his stomach until breakfast. The closest he'd had to a decent meal was at the Nashville airport; not even peanuts on the flight from Vegas to LAX.

Niki moved into his path, hands clasped, almond-shaped eyes anxious and fighting to stay open against the hour, flashing alarm well beyond the message they sent whenever one of the kids misbehaved or Connie arrived and began one of her cooking takeovers. She looked like a little girl in her teens, not her twenties, in her pink cotton pajamas and robe, pink fuzz-ball slippers, and pigtailed hair tied with pink ribbon, but there was grave adult certainty in the way she said, "I waited up for you, Mr. Josh. Please. I sincerely hope you don't mind."

"You hungry?" he said, pointing toward the kitchen.

Niki wandered about while he took his first great bites out of the sandwich she had made for him, scrambled eggs and a slice of American cheese on whole wheat toast, and washed them down with milk. High in cholesterol. He was too famished to care.

Unable to wait any longer, she climbed onto the stool next to his at the service bar and said, "I'm afraid for Justin, Mr. Josh."

He was surprised. He'd been thinking maybe she wanted time off or a raise, either of which he was prepared to extend.

"How tell?"

She drew in her breath like it might be her last and settled her hands on the counter to keep it from flying away. "He is twelve years old."

"I know that, Niki. What else?"

"My brothers, home in Persia, I saw it with them, and what happened when my father chose to overlook what he also saw, my father saying it was boys being boys, and it would be over when they reached thirteen and were men who could deal with the future as all intelligent men do. Only all intelligent men don't, Mr. Josh, but my father was too blind or too proud to acknowledge that."

"What?" Josh said. "Too proud to acknowledge what?" It wasn't being bone-aching tired that kept him from understanding her. Niki was dancing around the subject, whatever it was, and suddenly looking like she regretted saying anything.

She screwed up her face and began snapping at her inch-long nails with her teeth, creating a rhythm of nerves that Josh finally put an end to by gently taking Niki's wrist and easing her hand away from her mouth.

"Maybe tomorrow would be better?" she said. "In the morning? You look in much need of sleep after so long a day. I apologize." She started off the counter stool, but Josh still had her by the wrist and guided her back down. "It was nothing," Niki said, her eyes pleading for release.

"Tell me what's on your mind and we'll both sleep better."

Niki wrestled with the request for several moments. "It's

Justin and—" Tangling up in second thoughts before: "It's Justin and that wretched Rusty Jr. I saw with my own eyes, with two of my own brothers, so I know."

At once, Josh knew what she meant.

"Paramount, right?" he said. "You saw them smoking, hiding out in the parking lot like bandits. So did I, and I intend to have a nice little sit-down with Justin, not to mention telling Miss Connie about Rusty Jr., whose idea it probably was."

"That—"

"Boys will be boys, here as well as Iran, although it sounds like your father went a little overboard with your brothers. I experimented around Justin's age, but smoking didn't become a habit until years later." He sent her an appreciative smile. "A filthy habit it took me years to break, but don't overload on worry—Connie and I will get it nipped in the bud with those two."

He released Niki's wrist and went at his scrambled egg sandwich again.

Her nails went back to her teeth.

She said, "That, yes, Paramount, I saw them smoking, but that's not what I meant, Mr. Josh. No. Not at all. It's what else I saw them doing. With my own eyes. Much worse than any cigarettes."

If Niki were an actress, he might have accused her of over-emoting, but sitting this close to her, there was no mistaking the reality of her passion. Her breath was racing at the speed of sound, her firm breasts pushing against her loose-fitting pajamas, her nipples taut with anxiety.

"I'm not sure how to begin," she said.

"At the beginning?" Josh said, reaching to take her hands in both of his.

"At the beginning," she said. "Yes. At the beginning."

What Niki told him made sleep impossible.

He gave up, finally, and wandered to Justin's bedroom. The door was open a crack, wide enough to see Justin resting peacefully on top of the blankets. After a few minutes, he moved on to Julie's room, her door open all the way, daddy's little girl curled up under the covers with her dolly, "Dolly Baby," her thumb in her mouth, fingers clutching the ragged remains of her foul-smelling security blanket, which no amount of coaxing or bribery had, so far, convinced her to surrender.

Back in bed, Josh shut his eyes and imagined Katie nestled in his arms, also unable to sleep, sharing his uncertainty over how to best confront what he'd learned from Niki. He pulled Katie's pillow to him and hugged it like a life preserver.

Chapter 22

Clyde flung the cell phone across the room, his eyes on an anxious wanderlust while he ranted about his inability to reach either Keshawna Keyes or Josh Wainwright, simultaneously working his fingers furiously to make certain Peppi understood his anger. "Wainwright goes to Nashville on my dime to see Kristy Palmer, I want to know what he thinks he learned from her that he didn't already know," he signed.

Peppi retrieved the phone and settled it on the bar counter. "She didn't tell you?" Peppi signed. He filched a cigarette from a tray on the bar, perched it between his lips and plugged the trach with a thumb while accepting a light from Clyde. Pushed out a splinter of blue smoke and transferred the cigarette to the trach hole.

Clyde swatted away the smoke. "No answer from that creature at either of her numbers, Nashville or El Paso."

"There's nothing she knows can hurt you."

"I'll be happier hearing it from her," Clyde signed. He helped himself to a clutch of the mood-minders stockpiled in an ashtray on the counter and washed them down with his Bloody Mary.

His cell exploded with a snatch of melody from one of the hits he had created for Garry Chaplin—like Billy the Kid, one of the ungrateful bastards in his life—signaling E-mail.

The screen lit up with Princess Lulu's name.

Her message was brief: *Today. Your place. Good time just us?*

Clyde, his surprise replaced by an ear-to-ear grin, quickly

pecked back an answer:

3 p.m.

He would send off Gidis and Egle, his cleaning people, early, as he always did whenever something called for absolute privacy.

His fingers answered Peppi's inquiring eyes, then explained what he wanted done. As an afterthought, he signed: "Turn off the security cameras and sound now, so we don't forget later. The girl wants to be alone with me. . . . Excellent."

He didn't have to explain to Peppi what he had in mind, of a different order than anything Princess Lulu might have in mind.

Peppi's expression told the same truth.

Princess Lulu arrived a few minutes before four, Peppi outside to greet her.

Clyde watched her pull up to the entrance peeking out from behind a corner of the floor-to-ceiling lavender velvet drapery of the second-floor bedroom he reserved for special occasions. His excitement at seeing her overcame the anxiety that had turned into irritation since he took up the observation post shortly before three o'clock, bouncing from foot-to-foot as the time passed, resisting the urge to explode that usually came whenever he was disappointed.

He wanted a drink, but had to be sober for the heavy-duty sales pitch he was going to hit her with. The same reason he had only popped one 'lude all afternoon. The two lines of coke he should have resisted, but he needed a little picker-upper around three-thirty, when he started to suspect she might be standing him up.

Princess Lulu had been on and off his mind, mostly on, since dropping into his life at EZ-XTC's recording studio. Because of her voice, of course, and what he could do with it—what he would do with it once she was his to do with as he pleased—but it was something else that had raised so strong an emotion in him.

No woman had ever reminded him of Angel Thompson the way Princess Lulu did.

Angel, Angel, Angel.

She helped make him rich.

She helped make him famous.

She turned his life around, then tried to screw him into the ground, and yet—

And yet—

He loved her today the way he loved her then and always.

Angel helped make him rich.

Angel helped make him famous.

He got her out of his life, but to this day never out of his mind.

He had fled high school to chase after his ambition, with the mountainous arrogance of somebody who did not need a second opinion to know his talent for music bordered on genius.

He was a self-taught musician who knew instinctively how to break down a song into its component parts, analyze a refrain, know where the hook was that made a song a hit, listen to a tune once and predict its future, spot lyric flaws that would keep a record from airplay and the *Billboard* charts, which he studied religiously, off the copy he stole every week from the corner newsstand at Crenshaw and Jefferson.

He hung around Buddy Bowen's studio, sweeping up and doing odd jobs, taking half pay in cash and applying the other half to studio time he'd use when Buddy wasn't working tricks on what passed for a board in those days, decades before the synthesizer came along and electronics began squeezing the life out of legitimate sounds.

Two tracks at first, one for the musicians, the other for the vocalist, because way back then Sinatra was almost alone in laying down vocals live in front of orchestras led by cats like Nelson Riddle, Gordon Jenkins, and Billy May.

Four tracks by the time he'd taken what he could from Buddy and knew the board better than him or any producer or engineer bopping in to make sides on the cheap, ping-ponging the tapes to double-up to eight tracks and closing in on what would soon become his revolutionary "Symphony of Sound."

That happened after he sweet-talked his way into Gold Star, the absolute best of the indie studios anywhere in the world, and did a load of hanging out in Studio A, where hits were being made by the likes of the Beach Boys, Sonny and Cher, the Righteous Brothers, and Phil Spector. "Wrecking Crew" players like Hal Blaine, Carole Kaye, Don Randi, Steve Douglas, and Tommy Tedesco. The board overseen by master magicians like Stan Ross, Dave Gold, and Larry Levine.

Clyde watched and listened, mentally improving on everything he saw and heard.

When he was ready, satisfied he knew better, had saved up enough to buy his way into the cheap daylight hours in "A" and hire his pick of the Wrecking Crew, he went after Angel.

She had sent him in a spin the first time he saw her walking the campus. He crashed for keeps at a school talent show, when she stepped out of the chorus and grabbed hold of the mike like a pro to perform some early Lena and Billie, then caused a near-riot of a standing ovation with her encore, a scat number that came close to matching the incomparable Ella with a series of runs that took the scales with one clean note after another.

Clyde couldn't have been closer to the truth and majesty of Angel's voice, having jumped at the invitation to accompany her on piano. That's what put them together for the first time, at a few skimpy rehearsals that taught him how to anticipate her vocal routing, handle her vamping, and know when to quit the keyboard and let her fly solo.

Afterward, Angel said, "You real good for a white boy."

"You could be better," Clyde said, at once regretting his words, as her hooded black eyes sucked in the insult and turned to burning him at the stake.

She raised her height by a mile, thrust back her shoulders, and—dismissing him with an imperious sneer and the snap of her fingers—marched out of his life.

He didn't know how to apologize. He'd never felt the urge or the need. He went back to idolizing her from a distance. Angel turned her back on him whenever she caught him at it. He quit school after a month or two of this, but never blamed her, as if anybody could control his destiny for any reason.

Not even her.

Not even Angel.

His Angel.

Impossible.

The next time they spoke, she was a junior and working the late shift at a Chicken Stuff take-out window.

He knew that much about her because of nights he'd park his Ford jalopy down the block from her place and track her comings and goings, boiling whenever he saw her with some guy, any guy. Often, he'd close his eyes and imagine it was him; dig into his pants to share a happy minute with her.

"Take your order?"

He was out of her sightline at the menu board, five cars ahead of him. She didn't know his voice at first, when he ordered the Deep Dish Fry Pie, slaw, black beans, and a jumbo cola.

"Something more?"

"Yes. I want to make you a star."

"Say what?"

"I want to take you into the studio to make a record, sing a song that's going to put you on the map, make you famous."

"Who this strokin' my bush?"

He told her. For a few seconds he thought the name meant nothing to her, until Angel blew a throaty laugh out of the loudspeaker. "You the piano boy who put me down at school assembly. 'Sted of famous, you get up here, you remember to put a nice tip in the tip jar, all's I need from you."

"You're off duty at midnight. Give me five minutes."

"That a jumbo cola or a super jumbo cola?"

"Five minutes, Angel. Famous. All the trappings that come with it."

"I get minimum wage by the hour. Time-and-a-half for overtime. Double-time for any special occasion."

"Ten bucks do it?"

"Twenny, in front, you feel like throwing away your money on conversation. Might give you some mouth, though, you remember to say please."

"*Please,* but you can save your mouth for where I really want it, in front of a mike in a recording studio." It was not entirely true now, but he had his dick back under control by the time Angel's shift ended and she climbed into the passenger seat of the Ford, which Clyde had parked in a remote corner of the Chicken Stuff lot.

She smelled of grease and was chewing bubble gum, making a bubble that popped and settled on her broad nose and high cheeks. She peeled and plucked at the residue after stuffing the twenty inside her bra, which she pulled out far enough for him to catch a good look. Didn't quit until she was sure he had. Said, "Got another where that one come from."

He snatched her hand. "I paid for you to listen. Now listen."

The bra snapped back against her tawny skin.

"Damn," she said, pulling away, eyes growing with recognition that he meant it. She angled between the seat and the door frame and locked her hands on her lap. "Clock's ticking," she said.

Clyde explained how he'd been spending his time and outlined his plan for her. She had never heard of Gold Star but knew the names he said recorded there and broke in time and again to name their hits.

"You saying you could make me like one of them, get me on the radio?" she said.

"Bigger."

"But you never done one before with any of them, like that Spector, he went and done it for the Ronettes? Ike and Tina, say?"

"I watched how it's done. I can do better. I can do better with you. Make you sing and sound in a way like never before. Put you on top of the charts and on top of the world. Listen up."

Angel cocked an ear at him and listened attentively while he hummed the melody he had been working on for weeks. When he finished, she nodded and pushed her palm at him, signaling for quiet, and hummed it back with a marvel of invention; then, again, but now scatting nonsensical words she made sound like they were drawn from some Bible of the soul.

"Better than that?" she said, challenging him.

"Or you can go back to Chicken Stuff and swallowing dicks for tips."

Her slap came out of nowhere and set half his face on fire. "No need ever talking to me like that again, you have any serious hopes of doing anything but monkey business with me."

He returned the slap. "Better than that."

"Likes the way you do business," Angel said, rubbing her cheek. "How much you gonna pay me to help you get your dream come true?"

"It's your dream I'm talking here, not mine."

She ran the scales with her laugh. "Save your sucker talk for some other sucker. I work here to help out my family, so my mama, she don't have to spend no more time on her back than on her feet, you follow?"

"It'll be a gamble for both of us," he said.

"No, thank you," she said. She pushed down on the door handle and started out of the car.

Clyde caught her by the shoulder. "Same as you're making here. Minimum."

"Time-and-a-half and double-time?"

"Yes."

"You able come up that kind-a bread regular?"

"Absolutely," Clyde said, only a vague idea of how he could make it happen, but already blessed with a gift of gab that could keep a conversation moving his way.

Angel ran a finger around her lips, used it to dry brush her teeth while she thought about it. She said, "You pay me like for a regular shift before I open my mouth, every time, and any extra for overtime right after, or I don't ever show up next time, you follow?"

"My turn now?" She flipped over her hand. "Every dollar you make in front, I get back first, once the record starts showing a profit. Next, I get back every other dollar I put into making the record and making it a hit. Then, we share together. Fair enough?"

"Sounds too good to be true. So where's the catch? When's it you try screwing me?"

"We'll put it in writing, so there's no misunderstanding. Your mama will need to sign it for you, because you're underage."

"Who's signing for you, piano boy?"

"I'm eighteen, legal as they come."

"Speaking of which. . . ." She sank forward, her fingers creeping toward his zipper. "Let's celebrate by getting your twenty dollahs off the books right now."

The time Clyde spent in the studios had taught him that the business side of the business was conducted by people who, growing up, probably cheated at Monopoly. There was always a record or publishing company honcho, a personal manager, a business manager, bragging about how his contracts weren't any better than his handshake or his word of honor.

The person they all seemed to admire most, treating his name with a reverence usually reserved for the Pope or the Dali Lama, was Paul DeCarlo, who sometimes made the *Billboard* news pages in stories about big deals and, less often, news headlines in connection with federal investigations into industry practices.

Clyde couldn't get through to him on the phone, so he camped out in the outer office of DeCarlo's undistinguished three-room suite in a high-rise full of companies linked to music at Sunset and Cahuenga. That didn't work any better. A purple-haired secretary with a face full of prune wrinkles felt sorry for him. She let him sit around for hours on end reading old magazines, like he was competing in some contest for squatters.

No one else ever came or went. It was always them, him and Prune Face, until the third day of his second week, when a kid about his age, only dressed smarter, in clothes worth what Clyde figured he earned in a year, stepped inside, sent the secretary a fingertip salute and smile, and said, "Mr. DeCarlo is waiting for you downstairs in the coffee shop, fella. Middle booth by the window."

DeCarlo ignored his offer of a handshake and pointed to the opposite side of the booth.

Clyde slid onto the faded red naugahyde and, squinting against sunlight slanting directly into his eyes, waited patiently for the man's attention, hands locked on the table, tennis sneakers alternating quiet taps to mark the passing seconds.

He was in his mid-to-late forties, as ordinary-looking as a bank teller dressed for Sunday golf on a municipal course, except for the Gucci gold chains around his neck that told a different story and reflective sunglasses that hid his thoughts from probing eyes. A body that could stand to lose fifteen or twenty pounds. Hair the color of horseradish and neatly trimmed, contrary to the mile-long hair and bushy sideburns look of the time. A voice never raised above a whisper during their brief conversation.

DeCarlo spent another few minutes working over his coffee, which he drank black after pouring it carefully from the cup into the saucer and using both hands bringing it to his lips. He took a few sips before settling the saucer down and waving away an anxious waitress in a skirt too short for her stumpy legs, studied Clyde's face for an eternity before nodding some kind of approval.

"You're the kid hangs out at the studios telling everyone how great he's going to be with his songs and producing and shit, right?"

"Am, Mr. DeCarlo. How great I *am.*"

DeCarlo flicked a smile so brief it was barely noticeable. "What else are you, kid, besides great, that has you haunting my office all this time, like I got nothing better to do than waste my time on you?" He eased the cup and saucer aside and settled his elbows on the table, forming a pyramid with his splayed fingers. The sun bounced a rainbow of light off a pinky ring diamond the size of a golf ball.

"No waste when you consider I'm prepared to make you millions of dollars," Clyde said.

DeCarlo laughed. "I already got millions of dollars, which translates to me as you'd like some of it." He patted his mouth, acting out a giant yawn. "You have my attention for another thirty seconds, starting now."

"An investment you'll never regret," Clyde said, and jumped into the sales pitch he had practiced for days.

DeCarlo looked up from his diamond-studded gold wristwatch and signaled him to quit. "Enough, kid. . . . You know how often I hear that from music business yutzes who think they can cash in big time by reinventing the wheel?"

"Except they all lack one thing, Mr. DeCarlo, they're not me. Buy into me and you get all four wheels. The whole car. You get all of General Motors."

"Christ, I think he believes it," DeCarlo said, talking to the air.

"I don't bring you a hit in sixty days, start turning you a profit by sixty after that, you're welcome to kill me."

DeCarlo brought up a growl from the base of his throat. "What's that supposed to mean?"

"I hear rumors."

DeCarlo checked around and dropped his voice another decibel. "What you hear are the rumors nobody will ever prove, hard as they might try. Something about your style I like, kid. Tell me what it is you need, it's yours. You disappoint me, you'll go to your grave knowing how true rumors can be." He spit into his palm and held it out. "Shake."

Clyde made the sixty-day deadline with breathing room, but barely.

Except for Angel, nothing was ever perfect enough to suit him.

He treated the booth jockeys and the Wrecking Crew cats like early losers on Ted Mack's Original Amateur, dumped session after session chasing after elusive notes he was determined to translate from his mind onto tape, and snorted and popped his way through a month of expensive all-nighters working the board by himself, wildly adjusting levers and dials.

Angel often kept him company.

She had bought in early to what he was trying to accomplish. She was there if he needed her to tease a phrase in a different direction or drop in a lyric change, once or twice contributing a word that gave him what he was after.

"Off the books, no charge," she'd say if he tried sending her home. "Sticking close to protect my interest, piano boy."

It was four, maybe five in the morning, time a blur, when it finally came together—

A single that gave him everything he was after, the sound that would set new directions and challenges for rock and roll.

The proof was in the playbacks.

Mono.

Stereo.

He'd created a monster, the musical equivalent of paintings by cats like da Vinci and Rembrandt, a record for the history books.

He'd respected Angel's hands-off demands all this time, no interest in sex, actually, getting off on automatic pilot anytime something else fell picture-perfect into the grooves.

This night was different.

This night Angel encouraged him.

She killed another brew, tossed the can aside, and declared, "The celebration what we both earned, piano boy."

They made delicious love on the booth floor.

Clyde's deal with DeCarlo specified that the single would be pressed and released on Big Horn, one of the labels in which he owned a silent minority stock interest.

Within two weeks, the record was a pick hit in *Billboard, Cash Box* and *Record World* and airing on all the key stations throughout the country.

Two weeks after that, the record was Number One in *Billboard, Cash Box* and *Record World,* airing on every rock-and-roll station in the U.S. and breaking big in England, Germany, and Japan.

Two weeks after that, Angel announced she was expecting.

"You going to do the right thing and make an honest woman of me?" she asked.

"Even if you weren't," Clyde said.

Two weeks after they eloped to Las Vegas, she no longer was.

Angel had suffered a miscarriage.

The need to pull together an act that Angel could take on the road helped rescue her from depression. The need to complete a follow-up single and the rest of Angel's debut LP became his salvation. They would be confirmation of his genius, to go with the wealth and fame now starting his way.

When it arrived, when both were sitting on top of the world he had made for them, Angel moved out on him and filed for divorce.

She said, "My mind, never been only much more'n a business arrangement you and me we got between us, piano boy. Now gonna run off and lead my life on my terms, not yours. Got new people to take care of me good and proper."

She was taken care of good and proper, all right.

He saw to that.

He mourned her death like he meant it.

More so when he recognized and could admit to himself he really did.

So what if Princess Lulu might be, as Angel was, a disaster waiting to happen?

She was also an updated, upgraded, better-educated version of Angel, already irresistible to him. Whatever had motivated her to tell him in EZ-XTC's record plant, *I want you to do for me what he can't,* whatever motivated her to come here today, Clyde was determined to own her before she left.

He waited until after Peppi had pointed her up the hill, then come around her late-model Beamer and helped himself to the passenger seat, before crossing from the bedroom window to the private elevator and pressing the button to his basement studio.

He was settled at the console, racking a tape, when she and Peppi stepped from the other elevator and headed for the booth.

Peppi guided her through the door and retreated after accepting her thank-you with a nod.

She was dressed to be noticed, seductive in an ice-cream-white stretch pullover with a v-neckline that showed off her dangerous curves and long-legged elegance. No bra or panty lines. Heels that added three or four inches to her height. Small pearldrop earrings, but no jewelry that might draw attention from her face.

She finished surveying the studio and said, "Cool, although the board's about a year out of date. This where we're going to work, me helping you make a comeback while I get out from under my daddy's shadow, show him what his little princess can get done without his smothering indulgence?"

"I've never been away."

"Or the eight-track. There will be one problem you have to understand in front, Clyde, and it's major league, otherwise I'd have trouble nights getting in my eight hours."

God, she was magnificent. "What problem?"

Princess Lulu ran a finger across her throat. "Daddy learns what's going on, he'll be on your case quicker than you can say Tupac Shakur or Notorious B.I.G., get my drift?"

"Your 'daddy'. You mean EZ-XTC, correct?"

"The man himself. Mr. Ezra Charleson. Mind you, not that I'm accusing my daddy of anything as bad as that, but that's his world, not mine. I don't want to be anyplace near longer than I have to, and that's already been long enough; too long. You are my passport out of his world. So, what do you say, Mr. Clyde Davenport?—as if I don't already know the answer."

"You certainly love the sound of your own voice."

"More than you do? I don't think so. Oh, hell—Yes."

"I didn't go to Dead Dogg Records asking for you for my Big Buddies of America show. I was after Cake Mouth. I take you, I get him. What makes you think I'd want you for anything but the show?"

Her smile brought out her dimples.

"Oh, you want me, you do, Mr. Clyde Davenport. Before, those five minutes you asked for, I saw it on your face, I smelled it on your body, steaming out your pores. I see and smell it now, but you know something else? True confession. I've always had a thing for older men."

"There's a forty year or more difference in our ages."

"More. You weren't going to let that stop you, were you? I'm not planning to let it stop me. Tell me you were going to let it stop you and I'll call you a liar to your ancient face."

Absolutely magnificent.

Clyde adjusted a knob and threw a switch.

The studio filled with the sound of Angel—

The single that put him in business.

"Think you can match that?"

"Angel? Better. Want me to prove it now?" Princess Lulu picked up the lyric line and in seconds, word for word, she was singing counterpoint harmony.

Clyde waved her off and cut the sound.

"Prove something else first," he said, barely able to contain himself.

"Game to go," she said.

Chapter 23

Josh woke up late, to an empty house, the kids at school and Niki at UCLA chasing after her grad school credits. So much for pulling Justin aside for a heart-to-heart, spare-no-punches conversation, and maybe just as well until he could speak with Connie, learn what she knew and cook up a strategy that would also yank Rusty Jr. back in line. Here was one more occasion when he had reason to miss Katie. She would have known instinctively how to handle the situation.

He returned Connie's phone call from last night. Got the machine. Left a message.

He tried connecting with Keshawna. No luck at any of her numbers. The office had not heard from her either. He left messages letting Keesh know he would not return any of Clyde Davenport's calls until he had her update on her overnighter at Mission Possible and any fresh news about Bluto Parks.

As an afterthought, he said: "Laszlo Lowenstein, that's Peter Lorre. Try Kathy Sue Nail, and no fair Googling."

In his mind, Josh wasn't convinced that Bluto would turn out to be anything more than a wild-goose chase, a wind-damaged straw unable to explain why he'd turned up dead on the list from Davenport, only to have Davenport on a later date talking to Billy Palmer about reuniting the two of them in a recording studio.

What might prove more substantial was anything he could learn from the receptionist at Uncensored Productions, who'd seemed so anxious to explain how Davenport connected to Merv Bannister.

He'd stuck into his wallet the slip of paper on which she'd written her number.

He dialed her on his land line.

Her machine answered with mumbo-jumbo on how to leave a text message.

He replaced the call on his cell.

Made a bath his next priority.

Josh did some of his best thinking lounging in the tub, when he wasn't doing some of his best thinking on the road, a habit that used to drive Katie to distraction. She often predicted he'd wind up crashing into somebody's back bumper if he didn't concentrate on keeping his eyes open to traffic instead of the distant sky, where he seemed to believe he would find his solutions. Over the years, that only happened twice, and that left turn into the Volks—positively the fault of the other guy running the red at a three-way intersection on Melrose like he didn't want to be late for his own funeral.

Today, the tub was no help. No matter how he let his mind wander with what he knew, the information got him no closer to—

Anything.

The good news first:

Davenport remained the prime suspect in the murder of Ava Garner.

If the case went to trial today, there wasn't enough "reasonable doubt" to keep any jury in the world from convicting him.

The bad news:

Nothing put Davenport's imprint on the murder of Billy the Kid Palmer.

The Davenport connection to Billy's suicide was no stronger now than it had been over the years on any of the earlier deaths of the rock artists that quit him, however similar.

The strongest link remained Josh's personal conviction, not any verdict that any jury in the world was likely to bring in on the strength of evidence that didn't exist.

One piece of good luck could change that.

Was it going to come from Bluto?

The Uncensored Productions receptionist?

Neither?

Would any of this make a difference in his life, except for the life he was prepared to swear under oath, proof or no proof, that Davenport had taken from him—

Katie's life?

If he had to be honest with himself, the answer would be "No."

Davenport would remain one of the droppings on the bottom of the birdcage he had left behind when he quit the force, no more, no less—

A name among names in investigation files closed and consigned to archive shelves in the lower reaches of the Hall of Records against recorded findings of accidental drowning, death by overdose of illegal substances, a fatal freeway mishap, a home fire, a suicide, other cute tricks meant to hide a homicide—

Nothing to warrant the open file a murder would warrant, except in Katie's case—

Death from a bullet wound inflicted by a person or persons unknown.

"But I know it was you responsible, Davenport, you sick dick!" Josh said, his eyes narrowing, a fist pounding the water, his pulse quickening on a flashback to the night he'd decided he was going to kill Davenport and to hell with the consequences. He was high on pills and on the bottle. Highest on getting revenge. Keesh saw it on his face, smelled it on his breath, and tried tough loving him out of it after Connie had called her panic-stricken, describing how he was acting like a madman. Keesh'd come running, cornered him in the den, where he was weighing whether to go with the Magnum, the Glock, or something heavier, and shouted: "Put those guns away, idiot."

"Who ast you?"

"Joshua, damn it. Stop thinking about your sad sorry ass and think of the kids."

"Outta way, you know what's good."

He pointed the Magnum in her face and staggered toward the door. She blocked his way. When he couldn't navigate her aside, he whacked her on the side of the head with the Mag. Her body followed the swivel of her head and after that a two-handed shove sent her crashing to the floor.

His classic '57 red T-Bird roadster was parked in the circular drive.

Keshawna appeared in the doorway, giving him orders while he fumbled for the key. He waved the Mag in her face, emphasized the warning by firing a shot into the fat black rain clouds hovering overhead in the harsh night air.

Went back to fumbling for the key on the keychain.

Got behind the wheel and struggled to make the key fit.

Keshawna was on him in a matter of seconds, before he could pull the door closed, the barrel of her Glock pressed against his temple.

"Quit it now, Joshua, or I'll—"

"Blow my brains out? Don't think so, Keesh. Don't."

He turned the key and the 312 V8 kicked in.

"You mean can't, not with nothing to work on, you brainless moron."

Josh gunned the engine.

Keshawna took three quick steps away and fired.

Then again.

Blitzing the front tire, then the rear one.

The T-Bird sank into lopsidedness.

The rain clouds were developing cracks, showering them in a drizzle fast growing in intensity while Josh, cursing the sauntering moon, managed to get a grip on the Mag and sight Keshawna in a two-handed aim.

"Bird's a fucking classic," he said, his anger abruptly shifted off Davenport.

Keshawna, her Glock sighted on Josh, said, "We'll clock ass on Davenport, but the right way, Joshua. The right way, with me there for you all the time, all the way."

"Fucking classic," Josh said, and—

Fired.

Keshawna's earlier shots had awakened Justin and Julie. They'd come running out to see what was happening, Josh's erratic aim sailed past Keshawna's shoulder toward Justin and Julie.

Justin yowled and fell to the asphalt.

Julie ran screaming back up the stairs and into the house, and—

Even now, sitting in the tub—

The memory of that night grabbed Josh by the neck, constricted his chest, and sent him back deep inside the moment, remembering how he'd howled with certainty that he'd just killed his son. How he'd tossed aside the Mag, cracked open the door, and stumbled, fell and crawled to him on his knees, begging Justin to be alive.

There was a trace of blood where his shot had nicked Justin's ear and blood on the hand his son was using to cup the modest wound. He was fine otherwise, better than Josh, who broke into uncontrollable tears, hugging the boy and begging forgiveness, looking up at Keshawna and telling her, "I need help, Keesh." Again and again. Repeating himself as best he could, each time each word forced through a battery of throat-clogged anguish.

Within days, he was in rehab.

Josh shook the tears loose from his face, climbed out of the tub, and toweled off.

He studied his face in the mirror, accepting there was nothing he could do or cared to do about the wear-and-tear brought on by aging, but maybe the sadness in his eyes would disappear the day Davenport was brought to ground, Katie's death finally avenged.

He was in the middle of shaving when he heard his cell phone singing.

Josh double-timed into the bedroom.

"Marilyn Pope returning yours," she said.

"Who?"

"Me. Marilyn Pope. Uncensored Productions? Merv Bannister? Clyde Davenport? Remember?" He was hearing her name for the first time. "How you fixed for a late lunch, Mr. Wainwright? I think you'll find what I got to say's worth the price of a meal. Besides, a girl's gotta eat."

His phone rang again about twenty minutes later, Keshawna returning his calls this time, deciding, "You sound the way I feel."

"Tell me something to make me feel better."

"The firm's springing to lease you a new Lexus."

"I was happy with the old one."

"So, apparently, were the beaners who hustled it down Tijuana way and stripped it clean. Anything in the glove or trunk you were especially fond of?"

"Besides the million bucks in diamonds, emeralds, and rubies I had stashed in a paper bag in the tool box?"

"Besides. Already mentioned the bag to our insurance people."

The banter gave away to serious talk a minute or so later, Keshawna saying, “Bluto Parks never showed his puss again at the mission. I slipped Raul a fifty to play snitch for us when and if.”

“Davenport?”

“I was ducking his calls wanting to hear all about your slithering around Billy Palmer’s widow until I reasoned, what the hell, I could tell Clyde no news is good news as well as you. Only he’s currently incommunicado. Got no pickup on any of the phones. All the surveillance switches been thrown, locking us out of sight and sound at his place.”

“The firewall I wanted here?”

“You tell me.”

Josh had her hang while he moved to his computer. Logging onto Davenport’s security system, he drew blank screens. He ran the screens back in time and got more of the same.

“Black as the bastard’s heart,” he reported.

“I’ll get our techies right on it. Not more’n a couple of hours max to run the lines and spot the fix point. You coming in?”

“Depends on how my lunch date goes.” He told her about Marilyn Pope.

“Anything else I should know?”

“She wears a ring through her nose and chews bubble gum.”

“Where you meeting her, Chuck E. Cheese’s?”

He thought Jean-Jacques, the maitre d’, had misunderstood and was guiding him to the wrong table, maybe out of some remembrance and sentiment for all the years he and Katie had been here for lunch or, more often, dinner, on nights the music industry crowd had made their special preserve, packing the dining room and the circular bar, especially the bar.

It was the table Katie was always given, one of several that let them observe the comings and goings of sundry famous faces as easy as it was for one and all to notice that Katie Sunshine was in the house.

En route, Jean-Jacques reflected brightly on those days, his once-brisk steps closer to a shuffle and burdened by the modest stoop of a man in his late seventies, but still resplendent in his classic tuxedo with the broad lapels and fresh carnation in the lapel to match his oversized crimson bow tie.

He pulled out the satin-covered chair across from the woman, who sat where Katie had always sat, and sensing Josh's hesitation wondered, "One of the others, Monsieur Josh?"

"Not that," the woman answered for him. "It's cool, Monsieur Josh. Really. I'm Marilyn."

Instead of the gum-chewing girl in her early twenties, he was looking at a mature woman maybe ten years older. Instead of off-the-Gap-rack trendy, her clothing was more of a costume, a sexy red dress made for dancing the bossa nova, her breasts as upbeat as before, but more skin on view in a neckline that plunged like the stock market had in 1929. Instead of a nose ring, tangled gold and sterling silver loops dangling from her pierced ears. Instead of jet-black hair, strawberry-blond strands falling playfully onto her shoulders from under a straw hat with an upturned brim and a hatband made of turquoise and onyx beads.

She raised her wine glass as if toasting him, flashed a smile, and said, "I got here earlier than I figured, so started without you. The house red, more exquisite than it has any right to be. My compliments, Jean." She pronounced it *John.* He gave her an appreciative nod, helped Josh settle in his seat, and retreated with his drink order and her request for a fresh carafe.

"Diet Coke the best you can do?" she said.

Josh recognized the woman's fattened lips, but her voice was richer, more mature than he remembered, a velvet quality absent in their later phone conversation.

"Sometimes, I take it straight and damn the calories," he said.

"Brave of you. I love that quality in a man."

"You may be Marilyn Pope, but are you the girl I saw at Uncensored Productions?"

"No . . . I'm the *woman* you saw at Uncensored Productions," she said, deepening the texture of her words. Reading his confusion, she giggled and reached over to pat his hand. "In case you're also wondering, the rack is a hundred percent real, but the nose got worked over a little, and I didn't grow up with this gorgeous chin. Marilyn Pope's my stage name. I took the Marilyn after you-know-who, Pope because I figured it's memorable when I'm on a call, you know—the first female pope?"

"A call. You're either a call girl or an actress. Which?"

He was half-serious.

She took no offense.

Her laugh hit every corner of the room, drawing attention from what remained in mid-afternoon of the luncheon crowd. She briefly basked in the notice. "A little of both, but more of the latter," she said.

She ticked off a flirtatious wink for the flighty waiter delivering their drinks, declared herself famished, and ordered the prime rib, rare; a Caesar salad, extra dressing on the side. Groaned, shaking her head in disbelief when he asked for the spinach and cheese omelet.

"Cheers!" she said, swallowing what remained of the wine and refilling her glass. "I get time off for good behavior at Uncensored. Also for bad behavior." Her eyebrows aimed for the wallpapered ceiling. "You caught me the last time fresh back from a casting call for a mosh-pit chick, and still in the mood. Before meeting you today at Chez Glitz, it was an open casting call for a high-maintenance society type for a new HBO series."

"What about the real you?"

Marilyn Pope drew a wistful breath. Her eyes retreated to

some distant place. She said, "The real me disappeared almost the day I got off the Greyhound from Kansas, and I'll tell you something else, Mr. Wainwright. I've put on the ruby slippers and clicked my heels three times a half a dozen different times, but it doesn't work that way in real life." She attacked the wine glass again. "Enough about me, right?"

"Things you said I should hear about Merv Bannister and Clyde Davenport."

"And Ava, the poor kid, chasing a dream that turned into a nightmare."

"Vic Swank ties her murder to Bannister. You?"

She made a fist and shook her thumb downward.

"Merv pimped Ava, the way he pimped a lot of us, playing off our dreams to get us to do what he needed to flesh out his dirty passions, but kill her, no? Women made money for Merv, but only that, and Ava made him bundles once she got into the spirit of the game and came to enjoy it. Shoot her dead? The only gun Merv Bannister's courageous enough to fire is between somebody's legs, or his own. I know the song and dance Vic laid on you, but it was Davenport done the dirty to her, crazy, fucked up, possessive pervert that he is."

"How do you know?"

"The walls have ears, and so does my switchboard, Mr. Wainwright. I hear things."

She paused for another slug of wine.

He urged her for more with an inward wave of his fingers.

"I heard Davenport on the phone with Vic, telling Vic how to play you if and when you came snooping, certain that you would sooner or later. Explain to you how Merv was out to get even with Davenport for stealing Ava away from him."

"Why would Vic go along with it? Davenport have something on him?"

"You'd have to ask Vic that. I only know what I know."

"Why tell me? Not just for a nice meal."

"Assuming it ever gets here." She looked around. "I hope you don't leave a big tip when the service is lousy. . . . No, to keep Davenport from getting away with murder. More than once, before he fell head-over-heels for Ava and went exclusive on her, I came away from his place battered and limping, lumps the size of eggs. More than once, he rammed a gun into my mouth, my ear, one of my other cavities, and threatened to pull the trigger. One time, I thought I was off to meet my maker for certain, except his guy Peppi Blue stepped in and saved my tattooed ass." She dabbed at the tears welling in her pale blue eyes. "If he doesn't get stopped, he's going to kill again."

"I heard a motive for Bannister. You haven't given me one for Davenport."

They were interrupted by the waiter delivering their order.

"I'm famished. Let's save that for dessert," Marilyn Pope said. "I understand the pecan mousse pie here is spectacular."

Chapter 24

Josh finished pouring a coffee from the fresh pot on the hot-plate and rejoined Keshawna in the conversation corner of her office, where he had spent the past twenty minutes briefing her on his lunch with Marilyn.

"The possessive bastard Davenport shows up without notice at Uncensored Productions to catch Ava taping one of those 'Whatever Happened To' bits for the next *National Search for Miss American Showgirl*," he said. "Instead, he catches his protégé tangled up in a three-way in Merv Bannister's dressing room."

Keshawna rolled her eyes. "Who was the other guy?"

Josh corrected her. "The other chick," he said, pausing a moment to build in his version of suspense. "Marilyn Pope."

She reared back in surprise, her eyebrows charging for the ceiling.

"And scratch any assumption that the man in the middle was Bannister taking a heavy breather from his sexual preferences," he said.

"Don't make me guess," she said, amusement setting in.

"Bad enough you haven't guessed who's Kathy Sue Nail."

"AKA Kate Capshaw. Steven Spielberg's old lady. I genuinely loved her in that Indiana Jones movie."

"You Googled, cheater."

Keshawna flashed her teeth like she was taking the Fifth. "Ava and Marilyn were joined by no less than this year's host of the show, the Prince of the Las Vegas Strip."

She tilted her head and looked at him like she hadn't heard right. "Connie Reynolds' ex?"

"Russ Tambourine himself. Definitely a small world, isn't it?"

"And what's it coming to?"

"A hot sandwich for lunchtime, but it wasn't in the rider in the scumbag's contract," Josh said. "Davenport somehow tracked down Ava, took one whiff of the scene, and he went ballistic. Marilyn's the top slice of bread at the time, she says, so first he pulls her off and tosses her aside. Next he's on Tambourine, beating on him like some Ringo Starr, trying to get him up from Ava. Tambourine has age and muscle on his side. A hard kick in the gut gets Davenport sailing across the room. He struggles back onto his feet, cursing at Ava and Tambourine, only now Davenport's flashing a gun. Waving it in their faces, like he can't make up his mind who he wants to do first. Tambourine makes the choice easier by pulling Ava in front of him and using her as a shield.

"Tambourine starts blubbering how it's not his fault, how the fuck-and-suck was all Ava's idea, and Ava is begging Davenport to calm down and put away the gun. Davenport is dripping saliva at the corners of his mouth, looks to have decided it'll be Ava. He pulls back the hammer. Marilyn, on her feet by now, grabs the Emmy Award statuettes on Bannister's dressing table and catches Davenport's gun arm. His shot rips into the dressing room floor. The door crashes open. Crew guys pounce on Davenport, wrestle him down, and grab the gun away, while he's cursing and doing the Yogi Berra, how it isn't over until it's over, while they drag him off. It was all over and done in less than three or four minutes."

Josh tested his coffee for heat with an index finger, moving it from the cup to his tongue. Satisfied, he took a gulp and waited for her to say something.

Keshawna weighed what she'd heard for several moments before translating a skeptical gaze into words.

"Joshua, explain to me how none of this came out before your chitchat over an expensive meal with Pope Marilyn. Not in any of our prep work, including any paperwork by our boys in blue or the D.A.'s office. Nothing you got from Vic Swank. Nothing on TV or in the newspapers or magazines. Not a squeal in the scandal books, where you'd figure enough people were around the set to see or hear and someone'd pick up a phone and look to cash in."

"I can't," Josh said. "Not yet."

"Soon would be helpful. Meanwhile, our boy Clyde had the means, the opportunity, and now a weighty enough motive to want Ava out of his life, and hers. That smacks to me of guilt beyond a reasonable doubt in any man's Jury Land."

"Works for me."

"Except it's not the work Davenport is paying us to do."

"Speaking of which, surveillance monitors up and running again at my place?"

Keshawna checked her watch. Almost four. "Our crew's closing in on the problem. Five, five-thirty latest, you should be back in business."

"Here?"

"All systems operational, but the client still has everything geared to off."

"To hide what?" She turned her palms up. "What's on-site say?"

"Pulliam says nothing to suggest trouble. Peppi Blue hanging out at the entrance gate, dragging one smoke after another through his neck, like he's waiting on someone."

"Maybe I'll head on over and wait with him."

"And maybe ask Davenport about Russ Tambourine and the three-way?"

"Keesh, m'dear, you are still one hell of a detective."

"You driving the old family relic?"

"The Bug that took a licking, but keeps on ticking."

"Can't have you embarrassing us any more than usual. Use the company Mercedes until your Lexus gets replaced. Also, when you get around to it"—she locked onto his eyes—"don't go crazy trying to ID Johnnie Collier by any other name."

Keshawna waited until Josh had left the building and added enough time for him to have hit the road before switching her desktop screen back to the Davenport coverage. The pictures and sound kicked in immediately. Also, her guilt over not telling him that she had her own ISO coverage of the Davenport's mansion, or that it had never quit transmitting here or at her home, because of the net override and IP she ordered for herself, not him.

She did that, she'd have to tell Josh why.

Sixteen different locations played on the screen at one time, miniature images she could bring up to full-size, if there was something worth probing. A few strokes of the keyboard took her from the grounds to another set of sixteen images inside Magic Land, a few more and there would be another sixteen locations, ultimately everywhere throughout the Italian villa, except where Davenport demanded complete privacy, a couple bedrooms and the toilets.

What had she told Davenport?

I advise against it, but you're paying the freight and that makes you the boss.

That's what—

What Davenport wanted to hear.

With all their clients, what they wanted to hear invariably worked better than the truth.

Something caught Keshawna's attention. She filled the screen with the area around the guard's post at the main entrance off Mulholland. Peppi Blue had stopped pacing. He'd plucked the filter tip from his windpipe, crushed it under his foot, and was now hurrying toward the gate.

Saying something to the driver in the Beamer that had just pulled up.

Pointing the driver up the hill.

Coming around and getting into the car.

The light of late afternoon and the camera angle had combined to obscure the face of the driver. Keshawna wasn't quick enough with the adjustments to catch a look before the Beamer headed for the mansion. She keyed in a close-up on the license plate and clicked off a picture.

The Beamer angled into a parking slot. Peppi helped the driver from the car, took her by the elbow, and guided her up the stairs and through the main entrance. It was a her, that part for certain; she appeared to be a black woman. Tall. Slender. The confident stride of an athlete or a model.

Keshawna remembered when she walked that way. So long ago, so much younger.

Keshawna Keyes, queen of the Jefferson High campus.

Keshawna Keyes, star of Jeff High's basketball team.

She shook her head free of ancient history.

She switched over to the interior cameras. She caught Peppi and the woman as they rounded a corner directly off the vestibule. She fumbled the keystrokes that brought in the cameras around the turn, made the correction and made the turn, but those few seconds had proven costly.

Peppi and the woman had disappeared.

Keshawna quickly ran through all the interior cameras once, then again; the second time with all the sound probes at peak. However it had been made to happen, Peppi and the woman were gone.

She ran playbacks. After fifteen minutes, halfway through the angles, her eyes growing red with strain, something again caught her attention on the live feed. The company Mercedes, Josh pulling to a stop across Mulholland Drive, fifteen or twenty yards west of the entrance gate.

Chapter 25

Josh waited for a break in the traffic and triple-timed across Mulholland Drive to the guard station at the entrance to Davenport's villa. It was not yet five o'clock, but the rush hour was already underway on the twenty-one miles of hairpin twists and turns along the peaks and canyons of the Santa Monica mountains and the Hollywood hills, connecting east to west, the city with the San Fernando Valley. The sky couldn't decide between dusk and darkness. Views that were staggering by day were only now electrifying into the carnival of light that nightfall would bring.

Earl Pulliam was in the booth, hunched over a paperback, a CD player plugged into an ear and drawing strength from a bag of potato chips; oblivious to the images the roving security cameras were popping onto his monitors and, worse, Josh's noisy twig-crunching, pebble-kicking approach.

Pulliam was another of the cops who had scrammed the Blue Crew before IA could tag him with anything more serious than the occasional rousting of a street hook in the service of recreational lust, a habit not exclusive to him.

Inside talk credited Pulliam with more serious offenses, drug-peddling and murder among them, but no one willing to step up and take the rumors outside the Blue Wall of Silence, maybe because his rabid disposition would place him first in any man's "Mr. Keep Him the Hell Away from Me" competition.

Josh considered him a loudmouth and a blowhard, a festering

hemorrhoid who delighted in bending rules and breaking necks, a bully who took special delight hammering on ghetto kids for real or invented reasons, always bragging how he was providing a public service by teaching them what to expect if they grew up into gangstas peddling sex, drugs, street violence, and death. Explaining with overblown Messianic passion how he was performing a public service, doing his bit to alleviate crowded conditions in the state's prisons and jails.

Josh had never forgotten how a seventeen-year-old Pulliam arrested for speeding and parked overnight in a division holding cell, who had screamed non-stop at his treatment by "that brain-damaged Gestapo cop," turned up dead the next morning. The M.E. ruled it a suicide by hanging, but there was a civic outcry bordering on another Watts Riots. The boy's body was exhumed and an autopsy resulted in a coroner's jury finding of death by choke hold.

Suspicion fell on Pulliam, who'd hung around after his shift ended, but that was as close as a Review Board could get to implicating him. When he was asked what a detective was doing pulling over someone for speeding, Pulliam gave out one of his smug looks of disbelief and said, "Sir, any crime is a crime, no matter how insignificant, and law enforcement officers are on duty twenty-four hours a day."

Before Josh joined up with her, Keshawna and Pulliam had worked plainclothes together out of Hollywood Division. Pulliam transferred out after a locker-room flare-up that sent another detective away on long-term disability with a busted jaw. Publicly, Keshawna refused to discuss the incident. Privately, she defended Pulliam and made a joke of the incident, telling anyone who asked: "It was a righteous bust," but volunteering no specifics.

Keshawna brought her ex-partner on board at International Celebrity Services the same week he quit the department, insisting to Josh his tactical savvy and skills more than offset any downside risk. She made it her personal brief to keep him in line, a task that sometimes tried her patience, but never enough to earn him a pink slip.

Josh tolerated Pulliam for a wholly personal reason:

Pulliam cried at Katie's memorial service.

At the home gathering afterward, his eyes still flushing tears, he worked his way over to Josh and the children. He hugged Josh warmly, then got down on his haunches to spend some comforting thoughts on Justin and Julie. Something about Pulliam made the kids uncomfortable. They yanked their hands free of his and headed across the room to Connie.

Rising, he drew a heavy breath, gripped Josh by the shoulders, and said, "You were so lucky to have as wonderful a wife as I always heard from Keshawna and all spoke about today. She'll be as welcome up there in Heaven as surely as she'll be missed here on Earth, so that's got to be a great comfort."

"Thank you, I appreciate . . . ," Josh said, unable to shake loose of Pulliam, who wasn't done.

Pulliam's smile grew strained and a darkness settled behind his steel-rimmed eyeglass frames. "Did it myself five times, Josh. Five times. Every time I got myself a dud, along with three or four kids you'd never spot in a pig litter. They all can't be a Katie Sunshine."

He wondered then and often since if Pulliam meant any of it, but he had cried.

He had cried.

He needed to believe everyone's tears, even Earl Pulliam's, were as real as his own.

Josh tapped on the booth to get Pulliam's attention.

Pulliam shunted his specs down the bridge of his nose, over a hump that never set properly after the bone was broken in an after-hours barroom brawl at Code Seven, a cop hangout on Broadway within walking distance of Police Central, and looked up from his paperback. He registered surprise, then signaled recognition with a salute at the forehead, removed the ear plug, and joined Josh at the counter.

"Hey, boss, how they hanging?"

Pulliam, in his mid-thirties, still had the Marine-toned body and buzz cut he'd brought with him to the LAPD training center, a muscular physique he emphasized by buying his drab olive security outfits a size too small. A perched goldfish kind of mouth that made it seem he was always getting ready to spit a pit. A bulldog's neck with a long, scabrous white scar not entirely hidden behind the bandana knotted cowboy style he wore like a body part.

He didn't wait for an answer. "Mine, too," he said. "Your son and daughter?" Trying to make it sound as if he cared.

"Fine. Thank you."

"Healing ain't no one-night stand." That smooth farm-boy drawl somewhere out of the South.

"No." Josh short-circuited their feigned pleasantries after another minute. "I see the cameras are working again," he said.

"As exciting as watching the grass grow, but not all. We still can't connect inside the place. Checking up, that what brings you here, or you get lonely for my company, boss?" A dismissive tone to his forceful baritone.

"Ideas why?"

"Davenport probably ain't finished boffing the chick."

"What's that about?"

"Some black beauty in a BMW. Minute she pulled up, Peppi Blue was here to hurry her up."

"You log her?"

"Instructions from on high not to. Same as we're to keep out anybody else and keep our own distance for the duration, or until we hear otherwise."

"The Beamer's license. You get that?"

"You see any peach fuzz on my face?" Pulliam wheeled around, tore the top sheet off a memo pad and handed it to Josh. "Ran the plate to whack some time."

The Beamer was registered to Dead Dogg Records.

At once, Josh figured he knew who the driver was:

Princess Lulu.

Davenport had sailed through his face-off with EZ-XTC well enough to connect with her.

Pulliam said, "You look like bells're going off in your belfry, boss."

Josh ignored his curiosity. He turned to head back to the Mercedes, saying, "I think I'll drive up there and see what's keeping the systems shut down."

Pulliam called after him, "Think again, boss."

Josh quit mid-step and wheeled around. "Meaning?"

"Told you they told me nobody else gets in and through until I hear otherwise."

"I'm telling you otherwise."

"So you'll have yourself an excuse to try busting me with Keshawna, for ignoring a client's instructions? You're not the first who's tried stunt-fucking me, only not as subtle as some I've come up against." Pulliam baring his famous fangs.

An inward breath caught in Josh's lungs. "What if I order you otherwise?" he said, his face frozen with extreme intensity.

Pulliam seemed to be laughing at him. He said, "You never hear that the customer's always right? I'd need Keshawna to tell me to toss aside the ICS rule book."

Josh said, "And I'm telling you the goddamn gate better be open in a minute, when I come roaring back in the car, or I'm blasting through."

"And I am telling you trespassing is trespassing, *boss.*" Pulliam couldn't have made the word sound uglier.

Josh weaved back to the Mercedes through traffic breaks he created by waving his arms like a distressed crossing guard, almost getting clipped by a westbound Porsche, whose driver had one hand on the wheel and the other clamping a cell phone to his ear.

His own cell sang out while he anxiously gunned the motor, waiting for a chance to break across both lanes and onto Davenport's driveway.

"Josh, thank God, you answered." Connie, her voice drenched in desperation. "It's Rusty Jr. and Justin, Josh. They—"

The phone quit.

Dead battery.

He reached over and popped the glove, hoping to find a charger.

No charger.

He pounded on the horn non-stop, ignoring the cascade of angry honks, mouthed curses, and middle fingers aimed at him and, after six or seven minutes that felt like forever, managed to angle his way into the traffic flow.

Chapter 26

After trying and failing to reach Josh again, Connie Reynolds looked at the telephone like it was her worst enemy. She again gave serious thought to calling the police, again ruled it out. For now, anyway. Not sure why, but hoping her panic was over nothing and the boys safe. Missing. Disappeared. Gone somewhere of their own choosing, but safe. Safe, safe, safe.

The phone rang.

She snatched it up.

"Josh!"

Momentary silence, then—

"It's Niki, Mrs. Connie. Calling again to see if you've heard from them yet."

"Damn it, Niki. Didn't I say last time I'd call you when and if I knew anything?"

She slammed down the receiver.

She hadn't meant to snap, but her nerves had frayed beyond redemption in the almost two hours since Niki's first phone call, wondering what time she'd be arriving with Justin and Rusty Jr., to help organize tonight's family dinner.

"Arriving with—? I don't understand, Niki. Rusty Jr. told me this morning you would be picking him up after school, along with Justin and Julie, so he could check out Justin's new *Star Wars* video game."

"I heard almost the same thing from Justin at breakfast time, Mrs. Connie, only you were taking him home with you and

Rusty Jr., he said, for Rusty Jr.'s new *Star Wars* game. So, I only fetched Julie."

"Niki, Rusty Jr. doesn't have the *Star Wars* game."

"Not Justin, either, Mrs. Connie, not yet. He saving up for it."

Conversation was replaced by a shared panic expressed in silence, neither anxious to vocalize what had to be mutual fear. Children went missing all the time in Los Angeles. Few disappearances had a happy ending.

Connie needed Josh to tell her what they should be doing.

Why she'd phoned him.

What, Josh?

Wait it out a little longer?

Call LAPD and ask for an Orange Alert?

What?

As independent a woman as Connie had always considered herself to be, claimed to be, that was in the rough-and-tumble world of show business. Family was different. Family meant—

What?

What she had growing up, loving and nurturing parents.

What she always coveted for herself—what Katie had found with Josh—instead of falling into the kind of miserable lowlife Russ Tambourine turned out to be.

What she desperately wanted for Rusty Jr., what her son deserved, a father to help him through the hurdles of childhood that a mother alone was incapable of providing. Or, was it only her, not every mother?

She ran a finger through her hair, adding a curlicue to one strand after another.

Those damn kids, like it wasn't already lousy enough she had to sit down with Josh and tell him about Russ's call last night, screaming like a lunatic about Josh's invasion—his word—of his dressing room, blaming her, threatening her with far more violence than she could imagine or had ever experienced at his hands if she didn't immediately call off her lousy rotten excuse for a knight in shining armor. *Wainwright shows his face again, people here ready to rip it off for me,* Russ said, dripping still more venom. *Then it'll be your turn, bitch.*

An hour and a half later, immobilized by worry and another Valium, Connie was startled out of her frozen stare by what sounded like fumbling at the front door. Not sure, she waited until she heard the noise again. It sounded like a key unable to fit into the lock. She pushed out of the armchair and raced from the den, still gripping the framed photo of Rusty Jr. taken for the school yearbook. Someone was alternately pressing the door chime and pounding on the door.

She turned the lock and pulled the door open.

Discovered it was her son standing on the porch.

She shouted his name like it was an answered prayer.

Rusty Jr. looked up at her through unfocused eyes and pushed past her on uncertain legs unsure of a direction.

Connie wheeled around and tracked after him.

She caught him down the main corridor, halfway to his bedroom, and demanded his attention.

"That hurts," Rusty Jr. said, trying to break free of her arm lock.

"Where have you been? Where's Justin?" He didn't appear to understand the questions and continued struggling. "I want answers, Rusty. Answer me."

"Leave me alone and go to Hell," he said.

She released him and slapped his face hard, then again from the other direction, in those actions exhuming herself of anger, frustration, and relief in knowing he was safe.

He made a failed attempt at kicking her. He was wearing a Green Day T-shirt and his arm was now extended in a way that revealed to Connie the all-too-familiar sight of a fresh puncture mark inside his elbow. He was high on something besides life.

He pedaled out of her reach and in seconds was locked inside his bedroom.

Connie pounded on the door, demanding he let her in.

He taunted her through the door, using words and expressions she already knew from her years of taking mental abuse from his father, until he tired of the game and went silent.

Connie slumped to the floor, pleading with Rusty Jr. until her voice gave out; replaced by tears and the sound of her fists desperately pounding the floorboards—

How Josh found her, Connie not sure how much later—

Josh on his knees beside her, lightly patting her face to draw her attention, his face a study in apprehension, saying something about his cell phone and the traffic and her door wide open and what was she doing here like this and what about Justin and Rusty Jr.? Was Justin in there with Rusty Jr.?

Connie pulled herself together and answered his questions, told him everything she knew, about the boys, about Russ, the words gushing from her like a broken fire hydrant.

Josh raced after the phone and was back in a few minutes.

"Niki says Justin got home about half an hour ago," he said, helping her up. "That's all she knows. She can't get a word out of him. I need to go home. Will you be all right?"

How could she answer otherwise?

"Fine. Go."

"Christ. I hate leaving you like this."

"Go, I said. Justin needs his father. I'll call nine-one-one, I have to."

She waited until she was sure Josh had left and turned back to Rusty Jr.'s bedroom door. She pressed her forehead and a palm against it, knocked softly and, putting as much love as she could muster into her words, said, "Rusty, baby, it's your mommy, sweetheart. Let Mommy in, please, won't you sweetheart? Rusty? It's Mommy, baby. . . ."

Chapter 27

When Josh got to him, Justin was sitting on the edge of his bed, feet dangling, bundled inside his arms, staring expressionless across the room at the framed poster of Katie that came out of her final photo session, promoting what would be an engagement she never got to keep at Lincoln Center in New York, "An Evening of Sunshine," a one-woman show encapsulating her entire career in a biographical monologue, photographs, film and, of course, the songs from her catalog of hits, Katie backed by the musicians who'd been with her for years and the New York Philharmonic Orchestra.

The poster, mounted under glass, was the same size as the giant painted billboards that lined the outside walls of Tower Records on Sunset and took up half the wall. The rest of the wall completed Justin's memorial to his mother, several smaller posters and photographs and a shelf with half the Grammys and other awards she'd won. The other half were on a shelf next door, in Julie's room.

The poster frame needed straightening. Josh took care of it, touching Katie's cheek and imagining he felt the warmth of her smooth skin, before settling alongside Justin, sharing the silence while he managed his thoughts. Resisting an urge to lash out at Justin for the deception and disappearing act a relieved Niki had described for him in anxious sentences burnished with frequent thank-yous to *El Dio* for returning Justin home safely.

"I miss her, too," he said, studying Katie's smile and the way she seemed to be reaching out to the audience, returning their love.

Justin nodded agreement.

"Your mom would've grounded you for life, the stunt you pulled today."

No reaction.

"You had Niki scared half to death."

No reaction.

"Want to talk about it? Anything you want to tell me?"

Justin dropped his chin and glanced over his shoulder at him, his eyes surrendering to guilt and unable to land anywhere. "I had to take a taxi home from the mall. Niki had to pay for it. I'll owe her back from my allowance."

"She's not worried about the money. She's worried about other things. So am I. What were you and Rusty Jr. doing at the mall, Justin?"

"Hanging out, you know?"

"I don't know."

Justin took his time answering. "There's this girl we went to meet over there, who wanted to see us again?"

"This girl? From school?"

"No. You remember we went to Uncle Lon's movie at the studio? The party after? This girl came over and said hello to us. She and Rusty Jr. got to talking, so then she said for us to meet her outside in the parking lot?"

A picture was coming together for Josh—

What he'd observed that night, what Niki later told him she had seen.

"That where you got the cigarettes I saw you and Rusty Jr. smoking, from the girl?"

The question put a scare into Justin. "They were Rusty Jr.'s, Daddy. We don't do them a lot, never, and the one she gave him, I only took a puff is all. It tasted funny and made my head spin, so only the one puff. After that, I needed to sit down somewhere and so did Rusty Jr., who let the girl show him how to do it right, she said. So, he did, like he was eating the smoke, what he could, and then he got to acting funnier and funnier."

"Is that when you started touching each other?"

"Besides the cigarettes, you saw that?"

Josh didn't want to reveal it was Niki, not him, further fuel the troubled relationship Justin had with her. "Yes," he said.

"She dared us, the girl, and said she'd show us her thingies and let us touch them if we did. So, we did. Only then she said she could do it better and did we want her to prove it? With her hands and then with her mouth and after it felt real good she said we could do it again soon, maybe at the mall. Maybe even more. She wrote down her phone number and gave it to Rusty Jr. and told him to call."

Josh said, "Tell me what happened at the mall, Justin."

Justin showed reluctance.

Josh ran an arm around his shoulders and patted his thigh. "It's okay, fella. We're doing fine here."

It was the assurance Justin had needed. "We got there and met where she'd told Rusty Jr., and then she took us to where her van was parked on the roof of the parking garage, way back over in a corner. We got inside, and. . . . We got inside, and. . . ." Justin's voice was trembling. He couldn't get the memory out.

Josh said, "And the girl did it again?"

"Only the cigarette before she touched us a little and said what else she was going to do for us. Only, first we had to do something for her. She shows us this needle, Daddy. I know what it meant from seeing it in movies and on TV. I wasn't going to do it, but Rusty Jr. was all for it, like he was showing off for the girl. Calling me out and double-daring me not to be a baby while she was wrapping this rubber tube around his arm. So. . . . So, I said okay I would do it."

Justin emptied his cheeks of air and went quiet.

Josh eased his arm off Justin. He unbuttoned Justin's shirt cuff, but was stopped before he could roll up Justin's sleeve and check for a puncture mark.

"I didn't. I couldn't do it, Daddy," he said. "Rusty Jr. was right. I was chicken. I got out from the van and ran back inside the mall, just walking around and around and thinking what to do next. Finally, I got a cab to drive me home, and I will pay Niki back what I owe her, Daddy, I will."

"You're no chicken, Justin. What you did was very brave," Josh said. "I'm proud of you." His smile drew one of relief from Justin.

"So I'm not grounded?" Justin said.

"Of course, you're grounded," Josh said, and turning to Katie's poster, "but maybe not for life. I'll check it out with Mommy and let you know."

Later, on the phone with Connie, she told him she'd talked her way into Rusty Jr.'s room and he was fine now. Sleeping.

She said, "How about there, you and Justin?"

"Also fine," Josh said. "What's Rusty Jr. told you about the day?"

"Nothing. Not yet. I thought it would be best if I held off until tomorrow."

"I think there are things you should know now." When he finished repeating what he'd learned from Justin, he said, "Rusty Jr. needs help, Con, and the sooner the better, or no telling where his wild streak will take him next."

Later, when the phone rang, Josh thought it might be Connie calling him back.

It was Marilyn Pope—

Her call on a relay from office voice mail, saying: "Hey, there, cutie, you need to do something about your cell phone. It's R.I.P. to the world. How's this for vibes? Just heard from Merv Bannister. He's anxious to pitch me on some extra-special, high-paying gigs. We're meeting tomorrow at my dump. You still want him, you got him."

She recited the time and her address, repeated both, slower the second time. "You care to stick around after he's gone, you can have me," she said, and broke into an insinuating laugh that lasted until the message timed out.

Chapter 28

Marilyn Pope lived south of Wilshire on one of the nondescript streets below the L.A. County Museum of Art, where two-story, four-family apartment buildings lined up like opposing pawns on a chessboard, medieval castles and Spanish-style haciendas and architectural bad ideas that were the rage in the twenties, joined by palm trees tilted by decades of strong winds gusting in from the ocean.

When he got there at three o'clock, Josh discovered the building had been yellow-taped.

Four squad cars and an unmarked were parked in the driveways on either side. A second unmarked and the coroner's meat wagon were parked out front. Nosey neighbors milled around, exchanging gossip among themselves and breathless speculation with the news teams scrambling for coverage.

Josh double-parked behind the "Eyewitness News" truck and headed for a familiar face, Bobby Romanin, a detective he had gone through the Academy with. He was working the street after anyone who might have seen or heard something.

"Business or pleasure?" Bobby said, after they'd shared a fraternal handshake and some glib catch-up.

"Just happened to be in the neighborhood, passing through, and spotted the action. Who's the vic?"

Bobby threw a disbelieving hand at him. "Passing through, my ass. You haven't lost that lean and hungry look, Detective Wainwright. A part-time hooker, a real traffic-stopper of a face and figure, name of Marilyn Pope. Mean anything to you?"

"Nothing," Josh bit down on his back molars to help sustain his noncommittal look. Getting pulled into an official investigation was nothing he needed or wanted. "A john do the dirty deed?" Fishing for details.

Romanin still not fooled, but playing along: "Open to question. The vic's next-door neighbor saw someone who could fit the bill double-time down the stairs about a half hour before waltzing over to share wake-up coffee and doughnuts, their regular morning routine. The door's ajar. Unusual. She goes in calling for Marilyn. Finds her in the tub, wrists slit, bathing in her own blood. So could be suicide or could be the john taking water sports to a new level."

"The john come with ID?"

"None the neighbor could make. Face lost inside a Dodgers cap and shades, a beard and a 'stache that from the sound of it puts mine to shame." He tamped down the salt-and-pepper brush he had sprouted years ago to hide the harelip that put a distinct burr to his voice. "A Cauc, casual dress. Everything else was the usual average this and that. Care to visit the scene?"

"Curiosity handled, thanks, Bobby. I'm late for something."

"No apology before you go?"

"Apology?"

"For treating an old pal like Dickie Dumbbell?"

"Proves what I've always said, Bobby. You're one keen detective."

Bobby called at his retreating backside, "Josh, you better remember you owe me."

Josh fist-pumped the air and answered: "Like an elephant, Bobby."

He would have liked to have eyed the scene, squeezed some specifics out of the coroner, but neither would clarify the contradictions raised by what he had learned from Romanin.

Vic Swank blamed Bannister for Ava Garner's murder, enraged over losing her to Clyde Davenport. Josh knew he was safe in assuming the "john" the neighbor spotted was Bannister, who could have wanted Marilyn out of the way to keep her from blabbing about something she had learned that tied him to Ava's death, except—

Marilyn had told Josh with the same certainty he got from Swank that Bannister was too much of a wimp to kill anyone. She said the killer was Davenport, whom she'd conked senseless after he busted in on Ava's dressing room three-way with Marilyn and Russ Tambourine, went berserk and pulled a gun. That gave Davenport, nut case that he was, a reason to crave revenge against Marilyn, so—

Who was the stronger suspect, the wimp or the wacko?

His preference was Clyde Davenport, of course, but still hadn't made up his mind—the current collection of facts too skimpy—by the time he ramped down to his parking slot in the Century City Towers underground garage.

Marilyn's murder didn't fit the pattern on the Davenport list of eleven deaths linked to "Mr. Magic." The revenge motive didn't work here. Marilyn wasn't one of the artists he worked his mojo on and made into international stars before they left him and ultimately, collectively, helped bring about the downward spiral in his career. She hadn't mentioned any connection to Davenport beyond eavesdropping on the conversation he had with Vic Swank, but—

There was something specific that echoed two of the deaths on the list—

Supposed suicides, in the bathtub, slashed wrists.

Emma Thorne, in her Mayfair mansion, adrift in blood and drugs.

Toenail of Raw Emotion, in his Plaza suite the morning after the last of three concerts at Madison Square Garden, his veins sliced open with a sculptor's precision.

Josh pulled into his reserved space in the Towers garage and headed for the elevator bank. A squeal of brakes and burning rubber said a car was taking a corner too fast. He turned and saw the car veering off the lane, aiming straight for him. He dove out of the way, landing with a thud on the trunk of a Jag, and fell backward onto the asphalt.

Smacking the base of his skull hard.

Bringing on a momentary faint.

The attack car had stopped about fifteen or twenty yards away.

Josh heard the motor being gunned and heavy steps clomping toward him.

He got to the .38 on his hip, was working into a sitting position, when the weapon was kicked from his grip and a Glock shoved against his temple, a voice he couldn't place playing menace for all its worth, telling him: "You best have a wallet, Mercedes man, and it best come with negotiables."

"Inside jacket pocket."

"You get it out for me, real slow like, dig?"

"You'll mistake me for a turtle."

He got the wallet out, handed it over and was rewarded with a gun butt blow to the head that knocked him onto his side and into a fetal position.

A boot crashed down on his thigh.

A kick breezed past his groin and caught ribs, causing his pain to explode violently.

The sound of footsteps retreating.

Seconds later, burning rubber as the car sped away.

Josh stayed curled for he didn't know how long, ignored by passing cars and passers-by on foot, who probably figured him for a bum sleeping off a bender.

He was glad to be alive, glad the Glock hadn't painted a garage wall with his blood, but increasingly convinced as he thought through the attack that this wasn't another of your typical on-the-fly L.A. muggings.

All he'd lost, in addition to some dignity, was his wallet.

It would have been simple in that brief encounter to snare his watch, his cell phone, shake him down for anything else of value, take off with his .38. There were at least two of them, so even the Mercedes.

Only the wallet, though.

Grabbed for show by muggers waiting for him, to deliver a warning from someone about something.

Had to be it.

Who?

What?

Josh's head, all of him, was hurting too much right now for him to stay focused on the questions and whatever else was nagging at him, begging to be remembered. Holding his rib cage to keep it from breaking apart, he struggled to his feet, found and holstered the .38, and aimed for the elevators.

The call came while he was being patched up by the ICS resident paramedic, John Gant, a Special Forces vet who got his basic training in Nam and applied it again in Desert Storm—

Merv Bannister—

Nervous, on the edge of panic, insisting, "We must get together, sir. Soon. Quickly. As fast as possible. A matter of life and death."

"It's already a matter of life and death," Josh said, wincing. It hurt to talk. "Who did you have in mind, specifically, Mr. Bannister?"

"Both of us, sir. You and me."

Chapter 29

Clyde was intentionally late for his meeting with EZ-XTC, confident his was the upper hand this time. That didn't prevent EZ-XTC from answering in kind, with silence for their first five or six minutes together. Settled comfortably behind his desk, shoes off, feet propped on the return alongside a mile-high stack of clear-view files, hands locked behind his head, bloodshot eyes staring placidly at Clyde over the rim of his shades as if his chair were empty.

Princess Lulu's voice serenaded them in non-stop hip-hop pouring from speakers turned Coliseum level, EZ-XTC nodding to the beat, while Clyde nursed a smile meant to disguise his horror at songs that defined a culture but, however brilliant her vocals, defiled the word *music*.

Midway into the next cut, EZ-XTC leaned over and quit the sound.

Acknowledged Clyde's presence by wondering: "You hear anything wrong with that, old- timer?"

"It's nothing I could ever come out of the studio with," Clyde said, confident EZ-XTC would take it for the compliment it wasn't.

EZ-XTC nodded approvingly. "Knew you could be right about something," he said. "Tell you now, it got hit writ all over it, whole damn album. Surefire triple Platinum out of the gate, but telling you something else, Mr. Davenport. That ain't good 'nuff for Princess Lulu, she say."

Clyde knew what was coming, but showed the surprise called for in the game plan he had laid out for his princess.

His princess.

Lulu was his now, not her daddy's, although Ezra Charleson would not find out the full extent of what that meant until it was too late for him to do anything about it.

"What is good enough for her, Mr. Charleson?"

"The jive turkey talk you fed her them five minutes you spent together, so why you pretending otherwise? Where you think you coming from?"

"I left my meeting with her fairly certain there should be a place for Princess Lulu on my Big Buddies of America concert stage, with or without Cake Mouth's participation. A lovely and charming personality to go with her voice."

"Enough with that big bullshit of America fucking talk, dig? She come out laying a rap on me 'bout how she think you're the fucking genius what can make her bigger than big and that goes to show what fools even the smart children can make of themselves not even trying. What you say to her anyhow?"

"How I was convinced of her talent based on what brief performance I'd just heard and would seriously consider using her for the concert. She said thank you, seemed to be familiar with my whole recording history, and said a number of flattering things."

"Convinced after she flattered you up your flabby ass."

"Before. Why you asked me back today, Mr. Charleson? To practice the interrogation techniques you learned during your frequent run-ins with the law?"

"You the dude ready to stand up to a murder rap, not me." He came around the desk and settled in the visitor's chair opposite Clyde, flashed an insincere smile broad enough to display his gold inlays. "Here's the deal, and understand it's for Princess Lulu, not because it's something I want."

"Spell it out and I'll tell you if it's acceptable to me, Mr. Charleson."

"Oh, it'll be acceptable, Mr. Davenport. Fo' shizzel, my nizzel. You can bet your life on it. Guaranteed." EZ-XTC lost the smile to make sure Clyde caught the underlying truth in his claim.

"Why do I think you're threatening me, Mr. Charleson?"

EZ-XTC slapped his palms together. "You are one smart dude. Anything besides your past ever get past you?"

"Nothing to speak of," Clyde said. "Please, Mr. Charleson, share this deal of yours with me. I'm all ears. I'm sure it will be wonderful."

It was everything Clyde expected, the old record industry smoke and mirrors combined with new tricks of the trade developed and perfected by the latter-day suits who respected the bottom line more than the music and ghetto gangstas who quickly began stealing from artists with the same ease and aplomb they'd once used robbing 7-Elevens.

"You produce Princess Lulu," EZ-XTC said, "enough sides for an album after the first single we'll use to introduce her on the Big Fucking Buddies of America concert."

"No interference, my studio. Nobody looking over my shoulder."

"Our studio. It's state-of-the-fucking-art."

"Mine is state-of-mind. My studio."

"Your studio, you pay all production costs, but Dead Dogg owns the masters."

"I own the masters."

"We share ownership of the masters fifty-fifty."

"I recoup all my costs first, from dollar one."

"From dollar one after Dead Dogg recoups all our costs, pressing, distribution, marketing, promotion, the videos, and etcetera costs. You know the drill, Mr. Davenport, so no sense in our reinventing the wheel."

"Or your hustle, trying to sell me the Brooklyn Bridge, Mr. Charleson. You're welcome to recoup, but only after I do, and based on one set of books open for inspection by me or by my designate twenty-four seven."

"So long's your designate ain't the IRS. . . . Dead Dogg keeps all of the publishing."

"Dead Dogg splits all the publishing with Mr. Magic Music."

"Your songs, nothing else. That's fair, Mr. Davenport."

"All songs in which Dead Dogg has an interest, equally, Mr. Charleson."

"This one album only."

"Every music and visual format current or that may come into existence anytime in the future. The world, foreign and domestic."

"Outer space and Mars, throwing them in at no extra expense, Clyde. You want the other planets, you got them, except Pluto, where it belongs to Mr. Walt Disney."

"Appreciate the gift, Ezra."

The sparring went on for the better part of an hour, a give-and-take with neither one conceding any points, frequently revisiting items where they had agreed, this time agreeing to disagree.

There'd be a new agreement reached or new agreement on their old agreement, then they'd move on. Clyde played at it as if he were engaged in serious negotiation, not doing or saying anything to make EZ-XTC consider he was getting less than parity.

A few times, he played out a deal point in a way to give EZ-XTC the impression he had won some small victory. EZ-XTC clearly needed the ego gratification.

Clyde enjoyed practicing some of the old tricks he'd had no recent call to use. He longed to tell EZ-XTC what a fool he was being played for, but that was for later, just as Princess Lulu would learn later that she had been screwed by him more ways than she could possibly imagine from the second she assigned him power of attorney.

She would be enraged at first, but he'd make her see his deception was also in her best interests. He was confident she would love him all the more for it and gladly become his wife. What intelligent woman wouldn't?

Memories of Angel Thompson played out in his mind again.

Angel, saying she was pregnant to excite him into marriage, lying about a baby the same way she lied about her loving him; deceptions meant to segue into his bank accounts more than his life, under California's community property statutes governing a marriage.

A new lie, her supposed miscarriage.

After that, her supposed depression, which he bit into like his favorite chili dog at Pink's, the hot dog stand at La Brea and Melrose, where he'd closed so many of his deals, most famously with Herbie Alpert and Jerry Moss, the "A" and the "M" of A&M Records, while they stood in the customer line that always stretched half a block, no matter the time of day or night.

This was the deal made a star of the late ingrate Skye O'Neal, one Platinum after another on the A&M lot that once had been the studio where Charlie Chaplin turned out his silent movie classics. What was it *Time* magazine had said about him? *Davenport is achieving the same kind of brilliance with sound as Chaplin did with silence, and at the same historic location.* How it would have proved something to his chronically criticizing nag of a mother, to this day neither missed nor mourned by him as much as his father, who didn't need *Time Magazine* to know the truth about his son's musical brilliance.

Her lies and the outcome depressed him more than Angel, only his depression was real. Angel had been the first person of either sex to so utterly deceive him and make a fool of him, respond to his genius with disloyalty. Angel, intelligent, but also cunning and deceiving, whose treachery he could not let go away without punishment.

Clyde turned for counsel to Paul DeCarlo, a master at repaying loyalty with loyalty, who had a strong financial interest in the success of Clyde's musical enterprises.

This was one of the rare times DeCarlo signaled him to quiet. "What I don't know can never come back to haunt me," he said. "Share your problem with Peppi Blue. After that, step back. Always step back, Clyde."

Peppi, even now waiting for him outside Dead Dogg Records, had been at his side, his trustworthy right arm, almost since the day he had led him from DeCarlo's office to their first meeting downstairs in the coffee shop.

Once their agreement was in place, DeCarlo told him, "I want you to have Peppi Blue with you as we begin our adventure together, Clyde. He's young and eager like you, with talent in a different direction, taking care of business with radio stations and record stores that can help guarantee you a hit. You'll make a fine team."

"How's he do that, Mr. DeCarlo?"

DeCarlo closed his eyes to the question, smiled benevolently. "I wouldn't know," he said. "I simply mention to him this and that, and then I step back."

Clyde never once doubted that Peppi was also there to keep DeCarlo informed, but it was a subject he knew better than to raise. Besides, Peppi never disappointed. He took to the phones and the road with every new record Clyde produced, working on an unlimited expense account that could withstand the toughest IRS scrutiny and did, especially in years when the government made headlines investigating the rumor of payoffs in cash, drugs, and merchandise to decision-makers at retail, radio stations, and people at the trades able to manipulate what records made it onto the hit charts, and at what position.

Peppi saw the turmoil Angel had put him through but said nothing until he recognized the rage eating at Clyde's insides was impacting his ability to work.

He told Clyde: "Not all hits are in the record business."

Clyde didn't have to hear more. The rest of Peppi's meaning could be read through the nicotine clouds emanating from the Camel always parked in the corner of his mouth, in Peppi's unblinking eyes. He nodded understanding.

Within the week, Angel was dead to banner headlines around the world, the news stories explaining how she had been run down by a hit-and-run driver after her Porsche incurred a flat tire on an unlit stretch of Benedict Canyon, apparently while Angel was standing in the roadway signaling for assistance. Clyde attended the funeral service and wept openly. His were the largest floral arrangements guarding her casket.

His tears were genuine years later, after Peppi was diagnosed with the throat cancer that would rob him of his voice, replace his larynx with a porthole about the size of a dime where his Adam's apple had been.

Whatever it takes to keep Peppi alive, whatever it costs, Clyde told the doctors. A blank check. No amount too great. No price possible to return the unwavering loyalty with anything but unwavering loyalty.

Peppi learned during the months of post-op rehabilitation how to speak using air as a laxative for words and sentences, by covering the hole with a thumb and sucking air into his mouth through a prosthetic voice box.

He found the sound, a gargled sandpaper growl, ugly and annoying.

He used the hole in his throat to park the cigarettes no amount of arguing could convince him to quit and, with Clyde tutoring him, quickly mastered sign language. Lipreading proved more of a struggle for him, but at Clyde's urging he learned that as well.

He rarely spoke after that.

Back on the road, he made sympathy his ally. He delivered his deal terms in notes scribbled on the spot, the sheet from his pocket pad destroyed immediately after they were agreed to, usually with a flick of his solid-gold Ronson lighter, a Christmas gift from Clyde.

EZ-XTC slapped him on the thigh.

"So, we all done here now and got ourselves an arrangement, Clyde?"

"One of us does, Ezra. Not me, not yet." EZ-XTC traded a puzzled expression for a hand gesture asking him for more. "Your tapes will sit on the shelf for the duration. I don't need you competing, getting in front of what I'm doing for Princess Lulu and what she wants for herself."

"What the duration?"

"If my record stiffs, you're back in business. If it succeeds, and it will—forever. But you get to recoup your investment from the net we're sharing, with a little markup for your time and efforts. The exact percentage to be mutually agreed upon later."

"I say no?"

"I'm gone from here and no hard feelings, leaving you to explain to Princess Lulu what went south between us."

EZ-XTC checked his high-gloss, perfectly manicured nails and worked them over with a thumb rub. "What else you thinking, Mr. Davenport?"

"What you had to be expecting all along, Mr. Charleson. In for a penny, in for a pound. The album goes Gold, I get a second album. Platinum, the third album. Double Platinum—"

He signaled Clyde to stop. "What else?"

"A producer's bonus on every million singles and albums sold."

"What else?"

"My name's on every release, singles and albums. Every piece of print, the labels, album jackets, trade and consumer advertising, videos, everything, my Mr. Magic Music company logo along with Dead Dogg's."

"Nice of you to include me."

"You let me through the door, so it would be rude to slam it in your face."

"What else?"

"Promotion. You take care of your people. Peppi Blue takes care of the rest."

Peppi's name bought a smile from him. "Kind of you to finally get around to offering up something I can stomach along with my grits," he said. "That man's got props. People I respect talk about Peppi Blue like he still King Shit come to making hits happen. What else?"

"You hear anything you can't live with?"

"You, dawg, I catch you trying to fuck me over."

CHAPTER 30

Clyde spelled out the deal he had struck with EZ-XTC heading back to the villa, sitting up front with Peppi, the passenger window open just enough to let fresh air challenge the smoke from his Camel. "The idiot said a handshake works as well as lawyer's paper with him," he said. "I couldn't have agreed any faster or been happier that I didn't have to be the one to suggest it."

Peppi tossed him a glance that said he was troubled by something. He mashed out his cigarette in an ashtray overflowing with butts. He plugged the trach and alternated gulps of air with his foghorn growl, saying, "The girl is. His daughter. Worse than playing. With fire."

"Not the first time I've played with fire, Peppi. I'm not the one who got burned."

"It cost you. Dearly."

"I've told you how many times before, you wouldn't say that if you had known my sorry excuse for a mother. You would have helped me pour the gasoline and set fire to the mattress."

"And your father. Remember?"

"I pleaded with him, begged him, after he wrestled me free of her, but he wouldn't leave without her. That venal creature, her last act on earth was depriving me of the one person I loved most in all the world."

Peppi growled, dismissed Clyde with an angry wave, retreated back to silence.

Shoved a fresh filter tip in his trach and lit up.

Clyde saw no reason to debate Peppi's mindset.

What Peppi was saying now was nothing new.

They'd disagreed at length the other night, after Princess Lulu left Magic Land and he displayed the documents she'd signed, naming him her personal manager and assigning Clyde and Mr. Magic Music full power of attorney over her career.

"Whatever terms I come to with her daddy will be null and void at my option, once I've transferred rights and authorities to our dummy corporations overseas, to the same places where the money will be banked, invisible and beyond anybody else's claim."

Peppi responded with fingers close to flying off his hands.

"Bad business," he signed.

"Bad? It's always proved successful for us in the past. Always."

"She's a smart girl. She agreed too quickly. Signed too quickly. Hopped into bed with you too quickly. What's her game?"

"Game? She knows I can make her the biggest star in the world, that's her game."

"What's her plan, Clyde?"

"Her plan?" He dismissed the question with a wave of his hand. "I plan to marry her, that's my plan."

"And when her father learns this? Those people kill on a whim. Murder to end arguments. Eliminate their competition. For revenge. There's disrespect somewhere and somebody winds up dead."

Clyde made light of it. "That means EZ-XTC and I have much in common. Wouldn't you agree?"

"I'll let you know," Peppi signed, his face furious with disapproval, and fled the bedroom that reeked of Princess Lulu's scent, her cologne—

Clyde's enchantment.

Princess Lulu arrived at the villa within an hour of Clyde's meeting with EZ-XTC.

Following his instructions, she parked at the rear of the estate and entered through an unmonitored security door mostly hidden inside the twelve-foot wall of bush and brick after Peppi buzzed her through. He met her halfway on the cobblestone path that led to his cottage, then downstairs to a tunnel connecting the cottage to the basement level of the main house and into the recording studio booth, quickly retreating as Clyde opened his arms to welcome her.

Their embrace led to a kiss that was long and lingering.

It left Clyde breathless, hungering for more, his hands searching her body for the fastest way inside her jeweled halter top. Princess Lulu helped him, dropping one shoulder strap, then the other. When he still fumbled, she took a step back, removed the halter, and tossed it across the booth. She was braless and beautiful and not about to quit there.

She wriggled out of her stretch jeans and threw them aside, reducing her to a black thong that was gone a moment later, leaving bare more than her intentions.

She ordered him to undress, studying him like a textbook until he was also naked, drew her mouth into a wicked smile, and licked her lips hungrily. "Anyone tell you you're too ancient to board the love boat, you send 'em on to me, Mr. Davenport."

She guided him to the floor and inside her, whispering, "Need to share my happiness over your coming to terms with my old man," her words as intoxicating as her cologne. "More where this is coming from, Mr. Davenport. Lots more."

"It's as if I knew the future would bring you into my life," Clyde told Princess Lulu later. They were seated at the studio soundboard, still naked, temporarily spent, calling it a time-out from celebrating what he had declared "a union of two great talents," listening to a tape reel he'd pulled from the reference cabinet.

The music that attacked them in Quad was classic Davenport Symphony of Sound, only richer, more vibrant, taking unexpected, innovative flight in ways that mixed and matched every mode of music and turned it into something revolutionary and irresistible.

Revolutionary and irresistible.

It was his conclusion, of course, shared and encouraged by every studio musician he had contracted for, the old dependable cats and those who'd followed them, paying double and triple-time to get what he wanted, dismissing any who didn't match his expectations or thought it was their right to offer recommendations or riffs that strayed from what played note for perfect note in his head.

This was the first of a dozen reels he intended for Princess Lulu to hear before sending her on her way.

Late into the first assembled cut, she slipped onto her knees and kissed his feet. "Not that I needed it," she said, "but already I'm hearing new proof of your genius. It's overwhelming and inspiring. I'm honored to be your partner."

Clyde found the use of her word *partner* curious, but employed it to his advantage. "In all things," he said. "Business and—"

She interrupted him. "Pleasure." Gave his toe a playful suck and crawled up onto his lap. "And my Svengali?" she said. Expressed as much as a demand as a question.

He'd intended to say "Life in general," as a preview of his intentions, leaving it at that until their first sides together were completed and in the can, when he'd have her tied completely to him, emotionally and otherwise.

Instead, he said, "Your Pygmalion, my wonderful Galatea."

"A beautiful sentiment, sir. Beautiful words to go with your beautiful music," she said, running a finger around his lips as prelude to a kiss.

"More beautiful words to come tomorrow, the lyrics I wrote and saved all this time for a wondrous voice like yours."

"Now? Can I hear them now?"

"Tomorrow. When we're fresher and more tuned to the task than—"

"Each other."

"Each other."

"Promise?"

"Promise."

"From your lips to mine," she said, and finished the kiss she'd started.

They were interrupted by the bulb-sized red light flashing on the com phone—

The ICS security guard at the front gate saying, "Josh Wainwright is here to see Mr. Davenport?"

Clyde said, "Give it five minutes, then let him through." He reluctantly slid his hand off Princess Lulu's breast and eased her off his lap. "A business meeting that's already been delayed too long," he said, his apology as sincere as his frown.

He gathered up her clothing, turned over the bundle to her and guided her into the private elevator, pressing the button that would take her upstairs to the bedroom.

"I'll make this as brief as possible," he said.

She stroked his cheek and said, "Take all the time you need, Pygmalion. We have all night."

Twenty minutes later, humming the first melody he intended to work on with Princess Lulu, Clyde held for a moment in the den archway, like a stage actor awaiting his entrance due from an anxious audience, before crossing over to the glossy cherry-red leather lounge chairs by the fireplace.

He eased into one and signaled for Wainwright to join him.

"How kind of you to finally find time for your client," he said.

Wainwright plopped onto a bar stool across the room from him. "I tried it last night and was turned away at the guard gate, or you'd have gotten my update then."

"By one of your own employees; how quaint."

"They're trained to follow a client's instructions, however stupid they can be sometimes."

"My time clock, I set the hours. If you'd phoned first, the way I phoned you—and phoned you—maybe a different story."

"Should I go stand in the corner, or do you have a blackboard and chalk and something special you want me to write a hundred times?"

"Take me out of the dark, that's what I want. Tell me what's been going on in your life, looking to save mine when you're not so busy trying to steer me into the gas chamber."

He adjusted the lounger to a reclining position and settled back with his eyes shut, his fingers pressed to his temples, giving over full concentration to what Wainwright had to report and his manner of expressing the news, alert to the slightest adjustment in tone.

At times like these, he supposed most people would be focused on facial expressions for some underlying truth. For him, it was the lyrics. Always the lyrics. Where the hook came in to send a story spinning in a new direction.

Wainwright's reporting was rich in detail, the kind you wouldn't expect in a detective's report, all of it presented matter-of-factly. Nothing about Nashville and the visit with Billy the Kid Palmer's widow set off alarms, until after he paused to work on a handful of almonds and cashews snatched from the crystal bowl on the bar counter.

"One other thing?" Wainwright said, investing his voice with sudden memory, like he'd seen one too many of those old *Columbo* mysteries on television. "Kristy Palmer was positive she heard you say you wanted to re-team Billy with Bluto Parks?"

No cause for denial.

She had said as much on the news.

"I did. Yes. So?"

"Just that, on the graveyard list of your old acts you got me, you had Bluto Parks dead." All Wainwright lacked was an old rumpled trench coat.

"I did." Clyde moved the lounger back to an upright position and opened his eyes to the question on Wainwright's face. "For a good reason. Bluto Parks is dead."

"We both know that you perform magic bordering on miracles in a recording studio, but you'll have to explain that one to me. Billy the Kid and Bluto the Corpse?"

"I told Billy what I did as encouragement, give him greater hope for a future that would take him out of his wretched present. I intended to use a vocal doppelganger. A sound-alike. I own all the rights to the act and the name, lock, stock, and Bluto. Bringing in a voice double, it's done all the time. Somebody quits or dies, somebody else takes over to keep the franchise alive. Like Sam and Dave, you remember them? Sam Moore quit the act. Dave Prater went back on the road with Sam Daniels. Dozens of stories like that."

"So, that's who called her?"

"Called her?"

"On her answering machine when she got back to Nashville from her new home in El Paso. Bluto, alive and kicking and enthusiastic about reuniting with Billy the Kid. That also a doppelganger? Bluto Doppleganger?"

Clyde answered him with a look of disbelief.

At the same time his mind racing after some acceptable response.

He said, "Not of my doing or knowledge. He's dead and that's that. Why he was on the list."

"And you know that for a fact because—?"

"Ray Gray. A past president of the Recording Academy. I cut some profitable publishing deals with him while he was running the Lamplighter Music catalog for Barry Frost. Ray starts every morning with a bowl of Raisin Bran and the *Times* obituary page. Then makes sure all his friends know. I took Ray's word on it. No reason to do otherwise."

"So, maybe, he confused Bluto Parks with another Bluto Parks? Such a common name. You mind if I check this out with Mr. Gray, to keep the loose ends from getting any looser?"

"Doing that would make you the miracle worker, not me, Josh. Clearly you don't follow the obituaries. Dear, wonderful Ray Gray suffered a heart attack and went up to that Great Music Company in the Sky two months ago."

Clyde caught the corners of Wainwright's tight-lipped mouth tilting upward briefly and ever so slightly, as if resisting a deserved show of appreciation for the quickness of his mind. He threw a look at Peppi, who seemed to be more interested in fitting a fresh Camel into his trach hole than in the conversation.

Wainwright said, "I'll check it out for myself later, how's that?"

"Be sure to let me know," Clyde said. "Let's move on."

"You're the client," Wainwright said, in condescending singsong that retracted into a "Just the facts" monotone, like Jack Webb on *Dragnet* instead of Peter Falk as Columbo. "I visited with Vic Swank over at Uncensored Productions, to talk about Ava Garner."

"Vic phoned afterward, told me about your chat. I've done a good deal of work for the company. We enjoy an excellent relationship and have for some time."

"So he said. He thinks Merv Bannister killed Ava, not you."

"A man after my own heart. Did he explain why?"

"Gladly. How Bannister and Ava were some kind of an item and Bannister went ballistic shortly after the *National Search for Miss American Showgirl* pageant, where you were a judge and judged her as someone worth possessing."

"Managing. I became Ava's manager and mentor. Not her murderer. She was meant for great stardom, and I'd have brought her remarkable gifts out of her as completely as I did for so many others, including"—a face-lifting smile—"Katie Sunshine."

He could not resist the jab. Enjoyed seeing Wainwright wince.

Wainwright instantly struck back. "Marilyn Pope, unlike Swank, thought you were the guiltiest son of a bitch who ever walked the planet."

Clyde held onto his cool like a subway strap. "The receptionist at Uncensored? She the new authority on guilt?"

"Not anymore. She's dead. Neighbor found her this morning."

"I didn't know."

"You should get out of the studio more often, or whatever it is keeps you occupied, Davenport. Slit wrists in the tub, a lot like two names on your list—"

"Toenail. Emma Thorne. What are you saying, Marilyn Pope is another one of my supposed victims?"

"A comment on coincidence. For now looking like a suicide. Why? Some reason you might want Marilyn dead?"

"I don't know of one, do you?"

"Might have, if she'd been able to keep the meeting she wanted with me. I got to her place too late for that."

Clyde heard a fresh cadence in Wainwright's voice. Slight, but enough to know he was slowing down his words to keep them from racing ahead of his thought process. Withholding or inventing information? Not enough yet to tell.

"More to the point, did she tell you what might be the reason behind her thinking I killed Ava?" Casual. Important not to appear overly concerned, give Wainwright reason to believe the switch-hitting whore meant anything to him.

"Not really," Wainwright said, after two too many beats. "Only that Bannister also would be at our meeting, to explain why he couldn't have killed Ava. No sign of him when I got there."

He was definitely holding back on something, but not quite making an art of his silence, like he was taking Clyde's measure.

"What else?"

"Russ Tambourine?"

"Sang a pair of numbers on *National Search for Miss American Showgirl.* Flat and off-key. The talent of a dead dormouse. Perfect for the tourist trade in Vegas. What about him?"

Wainwright jutted his lower lip and wagged his head.

"Then I have business to get back to. Let's resume when you have more news for me," Clyde said, working up from the lounger. He directed Peppi with his chin to come out from behind the bar and escort Wainwright.

Halfway to the hallway, Wainwright snapped his fingers and threw his hands away. "There was something else," he said, playing Columbo again. "Marilyn mentioned how she eavesdropped on phone conversations. Something about overhearing you and Swank talking about me and Bannister? Ring any bells, Davenport?"

"I told you. Vic called me after you left."

"I got the impression from Marilyn that she meant a conversation you had before I sat down with Swank."

"In which case, I don't know what she was talking about."

"More the shame Marilyn getting herself dead and Bannister disappearing before I could clear that one up for us."

For us. Cute. Was Wainwright turning into more of a liability than an asset? He'd discuss it with Peppi, but first—

Wainwright gone—

Clyde fished out his cell phone and called Vic Swank.

Chapter 31

Josh followed the roofless tunnel of an entrance walkway into the central courtyard of the Museum of Art, a set of buildings suffering from an acute case of architectural disharmony. The area was decked out with rows of folding chairs arranged theater style for a jazz concert starting shortly on a stage of makeshift risers.

Almost all the seats were taken, as well as those at the metal picnic rounds behind them, by patrons enjoying quickie meals purchased from vending carts scattered about the area under a cloudless sky and an unseasonably warm evening breeze.

Merv Bannister wasn't hard to spot in the crowd.

He had settled at a table on the aisle that gave him a commanding view of the entrance and put him on full display. He was signing autographs for fans who knew him from television and posing for photos with owners of picture-snapping cell phones.

Josh headed over, chuckling. So much for the fear Bannister had spent on his phone call, labeling their meeting a matter of life and death. Bannister was not the first celebrity he had met whose ego raged supreme and danger be damned.

Bannister passed back a signed napkin to a blue-haired woman gurgling with delight, adding a double-barreled smile and a thank-you, before looking up and extending his hand in Josh's direction, as if expecting the next piece of paper for his signature. A puzzled look replaced the smile, followed by a polite, "I'll need something to write on."

"I'm Wainwright," Josh said.

Hearing the name brought back his big smile. "Yeah, right. Of course. Grab that empty chair, saved it for you, and a glass of schnapps while I finish up with my fans." He pointed to the carafe of red wine on the table, then took a dollar bill from the next fan in line, wondering, "Who should I sign this to, dear?"

This went on for another ten minutes, while the sky turned from a luminescent blue and orange to charcoal and a full moon drew fresh support from floodlights on stanchions. Bannister signed a last autograph and retired the smile as the five-piece combo on stage finished tuning up and eased into something mellow out of the Duke Ellington songbook.

"I thought of this place because it was close to poor Marilyn's," Bannister said, like he was Columbus reporting on America. "Interesting. You ever been?"

"Often," Josh said. "Bring my kids here."

"Yeah, I suppose. Been wandering around, checking it out, ever since I got hold of you. A lot of paintings don't make any sense to me, but there they are."

"And here we are, Mr. Bannister. Tell me about our matter of life and death."

"Right," Bannister said.

"But, first—did you kill Marilyn?"

"Jesus fuck no," he said, jolted into loud reality that brought on harsh stares and hush requests from some of the surrounding tables. His eyes wandered anxiously, and his fingers began tapping out a tone-deaf beat to the music. "I had no reason—I found her like that, I got there. I got the hell out of there, in case they were coming back for me. Or for you and me."

"They knew about the meeting? Who? Who are *They?*"

"Whoever he put up to it, the way he put them up to killing Marilyn for what she knew?"

Josh raised his voice to be heard over the jazz combo, which had moved into something louder and more raffish that sounded a lot like Coltrane struggling on an uncooperative alto sax. "Who's *He?* What did Marilyn know?"

"That prick Swank. Vic the Prick Swank is who, that lying, treacherous bastard."

As far as Bannister got before excusing himself to deal with a fan who had approached the table. He pasted on the celebrity smile, held out his hand for whatever it was he'd be signing, only—

It was not a fan, and—

The man was holding a small silenced pistol.

The popping sound was buried under the jazz landslide emanating from the stage.

The shot caught Bannister in the right eye. It passed through his skull and whizzed into the asphalt aisle, along with a splatter of blood and bone. Showing the final surprise of his life, Bannister slumped forward. His head crashed onto the table and knocked the wine carafe over. The carafe rolled onto the ground and shattered.

The shooter twisted and aimed the pistol at Josh.

Josh closed his eyes to the inevitable.

Instead, something landed in his lap.

He reached for it blindly.

Caught himself gripping the pistol.

Raised it, drawing a reaction from people suddenly aware of something amiss, growing noisy and disrupting the performance, as Bannister fell from the chair.

Josh jumped up, searching for the shooter while accusing fingers pointed at him. He elbowed free of two guys acting brave on thoughtless impulse and turned the pistol on them. Trading in stupid for smart, they backed off. So did others who appeared tempted to corral him.

He thought he saw the shooter turn a corner at the far end of the Hammer Building, onto the path to the sculpture garden stairway. He chased after him, waving the pistol and shouting threats to clear the courtyard aisle. The shooter was heading down the steps to the garden.

Josh picked up the pace, refusing to acknowledge the new pain to his damaged ribs. He stumbled, fell, rolled the rest of the way down the stairs, and crashed on the grass at the base of a monumental Rodin sculpture. He used the base to struggle back onto his feet.

The shooter had reached the far end of the garden, near the entrance gate of the tall chain-link fence topped by barbed-wire coils. Instead of using it to escape to the side street, he turned in the opposite direction, disappeared behind a giant Henry Moore sculpture of horizontal lovers.

Josh filled his lungs with second wind, then another deep breath.

He got a two-handed shooter's grip on the pistol, inched forward with extreme caution. He reached a safe corner of the sculpture and prepared himself for a snap turn, praying he would not wind up facing the shooter's backup. Moved with the old battle cry kind of cop yell meant to startle a suspect off his mark and—

Found himself staring down two young kids in a clinch.

The teenaged boy he had been pursuing yanked his hands and lips off the teenaged girl and tossed them in the air, his eyes bursting with fear. The girl begged Josh not to shoot them.

Whoever the shooter was, this boy wasn't him.

Josh waved them to calm down.

He jammed the pistol inside his belt and fled through the fence gate.

Josh hoofed it to The Grove, aiming for the old Farmers Market complex at Third and Fairfax, using a maze of residential back streets, en route phoning an SOS to Keshawna. She found him about an hour later at the pit barbecue stand they frequented in their detective days, wolfing down chicken and ribs to thwart the food lust that attacked him whenever his adrenaline was pumping.

"The kill was all over the radio heading here," she said. "There's an all-points alert for someone named 'Armed and Considered Dangerous.' " She went for a chunk of rib that had fallen off the bone and was drowning in a pool of grease. Aimed it carefully into her mouth. Washed it down with a swig of his bottled water. "A scatterbrained description the Blues got from two kids he threatened within an inch of their make-out session sounded a lot like you."

" 'A lot' how?"

"About your height and weight, maybe a little taller or shorter, heavier or not so heavy and vaguely good-looking."

"Vaguely?"

"That should be enough to keep the Blues off your scent. And both kids said Hispanic. Was the light that lousy at the museum or is there something about your heritage you never mentioned, señor?" She peeled off some chicken and dipped it in grease, worked that over and went for the water again. "Eyewitnesses to the shooting yet to be heard from, so you're not free and clear." She found another piece of rib. "Two corpses in one day. You should consider hiring yourself out as a jinx."

Josh pulled the cardboard food container out of Keshawna's reach. "Bannister gave up a name before he got hit, Keesh."

That took the laugh track out of her. "Anybody we know?"

"Vic Swank."

"For what? Offing Marilyn Pope? Ava Garner? Both?"

"The name. Far as Bannister got before the big bang."

"So it means nothing, the name. No more than before."

"Not yet."

"Going to visit Swank again?"

"Thinking about it."

"What else you thinking about?"

"Johnnie Collier. Was thinking about that one waiting for you. If you had given me the full name, Johnnie *Lucille* Collier, I might have zeroed in on the right sex and guessed sooner it was Ann Miller."

"All's fair. . . . Could tap dance up a storm, that girl." She inched toward the ribs.

He slapped her hand. "Also, wondering if Davenport had anything to do with the hit on Bannister. Bannister played it like an iceberg, but I spotted concern when I said Marilyn listened in on his conversations with Vic Swank and how Bannister was supposed to show up at her place with things to tell me."

"I monitored you and Davenport sparring."

"I left Davenport thinking, hoping Bannister might know something that would pin Ava's murder on our client and hold up in court."

"Not what Davenport's paying us to find out."

"To protect and serve is LAPD. We're being paid to find out the truth."

"The real truth, Joshua, not the truth as you'd like it to be."

He wasn't up to another round of philosophizing with her.

He said, "Davenport and me sparring, and what else did you monitor?"

"Trade you for a rib."

He pushed the carton over.

She gave him one of her silly victory smiles and took her time picking the largest rib left.

"Princess Lulu there before you showed your vaguely good-looking face," she said. "She disappeared after that. One minute she's in the recording studio with Davenport. Next minute—poof! The system goes to black. The overrides are useless. We were in the dark until you turned up at the gate. She's still there for all we know. You left and the monitors went down again."

"Why am I thinking it has to be more than system bugs?"

"Either that or Davenport not only mastered the shutoffs, but added some nuances of his own for reasons of his own. I have the team quietly trying to sort out the problem at our end. So far, no answers and no solution."

"My money says Davenport's definitely hiding something, Keesh."

"Princess Lulu and what else? He was meeting at Dead Dogg Records about the time of Marilyn Pope's demise, so he's got clean hands if the suicide turns out to be murder."

"Clean hands, but bodies keep falling around him."

She tilted an eyebrow upward. "You tell Davenport you were meeting Bannister at the museum?"

"I forgot that part."

She gave him one of her *I ain't buying it* looks. "Even if you had, Davenport didn't have time to set the hit in motion."

"Unless it already was in motion. Unless he already had somebody on my tail, like those specimens who came at me in the garage."

"What for? He has us hired, you, hustling to cut him out from under a murder charge and paying dearly for the privilege, so why pull that shit?"

"The hire as cover-up for his true intent, to see my name carved on a grave marker when he's good and ready? Meanwhile, good-bye, Merv Bannister, as a precaution. Alibi in place, Mr. Magic off somewhere else doing something else when the evil deed is done. It's been one of his trademark constants, one death after the next."

"I might buy Bannister, but explain if you can why he'd want you dead, Joshua."

"He doesn't like me?"

"Besides the obvious."

Josh worked through the question sucking on a drumstick. "I found out something, I know something, that can finally put him down for one or more of the deaths decorating his past," he said, nodding agreement with himself. "Closer than I've ever gotten, and he's decided that's too close for comfort."

"Like what?"

"Like I don't know what, Keesh, any more than you can tell me Michael Douglas' real name."

"Why do I think that's a trick question?"

"Because it's a trick question. Practice for the trick I have in mind to play next."

"You going to share that trick with me?"

"The ribs and the chicken—I've shared enough with you for one day."

Chapter 32

Keshawna told Josh she would be calling it quits for the day, aiming for the gym after she dropped him off at the Mercedes and hung back long enough to satisfy herself nobody was on his tail, but—

She had something else in mind.

Nothing she cared to share with Josh.

Not yet.

Not the biggest secret she'd ever kept from him, but it brought on that old lousy feeling anyway, like an ulcer drawing blood while it devoured another chunk of her soul.

Josh's tricks were always playful, like the latest Chapter in their name game. *Michael Douglas.* Not Michael Douglas, whose father, Kirk Douglas, was born Issur Danielovitch Demsky. Some other actor, who had to change his name the way Stewart Granger became Stewart Granger because the movies didn't need a second James Stewart.

Her tricks?

Not so playful.

The biggest one of all, hidden to spare him pain and her shame and—

She bop-honked Josh good-bye and maneuvered her Boxster in the direction of Magic Land, using Crescent Heights and Laurel Canyon to get to Mulholland Drive, a route that put her at the tag end of bumper-to-bumper insanity caused by a four-car rush-hour pileup.

She reached the villa and did a drive-by that included the narrow service road up around the property, slowing when she spotted the BMW that had showed up on Pulliam's log with Dead Dogg Records registration. She moved ahead another twenty or third yards, around a downhill bend; parked and doubled back on foot, tracking the tall hedge with her Maglite until she located the answer to a suspicion—

A door sufficiently obscured that it had been missed by the ICS setup crew.

Judging by its location, the door backed the caretaker's cottage.

Took a keypad code to open.

Keshawna tried the handle and gave the door a modest shove. Whoever had used it last was sloppy and hadn't shut it all the way. The door slid open silently on lubricated hinges. She shielded the Maglite's beam with a hand and slipped onto the property, leaving the door slightly ajar.

She was right about the cottage. Dark, except for light burning through the drawn shade of a downstairs window. Peppi Blue in residence? The possibility suspended an itch to head up the cobblestone path and test the cottage door.

Keshawna moved off the path onto the lawn, intending to follow the wall around to the main house, when the light overhanging the door blazed on.

She darted behind the nearest oak and snapped off the Mag.

Pressed hard against the tree trunk.

Struggled to regain control of her breathing, now almost as loud as the sound of the cottage door opening.

Footsteps on the path headed for the door in the wall.

She rolled herself around the trunk to keep out of sight.

The footsteps stopped.

She dared a peek.

Peppi Blue and Princess Lulu, her punctuating whatever she was telling him with girlish laughter.

He released her elbow and was about to work the keypad code when he saw the door was ajar and pointed it out to her.

She shrugged and gestured an apology.

He pulled the door open.

She gave him a hug and a kiss on the cheek and disappeared.

He closed the door, tested it with a pull, and punched in a code.

Starting back for the cottage, something made him stop. He worked his head like a tank turret and appeared to sniff at the air, one short snort after another, as the pale starlight showed off the expression of uncertainty that had formed on his face.

Keshawna decided it had to be her damn perfume. She dug her nails into the trunk and felt one nail, then another, break under the pressure. Droplets of sweat dribbled down from her forehead and stung her eyes.

Peppi fished for his pack of cigarettes.

He popped one into his trach hole and put a lighter to it, let the smoke stream from the corners of his mouth while he studied the trees for—

What?

The source of whatever it was he thought he smelled?

Damn it, damn, damn.

Keshawna stopped breathing, certain he'd be crossing over for closer investigation any second. And if he caught her—

She had her reasonable explanation in mind, ran through it again, how she'd come to personally check out the security system and hopefully locate the flaw that kept causing it to break down. Tracking the perimeter, she found the door and—

Peppi fieldstripped the cigarette and headed back for the cottage.

Keshawna allowed herself ten minutes to regain her composure and started for the wall, quit after a few steps, remembering Peppi had coded the door. She would have to get out using the front gate.

Turning, her cheek connected with cold steel, not the first time she'd felt the mouth of a gun barrel pressed against her skin. Against a blinding light burning into her eyes, she extended her arms in surrender. In return, she got a smug grunt and an equally self-satisfied voice telling her, "The old days, boss, I could have figured your Mag for a weapon and dropped you on the spot."

It was Earl Pulliam.

"The old days, I was black enough you wouldn't need an excuse to drop me, plant your backup, and get away with it," Keshawna said. "Get the damn light off me."

Pulliam holstered his .45 and clicked off his Mag.

"Gone are the good old days," he said, making light of it, but she knew how capable he was of the game. His jacket was full of accusations, but never enough proof to put him away.

"You sneaking in here, how'd you pull that one?" he said, looking around for the answer.

Keshawna indicated the gate. "We screwed up on the security blanket. We're getting it corrected."

Pulliam gave the gate a once-over before deciding: "The bigger screw-up was our going along with the nut case client insisting no twenty-four-seven foot patrol as part of our coverage," barely disguising that superiority he was always trying to hoist over her. "What brought you back here anyway? Not exactly like you'd get turned away at the front gate."

"Like you did with Josh Wainwright."

"He's the one more likely to bust rules, not me, boss. Remember?"

"Dealer's choice, Earl. Anybody you turn away since then?"

"Anybody you got in mind?"

"The black woman who showed up in your report, in the BMW belonging to Dead Dogg Records?"

"The latest looker Davenport's probably sticking it to?" He shook his head. "Any encores going on with that black beauty, not on my watch, boss. Why her in particular?"

Nothing made it Pulliam's business. She shook off his question by posing her own: "What took you away from your post?"

"The nut case himself. On the intercom saying how his mute sidekick thought he might've heard something going on behind his cottage. So, here we are. Proof Blue's dumb, not deaf."

"But nothing else?"

"Like what else, boss?" The question toned with an itch of suspicion. Pulliam could find a conspiracy in a cough; equated being kept out of the loop with a personal insult.

She said, "Escort me to the villa, Earl. Let's show Davenport how well you deliver the goods," certain Pulliam would like hearing that more than he'd care to question her generosity.

"Never the one to ever let you down, boss, not me," Pulliam said, giving her a mobile thumbs-up.

Clyde Davenport joined her in the den.

"Wainwright and now you," he said. "So unexpected. So, why? Could it possibly be to make up for lost time in getting back to me with the state of my well-being, Miss Keyes?"

"Nothing works better than an apology in person," Keshawna said.

He accepted her answer with the condescending smile and floating hand gesture of a generous Caesar that quickly vanished. "Which, of course, doesn't explain your feeling it was necessary to sneak in through a back door. I hate to think what might have happened if Peppi, instead of telling me about a possible intruder, had armed himself and headed off to check for himself, and in the dark mistook you for the person who came after me the time before."

He glanced past her shoulder at Peppi, who was sitting quietly behind the bar and looked up from a *Ring Magazine* long enough to nod a brief agreement.

"You're right. I also apologize for that," she said.

"Correctly so."

"But shouldn't you apologize, for hiring us to protect you, then hiding gates, tampering with our installations, and making it impossible for our monitoring systems to monitor the way they should?"

Davenport blew noisy air out the side of his mouth. "Not as long as I'm paying for the privilege. I let you pry where and as I like when I like."

"Those conditions, how do you expect ICS to do its job properly, guarantee your safety?"

"Start by getting me out from under the shadow of my dear Ava's murder? Maybe begin by asking Wainwright to stop charging me with every death that comes along, the new one being the receptionist at Uncensored Productions who committed suicide earlier today?"

"Marilyn Pope."

"Her."

"I'll discuss it with him."

Davenport signaled approval, pushed out of the lounger, and straightened his robe. "It's late and I've had a long, tiring day."

She wanted to tell him, *Fucking and doing God knows what else to someone a fraction of your age can do that to your body, if not your soul.* Maybe one day she would. For now, it would have to be enough telling him, "Before leaving, I need to check out our surveillance systems, to verify they're back on track."

His stare froze on hers briefly. She knew he was searching for some other motive, but she'd had too much practice at these hide-and-seek games over too many years to fear he'd see through her enough to recognize he was right.

"They're back on track," he said, with a finality as sure as the word *Good-bye*.

"Where I come from, seeing is believing," she said.

"Why I had your technicians show me before they departed. I've seen. I believe."

"They don't sign off until I sign off, any more than you would allow anyone in the studio telling you when your sound levels and all that good stuff was where it belonged."

Davenport fussed over his robe and tucked his hands inside his elbows. "You're quite the consummate professional, as advertised," he said. "Peppi, please escort Miss Keyes to the door," he said, at the same time speaking to him with his fingers. "After she's satisfied herself that our security system is back on track." As if it were his demand of her.

Peppi waited until Davenport had left the den and started up the hallway staircase before setting down his magazine and coming out from behind the bar. He filled his trach with a filter-tipped cigarette and put a lighter to it, waiting for instructions.

"The A Box and master panel by the entrance door, as good a starting place as any," she said.

She fiddled with the box and the panel more than necessary, adjusting and readjusting beyond what had to be done to keep her ISO home and private office monitors on track even when Davenport thought he was shutting down the entire surveillance system. The show of diligence was for his benefit, on the likelihood he now was settled at a monitor checking her progress.

Next, she moved from the vestibule to the corridor she'd seen Princess Lulu and Peppi take before they had disappeared like a magician's trick from her office monitor. Nothing along the art-lined walls revealed how that slight-of-eye was pulled off.

She stopped at system checkpoints that didn't figure in what she was searching for and did more fiddling before telling Peppi the recording studio would be her final stop.

He guided her from the elevator through the studio into the engineering booth and settled at the console while she made a game of the B Box that controlled the downstairs area, voicing approval of the settings as a cover for a few more adjustments.

She turned to leave and noticed for the first time a keypad on the back door to the booth.

It wasn't part of the ICS system.

New, or added since?

Peppi must have caught her interest, because he casually moved from the console to a leaning position at the door that hid the keypad and guarded it from her.

What was behind the door?

The answer to Princess Lulu's disappearing act, perhaps, and—

What else?

Keshawna knew there was nothing to be gained by raising the question.

The answer would come soon enough, now that the surveillance system cameras could operate free of any intrusion by Davenport.

Chapter 33

Josh woke to an empty house, pulled from a sheet-tangling sleep by voices talking about Merv Bannister that he figured for the fading echoes of a dream until he saw he had dropped off last night with the TV bleating. He massaged his eyes to bring the picture into focus. The news anchors sharing a desk and perky mid-morning smiles finished rattling off Bannister's catalog of credits as the screen dissolved into a series of stills and showed footage of the genial host at his most genial.

Bannister grew younger through the years—his face tighter, his hair color lighter, his teeth brighter—in one hit show after the next, concluding with the *American Showgirl* special, Merv surrounded by the winner and the runners-up, Ava Garner among them, Russ Tambourine hovering in the background, his eyes hungry for another shot at the spotlight.

Josh clicked news channels and caught the end of a breathless report linking the Garner and Bannister murders and the suicide of Marilyn Pope, Uncensored Productions the connection. Vic Swank materialized onscreen displaying exaggerated sadness, extolling his fallen comrades and, in the same sad breaths, mentioning his new shows and the past hits currently moving their way through cable syndication.

Another channel focused on Bannister's murder, highlighted by a lengthy interview with the loving couple Josh had caught hugging behind the Henry Moore lovers. Their descriptions of the fleeing assailant had varied since yesterday, but still were nowhere closer to him than he ever expected to get to Penelope Cruz.

The report cut to composite drawings by a police artist based on descriptions from people who had been on the museum plaza when the shooting occurred. One, a face gone out of its way not to be recognized through a Cossack's fiery red beard and bushy eyebrows, an oversized pair of shades, a trucker's duck-billed cap. The other drawing, a face looking too much like his own, happily not enough for any quick flashes of recognition by eyeball witnesses already uncertain over who the shooter was, the Cossack who had raced off in one direction or the other face, who had fled in another direction after waving a gun to free himself from people attempting to wrestle him under control.

Waving a gun—

The blue-steel .38 silenced short-barrel sitting across the bedroom, on top of his dresser, decorated with his fingerprints.

Common sense told him to ditch it fast, but he could fit the .38 into the plan simmering in his mind since yesterday. He rolled over and into a sitting position, grabbed for the cell phone on the nightstand. Ran the directory. Hit the automatic dial.

"Josh," he said. "Calling to double-check. You still game?"

"Shady Acres."

Nothing like it was supposed to exist, but it did—

A postwar house on a side street within walking distance of West Hollywood Park, the Blue Whale, and the Sheriff's Substation, a good fit on a block full of genuine lathe and plaster, shingle roofs, sun porches, well-tended lawns, and—

Frequent foot traffic in and out of the other nondescript single homes, duplexes, and two-story apartments dotting the neighborhood, the look-the-other-way kind, white collar pimps and madams, drug dealers and private membership bathhouses working their hustle with a degree of comfort. It was an open secret among them that they were safe from the law so long as they were not stupid enough to drop a dime on Shady Acres.

Years ago, some of LA's finest had purchased the place as an investment. Spiffed it up. Did some bare bones furnishings, worked out a routine maintenance system, and passed out keys to what was christened "Shady Acres," although so long ago no one who remembered why was still around. It became a clubhouse for some, a hideaway for others, a base for sexual rendezvous best kept clandestine, and one other popular use:

Shady Acres was a prime Blue Wall of Silence one-stop for the interrogation of suspects that were safer to conduct away from the precincts, where techniques not taught at the Academy could be practiced at whatever length was necessary to inspire a confession.

If privacy was a consideration, there was a signal that told the co-op cops to steer clear for the duration, a lamp burning in the bay window facing the street. It was a trick applied soon after Shady Acres was acquired, suggested by a detective lieutenant who had seen it used by the actor Fred MacMurray in a movie called *The Apartment.*

The lamp was lit and in the window now—

Placed in the last half hour by Josh, who was inside on the key borrowed from Keshawna.

This was one of the few times he had ever used Shady Acres, the first time ever he had need for the lamp.

When the old-fashioned chimes cling-clanged, Josh leaped out of the pace circle he was digging into the shabby living-room carpet and crossed to the front door, checked the spy hole, and stuck a false smile on his face. "Hey, thanks for making it," he said. "Right on the dot."

Vic Swank stepped inside. He took a fast look around and crimped his face. "Who's your decorator?" he said. "The Salvation Army Thrift Shop?" He checked his wristwatch. "We have to make this quick. I'm meeting some potential heavy-duty investors from Japan for drinks, dinner, and a little extra-special sociability, if you get my drift."

"We could have made it another time."

"No time like the present," Swank said. "Besides, something I need to put to you."

They crossed the room to what passed for a leather couch and settled at opposite ends, Swank bringing on fast-paced conversation that began with Clyde Davenport's name.

"He called me all five-alarm fire, ranting about something you told him you heard from that cheap bitch Marilyn Pope," Swank said.

Josh made a clucking sound. "Speak not ill of the dead, Mr. Swank."

"Lucky to have a gig, the way she carried on around the plant, and now to learn she eavesdropped on my phone calls?" His eyes retreated into slits. "Anything that Marilyn Pope may have said to you, a guaranteed pile of bullshit, Josh."

Josh played out a minute to see how edgy Swank would get.

Swank looked at his watch again. Shot the gold-anchored cuffs of the high-collar silk shirt that gave him a modified Elvis look. Chest hair competing for attention with his eighteen-karat necklace, a sea-blue diamond rock at its core.

"Marilyn told me what she overheard between you and your pal Davenport made her change her mind and it wasn't Davenport who killed her pal Ava Garner," Josh said, thinking, *The lie, such a wonderful trick in a cop's arsenal.*

Swank drew back showing the kind of surprise that's hard to fake, but he got past it in a few seconds. "Which leaves Merv Bannister, the poor dead depraved SOB, same like I already told you last time we met, right?"

"You don't seem especially broken up about him, either."

Swank dismissed the idea with a gesture.

"I'm sad where it hurts the most, in my bank account. Merv getting murdered like that? Jesus! You care to guess how much it'll cost Uncensored Productions in the syndication market? Who wants to watch a dead guy hosting anything? Spent half my day fielding cancellation calls. Why the Japs I meet later are so important." He crossed himself. "So, what's it that the bitch said Clyde or I said to make her change her mind and pin the tail on Bannister?"

"Whatever it was sent Marilyn exploring his dressing room. She came away with this." Josh reached into the small grocery bag on top of a pile of old *Playboy*s decorating the coffee table and withdrew the silenced .38 that killed Bannister. He slid it along the couch to Swank. "It's not loaded. Check it out. Look familiar to you?"

Swank picked up the .38 by the barrel and palm-bounced it for weight. He gripped the blue handle, gave the silencer a little attention before deciding, "Nope. Should it?" and offered the weapon back.

Josh finished putting on the pair of latex gloves he'd pulled earlier from a supply cabinet in the Shady Acres med cabinet and retrieved the .38.

Returned it to the grocery bag.

Set the bag aside.

Said, "Definitely. It's the gun you used to air condition Bannister's head yesterday. Your prints all over it again."

"Again?" Swank shuttered his eyes trying to decipher what he had just been told. "What kind of a lousy trick—" His eyes flew open. "The police sketch on the news. That was you."

"Perfectly disguised by the sketch. And that was you hiding inside a silly beard—the way you can't hide your prints."

Swank served up a grotesque cackle. "Any more than you can hide your stupidity, Josh, that's what you really believe.

What are you really trying to do here, audition for the starring role in a new TV series called *Dumb Ex-Detective*?"

"Convince me it wasn't you."

"No need. The law of physics will do that for you, for any cops you call in, for the lawyer I'll have suing your surly ass for every dollar in the pot of gold Katie Sunshine left you when she left you for good. I was leading the Japs on a tour of the plant when he was shot." Swank aiming his chin like a challenge, his every word smugly drawn.

Josh fought back the rage building in him over Katie's name thrown in his face like that, fought off the urge to pull the .38 from his hip holster and use it on Swank.

He lost both battles.

He leaped to his feet and yanked out the automatic.

Startled by Josh's sudden move, Swank reared back and threw up his hands defensively, crossed at the wrists in front of his face. Josh brought down the .38 hard on top of Swank's head. Within seconds, a rivulet of blood was creeping past Swank's brow. He whimpered a demand for Josh to stop, too late to prevent the blow that broke skin and drew blood above his left eyebrow.

Josh took a step back, held his aim, waved his fingers at his palm. "I need to hear more, Swank. Like who it was you and Davenport contracted to take out Bannister. And Marilyn? Her, too? The suicide, too convenient for me to believe."

Swank moved his hand from his eyebrow, studied it for blood, and pressed it back. "You will regret this, I'm done with you, Josh. Count your days."

"You get to count first," he said. He stuck his thumb and middle finger in his mouth and whistled. Called, "Now's the time, Dr. Lueg."

The door connecting the kitchen to the dining room swung open and out marched a tall figure in a rumpled blue pinstripe suit and a loud tie that belonged in a burlesque routine, heavy black horn-rim frames, and a bushel of unruly hair dyed the same garish borderline brown color as his waxed mustache and elegant goatee.

He was carrying an old-fashioned black doctor's satchel, which he settled on the coffee table and proceeded to open. He removed a loaded hypodermic needle, gave the lever a squeeze, and flashed a taut smile and a nod at Swank. "Ready whenever you call it," he said, with a trace of Scottish accent.

Josh said, "Roll up your sleeve, Swank."

"Fuck you and your truth serum or whatever the hell."

"Doc?"

"Nothing lost if I puncture through the material, Josh. Or, the chest as good a place as any. Shoot it into his mouth. Plenty of options."

Josh said, "The good doctor works for the city's vaunted crime lab, Swank. He owes me a payback on a small favor—"

"Eternally in your debt, Josh."

"I requested his help with you tonight, if it became necessary. It's become necessary. Doc, please tell Mr. Swank what happens next."

"Sir, it's like this," Dr. Lueg began, his words joined by a benevolent bedside smile. "I'm about to administer you a dose of HIV-positive blood drawn from a suspect in the throes of a death caused by an advanced, extremely unfortunate and ugly case of AIDS. Sadly, it will send you off on the road to a similarly sad conclusion."

Swank pushed himself into a corner of the couch. "This is crazy. You wouldn't."

"I would," Josh said. "Count on it, unless you decide you have things to tell me that I want to hear."

"You're talking murder, Wainwright. You won't get away with it, either of you."

"Run, tell your story after you're out of here. After the doc and I tell ours, who do you think they'll believe?"

"I'll see you dead first, you crazy son of a bitch." He shifted his gaze to Dr. Lueg. "You, too."

Dr. Lueg shrugged. "It's a particularly virulent strain," he said, and turning to Josh: "Can we get this over with, Josh? I'm the honored guest at tonight's meeting of state criminalists and would hate to miss out on the cocktail reception."

"Your breath smells like you already started without them."

"Don't I always?" He inched closer to Swank. "Now?"

Swank pushed deeper into the couch. Josh gave him a moment's study. The color had drained from his face. His jaw muscles were twitching furiously, his eyelids blinking an urgent Morse code of fear. He was raining sweat and tears. Josh shrugged. "No time like the present, Doc."

"God damn you, you bastards," Swank said, his words boomeranging off the wall across the living room. "Russ Tambourine did it. He's the one you want."

Chapter 34

Russ Tambourine?

Swank's declaration was nothing Josh expected to hear.

He motioned for the doctor to step back.

"Convince me, Swank," he said.

It took Swank several minutes to pull himself together. His breath was labored and the words didn't come easy. He raised his shirt, used the hem to pat his face and hands dry. Snarled at the doctor, who stayed near enough to stab him with the needle.

"There was this three-way, Russ, Ava and Marilyn," Swank said, his eyes cemented on the needle.

"Tell me something I don't know."

"A set-up."

"A good beginning," Josh said.

"Marilyn and Ava roped Tambourine into the action. They gave it new twists on the word kinky, Tambourine a happy camper inventing beyond anything you find in the Kama Sutra. He's the only one who doesn't know Bannister is capturing it all on video, for use in blackmailing the big bucks out of Tambourine. No pay, the video goes up on the Internet, as is. Something there to offend everybody, make Pamela Anderson and Paris Hilton look like Girl Scouts and guaranteed to put his career in the toilet for keeps. Bannister's going to split the paydays with Marilyn and Ava, the way he's done before with other patsies. Only, Tambourine won't bite on the blackmail. He can't, it turns out.

"Tambourine is a chronic loser at the Vegas tables, markers out that'll keep him signing off on paychecks until the week after forever. He brings his situation to the attention of certain people who see him as a gift that keeps on giving. They turn Tambourine on to a couple of LA handymen-for-hire, if you catch my drift." He shot a finger gun at Josh.

"The ones who came after me in my building?"

"I don't know anything about that."

"But you're certain Tambourine put goons up to doing Bannister?"

"Certain."

"And Marilyn Pope?"

"Probably."

"And before them, Ava Garner? Wiping out all three threats?"

"No. Maybe it was on Tambourine's mind, but I told you before—Merv murdered Ava."

"This time tell me what makes you so certain."

"Merv, he told me. Good enough?"

Josh signaled for more.

Swank worked over his sweat again and pushed out a few tons of noisy air while steering his anxious eyes from Josh to the doctor's hypodermic needle and back.

"After Ava's out of here and hooked up with Clyde Davenport, Merv can't let go of how he feels she betrayed him. He takes to stalking her. That night, Merv's camped outside Clyde's digs, whacked, as looped as a Magic Mountain rollercoaster, when he hears Clyde screaming and Ava screaming back. He sees Clyde is chasing her, threatening her with the Uzi he's aiming at her like a divining rod.

"Merv hustles from his car and crosses over Mulholland to the Magic Land entrance gate in time to see Clyde stumble over his own feet and hit the ground hard. Passed out. An iron grip on the gun. Ava is tighter than a virgin's twat, doped on something. Aiming a Glock in a dozen directions at once. Swearing she'll kill the old bastard before he can kill her.

"Merv smooth talks his way to Ava and gentles the Glock away. His first thought is to use it to do in Clyde, only until Ava says, 'Where'd you come from you perverted piece of shit? Out of the old bastard's asshole?' With that, Merv turns the Glock on her and *bang!*—Ava's gone. Now, his brain a Mixmaster running at warp speed, Merv hustles over to Clyde, works Clyde's prints on the Glock, drops it, and hotfoots it the hell away. Down the canyon, he pulls into a gas station pay phone, dials a nine-one-one. . . . The rest you know."

"Except why you didn't come forward and tell this to the police, being such a great friend of Clyde's. It could have kept him from being charged with Ava's murder."

"I was saving it for the court. Meanwhile, also, I was protecting my asset until I found a suitable replacement for him."

"Like Russ Tambourine?"

"Stranger things have happened," Swank said, beaming like a Cheshire cat.

The front door chimes sounded.

Swank checked his watch. "I told my driver to come up after me if I wasn't out the door in half an hour." He put a question mark on his face. "*Banzai* and all that, remember?"

Josh nodded okay and parked his .38.

Swank lifted off the couch and adjusted his outfit before sailing to the door.

Standing on the porch was a tall tree-stump of a man in a chauffeur's black uniform and ill-fitting cap.

Josh called across to Swank: "You realize your problem, don't you?"

Swank glided around. "The gun with my prints? We've crossed that base."

Josh swiped off the coffee table a digital voice recorder the size and shape of a Zippo lighter and held it up, enjoying the sight of Swank's surprise turn to anger. "What you told us puts you in line for a charge of aiding and abetting commission of a Class-A felony," he said.

"I used to be a Boy Scout," Swank said. He stepped to one side twirling an index finger, opening a view to the chauffeur pulling a .45 from a shoulder holster and moving into a shooter's stance.

Wordlessly, Swank moved back into the room. He snatched the grocery bag with the .38 off the table, snatched the recorder from Josh and dropped it in the bag, crossed to the doctor and snatched away the hypodermic needle.

Heading for the door, Swank halted on an afterthought.

He wheeled around and advanced on Josh.

Punctured his arm with the needle.

Stepped over to the doctor and caught him in the chest.

Dropped the hypodermic in the grocery bag and hurried out the door, the chauffeur moving in reverse gear, protecting Swank's backside.

Josh moved his hand to his arm.

He checked his fingers.

They were blood-stained from touching the jacket where the hypodermic had broken through and penetrated skin.

He said, "Your shirt's a bleeding mess, Dr. Lueg. Swank got you as good or better than me, and you know what that means?"

"Means the jerk let his temper get the best of him?"

"Marking him for two counts of assault with a deadly weapon, two more on assault with intent to commit bodily injury, and one big count of felony stupid."

"If it were the real stuff in the needle, not cranberry juice?"

"That would add two counts of murder—us—to Swank aiding and abetting in the murder of Ava Garner," Josh said. He showed off the backup digital recorder perking in a shirt pocket. "Swank wasn't the only Boy Scout in the room, bro."

"Can I dump the makeup now?" Lon McCrea said. Without waiting for an answer, he removed the horn-rim frames and tossed them on the couch, began peeling off the goatee.

"You looked enough like a doctor, you almost had me believing."

"The actor's art, and what do you mean almost? I had Swank half scared to death with that HIV business you cooked up."

"How do you explain away the other half?"

"AIDS, no laughing matter," Lon said.

That cut deeply into the common laughter they were sharing.

"Time to turn off the lamp and call it a night," Josh said.

Josh went home by way of Westwood Village Memorial Park.

He entered through the maintenance gate and made his way on foot to Katie's gravesite, a route he could follow blindfolded without any missteps. Tonight, a full moon in a cloudless sky was lighting the way and casting what he had come to call a "Heaven-sent glow" on her marker.

To it Josh added the plum white Nastranana he'd plucked this morning from Niki's floral arrangement in the entry hall and a loose multi-colored stone picked off the path. He settled with his legs crossed at the ankles and randomly attacked stray weeds missed by the park's gardeners while bringing Katie up to date. When he finished describing the ruse he and Lon had pulled on Vic Swank, Josh fished out the recorder and showed it to Katie, saying:

"See? It's good news and bad news, my sweet love. The good news is case solved, with it another murder or two that gets that louse Russ Tambourine out of Connie's life once and for all. Sending Vic Swank away is a bonus, but it's not what I was hoping to get out of him, and there's the bad news. This tape says Mr. Magic will get away with Ava Garner's murder and, damn it, I know Davenport's guilty. As guilty as he is of your murder. As guilty as he is of all those others. He figures in her murder somehow, but—no proof. Nothing to tie him to the crime. Is Davenport that smart or am I that dumb, Sugar? Where are the lies that I don't see?"

Josh looked at the recorder like it was trying to talk to him, reveal some secret.

All he heard was his mind spinning on empty, until—

"Sugar, what if there were no recorder?"

He gave the question thought.

"Sugar, Swank doesn't know this one exists, only the recorder he left with. . . . He'll destroy it, for certain. He can still take the stand at Davenport's trial and give him an alibi by pointing the finger at Bannister, but—will he now, knowing he'd be on the hook for aiding and abetting if the whole story comes out on the witness stand?

"Swank stays out of it and all he has to worry about are any charges filed by Lon and me. We're not going to do that, of course. I can't give up Shady Acres and, even if I could, Swank's attorneys would scream entrapment. His turning the hype needles on us? The worst charge any investigation would deliver is assault with cranberry juice.

"Swank's a savvy businessman, so I wouldn't be surprised if he's gotten rid of the recorder already. That's the smart move. Killing Lon and me an hour ago would also have been smart, but he didn't. Why? What am I missing? Fingering Tambourine? The story all made up, to buy time until his stooge came riding to his rescue? That it? That wouldn't be so bad for us, would it? It would keep Davenport in the guilty sweepstakes."

Josh looked at Katie's grave marker like he expected to hear an answer. He got a bleak silence matching his own. Broke it with a sigh. Told her, "After all this time, there's no reason for us to be in a hurry, either, my love."

He left after five or six minutes of quiet contemplation, during which he carved out a shallow hole next to the gravesite and buried the recorder. He was now guilty of concealing evidence in an ongoing criminal investigation. So what?

Chapter 35

Clyde arranged the day's appointments so he could be back at Magic Land by three for the studio session with Princess Lulu, although certain she'd be late by half to three-quarters of an hour, sauntering in with neither an apology nor an explanation.

It fed some need of hers to be in charge, as if she had already achieved the heights of stardom she knew he could deliver.

It was an attitude he had never tolerated in any of his acts, never, and, one day, after he had carried her to the top of the charts, he'd remind little miss Princess Lulu who was boss—in the studio, in the bedroom, in her life.

He wasn't describing any of this to Stan Hubbard, of course, only talking about her in the most glowing of terms as they shared coffee and sinkers at the conference round in Stan's office at *Record Box* magazine. Stan had been at the magazine since Tyrannosaurus Rex roamed the planet. He had bought "The Bible of the Music Business" two or three years ago and was now president and chief operating officer, but that didn't mean his hand was closed to the kinds of payoffs that fed his greed in all the years Stan was the go-to guy if you wanted your act on the cover, your record on the charts, or only the nicest things said about you in his weekly column, "Headliners and Honchos."

Clyde was saying: "I'm giving Princess Lulu the next-to-closing headline spot on this year's show for 'Clyde's Kid's,' that's the kind of belief in her I have already, Stan, and I know you'll share it with me once you hear her for yourself."

Stan gave his chocolate doughnut another dip in his coffee and wagged a hand while he chewed through a big mouthful and picked after flecks of dough trapped between teeth stained ugly yellow and uglier brown by the caffeine and Cubans that had turned his voice to sawdust. He swallowed hard, rinsed with coffee and wondered: "What Clyde's telling me about this new *schvartza* of his, the *emmis,* Peppi?"

Peppi, sitting across the table from Stan, to Clyde's immediate right, answered with an animated thumbs-up. Peppi had always been Clyde's link to Stan, his bag man for whatever payola Stan was into. The bucks. The broads. The Colombian. No price too great for an editor who always delivered. Stan wasn't alone in that category, only the most important connection, and too subtle in his dealings to ever get caught in the nets cast by the Feds or Congressional hearings into the industry's underbelly.

Stan said, "Not so long ago we were talking this way about that discovery of yours got murdered and you arrested, that Ava someone," and, trying for a laugh: "What really happened there, Clyde? You dig into your gun collection after she bit off your dick or did something really serious happen?" Stretching the word *really* a mile.

"I'm innocent until proven guilty, Stan."

"Yeah, me too," Stan said, and went after a sugar doughnut from the platter on the table.

"I'm still working on some tracks by Ava. I'll release her single on top of being declared innocent."

"Amen," Stan said. "You always were a master of timing. That should get you a lot of national press."

"And the cover of *Record Box*? Her single breaking at Number One on your chart?"

"I thought we were discussing the *schvartza,* what's her name,

Princess Poontang? And I'm all of a sudden wondering if this is the one I been hearing about from people over at Dead Dogg Records."

"She's mine now, Stan. A deal I worked out with EZ-XTC himself."

"Worked out all the wrinkles, Clyde?"

"Enough for now."

Hubbard crushed his forehead between his eyebrows, ran a hand through what was left of the mountain of hair once his trademark and now was reduced to a few unruly strands and closed his eyes to the concept. "Enough ain't enough with that black *momser,* Clyde. Anything less than all doesn't work with Mr. Charleson. Friend to friend, I'm telling you, be careful. Don't fuck with him." His eyes clicked open and shot up to the ceiling. "Jesus fuck! We're talking Princess Lulu here, right? She's his daughter. You're playing games with his goddamn daughter?"

"Strictly business, Stan."

"Since when with you?" Turning to Peppi: "Anything you want for Princess Lulu, on the house. My treat. Ask and ye shall receive. Just make sure the word gets back to Mr. Charleson."

Peppi sent him a fresh thumbs-up.

Clyde said, "And what would be a fair retainer for your consulting services when I'm ready with the Ava Garner release?"

Hubbard shook it off. "My welcome back gift to you, my friend."

"Ever the gentleman, Stan. When I get around to sending you a heartfelt thank-you note, to the usual address?"

"That works and, Peppi, tell Reggie to put it out in the garage. He'll know."

Clyde only talked about Princess Lulu in his meeting at United

Brothers, the black radio syndication company whose shows reached every major black market in the country, drawing a commitment for heavy rotation airplay that would have her single spinning three times an hour every hour, reasoning Ava was outside the demographic, so why bother? He would deal for the saturation airplay he wanted for her later in the day, at Engine Company Number One.

The United Brothers package totaled a couple million dollars, plus bonuses for every market breakout, until Clyde acted on the lesson he'd taken away from his meeting with Stan Hubbard. A conference room full of overripe smiles turned nervously grim after he mentioned Dead Dogg and Princess Lulu's relationship to EZ-XTC. At once, the price was cut in half, then by another third, the vice president-sales stuttering through apologies for his faulty arithmetic.

Engine Company Number One was a tight network of independent promotion men in breakout markets, whose ties to key radio stations were as strong as Peppi's during the time he was king of the hill, winning the *Gavin Report*'s "Promotion Man of the Year" honor year after year, until he declared himself out of the running.

The motto associated with them in informed circles was: *What we can get you on the turntables depends on what we can get from you under the table.* It was kidding on the square, and there were no discounts offered after Clyde explained what he wanted for Ava Garner to the Engine Company's West Coast guy, Tee Dragna.

"We'll need it up front, cash money," Dragna said. "Any refunds due, you'll get it after the first six weeks, when we decide if we want to keep working the record, in which case it'll roll over into the next advance." His accent bespoke a New Jersey connection.

"My credit no good, Tee?"

"Good as gold, but we're a cash-only operation. We got companies standing in line to get us on their team. We bumped you to the head of the line, Mr. Davenport, because it's an honor and a privilege doing business with a man of your stature and in the company of the great Peppi Blue."

"It is," Clyde said. Turning to Peppi he signed: *Pay the smooth-talking asshole.*

Peppi's mouth twitched a smile. He dipped into his attaché case and came up with an overweight envelope that he tossed across the desk.

"Enough bread there for six weeks and the next six," Clyde said. "Start now."

"Soon as you get the product to us."

"You'll have product in six weeks. Consider half of what's in the envelope a bonus, an expression of my confidence in you and your associates. Once you have Ava's record, I don't want you working any others for the duration. Call and let me know how much that exclusivity sets me back, Peppi will run it over the same day. Cash. We understand one another? We have a deal?"

Dragna whistled amazement. "You're talking big, big bucks, Mr. Davenport."

"Maybe to you, Tee. To me—chump change."

Clyde was spooning out the remains of his crème brûlée, savoring every mouthful of the caramelized custard as much as the deal he and Harry Emerson had forged over the outrageously large steak and lobster entrées the Palm was notorious for, when a shadow quit over their empty platters of French fries and fried onion rings, followed by a throat-clearing cough meant to gain attention. He looked up to find Vic Swank hovering at the booth with his ear-reaching smile.

"Hope I'm not interrupting," Swank said.

Harry, who'd built Eiffel Records from a storefront on Hollywood Boulevard into a multimillion-dollar international music and video franchise, had never been one to tolerate interruption. He set his goblet of Cabernet Sauvignon on the stained tablecloth. "You are," he said.

Swank held his smile and pointed to a booth in the middle aisle. "Happened to spot Mr. Davenport from over there, where I'm having a bite of lunch with somebody you'll recognize," he said. "Need some face time, Clyde."

Harry checked out the booth and shook his head. "Like every other blonde with tits that hang like my late grandmother's," he said, and sent Clyde a look that said *Enough with this guy.*

Clyde said, "Later, Vic. Call me at my place later and we'll talk."

"Face time, better. Important."

"Running late already. Check with me tomorrow."

"Today," Swank said, with out-of-character insistence.

"Another ten or fifteen minutes for us, Harry?"

"Ten seconds, if this bird doesn't pick up on the hints and fly away."

Clyde turned back to Swank. "Peppi is out front minding the wheels. We're in the Rolls today. Ride home with me and he'll get you back here to your car when we're done."

"Sounds like a plan," Swank said. "I'll break the news to Anna Nicole and see you there."

"Remember the scene in *On the Waterfront*? Brando and Steiger? 'It was you, Charlie?' " Swank, doing a lousy impression of Brando. "What it feels like being back here in the car with you, Clyde."

"That's what had you fucking up my meeting with Harry Emerson? A need to play movie trivia? You know who that is,

Harry Emerson? What I was setting up in every one of his Eiffels? The billboard displays out front, the end caps, the listening posts? All for Ava when I'm ready to release her single."

"I didn't know Harry Emerson any more than he knew me, except that he has a bulb of a nose that would have put Jimmy Durante to shame and he spits when he talks, so call it a draw, okay? And Ava, Ava's part of what we need to talk about."

"I'm listening, Vic. This better be good."

Clyde listened with increasing intensity and a growing alarm he kept hidden as Swank described his meeting last night with Josh Wainwright.

Several times, he had Swank repeat something, to be certain he'd heard correctly. About Merv Bannister killing Ava. About the AIDS-infected blood he had inflicted on Wainwright and the doctor. About the recorder. Especially about the recorder.

"You didn't destroy the recorder?"

"Almost, then I thought, 'Whoa, there, Vic. It might not do any harm to let Clyde hear how you're still protecting his backside; a man of your word when it comes to favors returned.' " Emotion seeped into his words. "Uncensored Productions would have gone into the shitter for sure without your help keeping our Chapter Eleven from becoming Chapter Eight."

Clyde waved off the sentiment. "Where's the recorder now?"

Swank patted the hanky pocket of his sports jacket. "Here, next to my heart, as you are, Clyde. Why I came on so strong back at the Palm. Play it now?"

"Save it for Magic Land," Clyde said. "Tell me again how it happened your driver was armed."

"Studio guard I use sometimes. A little problem here, a little problem there. One look at him, the problem goes away. Got scared after learning about Marilyn, then Merv, so I kept him on overtime last night. Lucky I did, or who knows what else

Wainwright had in mind for me."

"Lucky," Clyde said, but he meant himself—

Lucky that Vic hadn't destroyed the recorder.

Based on what he'd heard, it could clear him of the murder charge and turn the cops onto Merv Bannister.

There was a downside, though.

Back home, after he'd listened to a playback, heard everything that had gone down with Wainwright, caught the nuances of voice the way he could trap a single bad note sung among a million, he'd know what to do about Vic and his big mouth.

At Magic Land, they headed straight for the studio.

While Vic was doing a few thick lines of premium snow laid out for him by Peppi, Clyde blocked out the security cameras, wired the recorder to the sound system, and set up the board to run a protection dupe.

He snorted a couple toothpick-thin lines and wiped the residue from his nostrils.

Tongued off his fingers.

Flipped the audio switch.

Hey, there, thanks for making it, Josh Wainwright said. *Right on the dot.*

Clyde blocked out the world while listening through a set of headphones, playing with knobs and levers to mark snafu points, where a word or sentence was muffled by movement or the material sitting on top of the recorder.

The playback ended with Vic telling Wainwright, *I used to be a Boy Scout,* and a run of wordless movement followed by a click.

Clyde settled the headphones on his neck and nodded appreciatively.

What he'd been told by Vic held up.

What he'd heard was proof Bannister murdered Ava, not him.

No suggestion of complicity in crimes committed by Russ Tambourine, the deaths of Bannister and Marilyn Pope.

Vic's little game of blackmail, news to him, adding to the problem he'd surmised:

Vic himself.

The recording also proved Vic to be a blabbermouth.

He had told the story to Josh Wainwright under duress, but too easily. What could Vic be trusted to say in a courtroom, under heavy attack from a prosecuting attorney? If it went that far. More likely, Vic would buy a plea bargain rather than suffer prison time for aiding and abetting murder by his silence. Vic would recant, and—

Clyde Davenport would be back on the chopping block, looking more guilty than ever in the eyes of a jury. He had outsmarted the world for years on crimes he'd committed. He was not about to risk being found guilty of a crime the recording made patently clear had been committed by Bannister.

Vic had become a threat.

Vic had outlived his usefulness.

Vic was of greater value to him dead than alive.

Rather than destroy the recording, its value would remain strong if Vic were found dead under curious circumstances or disappeared for good.

No worries about him saying the wrong things on a witness stand.

Suspicion would sail over to Wainwright and his doctor friend, who had threatened Vic with AIDS, only to become his victim.

What a laugh.

The tables turned.

Talk about probable cause.

Wainwright, so dedicated to proving Clyde's guilt, now more likely to be the one judged guilty of murder, because of that AIDS business, although—

Clyde dismissed the idea.

A stunt like that was too out of character for Wainwright to have been anything more than a stunt, a bluff to get Vic scared enough to talk.

So, what?

In any event, Vic had to go.

Clyde turned to Peppi.

Peppi's expression told him Peppi was thinking the same.

So many years together does that, not only for husbands and wives.

So very soon, Peppi would have Vic Swank disappearing forever, guaranteed never to be found.

Vic helped himself to a short snort and said, "So, what do you say, Clyde?"

Chapter 36

Josh's migraine was worse than ever, a Samson bringing down the temple walls, making more than a few scattered hours of sleep impossible. He wrestled the covers to a draw, paced the bedroom, stared endlessly out the window at a black sky he prayed would open to a light from heaven saving him from the hell of his confusion. The answer arrived in the beginnings of early morning light, before the neighborhood early birds launched their wake-up chatter, while he was showering away the last of his doubts.

He joined Niki and the children at the breakfast table knowing what had to be done with the recorder, knowing he'd always known what he had to do with it:

The right thing.

It was also what Katie would want.

The right thing.

Josh had known this all along without having to ask her opinion or permission.

Burying the recorder instead of turning it over might get Clyde Davenport convicted of Ava Garner's murder, but where was the satisfaction in knowingly helping an innocent man—any innocent man—be found guilty of a crime he didn't commit?

It was an unsatisfactory shortcut to the revenge he sought for Katie's murder.

It was an unacceptable way to stop the bastard from adding more names to the list of dead music superstars he blamed for his own fall to irrelevance from the top of the mountain.

Justin was noticeably somber this morning, studying the pancakes he'd drowned in hot maple syrup and using his fork to push them around. Julie was racing through her corn flakes, bubbling with excitement about the trip her class was taking today to the Museum of Tolerance. She had just read *The Diary of Anne Frank.* On exhibit were letters and other artifacts that took Anne's story past the last page.

Josh wondered aloud if it was something suitable for children Julie's age.

Julie gave him one of her disbelieving stares.

Niki put it into words: "My parents taught me that the only way we can avoid the evil in ourselves is by confronting the evil in others."

"Confronting the evil or defeating the evil, Niki?"

"You can't have one without the other, Mr. Josh."

Julie said, "You know what I believe, Daddy? I believe that, in spite of everything, people are really good at heart."

Josh said, "How about you, Justin? What do you believe?"

"Rusty Jr. shouldn't have been sent away by Connie. He's a good dude, and—"

"Rusty Jr. got caught doing bad things, Justin. Getting you to do bad things. And who knows who else before he got caught at it. He'll come out of rehab a better person."

"How do you know, Dad? Just because you say so?"

Justin went back to jabbing at his pancakes, to the relief of Josh, who had no quick answer that would satisfy his son, much less himself.

Julie did.

"Because Rusty Jr.'s really good at heart," she said.

Josh left for the office knowing he had made the right decision about the recorder. On the way out, he swiped a rose from

Niki's entry hall arrangement.

Wallet.

Keshawna had scribbled the word on one of her rose-colored Post-its and slapped it onto his computer. He plucked it off and headed for her office. She looked away from her monitor and clicked on a screen saver while he found a comfortable position in the visitor's chair. Pressing the Post-it to his forehead, he said, "Wallet, Walt. A character in the old 'Gasoline Alley' comic strip, a funny geezer who always walked around in a bathrobe and slippers, but not Michael Douglas, if that's what you're guessing."

Keshawna popped her eyes to the ceiling. "Michael Douglas, the real name of Michael Keaton. Wallet. Found. Real wallet of Joshua Davenport." She grabbed it from her desk return and tossed it over. He caught it mid-flight. "All present and accounted for, except for any cash, credit cards, driver's license."

"My photos?"

"Katie and the kids, present and accounted for."

He checked to make sure. Smiled. "Where and how?"

"First thing this morning. It turned up in a dumpster along with others. Turns out it's the work of gypsies working the Century City turf the last week or ten days. Teams in and out of the parking garages wham-bam fashion."

"No connection to—"

"Any of our clients, Joshua. You just happened to be convenient for a wham and a bam. These gyps probably Russian, working independent of our Russian Mafia locals. You remember to put the brakes on your credit cards?"

"No chance."

"Find time."

"First things first. A heads-up for you on the little encounter I produced last night with Vic Swank, which had the lousy net effect of doing Davenport more good than damage despite my best efforts to the contrary."

"I have news for you on the same front," Keshawna said. She did a thing with her jaws and averted her gaze, mechanical motions he caught whenever she had something troubling on her mind. "You go first." She was buying time while she pumped herself up for sharing.

When he'd finished describing the events at Shady Acres and afterward at the cemetery, he tossed her the recorder. "Take a listen, then off it goes to our buddies with the badges."

She set it aside. "Already sounds to me like you don't come off looking so clean."

"It beats feeling dirty, Keesh. The way I figure it, a rap on the knuckles is the worst the D.A. might see for a private citizen only trying to do his civic duty."

She let the idea sink in and drew back her mouth in nodding acceptance. "If Swank holds to his story and plea bargains out on his culpability. Otherwise—"

Josh stopped her with a gesture. "Two murders, maybe three with Marilyn Pope," he said. "A good deal for the D.A., even though I'm temporarily trading my first son of a bitch of choice, Davenport, for the lesser son of a bitch, Swank."

"It's your call," Keshawna said, "which brings us to the call I got first thing this a.m." She picked up the recorder and toyed with it. "Davenport. Announcing he no longer needs our services, thank you so very much, and will we kindly remove our surveillance gear posthaste and submit the itemized invoice with backup his business managers will need for income tax reporting purposes, etcetera, etcetera, etcetera."

Josh thought about it. Slammed the desk with a fist. "Swank went running and blabbing to his pal. The SOB knows about the recording, how it gets him off the hook." He strolled the room shaking his head. "So, tell me, Keesh, I'm right, why didn't Swank step up to the plate and rescue Mr. Magic before this?"

"To protect his own ass? Still the reason, only now to get to Davenport before you did, with whatever cockamamie excuse he might have dreamed up?"

"Or because he was lying to me, protecting Davenport's ass along with his own?"

"Either way, he went to Davenport's last night. Our cameras caught him arriving and in the recording studio before the monitors went to black. Davenport overriding the systems again. No sign of Swank leaving, though, although the cameras were back up in time to see Davenport hop into a cab and sail away."

"Cab?"

"Cab, and no Peppi. I figure Davenport's flying off to Nashville on his own."

"Nashville?" Josh wheeled around to face Keshawna, spread his legs, a hand on his hip, the other hand urging more. "Something else you have to tell me?"

"Who Jeremiah Schwartz became, because there's no way in the world you'll guess that one."

He showed her he wasn't amused.

She said, "Davenport mentioned it's for Billy the Kid's memorial service tomorrow. Said Mrs. Palmer called, inviting him to come and say a few words about her dearly departed. More interesting is what Davenport didn't bother telling me, what I got from the widow afterward, when I courtesy called."

He waited her out while she held onto the next few seconds like they deserved a blare of trumpets.

Keshawna said, "The widow told me Bluto Parks phoned and left a message saying he'd heard about Billy's death and was heading for Nashville to pay his final respects at the service."

"Davenport know that?"

"She told him."

"A million to one that's the real reason Davenport is going, to square stories with Bluto before we can get our hands on him. It also explains why he'd suddenly want us off the case and out of his checkbook. . . . I'm going to Nashville, Keesh."

"Of course, you are. I booked you a ticket after getting off the phone with Mrs. Palmer. First class, round trip. My treat."

Chapter 37

Keshawna hadn't told Josh everything.

There were things he didn't have to know, like the secrets buried in the past and best kept that way.

She busied away the next several hours supervising the shutdown on all but her private links to the Davenport security and surveillance systems.

When the clock said Josh was in the air to Nashville, she took off for Magic Land.

It was one of those balmy late afternoons, unseasonably humid, humongous black rain clouds on the prowl, but not quite ready to unload. The rush-hour traffic was heavy heading up Benedict Canyon to Mulholland Drive, not bumper-to-bumper, but close after the swing past the Beverly Hills Hotel.

Keshawna didn't mind.

She wanted darkness as her ally when she broke into the villa.

She built in another forty-five minutes by pulling onto a shoulder and studying the copies of the blueprints she'd acquired from the Department of Building and Safety, using up a favor to quash complaints that the search meant digging into files and log books that hadn't been cracked in more than half a century.

The blueprints revealed secret villa entrances overgrown by time and foliage, the location and routes of a basement tunnel connecting the main house to the caretaker's cottage, and a later extension that added rooms and a second, private elevator to the villa.

She had chased after them when research on the original owner, the movie idol Alfredo Mantegna, turned up front-page stories documenting his arrest, conviction, and tumble from grace for luring young men to the villa for acts even Hearst's scandal-pandering *Examiner* and *Herald-Express* refused to describe past phrases like "soulless acts against nature," declaring Mantegna "Satan's lieutenant."

The blueprints explained how people were able to appear, disappear and reappear on the surveillance cameras. How she could get inside to see if Vic Swank or Princess Lulu were still there—

Especially Princess Lulu.

She would have to risk the presence of Peppi Blue, unaccountably absent from his usual position, glued to Davenport's ass when Mr. Magic hopped into the cab on camera, heading for LAX. The troubling thought carried her hand to the .45 Heckler & Koch pistol parked inside the waistband of her Armani sweats, then down to her black Nike high tops, where her .22 backup was stashed.

She ran her fingers through her hair. Her scalp was damp with perspiration. Always a good sign, sweat. It signaled her adrenaline was pumping; with it, faster reflexes. She was not courting trouble, but there was no guarantee trouble would not be courting her.

Keshawna cruised past the main entrance, slowing long enough to determine the duty guard was gone, the guardhouse dismantled, the gate drawn and padlocked.

She steered past the back entrance she had used once before, to another entrance hidden in the overgrown brick wall; parked the Boxster fifteen feet away; doubled back and dug through the brush until she got to a door latch.

It wouldn't budge.

She headed back for the car, plinked open the trunk, and reached for the doctor's satchel that contained a variety of burglary tools.

Another five minutes, using a mild explosive that came wrapped like a firecracker, she'd popped the latch and the lock and cracked the wall door wide enough to angle herself onto the grounds.

Adjusting her night goggles, Keshawna patiently worked her way to the rear of the dark caretaker's cottage. No lights visible through any of the drawn shades or curtains.

She paused behind a tree and studied the cottage for any sign or sense of activity, jarred after a few moments by the crackle and crunch of twigs and grass behind her.

She drew her pistol and wheeled around in the same action, expecting to discover Peppi Blue.

A pair of squirrels dashed past.

Leaped onto the trunk of a nearby tree.

Disappeared inside its thick branches.

Keshawna laughed off her brief panic, settled the pistol back inside her waistband and moved past the back door to a coal chute built into the wall.

No lock on the lid.

Rusted hinges.

She open the lid and flipped in a quarter.

The coin tinkled down the metal slide and landed quietly enough to convince her it was a safe route to the basement.

She climbed inside the chute one leg at a time, on her stomach, and inched her way down the slide.

Five minutes later, her sneakers touched asphalt.

She brushed off the dust and cobwebs of disuse, backhanded the sweat from her forehead, got her bearings, and aimed for where the blueprints told her the tunnel entrance would be.

Another five minutes of cautious approach brought her into the room behind Davenport's recording studio, the secret room revealed in the blueprints, and to the hidden elevator.

She rode it to the first floor, slid back the metal safety gate, and pushed at a wooden door that glided open and turned out to be the back side of a trophy case in the corridor. It explained how Peppi Blue had managed to disappear with Princess Lulu.

She rode up to the second floor.

This time the elevator door opened onto a secret bedroom decorated in lavender-flavored whorehouse chic and—

Princess Lulu.

She was sprawled on her back, on a circular bed large enough to handle the entire Lakers starting five, naked, her body inviting inspection, the recessed lighting too dim to make out if she was breathing or—

Keshawna swallowed panic air and moved to her, eyes bursting with concern that passed the moment she pressed her fingers to Princess Lulu's neck and felt a pulse.

Her own breath kicked in again.

With it came the lingering sardine smell of consummated fucking.

"Damn you, you stupid little fool," she said, louder than she thought, loud enough to make Princess Lulu's eyes burst open with the frightened stare of somebody leaping out of a nightmare.

Princess Lulu's shoulders twitched.

She moved into a half-sitting position, looking around desperately for a sense of location before her focus settled on Keshawna.

"Auntie Keesh," she said, drawing her lips into a smile that quickly disappeared inside disbelief. "What you doing here, Auntie Keesh?"

"Come to see you, but don't have to ask you the same question, do I, girl?"

"*Woman,* or ain't you noticed?"

"Smell it, too. It isn't singing, and cover yourself up before you disgust me more."

Princess Lulu reached for a pillow and pressed it for protection against her modest breasts. "It's fucking, is what it is. Better than I got all the years, so far, from life, because it's been my decision, not my daddy's. Dickin' my way up the ladder of success my way, not his way."

"By selling your body to Clyde Davenport?"

"By giving it away, but maybe selling my soul, and so what? He's going to make me a star, and that's what this is all about. He gets what he wants and I get what I want. More and bigger and better than anything my daddy has to offer me, which has always been only what would make Mr. Ezra Charleson an even bigger hero to his homies."

"Get that snot from your voice, Lu. . . . You ought to be ashamed of yourself talking that way about a man who did so many good and fine things for you growing up. College and all. Now, ready to make you a singing star like he's done for all those others? At what price?"

"Too late for you to start coming around again telling me what to think or offering me raggedy-ass advice, don't you think? Not to mention you, an ex-cop, upholder of law and order, down to defending a convicted felon, a one-time pimp and drug-pusher who so far's been smart enough not to get connected to any of those murders of rappers who dared come up against the mighty EZ-XTC or Dead Dogg Records, or one of his acts left him to get an honest count on their royalties by going into competition."

"You're talking about long gone history. Accusing your daddy of crimes he's never been charged with. Even worse, you're taking sides against kin. Your daddy, who, whatever else you think, loves you. The husband of my sister, Latasha, rest her precious soul, who died in giving birth to you. . . . That makes you a worse criminal than Easy Charleson can ever be."

"Don't bleed your heart all over me, you don't mind," Princess Lulu said, shaking her finger at Keshawna's face, her own flushed with disrespect.

Keshawna slapped her hard, twice. The back of her hand crashed against Princess Lulu's cheek. Her palm caught the other cheek on the rebound. Lulu's neck snapped right, then left. The suddenness of it all startled both of them.

Keshawna stepped back from the bed, weighing what to do now.

Lulu sat mindlessly, hugging the pillow for comfort, an ugly stare overriding her tears.

"You need to demonize someone, it don't have to be your daddy," Keshawna said. "Clyde Davenport's badder than your daddy will ever be."

"You gonna tell me about Ava Garner? Then I'm going to answer you the same way you answered me. He's innocent of the crime until he's found guilty, Auntie Keesh. The way the law works, remember?"

"And at least eleven other murders on Davenport's score sheet."

"You got the proof?"

"Working on it, girl. Pray to God in Heaven I find it before your name goes on the list."

"Woman. . . . A lot of me's dead already, so what's the difference? Let me know when you got the proof. Until then, we have nothing to talk about."

"I want you to get dressed and come away with me, Lu."

"When I leave, it won't be with you, so pack up your sermon and go on. Don't trip over the speed bumps on your way out."

"You'll leave with me and now, or I head straight to your daddy to drop a dime on you, tell him what's been going on between you and that crazy ass-wipe Davenport."

"What do you think that'll accomplish? Your word against mine. I'll deny it. Make like Daddy's little girl. It never fails me with him."

"Because he loves you."

"But never enough or in the right way." She put on a little girl singsong: *"Daddy, I don't understand why Auntie Keesh is inventing those awful stories, but they're not true, Daddy."* Her eyes flashed wide with innocence.

Keshawna scanned the room for clothing. None, except for an Oriental-patterned silk robe puddled on the yellow-stained polar bear rug between the bed and a door opened onto a bathroom. She was crossing to an antique armoire when a crimson bulb began flashing in the mirror angled on the wall behind the bed. She hadn't noticed the bulb before. It was mounted above a door across the room she figured fed onto the hallway.

Lulu read the question on her face. "Means someone's come in through the front gate," she said. "Probably Clyde's main man, Peppi, back from driving him to the airport and some errands. It could get really messy, he finds you here. Trespassing and all?"

Keshawna moved to the window and pulled aside a corner of the velvet drapes.

Peppi Blue had finished pulling the gate shut and restoring the lock.

He was heading for the limo.

She figured it would take him two or three minutes to drive up to the villa and park, maybe another two or three minutes to settle inside. How much more time before he came looking after Lulu?

Lulu read her mind. "First thing, Peppi will check on me," she said. "That gives you a five- or six-minute head start on leaving."

Keshawna grabbed up the robe and tossed it at her. "Let's go, Lu. Get your ass in gear, and let's go."

Lulu flung the robe aside. "What part of *Fuck you* don't you understand?"

"The part where you believe I'm leaving without you," Keshawna said. She moved back to the bed and pounced, straddling a startled Lulu and pulling her head up by the hair, stretching her neck, making it an easy target for the hard, side-of-the-hand diagonal karate chop that scored a direct hit on the depression behind Lulu's jawbone, causing instant trauma to the cranial nerves.

Lulu lapsed into vascular shock and unconsciousness.

"Sorry, baby," Keshawna said, then—

Moving hurriedly, she worked the robe onto Lulu, rolled her into a sitting position, legs overhanging the bed, and eased her onto feet that refused to cooperate.

She gripped Lulu's slim waist, lifted her featherweight body an inch or two off the floor and maneuvered her like a wounded soldier to the elevator.

The door wouldn't open.

The hum she heard made her realize it was descending.

She half-dragged, half-carried Lulu to the hallway door.

Locked from the outside.

That elevator hum again, the same, but different.

The elevator was returning.

Keshawna lugged Lulu over to the bed and gentled her down, then quickly crossed to the armoire and jumped inside. It was empty, except for an assortment of leather outfits and sex toys that belonged in an S&M hall of fame, either hanging or displayed on pegs for easier selection. It smelled of mothballs, sweat, and residue whose sources she wasn't about to guess at.

She drew and cocked the .45, left the door open a crack that permitted her to keep check on the bed.

Barely a minute later, Peppi Blue moved into her line of vision, bringing with him the stink of burning tobacco from the cigarette parked in his trach hole. At the bed, he hovered over Lulu and seemed to study her like a novice paramedic, briefly, then nodded approval and gently adjusted the robe to cover the parts of her body that had been exposed.

He dipped into a pocket for a ring of keys chained to his belt and turned toward the hallway door, but stopped after a few steps, checking the room with a mix of suspicion and uncertainty, sniffing the air for—

What?

Her perfume?

Her perfume, damn it?

Peppi aware of her perfume like that one time before, outside on the villa grounds?

His eyes veered toward the bathroom, then the armoire.

Keshawna lowered the gun barrel from the roof of the armoire to the door and held her breath as Peppi pulled out a Glock from under his suit jacket and started forward.

"Hey, there, Peppi Pepsi Cola!" Lulu's phlegm-stuffed voice stopped him. Her eyes, not yet fully awake, stared at the armoire like she knew what Peppi could find inside. "You get Mr. Magic safely tucked into his first-class carriage to Nashville?"

Peppi hurriedly restored the Glock inside his jacket.

He removed the cigarette from the trach hole and substituted his thumb, announcing in words and pauses for breath while turning in Lulu's direction, "Yes. You tomorrow. . . . He'll have the studio set up. . . . Musicians ready . . . by the time we . . . get there." He looked over his shoulder at the armoire.

Lulu got back his attention saying, "A little Nashville sound in the album mix; exciting. Ingenious, don't you think?"

"Long as I know him. . . . Everything he does." Fingers translating his words out of habit.

"And he's not so bad in bed, either. You wouldn't believe the sweet music he pulls out of me there." She angled onto her side and tossed her shoulders in a way that shucked off the robe. "I don't suppose I could interest you in a little poon tang while the cat's away? A little rub-a-dub-dub in the old bathtub? Make it our little secret, Peppi Pepsi Cola?"

Peppi shifted his eyes away from her. "Back in the morning for you," he said, with as much indignation as his gutted throat allowed. He re-plugged the trach hole with his cigarette and passed from view.

Keshawna heard a key turning in a lock, a door opening and closing, the key again, and moments later Lulu calling over, "It's safe now, Auntie Keesh. He's not likely to return," as she readjusted her robe and moved into a sitting position on the bed, knees up, legs crossed at the ankles. Rubbed her neck where the karate chop had landed. "I knew my offer would send him running. The dude's too loyal to ever think about sticking his salami in the boss' meat grinder."

"What if you were wrong?" Keshawna said, stepping out of the armoire, palming her forehead sweat into her hairline.

"Would have taken it up the ass, I had to, to keep him from finding you," Lulu said. "I heard stories about him from Clyde would turn you the color of Michael Jackson. Peppi would do you serious damage, he found you here by no leave but your own."

"How suddenly generous of you, Lu. What brought on the change of heart toward me?"

"My heart's always been in the right place, Auntie Keesh. Just don't need you messing with my life, giving me orders, telling me what to do and not do, when it's enough I got Daddy always trying to make me out to be his spitting image."

"And you figure it's better with Clyde Davenport than with your daddy?"

"It's different, what it is. I'm using him, in the end more than Clyde is using me. I'm the one who's really in charge here, in control of my own destiny. Clyde is part of my plan, not the other way around."

"People who thought like that before you are dead now. Come with me."

"Don't want to ride that merry-go-round with you again. Save it for another day, please. Besides, need to save my voice for the Nashville sessions coming up. You heard. Clyde, he's got it worked out to where I may even be doing duets with Willie and Dolly, how's that for nothing Daddy could ever score?"

She stretched out, rolled over with her back to Keshawna, who recognized it was not an argument she could win without another battle. Whatever else Lulu was or hoped to become, she was definitely her daddy's daughter.

Keshawna blew her a silent kiss and crossed to the elevator.

Peppi Blue was waiting for her when she stepped out into the room behind the recording booth, trails of blue smoke drifting from the lapsed corner of his mouth, the Glock aimed at her belly.

Chapter 38

Keshawna said, "It was the perfume, wasn't it?"

Peppi nodded.

He motioned her out of the elevator and, using the Glock as a prod, steered her into the booth and a tall stool at the rear, away from the doors, then stepped back and squashed out his cigarette in an overburdened giant ashtray while waiting for her to oblige his grim-faced order to unload her weapons.

There was no percentage in disobeying.

Keshawna laid the .38 on the counter, dipped down for the .22 in her high-top while idly searching around for some other kind of weapon. Nothing seemed right except, maybe, for the small fire extinguisher clamped onto the wall, but she'd have to be faster on her feet than Peppi was on the trigger to reach it and have it do her any good.

For now, a bluff would have to be her best defense trying to explain her presence.

"Came on over personally to double-check that all our ICS surveillance systems were properly removed," she said. "Called ahead, but got no answer. Found a way in, so there's still that and maybe some other security breaches to take care of before—"

He waved her quiet and corrupted his face into a look that translated as *What kind of idiot do you take me for?* Just as well. Nothing she could dream up was going to explain what she was doing inside the armoire. Peppi tapped his ear. Reached over and pressed a button on the cassette deck mounted above the control monitors. The murmur of the air-conditioning was overpowered by speakers pumping out her conversation with Lulu.

She kicked herself for not realizing before now that Davenport had his own damn system for bugging his private whorehouse. She offered Peppi a contrite smile and airborne hands. "Got me," Keshawna said. "What now?"

Peppi pressed his thumb over the hole in his throat. "We wait for . . . Clyde to . . . call back." He indicated the cell phone on the control deck.

"And tell you what to do, loyal old flea-bitten hound dog that you are?"

He ignored the slur. "Told Clyde he was playing . . . with fire. . . .Your tramp niece . . . too deceitful for her own good. . . . He won't let her get away . . . with anything. . . . Not once he hears the tape."

"EZ-XTC will be coming after both of you with a vengeance when his daughter turns up missing."

"Missing?" Peppi shook his head. "Accidents happen all the time."

"Nobody knows that better than you and your taskmaster, that the truth, Peppi?"

He twitched a tight grin and made that his answer.

"And me along for the ride?"

Another twitch.

Keshawna gauged her distance from the fire extinguisher again. She ruled it out and thought about her .38 and the .22, both closer.

Peppi's cell phone erupted with one of Davenport's more memorable Symphony of Sound melodies.

He reached for it blindly, his eyes fixed on Keshawna, whose sweep of the booth caught Lulu stepping quietly inside from the back room, her hands awkwardly gripping an Uzi, wearing a determined expression.

Lulu ordered, "Don't answer it, Peppi, you know what's good for you. I have a gun aimed right at you. I'll use it if you make me."

Peppi checked over his shoulder and verified the Uzi. He drew back his hand.

Lulu said, "Auntie Keesh, you come over here by me. Out of the way."

Keshawna started to rise.

Peppi shook his head. Held steady aim on her with the Glock, ready to squeeze the trigger as easily as he took a piss.

Keshawna settled back on the stool in a way that put her closer to the .38 and the .22 by a couple inches. At his age, late fifties, early sixties, Peppi's reflexes could not possibly be as sharp as hers, improving the odds in her favor, making it a gamble she'd willingly take if Lulu managed to throw him off guard.

The cell phone sang out again.

Keshawna saw Peppi was tempted.

Lulu called out another warning: "Don't!"

Peppi wheeled around to confront her.

Keshawna leaped at him. Her two-handed shove threw him off balance before he got off his shot. The bullet narrowly whizzed past Lulu. Thudded into the acoustic tile.

Lulu fired back. Her shots sailed over Peppi's head as he crashed to the floor.

Keshawna jumped after the fire extinguisher and slammed it down on Peppi's shoulder, cracking bone. She dropped it and went for the .38.

The Symphony of Sound melody sang out a fifth time.

Peppi appeared to shake off the blow.

He raised the Glock for another try at Lulu.

Gunshots. All from the Uzi. All of them ripping into Peppi, Lulu screaming, "I warned you! I warned you, didn't I? I warned you what would happen, motherfucker!"

Peppi too dead to acknowledge her or his cell phone before it quit singing.

Keshawna took the Uzi from Lulu and pushed it aside.

She nested Lulu in her arms like a newborn, Lulu swallowing noisy air, begging Keshawna to tell her what she had done was necessary.

"You killed him to save my life, baby. How much more righteous can it be than that?" Keshawna said, using a variety of words and illustrations until Lulu appeared calm enough to take instructions. The first was the most important. "I need you to give me your daddy's private phone number," she said, "whichever one he always answers knowing it's probably you."

Lulu sputtered out the number. "Why for, Auntie Keesh? What you need by him?" The shock of killing Peppi had reduced her to the bad grammar of her childhood.

Keshawna answered her by using her fingers as a quiet button on Lulu's trembling lips. "Go back up to the bedroom and get dressed, gather your things and come back," she said. She cupped Lulu's face under the chin and kissed her on the nose, then the forehead. "Go now, child."

Lulu struggled to her feet and made a move to pick up the Uzi.

"That stays here, baby."

"Not put it back where it come from?"

"Fine where it is. When you're all dressed and packed, I'll be waiting for you. Hurry."

"I don't understand, Auntie Keesh. What about him, Peppi, and—"

"You don't have to understand, baby. Please. Just go and do."

Lulu filled the booth with a sigh and headed for the elevator.

Once satisfied she was gone, Keshawna stripped the tape from the cassette deck and pocketed it. She fished out her cell phone and tapped in Easy Charleson's phone number. He picked up on the first ring.

"Not your princess," she answered his greeting. "It's Keesh, Easy. We got ourselves a major mess, you and me." She described the situation and heard him out. "Forget about using the main entrance," she said. "Keep on driving past, until you see a road."

Keshawna and Lulu were outside waiting for Easy Charleson by the old wall door when he arrived within the hour in a modest sedan, trailed by an equally undistinguished commercial van, vehicles that wouldn't appear out of place or raise concern from anyone who might venture up the service road.

Unlikely, but Easy was never one to take unnecessary risks. His attention to detail had saved him from countless arrests, starting back when he ran numbers in the hood, then pushed drugs and prostitution on his way to creating the multi-million dollar entertainment empire he began by peddling Dead Dogg rap on the streets the way he once sold dime bags.

There were three others in the sedan, including the driver, and six more homies in the van, who spilled onto the road and lined up waiting for direction.

Easy stepped from the car and hurried toward Lulu.

She wriggled free of Keshawna and flung herself into his arms, a blubbering mess of emotional turmoil.

Easy held her like a life preserver while Lulu explained, "I knew, I knew it, I just knew something was wrong, Daddy. Had the feeling. Had the feeling, so I got this gun from one of the cabinets where—and I went down in the elevator—and Auntie Keesh was in trouble, I saw. Him going to shoot her or something, I saw, and I warned him not to, but he—I—and it just happened after that, and—"

Easy calmed her with whispered words, hand-signaled his homies to move her suitcase and overnight bag into the car trunk. "Need you to go ahead now with Mountain, Gary, and Ali, Princess. Over to my place, while me and your Auntie Keesh finish up some business here. You okay with that? Join you real soon and we'll talk all about this."

"You say so, Daddy."

They traded kisses and he guided her into the back seat of the sedan, watched it make an awkward turnaround and glide back down the road before joining Keshawna, whose own frayed nerves had denied her any relief before Easy's arrival and seeing Lulu safely away from the villa.

Easy gave her a thumb and pinky. "Props, Keshawna. You did real good, the right thing by phoning me up," he said, and moved like he planned to engulf her the way he had Lulu.

She stepped back, out of reach, beyond the magnetic field she'd always felt around him. "I saw Lu needed her daddy. Besides, you're better than me at breaking the law, Easy."

"Not always, Detective Keyes," he said, a grin working its way up one side of his face, like he was on to dark secrets beyond any they already shared. "More to what's gone down here than you've told me yet. True?"

She ignored the question. "We go in through there," she said, pointing toward the wall door. There's a tunnel from the cottage to the main house and Davenport's recording studio."

"Ain't that damn something," he said, slapping his thigh. "Don't you worry none, Miss Jefferson High Campus Queen. When EZ-XTC and his posse perform their magic, there'll be nothing for the bitches in blue to find connecting our Princess Lulu. Like she was never here tonight."

"Except Davenport will know."

"Like she was never here tonight," Easy said again, gesturing for Keshawna to lead the way, snapping his fingers and calling to his homies, "Yo, peeps, is time for us to take care of business."

Chapter 39

Josh had the cab take him straight from Nashville International to Printers Alley.

It was verging on eleven o'clock and the stretch between Third and Fourth avenues, from Union to Church, was crowded with people whooping it up, cruising from one bar to the next on what once was notorious as the city's "dirty little secret."

A black sky contributed to a darkness relieved only by the neon-illuminated marquees overhanging the entrances that shouted out the names of the musical attractions and show times. Doormen worked the sidewalk, waving in potential customers with slick smiles and a promise of bargain-priced meals and drink to go with entertainment equaling anything in New York or New Orleans.

"Not no more what the Alley was back when it started up in the late eighteen hundreds," the cabbie said, after jotting down the destination on his trip sheet, a drawling encyclopedia of local history. "Was notorious for being 'The Men's District,' cafes, saloons, gambling halls, and speakeasies for them what worked at the three dozen printing companies that give the Alley its name, not to mention frequent drop-ins by judges, lawyers, politicians, and mucky-mucks aiming to be naughty.

"Y'all ever hear about Hilary House, the mayor for twenty-one of the thirty years the sale of liquor was outlawed, but always flowing freely in the Alley? Puffing out his chest and telling the newspapers what accused him of accepting bribes to look the other way, 'Protect them? Jesus all to Hell, I do better than that. I patronize them.' Came to be different in the seventies, when the printing companies moved on, and only four or five clubs survived, The Black Poodle, The Brass Stables, Skull's Rainbow Room, Boots Randolph's place, of course, plus the one y'all are aiming for, the Bourbon Street Blues and Boogie Bar. Change came here again less'n ten years ago, new clubs opening and the streets duded up Disney World fashion, but what's still the main attraction is the music, mister. Down home country or any way you like it, it's all there. Me? I'm still partial to western swing, anything else that come before country put on a shirt and tie and went city."

The Bourbon Street Blues and Boogie Bar was easy to spot—

A prime location and an animated neon sign across the length of the building, flashing "Georgie Wilson and Claude Hall with Sue Hathaway and The Original Cowtown Boys" in brassy, multi-colored capital letters. Underneath, in smaller caps:

TOMORROW. ONE NIGHT ONLY. MEMORIAL SERVICE FOR LEGENDARY BILLY 'THE KID' PALMER. Y'ALL WELCOME.

Josh paid twenty dollars at the door, pocketed the drink tickets that were included in the admission price, and checked his carry-on. He wandered into the showroom and found an open spot at the bar. The room was half-full, rickety wooden tables with linoleum checkerboard table cloths, barely any inching room between them and almost non-existent aisles. Waitresses in cowgirl outfits that went out of style fifty years ago and showed off cow-pen thighs and a fortune in cellulite. The smell of stale beer and smoke setting off an intolerable buzzing in his head that he couldn't extinguish with a quick shot of straight house bourbon that tasted like it was watered more often than his front lawn.

On the tiny stage, a band of musicians was playing the last off-key notes of a number he didn't recognize, any more than he knew who they were. They were all wrinkles and sagging chins and tucked into costumes straight out of a Roy Rogers movie, like some Grandfathers of the Pioneers, except for the middle-aged woman who was milking a yodel at the mike and had held onto a reasonably youthful buxom figure beneath her pink bubble dome hairdo.

They finished to polite applause and scattered beery demands for an encore, with the vocalist promising, "Me, Georgie, Claude, and the boys will be back following a pee and a puff with all the numbers on our new Greatest Hits album, so y'all stick to your chairs like used-up chewing gum, hear?"

Josh signaled the lady bartender for a second bourbon and caught an elbow in his side from a cute young thing dressed for action, who had squeezed in alongside him wondering, "You think y'all might stand me for a beer, mister?"

She didn't look old enough to drink, but this wasn't his town and that wasn't his problem.

He pointed her out to the bartender, tapped his chest, and added a nod. Within a minute, the bartender had brought over his bourbon and, without having asked, the Young Thing's brew in a tap mug. She took the drink ticket and a fiver and, without wondering if he expected change, stuffed them into her bra.

"Cheers," the young thing said, her voice a victim of the cigarillo hanging from a corner of her bruised lips. "Happy to say thank y'all in a very special way, show my 'preciation, you of a mind." Her meaning as obvious as the back page come-on ads in the *L.A. Weekly.*

Josh flashed her an appreciative smile. "Flattered, but otherwise engaged."

"I'm hanging, you come to figure otherwise," the Young Thing said.

She grabbed the mug, stepped away, and a few moments later was down at the other end of the bar, smiling and stroking the backside of a tourist-type in an ill-fitting ten-gallon hat and a camera strapped around his neck.

Josh checked his watch.

Kristy Palmer was supposed to be here by now, with Bluto Parks in tow.

Checking out the room, she said, when he called her from L.A. The stage. Working out some final details for the memorial service with the club's management. Giving Bluto a chance to feel the room and get acquainted with the band. He intended singing tomorrow at the service, a couple Billy the Kid and Bluto hits produced by Clyde Davenport, Georgie Wilson standing in for Billy. Clyde's idea, that. Clyde also insisting that he be permitted to pay for the service and, please, no argument. Everything to be first class and don't forget about flowers, Clyde insisted.

Kristy unable to rein in her emotions relating this to Josh.

Josh interpreting the news as Davenport once more sugarcoating himself as a saint to camouflage his next-intended sin.

He surveyed the room again and glimpsed Kristy passing through the door curtain to the right of the stage. She was wearing tapered jeans and a sweater that looked like it was painted on. She checked around, caught his wave, smiled, and threw an index finger at an empty table. Her inherent sexiness exploded as she sashayed her chunky body toward him, pausing on the way to accept handshakes and hugs from some of the patrons.

She was alone. No Bluto Parks.

"I'm honored you'd think to fly back to Nashville for Billy's memorial," Kristy said when they met at the table. She squeezed both his hands in gratitude and impulsively laid a kiss on his cheek, held him briefly in a bear hug that infused him with the full heat of her unbridled breasts before she eased onto a chair next to his.

Her sincerity reduced him to a bug, thankful he'd said nothing to let on it was only the crack at Bluto Parks that brought him here. He waited until a waitress had limped over to take their drink orders before asking: "Should we hold off until Bluto joins us? Where is he? Still working things out backstage with Georgie Wilson?"

Kristy lost her smile. "You can't believe my disappointment," she said. "Bluto isn't here yet." She asked for a tall-neck Lone Star, a gin chaser, double shot. Everything to go on her tab.

"At the club?" Josh said, and ordered his own Lone Star with a scotch chaser.

She shrugged. "Nashville, anywhere I know of yet, for sure. Been no word, nothing from Bluto, not since we worked out what I told you about when you called me up. I don't know what to think, and neither did Clyde when I told him."

"What were Clyde's thoughts?"

"He's thinking Bluto might have one-stopped for a shooter he turned into a party along the way. Sleeping it off somewheres, but bound to show up. If not, Clyde says he just might go on up there himself and do the numbers with Georgie, besides whatever else he has in mind to say about Billy and how great he was." She smiled, picked at a handful of stray hairs.

"Clyde backstage now with the band?"

The waitress returned with their drink orders.

Kristy toasted Josh and downed the Lone Star like a veteran. "Clyde's over at the house, hanging back with my kids," she said. "He thought it would be best to have someone sticking by the phone, if Bluto called again and was needy. He told me to go on ahead, in case Bluto walked in unannounced; also, knowing that I invited you to head straight on over here from the airport."

"I'm surprised he didn't leave his guy, Peppi, at your place."

"Except Peppi's not due until tomorrow. He's coming in with a new singer who Clyde's producing. He said he's thinking about pairing her with Bluto on some down-home cuts for her first album."

"Princess Lulu?"

"That's who. Clyde said he's already set the studio and the musicians. When I told it to Georgie and the others, you can guess how they got all over me, wanting me to throw in a good word about the band with Clyde, which of course I'll do."

"Of course."

"Think he will, Josh?"

"Generous to a fault, that Clyde," he said, wondering how much of this Keshawna knew.

He made some small talk about her late husband, praising Billy's contributions to music in words that inspired Kristy to glow with gratitude, before he feigned flight fatigue and asked her to drop him off at a nearby motel.

Kristy wouldn't hear of it.

She insisted he go home with her.

"Got a perfectly decent spare bedroom going to waste," she said. "Least I can do to thank you, and a nice home-cooked breakfast come morning. Also the chance now for a meet and greet with Clyde."

Only, Clyde wasn't there when they arrived.

Dylan, Kristy's fifteen-year-old, was in his bedroom at the computer, chat-rooming and carrying on multiple IM conversations at the same time. Hearing her approach, he switched the screen to an image of Darth Vader and did a teenage grumble about people invading his space unannounced.

"Oh, yeah," he said. "Mr. Davenport said for me to tell you he's gone to get Bluto Parks."

"Bluto called?"

"Somebody, Mom. Mr. Davenport said not to wait up for him. Said he'd get Bluto Parks settled and come by with him in the morning. Call over here first to let you know."

She introduced Josh to the boy, who couldn't have shown less interest, tapping his fingers impatiently on the desk, tapping his foot as musical signals announced the arrival of one new IM after another.

Later, alone in a small bedroom that smelled of disuse, Josh tried reaching Keshawna. Her call-forwarding was turned off at all the numbers. All he got was the polite, impersonal voice requesting a message at the tone. He briefed her on what he'd found and what he hadn't found, told her to return his calls regardless of the time, and not to worry about waking him.

What roused him a few hours later was the sense of someone crawling into his bed.

Kristy Palmer.

Despair in her voice, choking over her words. Telling him: "I just need to be held, truly, that's all, Josh. Just to be held. Been so lonely without Billy. Just need to be held. Okay, Josh? Okay? Hold me?" The smell of beer on her breath masking the gin.

Kristy, as naked as her emotions.

Josh took her in his arms.

In the morning, when he woke, she was gone.

Chapter 40

Bluto Parks' phone call changed little, except the timetable. Clyde had decided that even before he jotted down the honky-tonk's location and told Bluto, "Stay put, my dear friend. Don't go anywhere until I arrive. I'm on my way."

Bluto had to die.

Now—

The sooner the better.

Drunk or sober, Bluto would be a risk as long as he was alive, especially now, with Josh Wainwright in Nashville and dogging after him.

The original plan was to connect with Bluto at Billy the Kid's memorial service and have Peppi dispose of him soon afterward, Clyde distancing himself from Bluto's tragic demise in a recording studio, where he'd be creating midnight magic with Princess Lulu, an engineer, studio cats, and the usual idol-worshippers hanging around for the thrill of watching the master at work.

Clyde had entertained visions of Bluto falling-down drunk, a hit-and-run victim while on his way to join them at the studio.

Maybe the victim of a mugger.

Whatever worked best.

These were details for Peppi to deal with.

These kinds of details had always been Peppi's domain.

Wainwright's presence had put a crimp in the scheme. Maybe for the better. Being in Nashville, Wainwright would have time to drag Bluto aside after the memorial service, coddle him, fill him with booze, and wheedle from him—

What?

How Clyde had sought Bluto out and offered him a new career, fresh stardom as a solo artist, but only if Billy Palmer were dead?

Clyde hadn't said in so many words, that Bluto should kill Billy, but Bluto always was a quick study—read the lyrics once and know them cold, along with every note on the page—and he wobbled off energized by the bright new future he had been promised, only—

Bluto never got to Nashville.

He disappeared, fulfilling Peppi's prophecy that he would celebrate the proffered fresh start on life by stopping somewhere for a quick one, and disappear.

Exactly what happened.

Why it eventually fell to Clyde to go to Nashville himself and invite Billy to suicide.

History.

Ancient history.

But it bit deep into Clyde Davenport's Nobel Prize for Thoroughness.

So did his taking at face value Record Academy President Ray Gray's report that Bluto had died. The reason Clyde added Bluto to his list. The excuse Josh Wainwright had found to continue hounding him until he found a strong link, like—

Bluto Parks.

Still among the living.

But not for much longer.

Bluto's death preordained and long overdue.

Only circumstance to deal with now.

Again.

The *How* of it.

Tonight he would keep it simple:

Rescue Bluto from Karaoke Country in Pigeon Forge, hide him in a motel with a handful of sleeping caps and a bottle or two of hooch, and tuck him nighty-night under the covers while reassuring him they'd be going back into the studio and cranking out hits like the great old days. Return to Nashville saying he found the honky-tonk, but Bluto wasn't there. Leave the rest of it to Peppi after he arrived with Princess Lulu.

The plan wasn't perfect.

Hastily produced.

Loose ends.

Someone at the honky-tonk remembering Clyde.

Someone at the motel remembering him.

At least, no limo driver to be concerned about. He had been clever enough to have a car rental delivered for the drive, loaded with one of those blessed computer screens that mapped the drive to Pigeon Forge and kept him from getting lost.

Clyde regretted not having Peppi at his side already, but Princess Lulu had been in no condition to travel when the decision was made. So what if Peppi still didn't trust her motives, argued that his brains were in his pants when it came to her? There, too, yes, but most of all her talent was going to put him back on the charts.

So she can leave you like all the others when that happens? Peppi said every time the subject came up, his fingers flying angrily.

She does, I'll have you to pick up the pieces, he would answer every time, his fingers displaying a certainty Peppi didn't even attempt denying.

Clyde pictured himself in bed with her. The image made him smile. Got him hot, hotter than any other woman had gotten him in years.

He reached after his cell phone on the passenger seat and tried Peppi again. The same recorded voice, telling him the subscriber's phone was not presently in service. Not like Peppi, whose cell was always on, always charged.

He tried the house numbers.

Dead air, not even a ring.

Whatever the communication problem, it had to be minor, otherwise Peppi would be on the phone to him. He tossed the phone back on the passenger seat and checked the car screen to see how many more miles before he reached Karaoke Country.

Clyde raised the sound level on the radio and caught the tag end of a song he didn't recognize by a voice he couldn't identify. No disk jock to help him out. A straight segue into a Buffalo Springfield cut produced by Jack Nietzche.

In the long ago, when everybody was starting out, he offered Nietzche a chance to work alongside him, but Jack decided to go with Spector instead.

Clyde snapped off the radio.

Karaoke Country was a down-home honky-tonk the size of a cow pen sitting twenty or thirty yards behind a muddy field of pickup trucks and long-distance haulers. Clyde didn't know what smelled worse, the decrepit room with its sagging wood beam roof or the unruly blend of cheap cologne on the women, many of whom were cramping through a Texas Two-Step on a dance floor the size of a postage stamp.

The stage, built on a base of wooden milk crates that fell from use when wax cartons replaced glass bottles and cardboard caps, rose to a height of barely three feet and was currently shaking under the weight of a robust diva wrestling with the lyrics to a Loretta Lynn standard twice her age playing out on the bed sheet screen behind her. She held onto the microphone like it was her umbilical cord, smiling desperately while trying to keep up with the melody being fed the speakers by an unseen karaoke machine.

Clyde sensed she was a regular attraction by the way everyone cheered her on and more than a few tossed coins and bills onto the stage as added encouragement. When the song ended, she threw open her arms like she was embracing the world and threw kisses to the crowd. Froze when somebody called out: "What a crock! What a fucking crock!"

It was Bluto.

Clyde recognized his voice from the phone call, nothing like the Bluto Parks who once shared Gold records with Billy the Kid. He didn't look the part, either, not the rock star who once feasted on quail and champagne at the world's finest hotels. He looked like one of life's tragic also-rans, a ruin of a man who'd never had enough luck to be down on.

"Fucking crock!" he said, repeating himself like a broken record while climbing onto the stage, every drunken step unsteady, and close to stumbling off before he arrived. He grabbed the mike away from the woman and ordered her: "Get back to the zoo before they miss you, you elephant."

The woman burst into tears.

Bluto pushed her out of the way and showered the mike with spit demanding the crowd's attention. "I sang my heart out for you and got ignored like I was a nobody, you hayseed morons, like Miss Jumbo had it all over me."

"You stank worse than a mule's fart," someone declared and caught a fast answer from somebody else: "No reason for you to disrespect a mule, Tom Billy."

Laughter raced through the room.

"I sang for the Queen of England, you nut cases. Shows how much you know."

"You look and sound more like you made a career of sucking dick for the queens over to the back alleys of Swanson Boulevard."

A sucking sound, and in seconds the sound was coming from every direction.

Bluto arched his back and threw out his chin, challenging: "That's why you looking so familiar to me, cowboy?" He shook a middle finger at him. "And the horse you rode in on."

That got the room whooping.

Calls of *He got you on that one, Roy* and *You gonna let him get away with that, Roy?*

"Just got out and not looking to go back in so soon," Roy answered.

Bluto clasped his hands and raised his arms in victory. He threw the mike at the woman, who caught it on the fly, and settled on his hands and knees to collect the silver and paper money scattered on the stage.

The woman reared back and bleated into the mike: "Johnnie Lee, he's stealing the money I got rewarded fair and square."

The chant began anew, this time a chorus of *He's stealing the money, Johnnie Lee. He's stealing the money, Johnnie Lee. . . .*

Johnnie Lee was less sympathetic than Roy. He shouted, "Hell, no, he ain't. You back on off, mister, and leave my lady's money right where it is."

"It's rightfully mine," Bluto yelled back, and kept on collecting.

The chant resumed, only louder:

He's stealing her money, Johnnie Lee. He's stealing her money, Johnnie Lee.

Johnnie Lee pushed his way to the stage and tramped up the stairs.

He was bigger than his woman, maybe twice her size, mountains for muscles inside a Grateful Dead T-shirt. Half Bluto's age, or less. Without preamble, he lifted Bluto off the stage and threw him into the audience. Nobody tried to catch him. He banged noisily on a table that collapsed under his weight, sent him rolling onto the sawdust and peanut-shell-littered floor.

Bluto used the table to get back onto his feet.

He shook his head clear and revealed a switchblade, cutting at the air to clear a path back to the stage.

"Show you, dumb redneck motherfucker," he announced.

Johnnie Lee pushed out his palms. "Don't need that kind of trouble, mister, neither of us, so why don't y'all just back off?"

"Why don't you all just fuck off?" Bluto said, when he got onstage.

He leaped for Johnnie Lee.

Johnnie Lee sidestepped him.

Grabbed Bluto by the shirt collar and propelled him off the stage again.

This time, Bluto hit the sawdust and peanut shells on his feet.

He swayed backward, then forward.

His knees began to give out.

He tried to restore his balance by wagging his arms.

He fell.

He landed with the switchblade sticking in his throat, just below his Adam's apple, blood spraying the people closest to him. His arms collapsed and all movement stopped, eyes open and blind to the clench-faced cowboy checking him for a pulse and yelling for somebody to get nine-one-one.

The room turned silent, then noisy with alarm.

Customers raced for the exit.

Clyde joined them. He didn't want to be there when police arrived, find himself trapped in the investigation process. Others had witnessed what he'd seen. Good enough. He found the rental. A minute later was back on the road, letting the map on the dashboard screen direct him back to Nashville, confident Bluto was either dead or would be by the time he reached his suite at the hotel. He smiled at how divine providence had solved the problem represented by Bluto, in a way that Josh

Wainwright could not conceivably blame on him, hard as he might try.

Clyde went after his cell, more anxious than ever to connect with Peppi, share the news about their good fortune.

No success.

He punched on the radio.

The station was playing one of the country songs he'd cut with Billy the Kid and Bluto.

How appropriate.

He sang along.

The tables had been removed and chairs were being arranged in rows for Billy Palmer's memorial service when Clyde arrived in late afternoon at the Bourbon Street Blues and Boogie Bar. The band's portable keyboard, synthesizer, and drum kit were set on one side of the stage; on the other side was a freshly waxed podium and, resting on an easel, a mural-sized photo of Billy in his prime. Floral arrangements and wreaths, the largest from him, took up what space remained and decorated the floor in front of the stage.

Kristy Palmer and Josh Wainwright were huddled in a booth nearest the stage. He joined them, drawing a tired smile from her and a reluctant handshake from an indifferent Wainwright. He dragged a chair over. Facing them with his back to the room, and, giving it his best pretense, he said, "How we doing, people?" He looked around. "Bluto get here?"

Kristy said, "Hoping you'd show up with him, Clyde. I heard from my son how he called the house last night and you went off to fetch him."

"Indeed. Some out-of-the-way redneck honky-tonk. Miles from here. Bluto wasn't to be found when I arrived. Certified alcoholics are like that. I was hoping he'd find his way under his own steam."

"Your offer's still standing, appears y'all be the one singing some Billy the Kid and Bluto songs with Georgie Wilson," Kristy said. "Georgie and the band, they're out back taking five."

"The least I can do," Clyde said, moving a hand over his heart. Wainwright turned away, refusing to be taken in by the gesture. "I have a couple of tunes in mind. One I heard last night on the radio, driving back from the honky-tonk."

"Must have been tuned in to the Tex Arkana Show. Tex was always a major fan of Billy's and been playing him over and over. He intends on getting up and sharing some of his memories tonight."

"What a lovely, thoughtful gesture."

"Right up here with things you been doing for us, Clyde Davenport. That so, Josh, what I've been saying all along?"

Wainwright gave Kristy Palmer's hand a squeeze. He said, "I'll go get the band."

"You, too, Josh. Thoughtful and considerate. A sweetheart for caring as much as you do."

Wainwright slid out of the booth and headed across the room.

He was barely gone a minute when a door-minder approached, coughed for attention, and threw a thumb over his shoulder. "The black dude over by the entrance? Saying he got a message needs delivering to y'all, Mr. Davenport."

A message to deliver? From the hotel, maybe? Strange. The hotel had instructions that Mr. Blue was to phone him the moment he checked in, so who then? What was there to deliver? Clyde turned to have a look.

The dude was a husky six-footer, decked out in sweats and a baseball cap turned with the brim overhanging his dreadlocks. He looked vaguely familiar. He responded to the puzzle gulfs between Clyde's eyebrows with a mouthful of smile that showed off a gold incisor and another tooth sporting a sparkling diamond.

He held up a cell phone.

Wagged it.

Pressed it to his ear and unloaded another generous smile.

Clyde excused himself from the booth and headed for the dude.

Wherever he remembered him from, it wasn't the hotel.

His size alone would have kept him in Clyde's memory bank.

The dude handed him the cell phone.

"Hello, yes? This is Clyde Davenport."

"Know who this is, Clyde?"

Clyde recognized the voice in his ear at once:

EZ-XTC.

"Ezra, hello. What a pleasant surprise."

"Actually, not so pleasant. Got some bad news for you I wanted to deliver first hand. About your bro, Peppi?"

"What about Peppi?"

"An unexpected change in plans. He won't be joining you there, like you expect."

"What kind of unexpected change in plans?"

"The permanent kind. Peppi, he got himself killed dead," EZ-XTC said, a sadistic twinkle in his voice.

The announcement stunned Clyde, immobilized him.

It took him several moments to react.

"You murdered him? Is that what I'm hearing?"

"Not exactly, but you're a different rap. Ganking my daughter from me. Skanking her. Treating my little girl like one of your toots. Any dealings you and I had, they're officially over. Same as you are—over—and me around to hear it happen. Good-bye, Clyde."

Before Clyde could respond, the dude grabbed onto his wrist.

He pushed the cell phone aside.

Jammed a revolver under Clyde's chin.
Squeezed the trigger.

CHAPTER 41

Leading the band back into the showroom, Josh recognized the pop of a silenced weapon.

He turned in time to see the top of Davenport's head explode.

The door-minder and the few workers setting up the room ducked for cover. Kristy was bug-eyed, a hand pressed against her chest, gasping noisily. The racket behind him was the band retreating through the curtain.

Davenport's body hung upright in suspended animation.

The shooter sent a second bullet into his heart, added a safety shot that destroyed the rest of Davenport's face, and was heading for the door to the street before Davenport hit the ground.

Josh's cop reflexes kicked.

He charged after the shooter, leap-frogging Davenport to close the gap.

The shooter braked and wheeled around. Squeezed out an off-balance shot that flew high and hit the whisky-bottle chandelier. A bottle rained glass while the shooter improved his stance and took direct two-handed aim at Josh, who stood motionless in surrender.

The shooter nodded approval. He said, "Got me no brief on you, mister, so best you keep that way and save your skin, dig?"

"Dig," Josh said.

The shooter gave him props and turned.

Josh sprang, got a finger-lock around the shooter's body and struggled to bring him down.

He was out-sized and out-powered.

The shooter flexed to break the lock, tossed Josh aside.

Pointed his automatic and said, "Once more and you don't get no third chance."

"Tell me why you did him," Josh said.

"Why for it matter to you?"

"It does."

"You his homie or something?"

"Something. I was out to nail him myself for murdering my wife. Other people. I was closing in on the prick, getting evidence that would take him out legally and lethally."

"So what I done you was a favor. No charge, dude. Do yourself one now. Stay steady where you stand or I'm obliged to take you down."

"What was your beef with Davenport?"

"No beef my own with the mark, bro. Taking care of business for a brother who always treats me handsomely."

"Who?"

"Not giving up a name's the second favor I'm doing you, can you dig?" A siren's wail was growing louder. Someone, maybe a band member, had gotten off a call to the police. The shooter heard it, too. "Sounds like you're in line to do me one, bro. The law gets to asking you questions, you lose my face or for sure I'll come looking for you and yours. You dig? We on the same wavelength?"

"I don't know I can do that."

Jesus fuck!

What was he thinking?

Talking standup, like he still had a badge to back his play.

With every nervous blink, Josh caught an image of Justin and Julie, heard Katie ordering him not to be a damn fool, get himself killed and turn them into orphans.

The shooter cocked his head and crinkled his wide-set eyes.

Appeared ready to spend another bullet.

Josh called out, "Yes," sharing the word with the room. "Yes, can do."

"Bet you college educated," the shooter said. Showed off the jewelry store in his mouth, fired a shot that ripped into the ceiling, and fled.

Kristy was at Josh's side in seconds, holding him like she expected him to take off after the shooter, begging him not to, telling the world: "Thank you, Jesus. Thank you, Lord. Thank you, for not spilling his blood."

The murder set off a police and media frenzy that consumed hours. A combination of yellow tape and red tape made it impossible for Billy the Kid Palmer's memorial service to be held at the Bourbon Street Blues and Boogie Bar.

Arrangements were quickly put in place for it to move down the street to the Leather Cowpunchers Corral, where lines of the curious began forming and had stretched down and around the block three hours before the scheduled starting time, promising an audience larger than any Billy the Kid had drawn in the waning days of his career.

Josh was free to leave after he gave detectives his version of the killing. It was rich in detail, but all he could do was apologize when they asked him to describe Davenport's assailant. "He looked like a gun ready to blow me to Kingdom Come," he said, and later gave the same answer to reporters and TV crews that shoved cameras in his face.

It was enough of the truth to give the sound bite legitimacy.

There was no red-eye to Los Angeles.

The earliest direct flight he could get out was at sunrise.

Josh called the house to reassure Justin and Julie he was unharmed, then had to repeat most of it for Niki, then Connie, there with Rusty Jr., who'd been granted a night's leave from rehab.

He connected with Keshawna's voice mail and left word.

He sat fidgeting through Billy Palmer's memorial service, alongside Kristy, who managed to hold herself together until it was her turn at the podium.

She rained tears and in a voice choking with emotion recited memories that became an undecipherable babble of words before her legs seemed to fail her, causing Josh to leap onto the makeshift stage and guide her back to her seat and the comfort of her two sons.

Afterward, he helped Kristy and the boys into the limousine he'd insisted on renting for them, expecting that would be the last he'd see of her. She surprised him, turning up at Nashville International and tracking him down through the airport paging system.

"My being here's not what y'all think?" Kristy said, after they had settled over coffees at a StarBuckaroo's, her eyes falling off his and onto her paper container.

"How do you know what I'm thinking?"

"I could feel it, Josh, when you loaned me the warmth of your body and again last night, especially when I heard off Susie Hathaway in the powder room how you whipped out a credit card and snatched up the bill at the Leather Cowpunchers Corral, only I wasn't to know. Put my boys and me in a limousine, also that."

"A friend helping out a friend. I can afford it, Kristy. You can't. That was all. A gesture. No ulterior motives."

She reached a hand across the table and trapped his mouth. "Then maybe it is me having thoughts. Also, a need to say it's too early and I'm not yet ready for any long-term or meaningful relationship. You're a beautiful man, Josh, but Billy's too close still to my heart."

"And Katie Sunshine to mine," he said, and passed her a napkin for her wet eyes.

"We can stay in touch?"

"Call or write sometime and let me know how you and the boys are getting along."

"Thank you."

She spent the next few minutes quietly staring into her container, until—

"Really should be heading back home. Is it all right I kiss you one more time before I leave, Josh?"

No way he could deny the plea bargain in her voice.

No mystery in her kiss, then—to his relief—she was gone.

Keshawna was staked out waiting for Josh at the terminal exit.

She said, "Lots to talk about, partner."

"The good news first."

"You don't need to grab a cab home." She thumbed him to the company limo double-parked curbside in the passenger loading zone, Pulliam squatting against a fender working a smoke. He spotted them, squashed the butt under his heel, and got the trunk open.

"Can you do good news better than that?"

"This more to your liking? The shooter didn't pop you and sounded to me like they all bought into your fairy tale about not being able to ID him, every damn news broadcast leading off with the story and making you out some kind of a hero."

"But not you."

"Only the hero part. Fine for business, but I didn't hear anything about you chasing after the suspect blindfolded, so I'm betting you have him tucked in nice and available in that rogue's gallery you call a memory, filed under Temporary Amnesia."

Josh dumped his gear in the trunk. A minute or two later, Pulliam was inching into the traffic lanes, narrowly avoiding the tail end of an airport people-mover, while Josh detailed the encounter with the shooter for Keshawna.

"No doubt in my mind he was a pro imported for the hit," he said. "The last thing in the world I need is him carrying through on his threat and coming after me or, God forbid, the kids."

"I'd have done the same as you, Joshua. Family is family. We take care of our own, even before we take care of ourselves." She helped herself to a beer from the fridge and tossed one to Josh. "Who do you figure set the contract on Davenport in motion?"

"Someone who despised him more than me."

"You owe him big time for the favor. It cleans the toilet bowl and lets you get on with your life once we get past a problem that developed while you were in Nashville."

"A problem. Should I be drinking my beer or something stronger?"

"I'll tell you, then you tell me. At this moment in history, it's looking like the D.A. won't be prosecuting Russ Tambourine for setting up Merv Bannister's murder or anything else your recorder caught at Shady Acres."

"I see a scotch in the bar. I'll take it straight from the bottle."

"You want the official version, or the truth?" Keshawna said.

"The bottom line."

"Police Central passed, saying it's all too circumstantial, but more concerned about the public shit-storm it would create by exposing Shady Acres. Already enough scandal in LAPD, enough careers crashing and burning, without Josh Wainwright helping add to the list. Last I heard, certain of our former detective buds were seriously thinking about putting a bounty on your balls."

"And the D.A.?"

"The Blue Brass got to him first, so it became thanks but no thanks after some feigned enthusiasm over the recording. The official line is how you and your brother got Vic Swank's statements using deception, fraud, entrapment, witness intimidation. Name your poison. The recording, something no judge in his right mind would allow into evidence."

She borrowed the scotch bottle from Josh, tilted her head back and took a healthy swipe. Rinsed her mouth. Checked the 405 rush-hour traffic that kept Pulliam driving shy of no miles per hour. "I'm barely back in the office from Civic Center when I get an anonymous call on the unlisted. Area Code 702," she said.

"Vegas."

"Vegas. Some nose in need of adjustment, wheezing a warning, how the best way for us to stay healthy was to lose the recorder and go hands off on Russ Tambourine. I put in a call to one of our friends there and got the same advice. Tambourine's casino markers can't get paid off with him making license plates for the state at four cents an hour, so it's in their best interest to keep him on stage and endorsing over his weekly paycheck."

Josh thought about it. "Why they saved Tambourine's ass and scored Merv Bannister when he tried his blackmail scheme."

"Nothing volunteered, but it falls that way. Probably the same with Marilyn Pope and Clyde Davenport."

"Pope I can see. She was into the threesome. But Davenport?"

"Maybe Mr. Magic knew more than you and Lon got out of Swank. Somebody with Davenport's ego, the way he went nuts with his guns, why take chances? Easier to go for the solution before the problem has a chance to go public."

"And Peppi Blue, Davenport's constant shadow?"

"Maybe his day's coming. Come and gone for all we know."

"I suppose," Josh said, unconvinced, wondering why Keshawna was throwing the theory at him like Robert Horry going for a desperation, game-winning three-pointer. He chose to save the observation for later and took another taste of scotch, to fortify himself against the migraine building at his temples. "What if we Deep Throat it?" he said. "Take the recording to the media and turn them loose on Swank?"

"Like the tracks wouldn't lead back to us?" Her cackle caromed off the roof of the car. "Just how tired are you, partner? Too tired to recognize it's time to leave well enough alone?"

She dug the recorder from her satchel bag.

Flipped it hand to hand like she was juggling a hot potato, oohing and ahing a few times before she dropped it on Josh's lap.

"I have four more names for you," he said. Her back stiffened with curiosity. "The two you gave me, Jeremiah Schwartz, and my answer. Andy Devine, who Jeremiah became for the movies."

"Impossible you'd figure that one out." She threw a hand at him and went for the scotch. "Confess, Joshua. You looked it up."

"Your turn again," he said, refusing to part with the bottle. "Virginia Hensley."

Chapter 42

After dropping off Josh, Keshawna told Pulliam to head for Dead Dogg Records.

Pulliam bypassed the freeway, hit light traffic zigzagging the residential streets south, but made good time on Pico east, then crawled in the rush-hour blitz south down Vermont to Adams. He spent almost all of the forty-minute trip stinking up the limo with his smokes and layering her with the snickering innuendo she wouldn't be taking from him if their lives hadn't been so welded together in their last days on the force.

Bad enough he was a dirty cop.

Pulliam was a despicable human being.

She kept him around fully believing in the old dodge about keeping your friends close but your enemies closer.

When he got to mocking her about something she said to Josh, mimicking her with her own words, *Take care of our own, even before we take care of ourselves,* his Southern drawl full of drool, she'd finally had enough and told him to shut it down.

He adjusted his steel-rimmed frames, gave her one of his *What are you going to do about it?* laughs, knowing what her answer had to be: *Nothing, nothing at all.* Reminded her, "It's what the Blue Wall is all about, Detective Keyes, ain't that so?"

Security passed the limo through the gates, but only Keshawna had been cleared by Easy Charleson to enter the building. He joined her in his office about twenty-five minutes later, Easy never one for being on time to anything; all glitter and good vibes, wondering if his homies were treating her right. He helped himself to a coffee and sugar doughnut from the serving cart, settled beside her on the sofa, and said, "Why the sad mouth, Miss Jefferson High Campus Queen?"

"When you said don't worry about Davenport, you didn't tell me what you had in mind, Easy."

He grabbed her eyes for his own and said, "When you told me what your security camera had on tape, you gave me the why. I didn't need the wherefore. Did what any father would do to some lying old chicken shit bastard like that. What's righteous isn't always a stranger to the evil deeds we do, ain't you figured that out yet?"

"I intended for you to see the tape, so we could talk about it, nothing more." She removed the videocassette from her clutch purse and offered it to him. "Here."

He pulled away from her, like the videocassette might be contaminated, indifferent to the coffee he'd spilled on his silk threads.

"I know that kind of action from hood rats, Keshawna. I didn't have to see it going down with my own daughter. Besides, who do you think you're fooling, except maybe for yourself? You wanted Davenport dead and buried for what he did with Lulu, as much as I did after getting your call, you all terrified about her and Peppi Blue, knowing I'd come on the run. No time now to play act the law-and-order girl or throw the Good Book in my face like it's Sunday and you're on the pulpit at Adams First Evangelical."

"Yes, I wanted Lu safe, but—"

"Don't deny it. Admit it. Say it. You also wanted Clyde Davenport dead as much as any mama would for what he was doing to your daughter, what he was turning her into."

It was Keshawna's turn to recoil.

She whispered in a voice trembling more than her hands: "You swore you'd never say that out loud or tell anyone, damn you, Easy. Does Lu know, or—?"

"Hold on, woman. I've always kept my word with you. You, not me, decided she should be your sister's daughter, you fearing your reputation would suffer, what that kind of association with me could mean for your career. Latasha, dead, the needle still stuck between her toes, not giving birth, the way Lu's always been made to believe. You know where else you've been so lucky? Where I've been the kind of daddy neither one of us ever had growing up, that's where. Who's first in your life besides you, Keshawna?"

She had no answer for him.

It was a question she'd never been able to satisfactorily answer for herself.

Easy knew it.

He squashed her with a look and reached for the remote on the coffee table.

A few clicks and Princess Lulu's sweet voice filled the room.

"One of the tapes I rescued from the studio while we were cleaning up and helping Peppi Blue disappear for good and making it so nothing can come back to haunt any of us. Lu's got my voice to go with your looks, and tell you something else?"

She shrugged.

"Lu was right to want Davenport working her career. He had her on the Glory Road for sure, so I'm going to finish up the album his way, but sell it my way. And I'm calling up that charity of his, Big Buddies of America, saying how I'll pay up whatever he did, double that, to make it happen. Only nevermore 'Clyde's Kids.' 'EZ-XTC's Kids' now, with Easy's kid, Princess Lulu, front and center."

★ ★ ★ ★ ★

"You took long enough," Pulliam said, while she climbed into the front passenger seat.

"Just drive, Earl."

"Taking some smear from that lowlife, like our good old days, that it, Keesh? What say, boss?"

"Earl, just drive."

"Wouldn't put it past you, only now too high and mighty to share a taste anymore?"

"From the stink on your breath, I'd say you've been helping yourself to a few tastes from the bar back there."

"A little sour mash to help keep the blood circulating on a cold day."

"Charleson's hired us to work security at a show he'll be doing. We negotiated the details. Okay? Now will you get your ass in gear?"

"What kind of show? His old specialties? Showing young pussy how to spread 'em or kindergarten crack heads how to pass the peace pipe? You still stick up for him like he's your personal Alamo anymore. What's that about?"

Pulliam turned away from the wheel to challenge her.

He missed the stoplight, didn't see the Hummer tooling into the intersection.

Keshawna shouted out a warning too late to prevent the limo from getting bashed on the driver's side.

The limo did a full circle spin and slid across the street, battering a fire hydrant before slamming against a telephone pole.

The windshield was cracked and bloodied where it was hit by Pulliam's head. Pulliam was angled against the backrest, his hands still clutching the wheel, his muscular body deflated, looking more dead than alive—

Keshawna suffering intense pain and not so certain about herself.

CHAPTER 43

Josh was in bed sleeping off the time change and the scotch when Niki woke him, full of apology while she offered the phone, explaining it was the office, something urgent about Miss Keshawna.

The news about the accident blew him awake.

He played Indy 500 on the freeways and less than an hour later swung into a space along the red *No Parking* curb outside the main entrance to County General. He took the series of steps two and three at a time, cursed the slowness of the elevator as it chugged up to the third floor.

He raced down the wrong corridor looking for Keshawna's room, trying not to choke on the overpowering smell of the criminal-strength sanitizer used on the disintegrating linoleum.

An intern roamed over his clipboard with eyes rimmed by midnight circles and told him where to find her room, finger-pointing and drawing out the instruction like it was his one-line moment to shine on some television hospital show.

Keshawna was sharing a room rigged for six with a frail-looking elderly woman wired to a bank of monitors and hanging drip bags, who wondered: "Arnie, that you, Arnie?" as he passed by, and broke into dry tears when he said it wasn't.

"When you see my Arnie, tell him I need him," she said, and went back to staring blankly into space.

Keshawna, attached to fewer tubes, was asleep.

Josh hovered over her until he was satisfied her breathing

sounded normal.

He eased from the room, enough squeak to his sneakers to alert the elderly woman, who called after him: "When you see my Arnie, tell him I need him."

He relayed her request to the two nurses at the floor station.

They thanked him and traded gloomy expressions before explaining only the duty doctor could advise him of Keshawna's condition.

"Over there, that room," the heftier of the two Filipino women said, raising her face out of the *National Enquirer.* "He's with the other patient brought in, the auto accident. Much, much worse condition, you know?"

"Miss Keyes is one lucky lady," the doctor said. "Still some tests to run, but there doesn't appear to be any permanent damage. A few weeks rest and she'll be good as new." He and Josh were standing in the corridor outside Earl Pulliam's room. "Mr. Pulliam, he's fifty-fifty, but looks to be holding his own. Under heavy sedation, but you can visit for a few minutes." Josh went in, hoping Pulliam would be able to tell him what had happened.

Pulliam's lids flickered open at the sound of his approach, exposing eyes clouded by medication and barely functioning. His head was heavily bandaged, the exposed parts badly bruised. Breathing through an oxygen mask. The rest of him was strapped inside vapor-thin blankets, being ministered to by twice as much medical technology as was being spent on the woman in Keshawna's room.

"Hey, boss, how they hanging?" Pulliam said, rationing out the words, attempting to make a smile work. Failing. "See what a little fender-bender can do?"

"Doctor says you're doing fine."

"For a dead man in the making, so glad you're here. Confession good for the soul. Need to apologize for something, a little Semper Fi before the scorekeeper closes me out."

Pulliam asked for water. Josh went after the glass on the roller table and angled the straw into Pulliam's mouth. Pulliam took several heavy sips and nodded. Josh returned the glass to the table and settled in a card table chair close enough to catch Pulliam's whispered words, expecting to learn about the accident. It wasn't what Pulliam had in mind.

"Blue Wall," he said. "The bunch of us expected it to come down because of you. Certain you'd break the code and name names. You never being one to play the game with us. Keesh, she said no chance you'd give us up to IA, but nobody was buying it. I drew the short straw."

"What kind of short straw, Earl?"

Pulliam needed more water.

Josh fed it to him.

"The telethon, all them Jewish people dancing around and carrying on?"

"L'Chaim."

"I was working security back of the hall. One Manischewitz too many. Lousy shot and I clipped her instead of you."

"Her? Katie? You intended to kill me and you killed Katie instead?"

"Couldn't trust you. Take us down. Need you to forgive me. Okay?"

"Fuck you!" Josh said. He bolted up and kicked the chair aside. Halfway to the door, he wheeled around and marched back to Pulliam's bedside, fighting an urge to rip every cord from his body. Pull every plug. Kill the murdering bastard. "I need you to tell me this, Earl. Did Keshawna know? Did she know about the plan. She know you're the one who killed my wife? Damaged my children with her blood?" His stomach was one giant knot. His eyes were on fire. "Does she, Earl? God damn it—you answer me."

"Blue Wall," Earl Pulliam said, and closed his eyes to Josh's fury.

Keshawna was still sleeping, but no longer alone.

Easy Charleson was hanging by her bed.

Two of his homies were relaxing on empties.

Josh recognized both. One had been doing guard duty the day he and Davenport were at Dead Dogg Records. The other was the shooter from the Bourbon Street Blues and Boogie Bar in Nashville.

The shooter grinned and acknowledged him with a nod.

Briefly cupped his hand over his mouth.

Nodded and grinned again.

The elderly woman called: "Arnie, that you, Arnie?"

Easy Charleson said, "Hey, dude, heard you was floating around."

"You're the bigger surprise," Josh said, reining back his emotions.

"Came to rescue my old classmate from this sewer. Doing the paperwork now to get her parked over at Cedars-Sinai, a suite to herself on the celebrity floor, where they put me and my friends whenever situations call for it. Private ambulance downstairs waiting on us."

"Whatever you say," Josh said.

Charleson leaned back and poked his hands in his pockets, spent a probing look on him. "Get a vibe you're stressed out, bro."

"Nothing to do with you," Josh said. Fueled by angst, he asked, "Think I could borrow one of your homies?" He indicated the shooter. "Something needs doing he might be able to help me with."

Charleson's manicured eyebrows rose to his forehead, but he

left any curiosity he had unspoken. He checked out the shooter, who signaled he was fine by it and trailed Josh from the room.

The elderly woman called: "When you see my Arnie, tell him I need him."

Josh and the shooter settled on a corridor bench. Josh told him what he had in mind, gave him Earl Pulliam's room number, and said, "Whatever it costs, I'm good."

The shooter flipped away the idea. He said, "Admire the way you keep your word, dawg. Besides, hearing need for only a minute of my expert time." He gave Josh's arm a few hard slaps, pushed up from the bench and headed off.

Josh leaned forward and rubbed his palms in anticipation.

Sixty. Fifty-nine. Fifty-eight. Fifty-seven. . . .

Gripped his hands.

Fifty-six, fifty-five, fifty-four. . . .

Swallowed air by the gallon as he mentally ticked off the minute the shooter said he'd need to—

No.

Revenge, but not now, not like that.

Josh chased after the shooter.

He lost his footing on a freshly laundered section of the linoleum and jitterbugged into the wall. Bounced off and down onto the floor. Fought his way back onto his feet and took off again.

Josh broke into Pulliam's room insisting: "Don't."

The shooter had a pillow positioned over Pulliam's face.

"I changed my mind," Josh said.

The shooter turned away from the bed and tossed the pillow aside.

He said, "Was getting ready to bring you news, dawg. This dude's already dead as my great-granddaddy's dick."

Back at Keshawna's room, a gurney had been wheeled in. Green-smocked nurse's aides were prepping her for the transfer to Cedars-Sinai under Easy Charleson's watchful eye.

Keshawna was barely awake, but able to mouth Josh's name and smile to show she was glad to see him.

He was too full of rage to reciprocate.

There was a question about Katie's murder that needed answering by her and, until then, a wall stood between them.

He fled without saying good-bye.

A computerized parking ticket was tucked under Josh's windshield. He yanked it off, ripped it to pieces, and tossed it like confetti into the easterly wind sailing in from the desert.

Chapter 44

Josh woke up in his office, nudged by an early-bird tech who'd caught his snore.

He had spent the night rampaging through Keshawna's files, then Earl Pulliam's desk, desperate to find some reference, some link, some anything tying Keshawna to Katie's death or—what he really wanted—some shred of evidence that cleared her of complicity.

No luck.

Nothing on paper.

Nothing he could find on the computer.

All the while uncertain how he would react discovering the worst about someone he had always only thought the best about.

Keshawna.

His partner.

His pal.

Watching her back and never doubting she was protecting his.

Now this, and Josh hovering on the hope that Pulliam had played badass to the end of his rope, giving him a deathbed confession that sealed their animosity forever. Nothing he'd put past Pulliam, dishonest conniving prick that he was.

He remembered a bullet Pulliam had caught during a murder investigation. The suspect, high on crack, managed to separate Pulliam from his Smithie and plant the slug inches from his heart. The only reason the cocksucker pulled through, or so went bureau reasoning, was because Pulliam had no heart to begin with.

That was two or three years before the L'Chaim telethon.

If only the crack head has been a better shot.

Josh showered and shaved in the private bathroom he shared with Keshawna and threw himself into one of the spare outfits he kept handy before phoning the house to give Justin and Julie some daddy words before Niki drove them to school.

Niki had told them about Keshawna's accident.

They were anxious to know how Keesh was.

"The doctors are keeping her on heavy medication, so she's been asleep since she was moved to Cedars," he said. "I'll be going over there again later. Cheer her up a little."

Julie said, "I added her to my prayers last night, Daddy."

"Good for you. She'll be pleased when I tell her," Josh said, and let it go at that.

Justin held him for another minute, wondering if over the weekend they could go with Connie when she dropped Rusty Jr. back at the L'Chaim International Renewal Clinic in Palm Springs.

"If it's okay with Connie, sure," Josh said. "We'll make a family weekend of it."

The bad news came while he was at Katie's gravesite, integrating the roses he had picked up at the florist shop on the lobby level with the Nastrananas from home that still had a sparkle to them, a combination of fresh Lady Jane Greys and Anne Hathaways that had arrived with the shop's morning delivery from the L.A. Flower Mart at Wall and Seventh.

He wasn't through telling Katie about Pulliam, so he ignored the cell phone singing until he had shared his worst fears with her, and then he had to deal with a tourist who'd come to a halt behind him, announcing: "I was a big Katie Sunshine fan, like I'm guessing you."

The tourist was late forties, early fifties, and had the middle-age sag to prove it. He was holding a modest bouquet of daffodils in one hand, palming a small digital camera in the other.

"You mind?" he said, extending the bouquet. "Not as fancy as your roses." Josh took them from the tourist and added them to the arrangement. "Katie loved her flowers, especially her roses," the man said. "I read it in *People* magazine."

"I know."

"You mind taking a picture of me here?" He held out his camera, hopefully. "Something for the missus to see when I get back to Salt Lake from the convention? She's someone else who loves Katie. We got all her records, you know?"

"Me, too," Josh said, rising. He brushed himself off and settled the tourist in a kneeling position, so the grave marker would read.

"Smile," he said, but the tourist was beyond the suggestion. He'd pulled a hanky from a back pocket of his red and blue pin-striped slacks and was dabbing at his eyes, saying, "I'm for sure not a happy camper seeing Katie here like this, no sir."

Josh clicked off two shots and returned the camera. "Me, neither," he said.

"Ask you something?" the tourist said, rising. "Like Marilyn over in her crypt there. Like Elvis. Like James Dean. You think Katie Sunshine dying so young and tragic is why we come to think of her as we do, an icon? Besides her great talent, I mean? Why we fans care as much as we do?"

"We all have our reasons," Josh said, quietly, no desire to disrupt the tourist's obvious sincerity.

His cell phone sang out again. He used it as an excuse to wander off. It was Cedars-Sinai, an anxious nurse telling him: "Mr. Wainwright, you may want to be over here as fast as you can. Miss Keyes has taken a turn for the worse. A severe cerebral aneurysm. She keeps asking for you."

Keshawna was in intensive care when Josh arrived at Cedars and trafficked the long corridor to the unit, past lithographs donated to the hospital by the Gemini G.E.L. atelier on Melrose. He was buzzed through after identifying himself to the speaker box.

"She's fallen into a coma," the doctor said, guiding him to her room. "How deep we've not determined yet. She seemed fine and was resting comfortably until she began complaining about headaches and double vision. Those were the first signs. No clues earlier off the CT scan they'd run at County General. We did an MRI that gave us the signal. Then, this."

Keshawna was lost in a stockpile of monitoring gear, on a bed central to the small space, a single sheet covering her body. The sheet was askew, revealing naked shoulders and a single breast. There was an Oriental kind of symbol tattooed above her bronze nipple. It was new, or he would have remembered it.

The doctor half-looked away raising the sheet to chin level.

Josh couldn't be sure, but Keshawna seemed to stir.

The doctor caught it, too. "Involuntary muscle spasm," he said.

"Prognosis?"

"We need to observe Miss Keyes a bit longer, but I suspect we're looking at direct surgery," the doctor said. "That means we open the skull to keep her from re-bleeding into the brain and possibly suffering a new rupture or hemorrhage, either of which could cause a stroke or death." He fiddled with his stethoscope and cleared his throat, adopting a pained expression. "I'm embarrassed to ask this," he said.

Josh saved him the trouble. "Miss Keyes has company insurance. Anything her insurance doesn't cover, I will."

"Thank you," the doctor said.

"Can I have a few minutes alone with her?"

"A few," he said, and retreated from the room.

"Hey, Keesh, hey, partner," Josh said, not really expecting a response and getting none. He bent over and pressed his lips to her forehead. "Damn sorry I wasn't here when you asked, Keesh. This time I'm going to hang around longer, long as it takes." He fished her hand out from under the sheet and gave it a squeeze. "I need you to beat this thing," he said. "I need you to do me a favor. Tell me something. Level with me. Something I have to know for my own peace of mind."

Josh sensed, thought he saw, the barest of movement at her shuttered eyelids, the corners of her lips. An effort to part her lips.

Involuntary spasms?

"Keesh, you hearing me? Can you hear? Let me know if you can hear me."

Nothing.

"I'll be outside in the waiting room," he said. "They'll know to come get me."

He couldn't free his hand.

She had tightened her grip on him.

"Keesh, you do hear me, yes?"

He thought he heard her trying to pronounce his name. He removed her oxygen mask and moved an ear to within a fraction of an inch of her mouth.

Heard his name like it was coming from a million miles away.

Closed in on her ear with his mouth.

Heard the sound of escaping air.

"All I need is a yes or no, Keesh. Did you know it was Earl Pulliam who killed Katie? Yes or no. Can you tell me that?"

Josh returned his ear to her mouth.

He heard her struggling to sound a word.
He said, "Which is it, Keshawna? Yes? No? Did you?"

ABOUT THE AUTHOR

Robert S. Levinson is the best-selling author of *Where the Lies Begin* and *Ask a Dead Man,* as well as the Neil Gulliver and Stevie Marriner series of crime-thrillers: *The Elvis and Marilyn Affair, The James Dean Affair, The John Lennon Affair,* and *Hot Paint.* His short stories appear often in *Ellery Queen Mystery Magazine, Alfred Hitchcock Mystery Magazine,* "year's best" anthologies, and he's been voted an Ellery Queen Readers Award three consecutive years. A former newspaperman and television writer-producer, he also founded Levinson Associates Public Relations, at one time the largest rock-contemporary music firm in the world. He was on *Esquire* Magazine's first "Hot 100" list of music industry headliners and the first "Publicist of the Year" honored by *Billboard* Magazine. Bob served four years on the Mystery Writers of America national board of directors, six terms as president of the Hollywood Press Club, and is a past director of the Writers Guild of America-West. He wrote and produced the 2003 and 2004 MWA Edgar Awards galas and the 2006 and 2007 Thriller Awards shows of the International Thriller Writers organization. He resides in Los Angeles with his wife, Sandra. Read more at: *www.robertslevinson.com.*